UNDENIABLE

LAURA
STAPLETON

DEDICATION

Lieutenant Jon Stiles was a real person who gave his life in the Second Gulf War. I was asked and am honoured to name a character after him.

To my Mom for getting me started, to my Husband and Child who keep me going. You three are my first, last, and always.

.

CONTENTS

CHAPTER 1

Beth Ann Bartlett walked behind her husband, unable to breathe. So many people milled around her in the town. She resented Daggart for forcing her to come here. He knew she preferred the quiet and clean air of the family farm. She didn't need to come along on his visit to the saloon. Beth sneezed, stopping only for a second before hurrying to catch up to him as he continued. If the dust hanging heavy in the air didn't kill her, being pushed around by the inhabitants with their wagons and horses would. She clung to Daggart's back in hopes that his bulk might deter anyone from running over her. After she accidently clipped the heel of his boot with her toe for the second time, he stopped cold.

He whirled to face her. "Lizzie Lou, what have I said about kicking me like that?"

She gritted her teeth in disgust at the name he now used for her. Her stomach churned a little, sick over how this must look to bystanders. Beth stared down at her feet. She hoped a quick apology might diffuse his anger. "I'm sorry."

Gripping her upper arm, he shook Beth a little. "I don't care that you're sorry, woman. Quit doing it or there'll be hell to pay." Daggart leaned in, their noses almost touching, to drive home his point. "Understand?"

"I understand." Once he faced ahead of them again, Beth rubbed where he had held her. Her pride hurt more than her arm did. She bit her lip while following, concentrating on not touching him.

As they neared a dressmaker's store full of lovely fabrics and wools, Beth resisted irritating Daggart by tapping his shoulder and suggesting they go inside. Her pace slowed. Stealing a glance at her husband, she wanted to linger at the store window, browsing the lovely colors and newest textiles stacked inside. Even as they passed, she kept her eyes on the goods. With such choices, she wondered how anyone made a purchase without regret. She walked at the slowest possible pace, lost in thought over the store's contents. So engrossed, Beth bumped into Daggart when he halted without warning. Their collision pulled her from imagining new dresses from the latest fabrics, and she gawked at him.

"Wait here." His eyes narrowed. "You look simpleminded. Try to stay in one place for a while. I have some farm business."

Shaking her head as if just waking up, Beth saw the tavern doors a couple of businesses down the walkway. "In the saloon, Dag?" she blurted out at him.

He stood toe to toe with her, his hot breath fluttering her eyelashes. The angry slits his eyes had become foretold the probability of punishment once home. She broke their stare first, knowing the battle was lost without a word said between them. Daggart turned and strode into the saloon.

Last time he had "farm business" to attend to, Dag didn't leave until well after dark. Beth took a deep breath to sigh, then tasted the dust in the air from a passing cart and regretted doing so. The first time he'd made her wait while he drank and gambled away the night, she'd not remained by the swinging doors where he'd left her. Instead, Beth had waited in the hotel parlor across the street. She'd kept watch through the window on the saloon doors for him.

Beth glanced at the empty bench between the saloon and boot shop. Even though she wanted to revisit the hotel lobby, his harsh reaction that day still sent shudders through her. Lost in thought, she stared into the saloon.

Her reflection stared back at her. She didn't like being taller than fashionable and frowned when seeing her hair. Smoothing the tendrils escaped from her neat bun, she knew the action futile in the humid air. A saloon girl waving at her startled Beth out of her preening, and she turned away with an embarrassed smile.

She went up the steps and sat. An unfinished stocking waited in the small cloth bag she'd thought to bring on the trip to town. Beth took out the sock and arranged the pins. After every few stitches she made, some new activity nearby distracted her. Studying the various people strolling or riding past interested her far more than needlework.

As she watched, people of all types, rich and poor, country and city, paraded by her. Independence, Missouri was one of the towns everyone traveled through to go west. Since '49, the roads choked with men and sometimes their families. Gold or land fever afflicted all of them. Ladies and girls in sunbonnets passed by on prairie schooners, the men driving the oxen. Buggies with the wealthier citizens, one of them spiriting the mayor himself away to some destination, rolled past, along with cruder wagons carrying supplies to the various farms.

A couple of men on horseback caught her attention when they trotted up to the hitching post in front. The two seemed as different from each other as rocks and feathers. One wore the clothes of a foreigner, shirt starched stiff, shiny boots, and a new hat. He nodded at her, his clear blue eyes twinkling and his face clean-shaven. "Ma'am." Beth smiled at him, feeling shy at being addressed by a gentleman. She wondered if she should stand and curtsey.

The other man took a longer time in tying off his horse. She looked at him too, as he checked first his own and then the other man's knots. While pretending to sort out her knit pins, Beth saw him retie his cohort's horse. Crude patches covered the man's knees, and his beard and hair's length rivaled the longest she'd ever seen. His hair was much darker than the other man's, black, with the sun catching slight glints of silver. Her bag carried a small pair of scissors. If the man didn't trust barbers, she could gladly give him a trim herself, Beth thought.

Stifling a wry grin at her small blades attacking such a mess of hair, she glanced up when the boards vibrated from his steps. The mirth faded inside her when she saw his eyes. This man squinted, much as Dag had earlier. Where her husband's look threatened, the stranger seemed to examine her thoughts. The steel blue of his eyes felt as if they sized up her character in the brief instant he held her gaze. Breaking the stare and with a tip of his hat, he entered the saloon. The breeze as he passed smelled bad, as if he'd not touched a bar of soap in a while.

Beth nearly gasped for fresh air once he'd entered the door. Still his stench lingered, as if the odor was a living thing. He'd had such lovely eyes and a strong stride. Very pleasing though he smelled a lot like her husband, she admitted to herself with a bit of guilt.

She stabbed each stitch of her stocking as she worked, oddly frustrated. Why should it bother her that the only clean men in the world were foppish city boys? The Grahamites too, she had to admit, considered cleanliness the only path to Godliness. Beth liked when a person of that faith walked upwind of her. She sighed. Dag had never been the type to bathe, either. He smelled worse than their chickens most of the time, and only somewhat bad the rest. The gentleman she'd just seen reeked as if he stored small, dead animals in his pockets. At least Dag only smelled of his own body instead of an entire barnyard. She sneezed when a buggy passed by kicking up dust. The horses in front of Beth glanced up at her noise. She didn't want to think about Dag for too long. If she were lucky, he'd drink himself to a stupor, stumble home, and fall asleep before finding a reason to become angry yet again.

She stared past her knitting. Since entering the bustling city, her thoughts felt scrambled and distracted. Town gave her a nervous condition Beth didn't know she could have. Better to make up a tale for the scruffy man she still smelled as a mental escape from all the ruckus. Shutting out the noise, she created a new life for the stranger, imagining him a recluse who came to town when his booze bottle at home ran dry. Too obvious and common, she decided and reconsidered the fiction. Maybe he lived in a nearby campground, but not too close, thus avoiding any soap and water.

After finishing five more inches of knitting, she'd concocted an entire life of him as an orphan. The boy, scrubbed so much by the personnel running the orphanage, now as a man rebelled against anything unsoiled. Except for friends, considering the fine company she'd already seen him keep. He allowed his friends to wash. Beth glanced at his horse. Animals, too, he didn't seem to dislike being clean since his mount's livery gleamed in the afternoon sun.

Lost in her imagination, she sewed the toe of her stocking closed. Dag and the two men exited the saloon, startling Beth when her husband nudged her with his knee. They continued to amble past the boot store and the dressmaker's shop. She stood and pushed her needlework into her sewing bag, unsure of whether or not to go behind them.

Dag motioned to Beth. "C'mon, woman. We don't have all day to waste on you. Keep up or walk home," he snapped.

The gentlemen turned to her. The dandy spoke first, "Why, Daggart, you didn't tell us this fine lady is your wife." He took off his hat and bowed. "I'm Samuel Granville, at your service." Samuel held out his hand, which she took, still stunned from his elegant manners. He lifted her hand, stopping just short of kissing it, and released it with a smile. "This uncouth hooligan with me is my brother, Nicholas."

Nicholas wiped his palm on his pants before extending it to her. "Pleased to meet you, ma'am."

She took Nicholas's hand as she had his brother's, ignoring his grubby appearance. "I'm pleased to meet both of you as well."

Dag interrupted, shifting his weight from one foot to the other. "That's good. Are we done, yet? I have a couple of oxen and a wagon to buy." He didn't wait, leading the men down the sidewalk and turning into the general store.

Both men flanking her husband watched while waiting for her to follow. Beth's cheeks began to burn at Daggart's dismissal. She clenched her hands, unable to even peek at the men. Embarrassment felt like a lump in her stomach.

She hurried into the coolness of the building, thrilled with the familiar smell of spices and grains for animals. The general store was her favorite shop in town. The place sold everything she needed for the home and farm. Seeds, chicken feed, fabric and sewing sundries, wool, and the list of other items in the place made her want to spend hours there. The flour bags caught her attention, the bright colors cheering her. Their contents helped convince Dag to let her buy them as necessary. As pretty as the fabric was, flour sacks didn't compare to the bolts of cloth and locally woven tweeds.

Beth glanced at her husband and his friends chatting with the store owner. She rather liked Henry. He always had time for her and seemed glad to see her when she shopped there. Her husband held a paper, checking off or adding to items on the page. His actions and furtive glances in her direction bothered Beth. He was up to something, but she knew she lacked any power to stop him. Instead, she went to the fabrics.

She tilted her favorite bolt of cloth towards the sunlight to admire. The crisp white background enhanced the small, multi-colored flowers. The pale color was impractical for farm work. Plus, the several stepped dying processes put the fabric out of financial reach. Still, this one remained her favorite and she admired it every chance

6

possible. She ran her fingertips down the length of the bolt, enjoying the softness of the cotton. This was certainly too fine for her to ever wear. Beth slid the fabric back into place and glanced at her husband. If he left and she didn't tag along, he'd not be bothered to wait. She'd have a long, painful walk home. Wiggling her toes against the confining shoe leather, she winced and glanced at the scruffy man. How long had he been staring? Beth bit her lip and walked over to the trio.

Henry scribbled on a bill of sale. "I have everything but five pounds of the coffee. That's not arrived from St. Louis, yet."

Dag shifted from one foot to the other. "When does the rest get here?"

Checking the chart on the wall, he answered, "Day after tomorrow."

She stood there, a little in shock. He wanted five pounds of coffee when they had a pound at home? Why? She wondered. Were these two men making him buy supplies for them? Had her husband lost a lot of money in a card game? Thinking of how much he possibly owed caused her heart to race. They'd been lucky, in a way. His gambling and drinking sometimes spent every penny between them. Yet, the crops, milk, and farm eggs had all kept them fed. Beth swallowed the lump of tears forming in her throat, unable to follow their continuing conversation. A fierce winter had kept Dag home and away from using cards to distribute money to other gamblers. She'd dared hope this fall would be their best harvest since Pa died.

Henry cut into her musing. "Hello, Mrs. Bartlett. How are you this fine day?"

Beth opened her mouth to reply as Dag interrupted, "I'll settle up here." He reached into his pocket.

Scribbling a total at the bottom of the paper, Henry replied, "Fine, Mr. Bartlett," with a forced smile.

Her head started pounding, and Beth couldn't move

as the men headed for the door. All the hints he'd dropped, the ones she ignored, special editions of newspapers he'd brought home. Why he never wanted to plan next year's crops. She looked at Henry and then at the bill of sale, certain she knew Dag's plans. "Daggart Bartlett, are you going to California?"

Chest puffed with pride, he replied, "Yep, sure am and you're going with me."

She stepped back, putting a hand to her mouth. Suspecting and knowing were two different things. Beth swallowed down the rising bile in her throat. Nothing else of her family remained except their land. She could not let this happen. "No, I am not. You promised Pa you'd take care of the farm and me, and I'm holding you to that."

"I'm still bein' responsible for you." Preoccupied by the exiting men, he looked from them to her, adding, "You're goin' with me tomorrow."

Beth crossed her arms. This one time, she refused to uphold the vow she'd made to Pa. He couldn't expect her to do such a thing, not even if Daggart ordered her. She frowned in an attempt to keep tears at bay. "No. I'm going nowhere because someone must stay with the farm."

"We don't have no more farm." He waved a paper in front of her face. "I sold it and everything else to the highest bidder. New owners might let you live in the barn while you do chores for them." Dag grinned and went off, following the Granvilles.

Shock from his bargain held her in place. Her farm? All she had left from her family? Beth wanted to scream but couldn't. His turning to leave, smirking, drove her into action. Before he could step from the boardwalk, she grabbed his arm, turning him to face her. "I cannot let you do this. You are not selling my family's farm. You will go get our money, and buy back our land this instant!"

CHAPTER 2

Nick glanced at Sam. With their years of familiarity, he knew his brother agreed. This couldn't be good for Mr. Bartlett's plans. The man strode over, put his arm around his wife so tight she winced, and pulled her outside. She stumbled a little, as if Bartlett controlled her upper body so much her legs couldn't follow.

Seeing Sam tilt his head toward the door, he nodded. Both left the shop, walking into a heated discussion.

With her backed against a wall, Bartlett stabbed his wife's chest with his index finger after each word he growled. "You and the farm are my properties. Better than that, like I sold the farm, I can sell you to the highest bidder."

Anger immobilized Nick, while his sibling had the presence of mind to react. Sam stepped forward enough to send Bartlett backward. "No need for that, is there, sir? I'm sure the farm's sale proceeds cover the trip's costs." Sam spooned on the charm. "In fact, you bargained so shrewdly, you had money enough for two trips west."

Nick ran a hand through his hair, frustrated by the brewing squabble. They had plenty of time for this during the trip west. "Had money for two, now just one. You'd be a hired hand on your own farm had we not stopped your bad luck at the card tables."

Mrs. Bartlett stepped back, face white from shock. "You sold my farm then gambled away my family's fortune? We can't even buy back our home? Oh, Daggart, no!" She turned, wandering away a few steps, the back of her hand pressed against her lips.

When Bartlett snorted at her reaction, Nick glared at him. The other man's expression changed from derision to surly in an instant. "What are you lookin' at?" Daggart stood toe to toe with Nick, adding, "She'll shut her trap once I start finding gold. Wait and see. I'll dig up so much, I'll buy the whole county, maybe even the whole state."

Sam stepped between the two men. "Has anyone mentioned your keen trader skills? I'm betting there are a lot of posts out there for a dealer like you."

As his brother led the man away while discussing a future for him in Indian negotiations, Nick went to Mrs. Bartlett. She stood still, arms crossed, and seemed to not even breathe. From the lack of color in her face, he worried she might faint. "Are you well, ma'am?"

She glanced up at him and back to her husband. "Yes, thank you, and you?"

"That's not important right now." He saw the spots Dag's poking finger left, red already turning purple. Nick caught his brother's gaze. He considered Sam to be better able to chat with someone they'd both like to leave for dead. Mrs. Bartlett's face remained pale, her eyes large. He watched as her expressions betrayed her emotions. Clearly, her family's farm meant everything to her and she wasn't consulted in the sale. He considered his place to be anywhere else in the world but between a husband and wife. And yet, Mrs. Bartlett seemed like an injured bird needing care. Nick sighed when tears began rolling down her cheeks. He could tolerate a crying woman, but not one trying so hard to be brave like her. In an effort to distract her, he asked, "Didn't we see you sewing outside the dance hall today?"

"Yes, in a way." She lifted her chin, blinking. "It's more knitting than sewing."

She didn't meet his gaze, so he thought of how else to start a friendly conversation. Nick did a quick search of their surroundings. Mention the weather, he wondered, maybe people in town? Thanks to the women in his life, he knew more than he wanted about needle arts. If asking inane questions kept her talking instead of crying, he was willing to ask them. "There's a difference between the two, am I correct?"

Mrs. Bartlett gave him a wavering smile not quite reaching her eyes. "Yes, there's a bit of a difference." Digging around in a little cloth bag, she held up a stocking. "Only the toe will be sewn closed. Everything else of this is knitting." He took the small garment, careful with the pins holding the stitches. As he felt the softness of the wool, she added, "I'm getting an early start on winter."

Nick grinned, handing her the sock. "April is very early. I assume your Sunday summer dress has been finished for a while?"

Mrs. Bartlett's expression clouded as she put away her knitting. She didn't look him in the eye while replying, "No, I'm lucky enough to wear my Sunday best year around. It's enough for me."

Her admission stopped him cold. No wonder she'd spent her time in the General Store pouring over the fabric. He'd never met a woman who didn't love a new dress, and hers looked as if it'd seen better days. Nick wished for just an ounce of his brother's charm. Thinking of what Sam would say, he worked to reassure her. "Then, it's no wonder you look so fine, dressed up as you are."

The attempt to be sociable sounded feeble even to his ears. Nick saw the wry disbelief in her expression, but his effort gained him a slight smile from Mrs. Bartlett. Encouraged, he grinned back at her.

"You're an extremely generous man and almost as charming as well, Mr. Granville. Thank you for the compliment." She turned away from him a little, appearing to listen in on Sam and Dag's conversation.

He suppressed a sigh, knowing he'd been dismissed in her mind. Thing was, Nick wasn't sure he wanted to be finished so soon with her. His brain felt mushy, like when she'd smiled at him after he topped the steps to the saloon. Mrs. Bartlett's eyes, dark green like moss in the shade, framed by long, black lashes, lured him to stare if only to see what expression they next displayed. Also darker than her hair, Mrs. Bartlett's eyebrows arched or furrowed, depending on her thoughts. Nick liked how her feelings showed on her face. She'd make a horrible gambler, almost as bad as her husband. At the moment, though, Mrs. Bartlett looked pale and afraid, rousing every protective instinct in him. He shifted, blocking the other men from her view. "I gather your husband has surprised you with everything today?"

Beth sighed and shook her head. "Not really. If I were honest, I'd admit selling the farm for his dreams of gold has been Dag's goal for years."

"Not yours?"

"Not mine at all." She gave him a fleeting look, seeming embarrassed. "But then, it's the husband's job to dream and the wife's to make those dreams reality, correct?"

"I suppose so."

With a sly glance, she added, "Besides, what my husband doesn't get through force, he gets through brute force. Mules seem easy going compared to him."

Nick looked at Dag, standing taller and broader than Sam. Anyone would have a tough time finding a man big enough to bully Daggart Bartlett. Neither brother sat short in a saddle, nor would either pick a fight with a man like Bartlett. His size, compared to his wife's, irritated Nick yet again. In an effort to stay calm, Nick told himself he didn't know the whole story. Like maybe how Mrs. Bartlett henpecked her husband every second at home. Or possibly, she placed every chore at the farm in his overworked hands.

He glanced down at the woman next to him. Nick would bet his own farm she was the condemned one of the two. Here her husband stood, swapping stories with Sam, while his missus patiently waited. Nick's own wife would have made her excuses to visit the dressmaker's shop.

Shifting his stance, he fought fidgeting with impatience. Memories of losing Sally lured him to the nearest bottle. He had no time for that. A hot bath at the hotel and a visit to the barber still needed doing today. "Sam," Nick interrupted a story he'd heard many times before now. "They need their oxen, wagon, and supplies before dark."

Sam laughed. "Of course they do. Sir, ma'am, I'll see you at Becker's Camp next."

Shaking hands with the men, Bartlett responded, "See you there."

Nick watched the Bartletts walk across the dirt street, not wanting to see her go so soon. To Sam, he said sotto voice, "She told me this trip is Bartlett's dream, not hers. Makes a man wonder what the woman does dream of."

"Don't even think of asking, Nick." Sam mock punched him on the arm to get his attention. "She's his wife, and I'd kill you myself before letting him kill you over her."

Lifting his chin, Nick refused to admit his brother read his mind. "I'm thinking nothing of the sort about the woman. She's just another client to me. Anyway, who says you'd be in the fight?"

"You know me better than that."

Sam always had his back, even when they fought each other. If Nick attempted courting Mrs. Bartlett, he'd deserve a beating from her husband. He nodded before turning to the hotel across the way. "I've never needed to poach before now, and it's a habit I'm not starting."

"She's a little thing," Sam said before stopping them both so a wagon could pass. "A man has a right to do whatever he wants to his wife, but I'd have a hard time letting him hurt her."

He sighed, frustrated with a bad situation before it began. "Mrs. Bartlett has already been bruised, and you know I couldn't let him do worse to her."

"You might have to."

Angry, Nick glared at him. "I don't have to do anything. Doesn't matter if it's a mountain lion, bear, or spouse, I'm not letting anything kill a member of the wagon party."

"I know, but don't beg for trouble." Sam went first through the hotel door. "I agree with your argument. Let's hope it's never tested."

Hours later, in one of the establishment's feather beds, Nick felt far more human than animal. His body tingled from the scrubbing, while his face felt naked without a beard. He might grow his mustache, but for now, Nick liked his bare upper lip. He had to get new clothes tomorrow, his prior garments too worn. While borrowing from Sam worked well for today, he found it tough to be his own man in another's undergarments.

Nick smiled, wondering how many people who'd seen him in town would recognize him bare faced. He might have robbed a bank and gotten away with it. Until the barber spoke up, that is. He lay there, pondering how he'd plan the perfect bank heist.

Somewhere between him eluding an imaginary sheriff and catching a train back to the east coast, Nick must have drifted off. He woke with a start, pulled into consciousness by his usual nightmare. As he worked on catching his breath, Nick swung his legs to the side of the bed. The cold floor chilled his bare soles. He shrugged into Sam's clothes, hoping for anything but biscuits and bacon for breakfast. There would be enough of that meal in the months ahead.

After a slice of strawberry pie and coffee, he settled up for the food and room. He enjoyed the night of luxury, but too much made a person soft for the trail. Nick put his hat on as the general store caught his attention. Mrs. Bartlett and her dress came to mind, and he paused. Yesterday as the Bartletts walked away from them, he saw how her dress had been gathered in the back. A different fabric from the rest of the garment made up a ruffle at the bottom hem. He'd learned enough from Sally to know the woman's dress was handed down from someone shorter and rounder. Nick also saw the skill in the modifications. Even so, Sally would never have considered such clothes to be her Sunday best, nor would Nick have allowed her to do so. He'd had too much pride in his wife. He also would have demanded she have adequate clothing for a journey west.

Not wanting to question why he cared and pushing away his conscience, Nick strode across the street and into the shop. Henry greeted him with a nod, which he returned. He went to the fabrics near the back, examining the placement of each to find Mrs. Bartlett's preference. Light, with spots of color, he mused. Nick pulled what he remembered from his mother's sewing to be a light, delicate calico from the others.

Henry walked up behind him. "That bolt has enough for a lady's dress and bonnet, not much more."

He held up the fabric. "How tall a woman would this fit?"

The storekeeper rubbed his stubbled chin. "You were in here yesterday with your brother, right?"

Nick laughed, scrapping plans for ever robbing a bank near this man. "Sure was. You've got a good eye for faces."

He shrugged. "It's something I've learned over the years. May I?" Henry held out his hands for the cloth in question.

Nick complied and watched as Henry went around and measured it all against a yardstick fastened to the counter. Already, Henry had reached the end of the fabric. Would there be enough? He forced himself to wait patiently while the man measured the cloth a second time. Mrs. Bartlett was taller than Sally had been.

Henry frowned, shaking his head as he folded the fabric. "This isn't going to make Mrs. Bartlett happy."

Nick's heart gave a guilty jump at her name. "How so?"

He took out his sales pad. "It's enough for her a dress and sunbonnet. She looks at this every time they come in here." Henry patted the calico. "There'd even be enough left over for a pretty ruffle."

Nick had been correct and fought the urge to grin. She loved this pattern, and he wanted her to have it. "Are you sure there's plenty for a nice sized dress?" At Henry's frown, he grew nervous and felt transparent. He knew Henry saw the beads of sweat grow to the size of buckets on his upper lip. He stammered a little, "I wouldn't want it to be my fault if my wife, who happens to be Mrs.

Bartlett's size, runs short."

"Since my cousin is the tailor down the street and my sister makes dresses, I pick up on these things." Henry went around and headed toward the back of the store. "Could be wrong about the ruffle, but there's enough for everything else." Stopping in front of the sundries, he asked, "Did your wife say she needed anything else for her dress?"

Nick's mind raced. What would Mrs. Bartlett say? How could he give the fabric alone to her, never mind the sundries she'd need? He shrugged, tapping the counter, stalling. Didn't women need thread, needles, and scissors? Hadn't he heard Sally mention whale bones and ribbons, too? He tried to laugh. "I never know what that woman has for making our clothes."

Henry looked at him suspiciously. "If your wife made your shirt, she has more than everything to sew a dress."

"She probably does." Nick remembered the last time his nerves felt like this, when his first oxen and wagon hit quicksand. He doubted Mrs. Bartlett had everything she needed. "To keep me in her good graces, though, I'd better get whatever she wants for an entire dress." He smiled, hoping some of Sam's ability to charm showed through the bloodline. "I want to surprise her, and she'd be disappointed if something was missing."

Henry shrugged. "All right, mister. It's your penny."

Nick left the store, more than several cents lighter with a package in his hands. He had boots waiting for him at the cobbler's and a new set of clothes at the tailor's. After picking up his things, Nick put his boots in one saddlebag and his clothes and Mrs. Bartlett's package in another.

He reached the camp in a short time, spotting Sam on the far west side. "Hey there, you got room for another straggler?"

"Look at you in my duds! You're almost as much a lady-killer as yours truly."

"I'm glad you think so. Want your work clothes back?" Nick dismounted his horse, throwing the reins over the animal's head so he'd stay put.

His brother replied while walking to the private side of their wagon, "Yes, next washday is fine since you'll probably need them 'till then." Both checked for bystanders before undressing.

Sam put on his older clothes as Nick removed them. Nick went to get a set of his own new clothes. He opened the saddlebag, taking out both pairs of pants and shirts.

"Nick?"

"What?" He kept buttoning his shirt.

Sam held up a corner of the calico. "Since when do you need such lovely clothes?"

"It's not for me." Nick turned away, tucking in his shirttail.

"I figured," his brother retorted.

Slipping a belt out of the opposite saddlebag, he pulled on his old boots, acting too busy to talk. Nick then latched shut the incriminating bag, glaring at Sam.

"You're not going to tell me who's the lucky lady?"

He mounted his horse. "No, and you don't want to know."

Sam grabbed the bridle and hissed, "Damn it, Nicholas, you can't give that woman anything like this. It's too personal, and Bartlett will kill you. If you're lucky, he'll do it with his bare hands."

"Or worse, he'll hurt her."

"You have clearly gone mad." He let go of the horse and sighed. "Fine. Promise me you'll wait until Bartlett wouldn't mind a gift from you to his wife. Do it for her sake, if not your own."

Taken aback, he admitted, "Good argument. All right, I'll wait for a good time." Compelled to explain himself, Nick went on, "She only has one dress. Just the one. Sally had a dress for every day of the week and two for Sunday. I needed to get something for Mrs. Bartlett."

"You needed to get something for her?" Sam shook his head and mounted his horse.

"Yes, because how much do you want to bet, the woman won't have another set of warmer clothes for this trip?" Before Sam could interject, he continued, "You and I both know Bartlett was warned of the cold in the mountains we'll cross. He'll have everything he needs to get to the gold, but not everything she needs to survive."

"I'm not taking that bet." He moved his horse between Nick and the rest of the camp. "Before you see her again, you should know something. She's his, for better or worse. Right now, it's worse but has probably been better, else they'd not be married."

His brother's speech reminded Nick love might have been in the Bartlett's marriage at one time. Maybe she loved the man no matter his bad manners or lack of kindness for her. "At the moment, it's more concern for her well-being than anything else.

I'm not smitten with the woman or anything."

"Smitten, is it?" Sam continued, his tone sharp, "Once she agrees to travel to California with him, you'll feel foolish for this infatuation."

Realizing she'd most likely stay with her husband reminded him how much she wasn't any of his business. "Infatuation is a strong word for wanting to keep a member of our group alive until Oregon." Catching his brother's scoffing expression, Nick added, "Or California. She is pretty, though. You're right about me thinking so, somewhat."

Sam sat up taller in the saddle and smirked. "Of course I am. I may be younger, but I'm far wiser." Leading the way into the camp, he continued, "I can't blame you for liking the girl. She's the first to catch your eye since Sally died, and the woman's a princess needing rescue. What able-bodied man could resist? When I first met her, I almost kissed her hand." Sam shook his head. "But out here isn't like home. Here, fine manners like mine can be considered a declaration of intent."

Nick shifted in his seat. "Before I say you talk too much, do you know her name by chance?"

After shooting over a dirty look, Sam replied, "You don't need to know and I shouldn't answer, but I heard him call her Lizzy Lou once in camp. She responded, so I assume it's her name. Not that you can call her by that, of course."

"No, I wouldn't." As they wound around, edging closer to the center of camp, Nick saw her. She sat in the shadow of a wagon, unraveling a tube of knitting. "Go ahead," he told Sam, "I'll catch up in a minute."

"Damn it!" Sam growled. "You're going to deserve the beating Bartlett gives your sorry hide."

Nick shrugged off the warning and rode up to the Bartlett's campsite. He saw Bartlett's wife sitting with her back against a wagon wheel and dismounted to talk with her. "Hello, ma'am. How are you today?"

Mrs. Bartlett took the tail of squiggly yarn and put loops back on one of her little sticks. "Hello, Mr. Granville. I'm well. How are you?"

"Fine, thank you." After several moments, she didn't look up at him and he sat on his heels. He paused for her to say something, and when she didn't, he broke the silence. "What is it you're making?"

He saw her smile, the only part of her face visible under her hat. "A stocking."

"Another?" He nodded at a passerby then added, "You're either very fast, or the recipient is very short."

She took a fleeting look up at him, almost catching his eye. "Sadly, neither is true."

"Oh?" He'd hoped his response would prompt her to explain more. She remained silent, her head bowed while concentrating on her work. Nick wasn't willing to leave her so soon. The woman had to deserve the husband she'd married. He needed to learn something unsavory about her and asked, "How do you like camping so far? Are you looking forward to your first night sleeping outside?"

Mrs. Bartlett focused on her work, saying, "I was able to sleep outside last night." She paused, resting her hands on her lap.

"So soon?" Nick blurted before thinking. "You and Bartlett packed up your wagon faster than most, I'm sure."

"My husband and Mr. Henry packed everything." She swallowed. "I was asked to keep out from underfoot." Pulling out the sticks, she began winding the string into a ball.

Nick didn't think unraveling her work could be a good sign. "Did you make sure they put your things in easy to find places? I know my wife was very particular when we traveled over land."

She stopped working for a moment and sniffed. After clearing her throat, she replied, "I didn't have to be bothered with that. All of my things and my family's things stay with the farm. That was part of Daggart's deal with them."

Hearing her wavering admission, words failed him. If he'd forced Sally to leave her belongings behind like this, Nick doubted she'd be as calm. At a loss for how to comfort her, he said, "I suppose it's good to travel light."

She scrambled to her feet, dropping everything and glaring at him. "I wanted my garden and flower seeds, wools, linens, and family heirlooms. I had treasures; now I have nothing! None of this is good! None at all!"

Mrs. Bartlett stared at him and he gawked back, surprised by her temper. "No, ma'am, of course it's not good."

For a few seconds, he gazed into her eyes as she said in a choked voice, "Heavens, you're handsome! I'd have not recognized you by sight, only by your voice."

He tried to smile, but her blackened right eye and swollen cheek stopped him. Nick didn't know what to say at first, not wanting to embarrass her. As awareness dawned in her face, he knew his expression gave away his thoughts. She bowed her head, hiding her blushing face with her sunbonnet. "Can't blame you, ma'am, for the surprise. I've been told I clean up well, and I had a lot to do."

Fumbling, Mrs. Bartlett picked up what she'd dropped in anger. "Um hm, you're right, you do clean up very nicely."

Encouraged by her, he continued, "You probably had to identify me by voice, since my prior bad smell is gone."

She snorted before catching herself and put a hand over her mouth. "Pardon me! I'm sorry to be so rude, but it's true. Your odor did precede you before we met."

Nick grinned, pleased at hearing her amusement despite the subject matter of his smell. When she glanced up at him, his breath caught. Even bruised, those dark green eyes of hers affected him in ways he didn't have the luxury to think about right now. He had the urge to see if he could amuse her again. "Sad to say, the laundress boiled my pants all night before burying them as a last resort."

Mrs. Bartlett snickered outright and retorted, "Did she do that so dogs wouldn't mistake them for dead animals?"

The tart comment and sly look from her uninjured eye surprised Nick, making him laugh. "No, she had to bury them deeper since wolves joined in on the hunt."

Her mouth dropped open. "They lured wolves into town? Good heavens!"

He worked to keep a straight face. "Absolutely. The dirt flew for days."

"What? No! Days?" She smiled at him again, "Oh, you're horrible!"

Daggart interrupted, "What's going on here?"

So caught up in amusing her, Nick didn't notice her husband until he stepped between them. Taken aback, he paused before asking, "Hello, Bartlett, how is everything in camp?"

The other man ignored Nick. "Elizabeth, you're talking vulgar like." He stepped closer to her, making Mrs. Bartlett lean against the wagon. "*Other* women wouldn't have been so crude. You better say sorry to Mr. Granville for what you said."

Afraid for her safety more than his own, Nick interjected, "That's not necessary; I know she wasn't serious."

Bartlett turned and glared at him. "What you know don't matter. She wronged you and needs to ask for forgiveness."

Mrs. Bartlett's head was bowed as she spoke. "He's right, Mr. Granville. I'm very sorry for the insult and won't let it happen again."

"That's my Lizzy. Now fix dinner. I'm hungry." Bartlett slapped her on the behind and then waited until she was out of earshot. "That woman is as dumb as a sod house. Good thing she's useful, or I'd have left her on that worthless farm."

Unless marrying Bartlett counted, Nick doubted Lizzy matched the man's assessment of her. Despite his disagreement, he nodded, "You could have. A woman can be a problem out there. Slows down a man."

Bartlett laughed and slapped Nick's back. "Some men are like you and your brother, rich as Midas and can visit every brothel between here and there. Others, like me and most everyone else, have to bring along their own female."

Nick, stunned, tried to respond as Bartlett walked away. Had the man compared Mrs. Bartlett to a woman for hire? Mrs. Bartlett deserved the love and respect due a wife, not the sole use as a bed warmer. Disgusted, he got on his horse to find Sam before his temper won out over his common sense.

CHAPTER 3

Rushing from their wagon to the campfire gave Beth no time to dwell on Nick Granville's appearance. She focused solely on cooking a midday meal that would taste better than the prior horrible breakfast.

Neither greeted each other as Daggart sat down and took a bite of bacon. "Huh," he said while chewing. "This ain't burnt." After the grudging praise, Dag held up what was meant to be a biscuit. "I can't eat this," and threw it in the smoldering fire.

She nibbled on the bread and frowned. Tough and gummy. Of course they couldn't eat the food. Even if she'd been experienced in cooking over an open fire, she'd still need her cow and at least one hen. Cooking up an egg with Dag's bacon and using milk instead of water would have improved his meal. Beth glanced over at him rifling through the back of the wagon for something else to eat. If he'd allowed her to stop by the farm yesterday, she grumbled to herself, he'd eat better today and on down the trail. But no. Like usual, he couldn't be told or even entertain a suggestion to do something beneficial for the both of them.

Beth gathered their plates, forks, and tin cups while keeping her motions slow and even. She tried to find a positive about dinner to help diffuse her anger. The coffee had tasted the same as usual, one small mercy. She searched for the calmest part of the Missouri river. Kneeling, she rinsed the dishes in water where it lapped onto a small strip of the sandy bank. The breeze here blew crisp and fresh from the water's surface. Minnows darted to and fro as she used her fingertips to scrub bacon grease from the plates. She almost enjoyed how the river smelled fishy. Would Dag have thought to bring a fishing pole? Beth shook her head. He'd shown no such foresight so far.

Last night's sleep had left her cold and sore. Most of the others slept under oilcloth tents of some sort. They had also used their horses' blankets as a mattress. She shook droplets from the dishes. Seeing Daggart stiff from sleeping on the ground gave Beth her only comfort after the hours of restlessness. It served him right. They'd had a lot of bedding at home they could've slept on here. If he'd thought before selling the farm outright, Daggart's mood would have been much improved.

She walked farther up the bank to where the ground wasn't so squishy wet. She could still hear the wagon party chatter from here, but it wasn't the overwhelming din. Sitting, Beth placed the clean dishes beside her. She stared out over the blue ribbon as it flowed. Seeing Mr. Granville had been an unexpected treat.

He'd spoken to her more today than any other person had in a very long time. Mr. Henry chatted almost as much, but usually stayed too busy to make wisecracks. Drawing up her knees, Beth hugged her legs. Samuel, any woman would agree, was the better looking brother of the two. He possessed buckets more charm, certainly. She wouldn't have thought of Nicholas as handsome yesterday, but today after cleaning up, he looked ages younger. He even seemed to borrow some of Samuel's charm along with his soap.

"Soap? Oh heavens!" she exclaimed before thinking. The dishes hadn't needed soap after breakfast or at the moment, but almost everything else would sometime soon. Beth released her shins and smacked her palms against the ground in frustration. She needed her own soap. Working with lye was grueling, the job she hated most even as the results made the effort worthwhile. Daggart's wild idea to chase gold ruined everything. The anger helped fuel her, and Beth finished washing up in record time.

She scooped up her belongings and stood to trudge across the grassland to their wagon. Prior generations of her family had worked hard on the farm, all for nothing now but a wagon and two oxen. The sale of the farm, going west ten years too late for the gold rush, and the gambling added to the nightmare. Knowing the Granville brothers pulled her husband out of the card game mortified her. She hated this familiar feeling of burning shame. The men's sympathetic looks had echoed those from the church members when her husband insulted her in public.

Beth put her palm on her left cheek and eye to cool the hurt. Keeping her head bowed so no one saw her face, she swapped their dishes at the wagon for her small bag of wool. She'd only brought enough to town to finish the first stocking. A little more remained, but not enough for a second. Unless…. She took out the completed stocking. A snip halfway between knee and toe, and the upper portion could be redone into another stocking. Beth smiled. Perfect, she wouldn't have to switch a single sock from one foot to the other as needed.

Some wagon trains, like this one, didn't allow dogs. Glad no animal might have marked his territory, she sat down comfortably on the shady ground. Her back against the wagon wheel, Beth began work on her knitting. She snipped a thread, unraveled the yarn, sewed the top of the sock, and began knitting its mate.

With her thinking the word mate, Nicholas sprang to mind. His appearance had surprised her so, she'd said the first thing she'd thought. She marveled at her audacity in calling him handsome. Her sunbonnet not only hid her black eye, it now hid her blushing face and Beth smiled. Thankfully, she'd notice no smell from him, unlike in town. While creating each new round in her stocking, she wondered about Nicholas's life. What man would let himself become so dirty, but then clean up so completely? Was he really a hermit, or had he traveled from the wilderness to here?

The thoughts buzzed in her head like telegraph wires at a train depot. First she'd dwell on Daggart and their argument, then on Nicolas and his conversation with her. In an effort to still her mind, she forced herself to concentrate on her work. After a few moments, the focus ended and the reflections began again. Nicolas looked wonderful in a crisp white shirt, impractical for the trail though it may be. She wondered if the suspenders would leave white stripes on a field of dusty brown after a day's ride. Probably, and he'd have to dry the shirt in the sun to brighten it. His pants looked new, too. Odd, since his boots, while polished, were old and a little scruffy. She didn't blame him. Beth would much rather have her old shoes than these new ones of her deceased sister.

Beth had some quiet time to think and reflect on Nicolas's speech. He didn't sound as educated as Samuel, who spoke with more of a posh accent. She'd heard similar speech from another person while in the dressmaker's store. There, a lady with a plumed hat had compared the sweet and quaint town shops to her sophisticated home stores.

When she looked up at Nicholas this morning, her dress felt much too tight around her chest. Beth smiled, remembering how the rest of his face lacked the slight tan of around his eyes. Such eyes, too. What had looked like steel in town seemed more like the dark blue-gray of storm clouds this morning. She drew in a breath at the memory, thinking he had such handsome lips. She was glad he'd shaved. Like an image in her mind to never forget, she'd hold close the first time he'd smiled at her.

But then, he'd seen what Dag had done and his expression changed in an instant. Chances were he'd known Beth deserved the hit. Her rude actions had broken the promise she'd made to her father on his deathbed. Even if correct in calling her husband a fool, she felt ashamed of yelling it at him like a curse word. People friendly to them last night now avoided her. Whether it was her loud voice or Daggart's slap, she didn't know.

"Mrs. Bartlett?"

Immersed in her own musings, Beth nearly jumped out of her dress in surprise at Samuel Granville's voice. She looked up before remembering her bruised face and then stared down at her lap. Unlike his brother, she noticed Samuel did have new shoes. "Hello, Mr. Granville. I hope you're well."

He sat on his heels, eye level with her. "I'm very fine today, ma'am, and think you'll be delighted to see what I've brought with me."

She glanced up, saw the sudden anger in his eyes, and hid her face again. Daggart must have hit her much too hard this time, considering his expression. "I don't know. I should stay here."

"I know accidents happen, my dear. It can't be your fault. Please, come with me for a moment." Samuel held out his hand to help Beth to her feet. As she stood, he continued, "It seems my brother and I were remiss in helping your husband with his travel list. There are things we assumed he'd bring from your home that aren't here." Samuel led her around the wagon to a buggy. "I've taken the liberty of packing a few things forgotten in your haste to travel west." He unloaded a trunk covered with a few blankets and quilts.

"Oh my goodness gracious!" Beth ran over and hugged the fabrics. "I cannot begin to tell you my thanks, sir. This is marvelous." She rushed to put the blankets in their wagon and went to the trunk. Afraid of the answer, she asked, "Is anything inside?"

"I certainly hope so. It was filled over the top before I left."

She tried undoing the latch, but her hands trembled too much. Beth wanted to cry with joy. Samuel helped her, and she opened the trunk. Everything she'd missed lay inside. Some items had been wrapped in scrap material, including a large jar she earlier wished they'd had for drinking water. Right off, she recognized and removed it from the trunk. "This is wonderful, Mr. Granville. We can have water or tea whenever we choose." She smiled at him, hugging the jar close.

"I'm glad to have been of service." He reached in the buggy one more time. "You two will need this for protection from the elements." Samuel held a large oilcloth Beth had stored in the barn. "Looks like the mice found this unappetizing, and Bartlett can make a sturdy tent from it."

"I'm so pleased with everything you've brought." She pointed out various things. "Here are my herbs, some seeds I'd saved from last year's garden, and oh! The family Bible! Thank you so!" Beth held the book to her chest. "You can't know how much this means to me. My family brought this from Britain. I'd considered it lost forever."

"Your pleasure makes the effort worthwhile, my dear." He turned and nodded to the east. "In a moment, Nicholas will be in your good graces as well."

She saw the elder Granville on horseback, leading her and Daggart's cow to them. "Erleen!" Beth ran up and hugged the animal's neck. "I'll bet you need milking," she said. Holding out her hand for the cow's lead rope, Beth smiled at Nicholas. "I can stake her in some grass. You two have done so much for me today; I'm sure you have chores of your own to complete."

"I'm sure, too," he replied, dismounting. "But right at the moment, I can't imagine anything more important than helping you load up your trunk."

She glanced at their wagon, unsure of what to do. Daggart told her last night the wagon held almost more than the oxen could easily pull. So much so that he insisted Beth walk to California. "There may not be room."

He strode over to the wagon, "Has to be. I can't let you go on the trail without anything of yours." Nicholas peered at the foodstuffs. "Bartlett agreed, and I'm making all this fit."

Samuel spoke up, "Nick, let me get Erleen situated and then see if we can figure out a solution."

Beth heard the warning in the older brother's voice. It caught Nicholas's attention, too. She began trembling from seeing their anger. Her voice more shaky than Beth intended, she said, "If my husband has approved, then we can carry everything. There's no need to fuss."

Both men stared at her for an instant at her interruption, mouths agape, then laughed. Samuel responded first, with a bow, "But, my dear, fighting each other is our favorite past time."

She glanced from one to the other, gauging Samuel's seriousness. Nicholas, she noticed, squinted at his brother in the same manner as when first seeing her black eye. Beth bit her lip and chewed a little. Pushing their banter aside, there may be a fight between them after all.

Dag strode over to them. "Looks like your cow is making the trip with us."

"Thank you for allowing this." She watched as he twisted the animal's ear in an attempt at affection towards her. "I'm sure you'll like our meals much more, now."

He scratched under Erleen's chin. The cow lifted her head, closing her eyes, and leaned into Daggart. "Speaking of dinner, were there any fishhooks in your rubbish?"

"I can look." She smiled at her animal's enjoyment, adding, "If not, I might be able to trade for one."

He gave her a withering look. "You don't have anything someone would want in that trunk of yours." Dag turned to the two Granvilles. "Well then, gentlemen, I say let's head into town and give the saloon one last visit."

Samuel shook his head. "As much as I'd like to, there are maps to study and plans to make."

Daggart narrowed his eyes. "What plans are there to make that you two don't already know? Didn't you say you'd traveled this route already?"

"Yes, I have, twice." Clipped words betrayed Samuel's irritation at the questioning of his credentials. "Nick has covered the trail thrice."

Also catching the other man's reaction, Dag softened his approach by asking, "Ain't it pretty dry between here and California? I'm not trusting Lizzy Lou to make me wine with that dried fruit you made me buy. It's a full moon tonight, so why don't we all go and have a round of cards at the saloon?"

She bit her lip. Hearing him call her by Lizzy Lou's name bothered her like the sound from a bent tin whistle. All the fuss over leaving home had distracted her. She'd not been able to introduce herself as Beth Ann to the others before Daggart had beaten her to the punch by calling her Lizzy first. Now if she corrected everyone to her true name, there'd be questions. Those answers would lead to secrets she didn't feel comfortable in telling anyone.

Irritated by her husband's voice as he cajoled the others into drinking, Beth slipped away from the group. Erleen needed care first. Her family treasures could wait a little while longer. She led her cow closer to a grassy patch near their new pair of oxen. She studied one of the larger animals. Uncertain if they'd fight, she tied Erleen a little distance away from the duo.

Beth grew hungry for fish after remembering the hooks. If either of the Granvilles had managed to gather all her belongings, there'd be a great meal before they decamped tomorrow morning. So as not to attract attention from her husband, she slipped around the wagon to her trunk. The three men were gone. Not seeing him or his horse and knowing her husband too well, she suspected he led a group to town for one last party. When he wanted to, the man rivaled even Samuel in his charming ways.

Searching her recovered belongings and not finding any sort of fishhook, Beth instead took a steel pin from her cushion. She pushed the pin in between the wood wheel and the metal rim, and bent it. While digging for a strong thread, she heard someone clear his throat behind her.

"If I let you use this, will you use it to catch me something too?" Nicholas handed her a cane pole with string and hook at the ready. "Assuming you can fish, of course."

"I could try." She smiled, thrilled to have a real hook instead of needing to fashion one herself. "No guarantees, though. I can bait a hook just fine. It's the fish that need convincing."

"I liked bacon and grits all right until your husband mentioned fishing. We're too far from trout streams, but I'd be glad to settle for bass or perch." He glanced over his shoulder and added, "Speaking of bacon, you'll need bait and I can help. Wait a moment."

She watched him walk away, his strides long and fast. With broader shoulders than his brother, Nick seemed the stockier of the two. Beth decided she liked his figure better. She knew her face glowed with her shame from the improper thoughts about a man's body. His kindness and good looks combined with her spring fever must explain her odd interest in him, she reckoned.

The two days she'd known the Granvilles seemed a much longer time. She unpacked and sorted her belongings according to need while contemplating her husband. Most other men won out over Daggart in the manners and husband area. Beth smiled when seeing the soap she'd made last year, so glad it had been packed as well. She wondered if the elder Mr. Granville knew he'd been so thoughtful. Beth breathed in deep, enjoying the fragrance supplied by last year's roses.

No man she'd ever met led her heart to feel squishy inside as much as Nicholas now did. Maybe not so much when he first arrived into town, but now, she'd place her own wager he was the best looking man in camp. Beth tilted her chin down to hide her face as a family walked past her.

Seeing her sister's shoes on her own feet, she sighed. It would be best, she thought, to not mistake the Granville's basic manners for real concern. Disliking her husband wasn't a good enough reason to fall for another man. She gathered her feelings and thoughts, pulling them into a direction more loyal to Daggart.

By the time Nicolas returned with a thick slice of bacon, she'd silently recited enough bible verses to refocus her wandering thoughts. "Mr. Granville, we have bacon already. You needn't have bothered."

"That's all right, ma'am. Sam and I have two wagons full of supplies to you and Bartlett's one." Nicholas held out a handkerchief with cut up cubes. "It's worth our handing over some meat to you later if you'll wait for a fish or two today."

"Very well." She smiled at him. "If there are any within nibbling distance, I'm sure this will lure them."

He grinned back at her. "If I were Sam, I'd say something like your face alone could bring in any male, fish or man."

"Oh heavens!" She occupied herself with her own fishhook and string, pretending to not be rattled. "If I were me, which I am, of course, I'd remind Mr. Granville I'm a married lady with an unruly husband who is quick to anger."

Nicholas leaned in close to her saying, "Good thing my brother keeps his distance, don't you agree?"

Beth looked up into his eyes, seeing his gaze brush over her bruises like a caress. What a lovely man, she thought, if someone so male could be such a thing. Beth examined his face. Would he shave every day or let the shadow of whiskers grow into a beard again? Maybe she could convince him to keep his hair trimmed. She sighed, enjoying the chance to really scrutinize him.

"Mrs. Bartlett?" he asked in a quiet voice. "Do you think the fish are hungry?"

"Mm hm." Fish? she wondered. "Um—" What was he talking about? "Oh! Yes, yes of course. There are fish waiting to be dinner, aren't there? Yes indeed. All right, good, good." Beth knew she babbled but once started, couldn't stop. "I'm sure you have many things to do at the moment. I'll be down at the river, coaxing fish to try some tasty bacon. I don't have yours or Mr. Granville's charm, so this will take me some time. Yes, I must be going now." Mortified, she turned and headed for the water.

In a haze of embarrassment, she set up the fishing poles. Once done, she only then thought again of milking Erleen. If Beth had not humiliated herself and run away, she could have had butter for frying the fish. Beth turned at the rustle in the grass.

"Ma'am." Samuel tipped his hat and held out a jar of milk. "Nick mentioned to me you'd not had time to milk your cow, nor had Mr. Bartlett, in fact." As Beth took the offered jar, he added, "I thought you might like a drink, or to keep this cool in the water."

She stood. "I have a better idea. While I'm waiting for dinner to jump on the hooks, this can be shaken into butter."

"Very good." Samuel turned as if to leave and then paused. "My brother did manage to barter an exchange?"

Laughing, Beth assured, "Yes, bacon for fish and now milk for butter."

"Thank goodness." He tipped his hat. "I'll leave you to securing dinner."

Hours later, the sun hung low in the sky and smells of other campers' suppers started her stomach rumbling. Two fish wouldn't be enough for four people, but no others seemed interested in the bait. At least she'd shaken enough butter to fry the fillets. Once at the wagon, Beth made quick work of starting a campfire, straining the buttermilk, and dressing the fish.

Neither her husband nor his horse greeted Beth. She looked towards town where the full moon rose large and orange. What if, out of habit, Daggart's horse carried his drunken mass to the farm instead of here? She smiled while stirring crushed, dried dill into the butter. It'd serve him right. With a sprinkle of salt, she rubbed the mixture onto both sides of the fillets. Let Daggart figure out where he was while in a drunken stupor. Beth almost laughed at the thought of his confusion. She couldn't ever make him pay with a beating as he did her. Instead, she imagined fate intervening to teach him his lessons. Although, Beth sighed to herself, maybe fate worked to teach her not to be so mean minded toward Daggart. How else to explain away all the horrible events of the past few years, she wondered.

"Hello, ma'am. Is supper coming along?" Samuel removed his hat and ran a hand through his hair.

Beth smiled at him to soften the news. "Sadly, I just now put it on the fire." She turned the biscuits. "The fish were lazy today and very few bit."

He went over to the pan. "They look fine!" He sat down next to her. "With everyone headed west, the ponds around here are almost fished out. You did well to find these."

She enjoyed feeling useful. Even better, there'd be the chance of fresh meat further down the road. The last time Daggart hunted, he'd shot off his hat. Any closer to him than the brim and she'd be a widow trying to work the farm alone. She needed to know better fishing lay ahead of them. "Will the fish and game be more plentiful as we go west?"

"At one time, both were far more plentiful than now." He shrugged. "Easterners, not thinking of those to follow them, shot more than they needed to eat. Between waste and shooting animals for target practice, I've seen far less to hunt than in years past." As Nicolas walked up, Samuel paused to ask him, "Have you had supper, yet?"

"No, I counted on dinner here." Nicholas removed his hat and combed through his hair as his brother had earlier. He nodded at Beth. "Ma'am. I see you've had some success."

"A little, I suppose. Frequent camping in this area has taught the fish a lesson, your brother tells me." She lifted one fillet with a spatula. Now cooked on one side, Beth turned each while adding, "Most of them struggled free once realizing they were hooked."

Samuel winked. "Surely after seeing you at the end of the pole, they jumped into your lap."

After a wry glance at Beth, Nicholas said, "I believe I

mentioned he'd have something horribly charming to say." He addressed his brother, "All that syrup reminds me, Sam. Let's have pancakes tomorrow for breakfast."

She smiled at the retort. "Does this mean if I promise to make breakfast, you two will bring it and maybe an egg or two?"

They looked at each other and Samuel replied, "We'll taste the fish first before committing our syrup."

"To see if it passes muster?" she asked.

"That's right," Nicholas replied, taking a seat on the ground. "There're a lot of good cooks in camp this time." He nodded over at his brother who was finding a spot opposite from him. "I'm sure Sam here can tempt a lady into sharing her cooking with us in case we're too much trouble for you."

"Oh? Is that so?" Beth put her hands on her hips. "When you find one so easily bowled over, let me know. If she's better, I'll sneak over and steal her secrets."

Samuel laughed and shushed the other man, "Be quiet, sir. Dinner smells good and if you insult Mrs. Bartlett, she might not share."

Seeing Nicholas's suddenly worried expression, Beth laughed. "Don't fret. We made a deal. You two get dinner tonight, whether it's fish or foul."

Though smaller than she'd have liked, Beth served the three of them a fillet each. She also dished the last one up on Dag's plate, in case he came back early from drinking. Several people on one sort of an errand or another strolled past the trio. Nearly everyone slowed pace when they smelled the food. Beth smiled to herself. Maybe now no one, especially Daggart, would joke about her cooking.

No one chatted during the meal, hunger making everyone chew much more than talk. Nicholas, the first to finish, sighed. "Ma'am, you served one of the best meals I've ever eaten. I recommend you troll the rivers with a net constantly so as to keep us fed." Samuel nodded agreement while biting into a biscuit.

She smiled while reaching out for their dishes to wash. "Thank you, I'll have to see what I can do about making a net, then. A little bit of herbs and spice helps anyone's cooking taste better." Beth, shy at Nicolas's attention focused on her, said, "Starving my dinner guests helps their appetite too."

Samuel grinned back at her. "We may have to concoct another

barter very soon to test this opinion of yours." He held out his own hand. "In the meantime, those who cook don't have to wash up."

"I don't mind." Beth stood to collect the dishes.

"Neither does Nick." Samuel took her plate and passed it along with his own to the other man. "He'll be glad to rinse off everything and return them to you."

"You'll want me to wash the pan?" Nicholas asked. At Samuel's shrug, he shook his head. "I thought so."

Beth had to protest her guests doing her work. "Oh no, no, I don't mind cleaning up after. You let me borrow your fishing supplies."

"I don't mind either." Nicholas looked towards the west. "In fact, it's getting dark, and you need to set up a tent of some sort. Since Sam has ours ready to go, I can help you once I'm done with these, if necessary."

She handed her items to him, chin lowered. "You're very kind, Mr. Granville. I'm sure I can manage just fine."

"Probably so, but I'm helping."

She watched as Nicholas headed toward the river, dishes in hand. He walked with an easy, purposeful gait she found strong and masculine. Beth shook herself free of errant thoughts to peer in the wagon. The twilight dimmed everything to dark blue hues. Once one end of the cover lay over the wagon's end and had been secured by a sack of flour, she pulled the other end away at an angle. She pulled out a small barrel of pickles, using it to hold the loose end of the cloth down on the ground. The tent fabric stayed just fine in the still air. Before too long, she'd need tent stakes handy for the windier nights.

From the corner of her eye, Beth saw Nicholas walk up, shaking dry his hands and their dishes. She busied herself with getting a thick blanket to cover the ground and a thinner one to cover herself and Daggart.

"Here you are, ma'am." He gave Beth her belongings and then looked at her shelter. "Looks like you have some cover rigged."

"I know it is crude at the moment. I plan on whittling some stakes to hold down the corners. Hopefully Mr. Bartlett can be convinced to cut a post for the middle, fashioning the tent something like a teepee."

Nicholas offered, "Since your husband is in town, maybe he'll bring back a set of metal spikes and pole from the store."

She choked back a snort, turning instead to place dishes in the wagon. "Daggart wouldn't have thought of doing so." Beth clenched her hands, working to keep her tone civil and light. "He tends to forget time so much I'm hoping he manages to come back before dawn."

Frowning, Nicholas shook his head. "Bartlett'll have to, if you want to join the wagon train this trip."

Imagining this man riding west without her bothered Beth. She didn't want to think why, ignoring the odd feelings for now. "We'll be left behind here?"

"Yes, until next year. As a captain of this group, I can't allow any unnecessary delays." In a fidgety move, he tapped a fork against the plate. "If we were to leave any later, we'd be caught in the snows."

Beth fell silent. Everyone knew of the Donner Party. The group's brutal fate dampened every wagon team's cheer as they started their own journey west. "You all couldn't wait even one more day? Even one morning?"

His gaze scanned the horizon, softly lit by the rising moon. "Possibly one day wouldn't matter. Then again, maybe tomorrow would be ten days too late."

"I see." She didn't want to see, but knew his and the other captains' responsibility for every person and animal there had to be a heavy weight. Her duties toward the farm and their four-legged occupants paled when compared to his. A jab of fear hit her stomach. She'd lost the farm, the one last place or thing on which Beth could rely. Swallowing down the rising bile in her stomach, she asked, "Do you have any suggestions as to what I should do?"

He paused, glanced around, and looked her in the eyes. "If Mr. Bartlett doesn't show tomorrow morning, what you will need to do is decide to stay behind at camp and wait, or to come along on your own."

"I'd have to be beholden to someone traveling by myself, and I'd rather not. Never mind the impossibility of leaving behind my husband."

He seemed to think for a couple of seconds, answering, "I don't know any other woman who has traveled unaided. But then, no one here is truly alone in a crowd. You could drive your own wagon, I suppose."

Samuel walked over, "Bartlett isn't back?"

"No." Nicholas turned to include him in the group.

Beth took a deep breath. She hated saying the words aloud, but admitted to the men, "He may not come back tonight. If he's sober in time, he might be here by noon." There. She'd said it. She'd told the two an ugly truth she'd rather never admit to anyone, not even herself.

"I want to wait for him," Nicholas said, crossing his arms.

Samuel shook his head. "It doesn't matter. You can't."

He turned to look west. "I know." He walked away, saying again, "I know."

Samuel smiled at Beth. "Well, if you'd be willing to wait a while, I could see about you joining up with a later party."

"Now that I've been forced to give up my farm and animals, the idea of traveling so far isn't as awful as I'd first thought." Her wavering voice didn't seem to convince him, but she had to further try. "I had made pets of my livestock. That's why I needed some convincing from Daggart to leave them behind. I hated giving up the animals, but he's assured me that we can get more after we arrive." She smiled, searching for a positive aspect. "While my husband is finding gold, I could be rebuilding our farm. If he strikes a good vein, we could hire someone to help me work the land."

Giving her a smile not reaching his eyes, Samuel responded, "Your cow is a good start if she survives the trip. Had it not been an ordeal for Nick to get her, he would have obtained the chickens as well."

"He rescued Erleen for me?" Beth smiled knowing no other person except her father would have done the same. A slight breeze from across the river sent a shiver through her.

Samuel shook his head, "You're chilled, and I'm only standing here and telling tales, unfortunately." He nodded in his camp's direction. "I promised it was Nick's story to give, and I'll let him be the one to tell you when he has time tomorrow." Taking Beth's fingertips, he bent as if to kiss the back of her hand. "In the meantime, I'll bid you goodnight and offer a silent Godspeed to your husband."

"Thank you, Mr. Granville. I hope he arrives soon too. Otherwise I will have to wait until next year." She shook her head, not wanting to think about being homeless and living in their wagon. Beth self-consciously admitted to him, "And I'd rather not do that, preferring you and the other Mr. Granville to be our guides."

"Thank you, ma'am, for your confidence. I'll be sure to pass on the compliment to my undeserving brother." He tipped his hat.

She stared at her feet in chagrin. "You're welcome, Mr. Granville. Goodnight"

After he left, Beth slid in between the blankets she'd set down. All her fears, questions, and speculations over the next several months kept her awake for a while. Once asleep, she dreamed of falling overboard while on a ship at sea. She struggled in her dream to take off the heavy petticoats pulling her underwater. Her grandmother had told her of journeying to America and the storms on the ocean, and the dream matched what Beth had imaginged. The high waves threatened to submerge her, and she tried to scream against the water choking her.

The pain woke Beth to find her husband trying to mount her while smacking her face when she moaned and shoved him away. He'd pushed her skirt up past the waist and now made loud, grunting noises. She squeezed her eyes shut because he sounded like the pigs they'd butchered a couple of years ago. Did everyone around them know what they were doing? She listened and heard voices outside the tent, could even see other wagons when she looked out the openings. Beth pushed against his shoulders, hard. "Dag, please! Stop it! Stop this right now!"

He continued to grunt, rubbing his lifeless member against her. "Shut up and be my wife."

Beth felt demeaned and wanted to disappear. Everyone in camp, she was sure, heard his high-pitched grunts as he tried to enter her. She shook him then hit his strong arms to distract him, whispering, "Daggart, stop it! Not here, not now! It's not private!"

He increased the frequency of his ineffective thrusts and the noise as well. "Damn you, Beth! Be Lizzy. I want my Lizzy Lou back, so shut up and be her."

She heard laughter from right outside the tent. "Daggart Bartlett," she hissed, grabbing him by the throat and squeezing to get his attention. "Everyone can hear you, even children, so you'll stop this right now."

He slapped her, hard. "I'll do what I damn well want with you." With every few words and resting his weight on his left elbow, Daggart hit her again. "You're my wife, and I'll take you however and whenever I want." He grabbed the back of her head by her hair and asked, "How long have we been married? How long are we going to be married?"

Beth knew the answer he expected and gasped through the pain, "'Til death do us part." Her bruised cheek stung, and she felt her heartbeat in her temple. Trying a change of tactics, she lay there, still, until Daggart considered himself finished with the task.

Her husband whispered against her ear, "You never, ever, tell me no where others can hear, or I'll make certain it's death that parts us."

CHAPTER 4

Nick watched the horizon. Clear skies over the vibrant landscape brightened the land. Along the Missouri river, the rolling hills kept his line of sight to the tens of miles. Still, he saw far enough to notice the deep blue of distant storm clouds against the bright green of spring grass. On his other trips, the promises of spring, and the sun's warmth filled him with anticipation of the frontier.

Not this time. Not after what he'd heard this morning at breakfast. Away from the women and children, the single men gossiped louder than old hens and cruder than a greenhorn's sod house. His breakfast soured in his stomach when they'd laughed over the grunting noises heard from the Bartlett's tent. He'd dumped the rest of his food into the fire and drained his coffee. The hot liquid distracted him enough to cool his anger as he left the campsite.

He shifted in the saddle, angry with himself and his reaction earlier in the morning. Nick knew he had no right to deny a married man his wife. Moreover, he knew his caring feelings toward Mrs. Bartlett exceeded common decency. The couple's relationship was none of his business. Mrs. Bartlett didn't need his protection when she already had a man. If he'd forgotten that, Sam reminded him of the fact this morning. He reminded himself of it again now for good measure.

In the valley, the wagons traveled alongside each other as much as possible. Still, not everyone could be in front. Most emigrants, worried about Indians attacking, let him and a few other men ride ahead as scouts. He snorted. They needed to be bothered about their own carelessness. People killed themselves by accident far more often. The idea of Lizzy meeting a similar fate raised the hair on the back of his neck. The metallic taste of fear tickled his tongue. "Damn it all to hell," he cursed under his breath. Better to imagine Bartlett versus his wife. Even then, he couldn't wish the man being mashed in two by a wagon wheel, trampled by cattle, or shooting himself by mistake.

"Hey, Nick." Sam rode up beside him.

Startled out of his dark thoughts, Nick replied, "Yeah?"

"It's about midday." After his horse snorted a protest at the slower pace, Sam continued, "Let's break for noon in a couple of miles. Give the youngest ones a rest."

He glanced over at his brother. Even after a morning of riding at a good pace, the man looked crisp. Not for the first time did Nick wish he himself had been so blessed. Feeling the grime on his face, he raised an eyebrow. "Sounds fine to me." Nick glanced sideways at him. "You want to say something else? Something I don't want to hear?"

Sam stared ahead of them. "I'm afraid so."

They rode on for a while until the silence struck Nick as funny. He laughed then said, "Get it over with. We've not got all day."

"I want you to avoid Mrs. Bartlett as much as possible for the next few days."

Nick's temper rose in him like acid in an overfull stomach. Struggling inside with his anger, he studied the sky ahead of them. He finally felt calm enough to ask, "How badly did he hurt her?" He already dreaded the answer. After a few minutes, he knew his brother didn't want to continue. "So," Nick growled, "How bad is it?"

Keeping his voice low, Sam replied, "Not very, but enough so I don't want you near her for a week."

"A week?" he exclaimed. "It'll take Lizzy that long to heal enough so I don't beat the guts out of him for hurting her?"

Sam glared at him. "Yes, you know how black eyes are. It'll take a while for the yellow to fade from," he paused for emphasis, "Mrs. Bartlett's face."

Nick gritted his teeth with Sam's accent on Lizzy's title. Lizzy? He needed to quit thinking of her with such familiarly. Anyone who'd called another man's wife by her given name would be asking for a fight. "You'd think Bartlett could keep from hitting her."

"I agree." Sam gestured, indicating up ahead. "Those rains are going to raise the Missouri. If they hold, we'll have floods tonight."

"Yep." He'd have to ride alongside the river, helping when the wheels of various wagons bogged down in the mud.

"Chuck and I can take care of the back half, if you and Lawrence can corral the first."

He struggled to keep the disappointment from his voice. "She's in the latter group?"

Sam laughed, letting him know he'd failed. "The very latter."

Nick snorted "Huh!" in response and shook his head. His transparency kept him from playing cards with Sam and using real money. No one else saw through him like his brother. "We'll be along the Platte in a week."

"I expect so. You'll not need to see her then, either."

The word need bothered Nick. While it was true he'd not wanted anyone since Sally, let alone harbored an interest in any one woman in particular, enjoying Mrs. Bartlett's company didn't mean he as much as needed her. Besides, people might think it strange if he kept a deliberate distance rather than talk with her as if she were any other woman. Nick grew more certain he must visit with Mrs. Bartlett to allay suspicion the longer he thought about it. He felt a smack on his arm and Sam turned his horse into Nick's.

The younger brother scowled. "Nicholas, I know that expression. Wait until the Platte and keep peace in the camp."

Nodding, he mustered his best, albeit transparent, poker face and pretended to agree. "You're right. I can wait until the Platte. Maybe even to Laramie's Peak just to ease your mind."

Not convinced, Sam scowled at him. "Let's stop for noon, and I'll check for stragglers." He rode off to the trailing people in their party.

Nick continued ahead. He waved and signaled to Lawrence to stop for mealtime. The ruddy-faced Scot galloped off to inform the southern travelers, while Nick began alerting the northern wagons. He much preferred his current position in the lead. Everyone else lagging behind helped him forget the crowds of people, letting him enjoy the solitude of the open country.

He dismounted and led his horse to the water, studying the bank of rainclouds inching ever closer. The Kaw Indians in this part of the area kept the game scarce. No one had seen anything worth hunting this morning, not even he and his men up front. The smell of broken vegetation and sound of Buck snuffling drew him from watching the weather. His animal chewed at the new grass, ignoring the river. "You'll wish you'd taken a sip soon enough."

While his horse ate, Nick's thoughts drifted. He'd bet Bartlett had done nothing in town but drink last night. The man deserved a hangover biting him like a devil. He looked back at the various wagons. If Lizzy was lucky, her husband hadn't gambled away what little they now owned. In helping Bartlett plan for the trip, he and Sam had learned Bartlett spent everything on the wagon, oxen, and supplies. But then, Nick had to concede, a lot of people did literally bet the farm on a better living in Oregon Territory.

In his opinion, Bartlett's gamble on the west was a bad deal. He retrieved a canteen and some dried bison meat from a saddlebag. Nick sat to lunch and to watch the river flow past while his horse drank. He'd seen the farm that Lizzy had been forced to leave. The place needed a little extra care certainly. But, all the things he knew a woman could do herself had been done with love. The animals looked well fed, the garden tilled and ready for planting. His heart hurt for her loss. Nick had done what he could while there, but knew he'd never be able to do enough to replace the loss of her home.

Standing, he hoped to see her among everyone else at the river. Nick wanted to tell her a new garden waited for her in Oregon, wanted to say this sacrifice was worth everything she'd have to endure in the next six or so months, but knew he couldn't give such a guarantee. Her husband planned to split off for California. Well, he thought, Sam will have to convince Bartlett to continue on to Oregon. Nick mounted his horse as Lawrence rode up to him.

"Mr. Sam wanted me to tell ye right away a lady was caught up under a wheel."

Fear raced through his veins. Not Lizzy. Had his dreading an event turned it real? "How is she?" Anger outlined the anxiety in him. If this was somehow her husband's fault, he'd skin him alive.

Lawrence bowed his head, his usual happy demeanor gone. "Bad, real bad. Won't last the day, I reckon."

Nick stared down at the pommel of his saddle, willing himself to breathe. Forget Sam's request of a week; he'd see her now, but first, to quiet his heart, he said, "Very well, she needs to be in a wagon and to be made as comfortable as possible in the meantime."

Restless, Lawrence pushed back the brim of his hat. He blinked at the sudden sunshine in his eyes and pulled the hat back down over his brow. "They're doin' that now. Mr. Sam wanted me to first tell you the Calhoons want everyone to attend the Missus' prayer service after dinner."

The Calhoons? Nice family, but not the Bartletts. His hands shook as he lowered them to his thighs. Lizzy had not been injured. Nick wanted to give out a war whoop in joy and anguish at the same time. He hated like hell they'd lost someone already, but for now, Lizzy was safe. "I'll be there this evening, then." He frowned at Lawrence, adding, "Next time Samuel says tell me something first, make sure that something is the first thing you say. Understand?" Lawrence gave a nod and turned his horse to go back to the main group.

He squinted against the sun and gave the signal to the others to get moving. Stuff Sam's week, Nick knew he must see her before then. He ambled along the river valley, inventing ways of accidently visiting with Lizzy. Time passed without his notice. A cloud bank hid the sun, cutting the heavy warmth. The sudden cool caught his attention and he heard the rapid staccato of hoof beats. He turned as Sam galloped towards him.

The younger man indicated the gust front and dust rising ahead of the coming wind. "We will need to stop for the night."

"As soon as possible." Dirt sandblasted him and flashes of lightning lit the insides of the clouds. The scent of rain hung in the chilly air. "This storm's going to be bad."

"Let's get started." With a kick to his horse's flanks, Sam rode back to warn the last of the train.

By the time everyone stopped, the wind had grown fiercer, preventing anyone from starting a campfire. He and his men helped put up shelter as needed. Despite the rush, Nick managed to visit the woman who'd been injured. Her family had given her enough laudanum to help her sleep. He left with an offer to pray for her recovery.

After a sharp crack of thunder, water poured from the sky as if from a bucket, soaking him in an instant. He shivered and searched around for Sam, certain his more couth brother was already in his wagon.

He rode through the camp under the guise of making a final check on everyone, knowing he looked for Lizzy instead. Wincing at the thunder's volume, he spotted their wagon and trotted over. Nick went to the slight opening in the oilcloth at the end. "You two all right in there?" A few moments passed with no answer. The couple had to be in their wagon. The storm raged too much for anyone to accomplish chores. Despite feeling rude, Nick peered inside the opening. He saw Bartlett lying down, one arm over his eyes and jaw slack. Lizzy sat opposite him, wrapped in a blanket, her eyes closed. She took off her sunbonnet and put a hand up to her face. He saw the bruises before her fingers hid them. Nick muttered a curse and when she glanced up at him in alarm, he stepped back with almost a stumble. Sam had been right; he hadn't wanted to see the burst blood vessel in the white of her eye. He'd been hit like that in a fight once and knew how the blow must have hurt her.

His hands shook and he clenched his fists to make them stop. Nick took in a deep breath to calm himself, but anger still burned in the pit of his stomach. He worked to shake the feeling off as he would pain from a stubbed toe. He needed focus and a plan, neither being with him at the moment. For now, he could at least help keep her safe for the night. Nick knocked on the wagon.

"Yes?" she shouted over the din of the rain.

"We'll have to stay here for the night, looks like," Nick hollered back.

Mr. Bartlett bellowed from inside, "For the love of God, woman, be quiet!" He held his head in his hands. "Ow, ow, ow."

Mrs. Bartlett pulled the sunbonnet even lower over her face and moved closer to the opening to talk. "I'd prefer to stay put tonight, anyway. It sounds terrifying out there."

"It's a little rough, sure." Now so near her, he didn't want to leave. Grabbing at any topic, he tried asking, "Is your husband all right?" Nick grinned, just shy of yelling, "He doesn't sound very well." Bartlett rewarded the efforts with a sickly groan at the noise.

She kept her head lowered so the brim of her hat covered her upper face. "He sounds better than he feels. He helped drain the tavern last night."

Nick smirked, "So he's paying for it again?"

She replied, "Sadly, yes."

He leaned closer to make sure only she heard him, "I'm afraid tomorrow will see him well again."

Lizzy tilted her head to give him a sidelong glance and a little smile. "I'm afraid you're right."

The color of her eyes captivated him. Nick forced himself to look away from their grey-green depths and checked on Bartlett. The man had wrapped himself in a blanket, cocooned like a worm in the dirt. Certain the man wasn't watching, Nick put his hand under Lizzy's chin, lifting her gaze to his. "If you need anything, Mrs. Bartlett," he softly said, "please tell me." He saw her shiver, amazed she could be chilled when he burned so warm himself.

"I'll remember that, sir." She took his hand from her chin as if to shake it like a man. "Thank you for the kind offer."

He held her hand for too long, wanting to ease her trembles. "It's a promise, ma'am." Nick let go of her. "You need to wrap up in a blanket too. No sense in you getting sick so soon in the trip."

Lizzy pulled the ends of her thick shawl closer together. "I wouldn't mind warming up a little, but don't worry, I'm very healthy. I'm not prone to the fever or hysterics."

He tipped his hat at her. "Good! Keep it that way. Take care." Through the small opening in the canvas door, he saw her reach for a blanket. Nick pulled the fabric closed for them.

As he turned to ride away, the large drops of rain hit him like pea-sized hailstones. He hurried the horse to his wagon, the only sort of dry shelter to be had. After tying off the animal, Nick climbed in. Sam held out a flask of whisky. "Is she better?"

Nick shrugged out of his wet buckskin jacket, hanging it on its hook. "I'm assuming Mrs. Calhoon is the same. I've not seen her since talking with you." Taking the flask, he drank a couple of mouthfuls.

Sam's laugh rang out, echoing off the oilcloth walls. "You're such a poor liar! You know I mean the only she you're not supposed to be near."

He glared at Sam, handing him back the whisky. "Have you been talking with anyone?"

"No, I haven't. I also can't imagine anyone else suspects you're a fool for her." He took back his flask. "Except Mrs. Bartlett, of course. But then, the lady is looking for a hero to save her from that husband of hers."

"That's not me. I'm not any woman's hero." Nick took off his boots to put on his other pants. He hated Sam's smug attitude, sitting there in clean, dry clothes.

Sam slipped a pack of cards out from one of the trunks. "You'd like to think so." He paused while shuffling the deck. "Usually I'm the one on the white horse." He shrugged, continuing. "This time, you're the penny dreadful's hero, saving the girl from certain doom."

Nick pulled on one of his cotton under shirts. He'd read a few of those novels and didn't identify with any of the larger than life heroes in them. "I'm not good at saving a woman from anything."

His brother cut the deck and shuffled, adding, "You can't continue to blame yourself for Sally."

"I can, every day. I'm also not playing cards tonight." He laid out his cover, rolling up a horse blanket for a pillow.

Sam nodded, dealing himself a game of Solitaire. "That's acceptable. You'll lose too much playing anything against me tonight. Your mind's in another wagon entirely."

Nick ignored the jab and looked over Sam's shoulder at the cards, unable to resist helping. He watched as his brother let the card tip to first one position, then another. He stifled the urge to tell him where to put it—the card and his observation. "My mind can't be anywhere near her. I need to focus on getting the train to Oregon, not on some married woman."

"Good. I'd prefer not to see you get into a fight on this trip." The younger man waved the card above the spread in almost a divining motion. "Which is something I can guarantee will happen if you tell me what to do with this two of clubs."

Grinning at Sam's dirty look, Nick moved back and settled in for the night. A few flashes of light brightened the sky. The thunder still rumbled afterward, but softly in the distance. He noticed Sam had already put out the bigger bucket to catch all the rain possible. Storms tonight meant gritty coffee tomorrow if they used creek water. Nick fell asleep to the shuffle of the cards and steady drip of the rain.

Morning dawned cold and bright. The clouds had moved off during the night and a light frost covered the ground. The sun's rays through the trees melted the slight ice with every yellow touch. Sam hunched over the campfire, coaxing a flame, so Nick grabbed the bucket hoping for enough water for coffee. Last night's chores led Sam to put the container out too late for enough. He stifled a groan and with the coffee pot, headed for the river.

Only he, Sam, and their hired hands stirred. Last night's rain must have kept everyone up late, he figured. Nick grinned. If he were a prankster, he'd yell "Indians!" and run through camp screaming like a woman. No one would ever sleep past daybreak again.

Lizzy's brown calico caught his eye as he strolled to an embankment at the water's edge. Nick grinned, easing his way down a sharp decline to the river bottoms. She'd help with the screaming woman part, if he could coax her into a practical joke. After sidestepping down, he paused to watch her, puzzled by how reluctant she seemed to approach the water.

She lifted her skirt a little before each step and then felt ahead with her toe extended as if checking for solid ground. Reassured, she stepped forward and began the process again. In this way, Lizzy edged closer to the river like a kid facing a whipping. He saw how she clenched and unclenched one hand, the other holding the pail in a white-knuckle grip. Lizzy was afraid of water, he knew and she had good reason to be after last night's torrents. The levels had risen since dusk yesterday. Nick watched as she carefully eased herself down, dipping her bucket into the stream. Not wanting to startle her, he announced himself by whistling a tune.

She turned toward him, and his heart sank at seeing her eye. Her smile told Nick there'd been no new hurts last night at least.

"Good morning!" Lizzy blushed, staring at her feet and letting the loosely tied sunbonnet fall to cover her bruises.

"Good morning." He went over, scooped up some water for coffee, and asked, "Is Bartlett starting a fire yet?'

Sighing, she replied, "I'm not sure. If I'd been thinking, I'd have started it before now." She kept her face lowered as he approached.

"But you wanted to get done what you'd been dreading, right?" She glanced up at him, her eyebrows raised, and he smiled at her surprise. "You approach a river like I do a hot spring. It only takes once."

"I've been told I'm too cautious at times."

Nick climbed up the embankment, turning to reach a hand out to her, which she took. "A little concern can be a good thing." He pulled her up like a five-pound bag of flour, her bonnet falling back with the motion. "The land can kill the careless."

She nodded at him with a somber expression. "Mrs. Calhoon's death proves it."

Staring back, he didn't let go of her hand at once. The day's new sun gave her hair a golden chestnut glow and deepened the green in her eyes. He wanted to cup her face in his hands and kiss her lips until she smiled at him again. In a quiet voice, he admitted,

"I'm glad you weren't hurt."

"Me too." She slid her fingers from his. "After hearing what happened to her, I prefer being at the very back of the entire group."

"You'll change your mind in the great desert." He knew she might worry about being seen alone with him. If he had any sense, he'd be concerned too. Nick started back to his own wagon and motioned for her to follow. "I've seen animals cough up blood and die just from inhaling the dust."

"Good heavens!" Lizzy stopped, frowning at him. "How horrible! Is there some way to fix bandannas for them?"

He laughed. "Your oxen would look funny, but I suppose a mask could keep them alive if the animals would wear them."

"They'd look like bandits." She smiled at him. "I wonder why thieves don't think to disguise their horses too?"

"Probably because I've never seen a horse on a wanted poster."

She shrugged her shoulders. "Thus, they don't need bandannas."

As they neared the campsite, he saw Sam rousing some of the lazier bodies, Bartlett being one of them. "I see your husband is still working on a fire," Nick said in an effort to be diplomatic. "Would you like to use ours for your coffee and breakfast?"

"Yes, please." She sighed. "Excuse me while I get supplies."

He rushed to get coffee boiling, and biscuits and bacon cooking. By the time all three were done, Lizzy and Sam walked over to him. "Breakfast is ready."

"So soon? I only brought water and coffee beans to start." Lizzy looked from one brother to the other. "I'd better hurry and get ours cooked before we're left behind."

"Instead," Sam said, "why don't you get your utensils while your coffee boils? Nick can throw on more food." He waited until she walked out of earshot before asking, "Will we have enough for noon, if need be?"

He nodded, "I'll make up extra."

Sam set out a wooden box for Lizzy's seat and checked for her return. "Bartlett hadn't even roused himself when I went to check on him. He'd also not gathered any firewood. She had tried herself, I saw, judging by the scrap and tinder collected."

"After being on the ground last night, nothing could burn."

"No, you're right." Sam held out his cup for Nick to pour the coffee. "I don't usually mind the very tender footed in our group, but Bartlett is starting to anger me."

The admission from Sam surprised him, making Nick admit, "You're a better man than I am in this case. I was angry at first sight."

"When you saw the bruise?" He stood, done with breakfast. "What happens in a marital bed is no one's business but those two."

He clenched his teeth to make himself say, "I know. I need to stay clear." Easing to his feet, Nick took Sam's eating supplies. "You can handle breakfast with those two while I handle cleaning."

Sam grinned and saluted him. "Will do."

Nick felt like a kid skipping school, only having to do the washing. Better that than playing nice with Bartlett. Every time he saw Lizzy's eye, he wanted to hit her husband and ask if Bartlett liked the punch. Nick used the coarse river sand to scrub off the bacon grease. He'd heard some men argue their wives deserved a beating or had asked for one. He wondered if those same men would ever deserve or ask for a trampling from a buffalo.

A movement on the far side of the river valley caught his attention. Slowly rising from a crouch, he squinted to better see. An Indian on his pony hugged the opposite embankment. The man wore a bright red shirt, blue pair of pants, and what Nick thought was a yellow sash for a belt. He didn't appear to wear war paint, convincing Nick the rider was a local farmer.

He headed back to the group, ready to get going. Nick laughed, spotting a row of children, various ages, staring at the Indian with large eyes. He knew some of the youngsters on this trip had never seen a red man. They'd get their chance soon enough to see more red men, women, and children besides. He strode past them. "Come on, let's get going. There're more Indians where he came from." This earned a yelp from each child as they ran for their parents. He laughed and went to saddle his horse.

The progress they made in the morning disappointed Nick. He looked back over the crisp wagon tops. The road they followed, usually hilly, had the added detriment of mud. Several times, the men on horseback stopped, tied the saddles' pommels to the stuck cart, and helped the oxen as they pulled the wheels free from the drying clay. After each unexpected stall, the small company of fifteen wagons seemed like fifty.

When Sam rode up to him, Nick knew what he'd ask and said, "Yeah, keep rolling to the next camp. Soon as we get there, we'll stop for the night."

Sam nodded, turned his horse, and galloped to the rear of the party. Nick began at the front, telling the head of every group or family of their plans. Those who'd not packed lunch foods protested. He assured them of stopping as soon as they reached camp, no matter the time of day.

Even as he said this, Nick knew the land between here and there. Very shallow creek ravines proved unavoidable and took time to cross. Two wagons in the lead were already stuck in a deep stream. Before he could ride up to help free them, a third barreled down the hill. The wagon picked up speed on the slight decline to the water, at one point pushing the animals supposed to be pulling it.

The oxen crossed the water, breaking free of the yoke when the first two wheels of the wagon mired. The force threw the driver headfirst into the opposite embankment with some belongings tumbling out after him. His wife and two small children, all screaming, peered over the seat like prairie dogs in their homes. Only after seeing the father stand and shake his head free of dirt, Nick chuckled. The man was lucky the heavy rains turned the ground where he'd landed into mush. Otherwise, he'd have broken his neck.

Those around on horseback, no longer waiting for tragedy, went to work heaving various carts up onto dry land as needed. Nick helped each across, his stomach knotting in anticipation when they neared the end. He saw Lizzy walking alongside the wagon as Bartlett led the team.

Nick had a few minutes before the Bartlett's turn, so he watched Lizzy. She still wore the ill-fitting brown paisley. He shifted in the saddle, impatient to give her the fabric purchased in town for her. There were empty hours between here and Fort Kearny to invent a story. He could ensure she had material for a new dress by then. The Bartlett's readied for their crossing. As Lizzy approached, Nick noticed a limp but couldn't tell which side she favored. Must be mud on her shoes, he concluded, riding up to the wagon.

After helping the Bartlett's across, Nick led his horse up the other side, following the wagon as it joined the group.

Sam trotted over as Nick remounted and turned his horse toward the creek. "Do you suppose Mrs. Bartlett wants to stay here?"

Nick looked toward the bank and saw Lizzy there. They watched as she'd pace to a narrow place in the creek, then go to yet another narrow place. Her actions mirrored what he'd seen earlier, if a little more frantic. "Damn," he swore under his breath.

Sighing, Sam shook his head. "I know. The girl doesn't belong here, Nick. Our dear Mrs. Bartlett is afraid of water. You know as well as I she's unfit for this journey."

Knowing this argument's path didn't stop him from trying. "We've helped terrified people across worse than this. Mrs. Bartlett will be fine. I think you're borrowing trouble."

The younger man snorted a laugh. "I am? What will she do when a ferry overturns?" He indicated her, still pacing the bank. "You know as well as I what she is facing. Bartlett needs to be a decent sort and take her back home."

Glaring at his brother, Nick retorted, "What home and what makes you think he'll give up California for Lizzy?"

Sam stopped watching her to stare at him through accusing eyes. "I don't suppose you are the one to convince Bartlett to do the right thing by 'Lizzy.'"

He searched for an argument in vain. Nick knew what answer his brother expected of him. "You're right. Her husband needs to send Mrs. Bartlett back to her family."

"I'm glad you see reason. Now if we can just convince him to take her to whatever relatives he has." Sam frowned at Nick. "Assuming he has relatives. Good lord! What if he was hatched?"

Nick appreciated him trying to lift the mood, even if it failed. "Not me. I won't be convincing anyone if it means she leaves."

Sam laughed. "I've owned mules more agreeable than you. Very well, let's hope she survives to California."

"Maybe not on your watch, but she'll survive just fine on my mine," Nick said through a clenched jaw.

The surly tone didn't affect Sam's grin. "Lawrence and Chuck are up ahead, so let's get going. Help your lady across, and sometime between now and the Platte, have Bartlett teach her how to swim." He turned to rejoin the others.

At his brother's fading hoof beats, he looked at Lizzy, hoping she saw his smile from this distance when she glanced up at him. She returned his grin and his heart felt odd in his chest. Lizzy bit her lip, looked back at the creek, and took a couple of fast steps toward the water. He shook his head, amazed. Even scared to death, she was going to jump. She stopped just short of leaping, stepping back up the bank. He saw her steel herself and try again. Nick gritted his teeth, vowing to protect such a brave and beautiful woman from Bartlett's fists.

CHAPTER 5

Beth looked at the muddy water, clenching then releasing her hands. Even though she couldn't see the bottom due to silt the passing wheels churned, the water appeared to be only a couple of feet deep. Pacing back to the only other narrow point, she trembled. If she hiked her skirt, could she jump the gap? What if she fell backwards into the water? She couldn't breathe from the fear of such a thing. Maybe some rocks stuck out in the middle and she could step from one to the other. Beth shook her head, deciding to look downstream for an even narrower place. She walked until the stream curved, not seeing any islands to hop onto.

"I have to get across," Beth muttered, frustrated with her fears. She went two and fro, mulling over which spot would be easiest to jump over. Though none of the currents flowed swiftly enough to overturn wagons, the force might pull her under and downstream. Tumbling with her head under the water like before didn't bear thinking of again. She gripped her hands to stop their shaking, her heart pounding as if trying to beat out of her chest.

Dag had gone ahead, angry at her dithering. Glancing up to check their progress, she saw the last wagon leaving the ditch. Watching how the men scrambled to get up the incline, she noticed Nicholas hanging back. Once the last few stragglers resumed the journey, he started towards her. "Oh dear," she murmured, ashamed. She needed to get across before he chastised her. So Beth took a deep breath and a couple of steps backwards, steeling herself to jump.

"Ma'am?" Nicholas's horse splashed as he rode over to her. "You need help crossing?"

"I shouldn't."

"Sure you should. No lady wants to get her shoes wet if she can help it." He held out his hand. "Hop up here, and I'll carry you across."

After wiping her sweaty left palm on her hip, she took his hand. She put her left foot in a stirrup he held out for her with his toe. He pulled her up with such force, she couldn't help but swing her right leg over the horse.

Seated astride that way, the position surprised her, and Beth looked behind to check how her dress fell. She laughed and tapped Nicholas on the shoulder. "Look, your horse looks very nice in brown."

He turned, seeing the skirt covering the horse's behind, and laughed. "She looks beautiful. If mares wore dresses, there'd be more colts and fillies in the world."

She chuckled at his joke then stopped, aware of her hands at his waist. He still looked at her, into her eyes, and her smile faded when his did. The same feeling of desire hit as it had when he helped her up the embankment earlier in the morning. Nicolas had such long lashes, but in a masculine face like his, they didn't seem out of place. Suddenly shy, she glanced down his nose to his mouth and the dark shadow of his beard. "We should get going."

"We should." He tapped the horse with his heel. "The others won't be waiting on us."

"All our food is rolling away even now." She had the odd feeling she'd disappointed him.

"Very good priorities, I see." He turned, urging the horse into a faster walk.

"One can live on only peace and quiet for a short time before the stomach objects."

"That's a good point." They continued for a little while before he added, "You're a smart woman to put the supplies first. You seem practical too. Maybe Sam and I should have consulted with you instead of Bartlett on what to pack for the trip."

Laughing, she retorted, "If I'd been the leader of us both, this whole fiasco wouldn't have happened."

"Fiasco?"

She looked at the back of his head. "Yes. The word describes my situation perfectly." So close to him, Beth saw silver glints among the black hair. He must be somewhat near her age. Peering over Nicholas's shoulder, she saw them draw closer to the wagon train. She gripped the back of his saddle, the cantle, reluctant to reach the others just yet, if ever. Beth examined how his torso tapered from wide shoulders to narrow waist. She longed to wrap her arms around him, to feel if he were in as good a shape she imagined him to be. A frustrated sigh escaped her.

"You sound impatient to get to your wagon." He turned his profile to her. "Don't fret; we'll be there soon."

An urge to lean against him and kiss his lips gripped her stronger than she'd ever expected. Seeing him in profile, feeling the warmth of him, Beth gasped, "I don't want to get there."

Nicholas stopped the horse, facing her as much as he could. "What?"

Heavens, what had she done now? Beth swallowed, afraid to say anything he might tell Dag. He looked intently at her, with some shock but no censor. Every time Beth stared into his eyes like this, she liked them more than the prior time. She couldn't stop trembling, trying to say something less true to her heart. "I, um, I don't want to not care." No, that wasn't she meant, but what else could hide her meaning and still sound similar?

When he smiled, his entire face beamed. He spoke in a low voice. "You, my dear, said you don't want to get there."

She put her hand on his shoulder, scared of what he'd now say to everyone else. "Please, I didn't mean anything by it." Beth bit her lip and then added, "I only meant riding a horse is preferable to walking."

He watched as the last wagon disappeared into a copse of trees. Nicholas cupped his hand and pressed the back of his fingers against her bruised temple. "I'm sure I know what you meant, Lizzy."

"Lizzy?" Even though his hand felt cool and soothing to her injured eye, him using her sister's name infuriated Beth. Shock at the familiarity mixed with the anger over the name filled her. She struggled to keep the hate from her voice, but couldn't. "I never want you to call me that again. I don't consider it my name."

He lowered his arm at Beth's tone, aware he'd angered her somehow. "I understand, Mrs. Bartlett. Please forgive me." His eyes narrowed as he faced ahead. "We need to get moving." Nicholas kicked the horse into a slow gallop, the fastest the terrain allowed.

The speed unnerved her, causing Beth to wrap her arms around his waist. Her breath caught as her torso came into full contact with his. His shirt hid a lean blacksmith's build. Beth struggled to not just melt into him. She could much easier pretend to be Nicholas's wife than she ever could Daggart's. Even on his best behavior, Dag couldn't compete with this man. She wanted to wrap her limbs around Nicholas Granville like a sweet pea vine wrapped around a trellis. The very idea left her short of breath.

He slowed the horse as they reached the end of the train. With that, she let go of him. Seeing the hard grit of his teeth, Beth couldn't let the prior incident pass by unexplained. She didn't want him angry with her too. "You don't and can't understand at all why I don't like you in particular calling me Lizzy."

Nicholas helped her down, and then dismounted. "I can't understand, you say? Try me."

She looked around them, seeing if her husband lurked nearby to overhear her confession. "I can't say without there being trouble." Beth stumbled, smiling when he grabbed her hand to support her. Being off the horse and on her own two feet reminded her of how much her blisters hurt. She'd have to find a way to stay off of her feet and ease out the aches.

Squinting at her, a thin trace of sarcasm sounded in his question. "So do you prefer being addressed as Mrs. Bartlett from me, but prefer 'my dear' from my brother, then?"

Beth heard her married name from Nicholas and shuddered. She looked away towards the camp and spotted Daggart's blue check shirt. He saw them, and while well out of earshot, he'd be close enough soon enough. Her palms still damp from holding Nicholas so close, her face burned. Rubbing her hands dry against her skirt, she absently said, "Yes, I prefer it, thank you."

"You're welcome, Mrs. Bartlett."

The sarcasm in his voice jolted her out of her preoccupation with her aching feet, sweaty palms, and approaching husband. "I'm sorry. What did you say before?" she asked as he led his horse to the right, away from her. He had mentioned something about his brother—my dear, no, my dear from his brother. Now she understood his apparent irritation. "Oh my goodness, Mr. Granville, no, I need to clarify! May I quickly tell you something in strictest confidence?"

He nodded an assent, and motioning him to follow her, she led him towards the leftmost wagons. She grit her teeth against the blisters rubbed raw by Lizzy's shoes. Once somewhat secluded, Beth checked to ensure they were alone and not overheard. Standing next to him, both facing the wagons to watch for anyone approaching, she leaned closer. Touching arm to arm she told Nicholas, "My name is Elizabeth Ann, not Elizabeth Louise. I can't tell you why, but Daggart insists on me being Lizzy Lou instead of Beth Ann." She glanced at him, feeling shy when seeing his eyes examining her face. The anger sharpening his features had softened as he listened. "My preference is for Beth, but I have no choice in this matter."

He studied her for a moment before saying, "Your explanation clouds more than it clears, but if you prefer Elizabeth Ann, maybe I can use Beth Ann when we're alone?"

No one had called Beth by her own name in such a long time. Now to hear it from Nicholas left her shaky inside. "When we're alone?" she whispered and looked around for others in their group. They had been alone together for too long already. And yet, the entire time seemed but a second to her. Every moment with him felt right, like she'd found her true place in life. "Yes, I'd like that very much."

He grinned, "Good, because I like Beth anyway. It suits you better." Nicholas gestured towards the wagon party disappearing from view over the next hill. "Much as I like chatting with you, ma'am, we need to get back soon or we're both in trouble for skipping chores."

"Oh! Of course." She followed, catching up with his long strides when he paused for her. They brushed arms as they neared the group. The contact tingled along her skin, and she glanced up at him. Beth didn't want to be Daggart's human pack mule in California; she wanted to be Nicholas's wife instead. The betraying thought shook her. She stumbled, her knees too unsteady to continue.

He grabbed her arm to support her. "Are you all right?" Concern laced his voice.

Samuel galloped up to them, the grass muffling the hoof beats. "There you two are. You saved me from launching a search party." He dismounted upon seeing Beth falter. "Mrs. Bartlett?" He glanced at Nicholas. "Nick? Is she all right?"

Nicholas put his palm to her cheek and forehead, checking for fever. "I don't know. We were walking; she stopped and turned white."

The fuss embarrassed her, and she refused to draw a crowd. Working up a reassuring smile, she said, "I'm fine." Goodness, Samuel was handsome too and seemed as fresh as morning glories. She smiled, knowing why all the girls fussed over him. In an effort to reassure the two men, she added, "We have a jar of rain water in the wagon. I'm sure it's thirst causing all this. After a little drink I'll be right as, well, right as rain."

"Ma'am?" Sam began.

"Yes, Mr. Granville?"

He returned her smile. "While we're in the woods, your husband will want to pick up a couple day's firewood. Just enough until we find buffalo chips."

"Oh." She wrinkled her nose, imagining the spring flower smell of today being replaced by the odor of burning chips.

He laughed. "Now, it's not as bad as all that. They burn clean."

Not quite convinced, Beth stated before censoring herself, "I'd prefer hickory or oak over anything out of a buffalo's end."

Samuel laughed at her forthrightness. "All of us do, myself included." He tipped his hat before swinging back onto his horse and riding to the front.

He gave her forehead one last check before letting his hand fall. "Mrs. Bartlett."

"Mr. Granville." Beth watched as he echoed Sam and rode to the front of their group. She saw her wagon and tried to take steps without limping as best as she could in that direction. Once she reached their cart, she could hold on to the back, letting it hide just how much her feet hurt. If little children could run and play during this trip, she could at least walk.

She sighed. The daily routine already loomed menacing ahead due to her feet. She tried and failed to motivate herself into wandering around while looking for the rare stick of firewood.

Daggart came around their wagon, startling her. "What'd they want? Where were you earlier anyway?"

"He wanted to encourage us to gather firewood now before reaching the plains." After the freedom of gazing at Nicholas most of the afternoon, having to see Daggart's fleshy, pasty face now disappointed.

He grunted, frowning at her. "You'd better get started gathering, then."

"I will," she nodded, reaching for the water jar he held. "I'd like a drink first."

"After me. I've been walking, not riding a fancy pants horse." He unscrewed the cap and drank deeply.

Seeing the water drain almost dry, she cleared her throat. "Dag, please."

He handed her the nearly empty jar. "You can have the rest."

Before she could help herself, Beth retorted, "Thank you." She put a hand to her mouth. Through her fingers, she added, "I appreciate it."

Giving her a mean stare, he strolled up to the oxen. She swallowed all the water, careful not to drink from where his lips had touched. Beth placed the jar and its lid back in the wagon before beginning the hunt for dinner's firewood.

Beth tried to encourage herself to search for this evening's fuel by making a game of finding new flowers and new types of birds. It didn't work. She'd rather eat a cold dinner of dried fruit than walk any more than necessary in these horrible shoes. She resented Daggart for burning her larger pair when he'd caught her secretly wearing them. Her efforts in modifying Lizzie's shoes to fit her own feet had been a disaster. Too loose in some spots, too tight in others, Beth sighed. Creating new footwear from wood and knitted wool would be better than these she wore.

She glanced up from the ground to look at everyone else. The wagons crashed through the woods, some needing an extra pull from those on horseback. Some families had two wagons to themselves. Beth imagined having so much as well, full of animals and plants to start a farm in California.

So lost in her thoughts, she didn't notice the unfiltered sunlight until a few yards had passed. She blinked, amazed at the emptiness. A few tree-lined creeks broke up the background of rolling hills. The blue sky dominated the landscape. Beth had never seen so much space in one area. Clear hilltops and open valleys were one thing, this vastness something else. The open prairie overwhelmed her. Insects buzzed and birds sang love songs to each other. Wildflowers swayed in the breeze, their scent adding to the torn grass smell left behind by the wagon train's wheels. She stopped, looking ahead, then back at the dense forest behind them. The blossomed redbuds and wild dogwoods gave red and white bursts of color against the bright spring green trees. She wanted to go back to her farm, to the safe canopy of the forest and the enclosed fields of home.

She saw Samuel ride out from the underbrush. Beth tried to smile a greeting as he and Lawrence trotted up to her.

"I've seen that expression before, mostly on a filly before she bolts for home." Samuel asked his hired hand, "Don't you agree?"

Lawrence grinned. "I wondered why she looked so familiar."

Squinting, Beth put her hands on her hips and playfully demanded, "Now, tell me how I compare to a horse."

Putting his hat on his chest, Lawrence replied, "Why ma'am, only in ways that are the best of the finest mare ever born."

She laughed and glanced at Samuel. "Has he been taking charm lessons from you?"

"Not at all. Every man in this outfit has been instructed to treat every woman with respect. I can't help it if other men's rude behavior makes us seem charming." He put his hat on his chest as Lawrence had.

Beth laughed at their crude attempt of innocence. "I'm sure. Hopefully the other gals buy what you're selling."

The two put their hats back on and grinned at each other. Lawrence started a retort, "They always put—"

Beth raised her chin and a hand to stop him. "No, don't say it. I misspoke. Polite ladies, even those comparable to horses, don't discuss the selling of anything."

Both men chuckled until something ahead caught Lawrence's attention. He looked to Samuel for permission, who nodded. The hired hand tipped his hat at her before riding off to the front. Beth turned to see him go, catching sight of Daggart talking with Nicholas.

"You're right, ladies don't." He glanced up and past her head, distracted. "I wouldn't expect you to ever discuss selling."

She heard hoof beats behind, and suspecting Nicholas, resisted the urge to turn around. "Thank you."

"Mr. Lawrence had it partially correct. The only possible way you could compare to a horse is if the mare were the finest Arabian." He wore an ornery expression. "Isn't that right, Nick?"

"We can discuss what you mean by that later. Right now, I'd like to get to camp before dark. There are no stragglers?"

"No one save the Bartletts."

"I've spoken to Bartlett about his lagging behind."

Beth felt uneasy. Judging by their expressions, more went unsaid between the men. Had she held back the camp due to her wanderings? If Nicholas spoke to her husband about the delay, Daggart would ensure she'd hear about it that evening. She glanced toward their wagon, now further ahead. The two men might see how tender her feet were as she started walking if she limped. She took a deep breath, determined to ignore the pain, and strode to catch up with her husband.

Dag gave her a surly glance as she walked beside him. "The captains talk to you, yet?" he asked.

His face scrunched more than usual, she noticed and wondered how to respond. Better with a short answer to pull more information from him. "A little, yes."

"They told me, Nick did, to keep you in line."

She doubted Nicholas would be so blunt but kept quiet, waiting for Daggart to continue. When he didn't elaborate, Beth asked, "Did either of the captains have any other observations?"

"He also said if you didn't keep up, I'd have to tie you to the wagon like Erleen."

Beth laughed at the image in her mind of both she and Erleen being led on a rope. She looked at the man's face and saw by his expression that he lied. Or at least told a half-truth. Calling his bluff, she teased, "You're right, if I don't, you'll have to tie me up like our poor cow."

He blinked in surprise. "Yeah, so, stay with the wagon."

Chuck came up to the couple, leading them to their place in the circle. Beth looked at the sun, still rather far from setting. "Did one of the Granvilles say anything about why we're on a hill and already circling the wagons?"

"No. They didn't have to." Dag unhooked the oxen from their yoke, leading them away to a nearby creek. "You saw the Indians we've already passed. You can't trust them, even the tamed ones. They'd as soon scalp you as look at you."

Beth had only seen the one this morning while getting water for coffee. Unless very well concealed, he'd had no weapon. He certainly didn't have a bow and arrow strapped to his back as she'd read about in the newspaper.

"Get Erleen to the water." He spotted some of the hands riding by, and as they drew nearer, his voice grew louder. "You'll want to milk her afterward, get us some water for tomorrow, and start my supper, woman."

One of the men, Chuck, tipped his hat and winked as he rode by them. Dag scowled at her. "Stop flirting with the men, Lizzy Lou, and get busy. We don't have all night."

She wanted to defend herself, but past arguments had taught her a lesson. Beth reached into the back of the wagon, grabbed the bucket, and untied Erleen to lead her to the creek. The cow drank with deep slurps while Beth rinsed the day's dust from the pail. Children splashed downstream, playing and yelling. The noise didn't seem to bother her cow, and Beth led her up the bank to where new grass grew through the old from last fall.

One of the younger children wandered over to her. Beth glanced at the little girl whose eyes widened. "What happened to your eye?" she asked.

"My eye?" Beth's cheeks burned as she realized how casual she'd been in revealing her bruises. Most times around everyone else, the sunbonnet hid the purple as it faded to yellow. The hat restricted her vision so much she hated wearing it and she'd forgotten the need to do so what with the distraction of Erleen and the water.

The girl pointed at Beth's face. "It's not pretty."

"No, it's not." Beth felt compelled to add, "A branch hit me while we went through the big woods."

"A branch?" The child stood there, staring at her. Then, she leaned forward to get a better look at the bruise. "Did it hurt?"

Beth smiled at the small girl's grown up and serious tone. "Very much, but it's getting better every day." She didn't like having to tell a lie to the child. The adults possessed too many manners to ask, or else they knew the truth without questioning her.

The little one nodded and turned when hearing one of the others yell for her. "Goodbye, ma'am!" she said and scampered away.

Beth settled in, facing west, to watch her cow eat and the sun set. Erleen pulled eagerly at the new grass. They'd not had time today to loiter, and she felt sure the cow must have longed to graze a few times. Various animal trails in the woods or valleys called to Beth as well. She wanted to follow them, if only to see where they led. After trying to wiggle her toes, she considered taking off Lizzy's shoes but decided against doing so. She figured putting them back on after a rest would have her too used to the relief. Better to wait until after dinner and take them off for the night.

With the cow having such a good nature, Beth milked her as the animal ate. She stood once Erleen had her fill of dinner and scooped up the bucket. Campfires dotted the land in the early evening light. The air hung heavy with the cooling of the day and scent of food. Walking up to the wagons, she had hoped Daggart started their campfire for dinner but no welcoming light glowed. She tied Erleen for the night and emptied the milk into a glass jar and sealed it with a lid. While fetching water, she kept a look out for her husband.

In the fading light of dusk, the creek appeared more sinister to her. She peered, trying to find the bottom, but the inky darkness of the liquid prevented her. Beth took a couple of deep breaths to keep calm. She reassured her fears, asserting she wasn't getting her shoes wet, just the bucket. Bending down a little, she strained to tip some water into the container to rinse off the milk. Beth cleaned out the bucket a little at a time. Finally, knowing she stalled the inevitable, she leaned further over, scooping as much as possible in one try. Satisfied with the heft of the bucket, she went back to camp. If lucky, she'd not need to get near the stream again this evening.

Their small campfire welcomed her. The near full moon hadn't risen yet. The people in camp played music, sang, and talked around their own temporary hearths. Beth supposed Dag had started the fire since his bedroll lay nearby. She put the water bucket on the fire to start boiling and searched their stores for dinner fixings.

Dag came around the wagon's end, stopping in his tracks upon seeing her. "You ain't cooked us anything yet?"

"Not yet, but dinner won't take long." She hated being late with his food.

"What is the damned hold up?" He kicked his bedroll out of the circle of light. Dag then stomped off to retrieve it while complaining, "First, we can't stop for nothin' until nearly tomorrow. Now you've been lyin' around all evening, not cookin' anythin' to eat. I'm hungry and I deserve a hot meal."

Beth clenched her jaw, not willing to argue with him. Any sort of discussion would anger him into violence, especially when he was hungry. In silence, she set up the bacon frying in the pan and mixed the cornbread. Beth didn't figure the cornbread could be as tasty cooked over the fire as in an oven, but it was his favorite and would quiet Daggart for now. When he settled down on his retrieved bedroll, she asked, "Were you able to hunt today?"

"No."

"I don't think anyone did." She left the food to take the

boiling water from the fire. Beth took his cup from the wagon and filled it with the fresh milk. "Are you going to set up our tent?"

"No. No one else is, either. There ain't no rain in the air, and it's warm out tonight."

After eating, Daggart spread out on his makeshift bed. Beth stifled a sigh while eating what remained of the food. She felt like to going sleep at the moment too, but poured cooled water into a jar for tomorrow and capped it. Dishes went into the bucket for later washing.

Daggart stirred when the metal and glass clanged. "Stop it, Lizzy. I'm trying to sleep."

She set the bucket down by the wagon wheel, unwilling to irritate him into hopping up and being mean to her. Her feet hurt standing there, plus, she didn't want to go to the creek for washing. Waiting until morning also didn't appeal to her, but at least there'd be light. Beth sat and pried the shoes from her feet, gasping at the cool air soothing them. The chill felt good on the bare skin. There were no new blisters or raw flesh, just deep grooves where the seams pressed into her insole. She wiggled her toes, even if they hurt, and began rubbing the sore spots. When her feet felt better after the care, she crawled into her bedroll. Her cloth sack of spun wool doubled as a pillow. She settled her head onto the cushy comfort.

"I sure do miss Lizzy."

Daggart's gruff confession surprised her out of her drowsiness. He'd mentioned her sister before this but not since her father died and not as if Lizzy was truly gone. His sadness triggered memories of her sister's death and their father's mental decline from the loss. "I do too, Daggart."

He snapped at her, "Then you better start doin' a better job than usual of bein' her. You keep your promise, I keep mine."

She lay there, staring up at the stars with tears flowing. Beth didn't sob aloud. This was an old hurt in her heart. They'd not been identical by a long shot, but she and Lizzy had been twins and still closer than most sisters. First their mother, then Lizzy, and finally Pa all left her with Daggart. She glanced over at him. He'd settled in at arm's distance from her.

If he'd been the same man Lizzy had married, Beth might not mind taking her sister's place. She struggled to keep from sniffling and letting him know she was crying. Lizzy died because of her.

She'd promised Pa and Daggart to make up for her horrible mistake. There was no sense in her wasting time wishing things were different.

The new day began too soon. Beth woke slowly, wiping the sleep from her eyes. She looked at the ashes, hoping a little spark remained for this morning. Daggart's bedroll was gone, as was he. She propped up on one arm, pushing the hair from her face. Her braid had come undone in the night, so she searched for the pin.

"Good morning, Mrs. Bartlett."

She smiled at Nicholas's voice, smoothing back the wisps and sliding the hairpin into place. "Good morning, I think."

"You don't know for certain?" He walked over to her and squatted.

Even when he was lower, she had to lift her chin to look into his eyes. She stifled a yawn. "Not until I'm awake."

"I can fix that."

She watched while packing her bed and wool for tonight as he put fresh wood on their embers. "Thank goodness," Beth exclaimed as flames flickered. "I thought they were dead."

Nick smiled at her. "Not entirely." He took the bucket of dishes. "If you'll find your coffee and put a little more wood on the fire, I'll wash these for you."

Blinking, she watched him stroll away with her dishes. Beth did as he asked, putting a few sticks on the fire and getting a scoop of beans for the coffee pot. She checked on Erleen and the oxen, and Nick returned shortly after.

"Great!" Nick poured water into the pot. "This will help you on your feet."

"It will. Thank you." She smiled. "Did you want some coffee when this is done?"

"I've had mine already. Excuse me while I rouse the other sleepyheads." He tipped his hat and left her there.

She frowned, unhappy at what this meant. Daggart had been right. Beth had held up the entire group. The Granvilles did talk to him. Dag hadn't been falsely blaming her yesterday. Her face burned in embarrassment as she mixed up biscuits as fast as possible and set them on the fire to cook.

A little while after the coffee began boiling, she poured a cup. Beth sipped, already dreading the day's walk. She waited for her husband as long as possible, keeping busy by making sure she'd packed everything else. She folded the biscuits into a napkin for breakfast later in the morning. Daggart could grab his own food while on the move.

All that remained was putting on her shoes. Beth picked them up and went to sit on the wagon tongue. Walking on the cool, trampled grass had felt good. She forced herself to put them on using the buttonhook to fasten them. One of the top buttons popped off, the pressure tearing a hole in the leather. She gingerly stood to her feet, wincing at the pain. Beth took a couple of limped steps toward the oxen.

She pulled both animals into place and fastened their yoke. Seeing her husband, Beth waved him over to her. She asked for his unneeded expertise, knowing he loved thinking himself the smarter of the two of them. "Have I done this correctly?"

He made a show of checking and double-checking the harnesses. "It's good." Daggart started the oxen on down the crooked road. "We're going in front today. I don't need you causin' trouble for us, Lizzy."

Beth fell in step beside him, forcing herself not to limp. "I don't plan on doing so."

"Hope not, because these men are our guides and guards to the gold, and you're not messin' it up for me." He glanced around. "I've seen you wander off, talkin' to one man, then another. I don't know what your plan is, but you'd better count on diggin' once we get to California."

"That is my only plan." She told him the truth. Whatever plans Beth ever had, Daggart tore through as if her wishes were spider webs. "Unless, you decide on a different life for us."

"Gold is my only plan." He glared at her. "Mr. Granville seems to be taken with you. I've see him smilin' and bein' polite and all."

Nicholas never seemed to need encouragement. Now nervous of how much Daggart suspected of her feelings, Beth swallowed. "I don't call him over specially."

"I'm thinkin' you might be doin' just that. In case you get ideas, you're not the only woman he likes to help around here. I've seen him bein' a bit too friendly with the other gals too, especially the married ones."

"I see." She bit her lip, chewing. Beth didn't know how to

feel. Foolish, because she thought he treated her with special regard? Embarrassed, since she had feelings he'd never return? Or sadness, certain she'd stay married to someone else?

"You better see real good. Just because he calls all the women 'my dear,' they all think he's a gentleman." Dag snorted, "Those manners are wiles dressed in Sunday best."

Oh heavens, he was talking about Samuel. She stifled a chuckle at her mistake. Still, Beth didn't think Samuel was as conniving as Daggart had said and asked him, "Why do you suppose he only pays favors to the married women instead of the eligible girls?"

"Crazy woman. The man doesn't want to get caught by some husband-huntin' devil." Daggart slowed and took her arm as if protecting her. "Look out, there's trouble up ahead."

She stepped away from him and forward a little to see why the fuss. The wagons stacked backwards from a ravine. Riders galloped north and south from the train's front.

"Go see what the holdup is but keep out of the way," Dag ordered her from where he waited. "Don't get hurt and hold us back, Lizzy."

Beth went, resentfully doing as he'd asked because she was curious too. As she made her way up front, other women and children joined her. All speculated as to the reason for stopping before noontime. Then everyone saw why. The ravine, seeming thin from a distance, instead gaped wide enough to swallow wagons. A high-pitched whistle caught everyone's attention. The rider to the south waved an arm in the air.

Samuel rode past at a trot, saying, "We'll head downstream for half a mile, cross the creek bed, and then see." The first wagon followed him toward the south.

She searched for but didn't see the north rider. The southern rider, now small, picked his way down to the bottoms. Wagons in front of Beth obscured her view. The wheels also kicked up more dust, the ground having dried from the rains of two days ago. A gritty wind blew from the west and she blinked away the grains.

From what she'd seen, the opposite bank appeared very steep. She trusted the captains and hands knew what to do. Walking back to Dag, Beth wondered how anyone could coax animals up the steep wall.

"Took you long enough."

Beth ignored Dag's tone and an argument. "We have to go south and across."

He let out an exasperated snort. "I didn't see any water."

She tried to remember seeing the glint of a stream. "No, there isn't any. The bed is dry."

"Did you get water this morning?"

She'd forgotten. Clenching and releasing her hands, she didn't want to admit to overlooking a task so important. "For us, but not for the animals."

He stopped the animals to glare at her. "Didn't you think we needed water for the oxen? How're you going to get milk from Erleen tomorrow if she don't get water today?"

His volume increased with each word. She saw others glance at them then look away in a hurry. Beth didn't blame them. She didn't want to be caught up in a fight either. "I'm sorry, Dag. We've always been near a creek of some sort. I didn't think about needing water until just now."

"There's a lot you don't think about, woman." He spit. "Am I going to have to do everythin' for you?"

She closed her eyes hard for a moment, willing herself not to snap back at him. "No, you won't. You're right, I do need to think more."

"See that you do," he sneered. "We need them in California. They'll be so helpful in the mines that I'd sooner bury you before them, Lizzy Lou."

Her chin snapped up at the name. Could he mean what he'd said? "You prefer a couple of animals to your wife?"

"When you're not being the wife I want, I do. You know the agreement."

Curse the bargain. Beth hated every minute passed since then. "I know you don't mean it, but very well. I'll make sure the big bucket is full of water if you make sure it's put in the wagon."

"Will do." Daggart pulled on the oxen, leading them to the ravine's slope.

She let him continue on, unable to bear being near him another moment. Other wagons behind her kept Beth from loitering in one spot too long. Curious, she walked to the edge of the chasm. No streams flowed below. Creeks, rivers, and other ponds had been so plentiful in Missouri. She never thought to store any water for the prairie. If tales about the great desert past the

Platte were true, she needed a better plan.

The northern rider galloped up, saw her watching him, and slowed to tip his hat. This one, different from the others, wore a green flannel shirt, open halfway down his hairy chest. Leather buckskin similar to Nicholas's coat, but with fringe, covered his legs. Like the other hands, he had pistols in a holster draped over the front of his saddle. She'd seen him around the camp but never spoke. Beth returned his greeting with a smile and nod as he rode past.

A long line of white-topped wagons snaked their way along the ravine going north. They traveled the slope into the slight canyon without incident. She followed at a distance from the dust cloud while not lagging too far behind everyone else.

The train rolled for what seemed like forever to Beth's empty stomach. She looked up at the midday sun. The procession hadn't stopped for noon. She hoped they made an early night of it. Though her feet ached, she kept going, knowing biscuits and water waited for her ahead.

Beth hurried up to the back of their wagon, finding Dag had already eaten his lunch. He'd left her water and a biscuit, something she'd not expected after their earlier conversation. She ate and a couple of drinks later, she wanted to give the last bit of water to their animals. Considering his earlier anger, Beth decided to consult Daggart first.

"What the hell?" He stood with the other men, arguing. "We have to unload everythin' just to get up the hill?"

His raised voice unnerved her and drew attention to him. She glanced around, hoping no one else heard his complaining. Beth walked up and peered to the front of the queue. The wagon at the foot of the ravine's exit buzzed with activity. Several people handed off the contents onto the ground. She watched as the person inside hopped out, signaled to the driver, and waited until the wagon topped the embankment. A line of people handed the boxes and sacks of belongings up to the cart. They made quick work of repacking everything.

She went back to Daggart. "I don't think it will be too bad. There's a lot of help and it seems to go fast."

He turned to her, hand raised. "Shut up!" Then, as if aware a few people saw his actions, he lowered his arm. Glaring at her, he ground out between clenched teeth, "I'm glad you reckon so. Let's see what you say unloadin' and loadin' our own."

She knew better than to argue but blurted, "The men and boys handle the slope. The women are driving the animals and watching out for the children." Beth yelped when he grabbed her upper arm. He wasn't gentle this time, or protective.

He smiled at the others as they walked by, dismissing them with a nod, and held her arm with a hard squeeze. "Since we don't have children, you'll help the men, won't you," Dag growled.

She bit her lip at the pain and knew he wasn't asking. "Of course. I'll want to make sure they do it right for you, won't I?"

"Good. Now get up there and make yourself useful," he said with a shove.

Stumbling, she caught herself from falling, turning her ankle a little. A slight stab of pain went up her calf that she ignored in her hurry to get out of Dag's sight. Beth breathed in deep, releasing it in a whoosh, trying to disregard the sting in her left ankle. She shook her head as if to shake away the hurt, having no way to avoid a limp. Between the tiny shoes and now this, she took each step with caution. Not everyone in the group strode hard and strong. Surely no one would notice her walking a little lame too.

She reached the latest wagon being driven up the incline. Addressing the nearest hired hand, the one she'd seen riding from the north, Beth asked, "How may I help?"

"Ce qui? Je ne comprends pas." He nodded toward Nicholas riding up to them. "Demandez-lui, s'il vous plait."

"Qu'est-ce que c'est?" Nicholas asked of the man.

Shrugging, the worker replied, "Je ne la connais pas. Entretien à elle."

"Ah. Hello, Mrs. Bartlett." Nicholas smiled down at her and tipped his hat. "I'm afraid Claude here doesn't understand. Maybe I can help?"

She smiled, her face feeling hot. "That's what I asked him, actually. How may I help with this?" She pointed to the current wagon being unloaded.

Nicholas addressed Claude, "Je serai là dans un moment. Allons." He frowned at her, shaking his head. "That's ridiculous. You can't help with this. Just stay out of the way and we'll handle it."

"Oh. I see." Beth chewed a little on her lower lip, fretting. She couldn't go back to her own wagon, angering Daggart. He'd say she didn't try to be useful. His horse snorted, and with a start, she realized Nicholas still stood beside her. Beth smiled up at him, "You will tell me if I can be useful in any way?"

He dismounted. "I appreciate you asking, but the men can take care of this much faster."

"Of course. I was being silly to ask." She looked down, hiding her face with her sunbonnet and feeling very foolish.

He sighed, smacking gloves against his hand, "If you must do something constructive, I'd prefer you wait over there." Nicholas gave her his reins. "Hold mine and the others' horses while we get across. Make sure they get something to eat while waiting."

"I will. Thank you for letting me help." She turned to lead his horse out of the way.

"Hold up." Checking to make sure Claude was out of earshot, Nicholas leaned in a little, speaking in a lowered voice. "I can't let anything happen to you, Beth. If the animals spook and pull free, you'd be crushed. Please stay back while we get everyone up the embankment."

She nodded, better understanding his unfriendly reaction to her offer. "I will, but what about you? I couldn't let you get hurt either."

Nicholas's chin went up and his eyes narrowed. Someone called his name in the distance. Holding his hand up in a wait gesture, he took a step closer. "Elizabeth."

The stormy grey of his eyes drew her in, leaving Beth unable to look anywhere else but him. She couldn't break her gaze any more than he could seem to break his. "Yes?" she asked, lifting her face for a kiss. Her lips parted as she realized what her gesture subconsciously told him.

He laughed. "No, no kisses." They heard him called again, more insistent this time. "Please keep an eye on the horses."

She nodded in assent as he answered the demand for his attention. She did as he'd asked, going up the incline to the mounts. Beth patted their necks, cooing at them to trust her and scratching their foreheads. She took two sets of reins in each hand, leading them around to give her a better view of each wagon's struggles uphill. Beth used the distance from everyone as a chance to watch Nicholas as he worked. He'd read her expression correctly. She'd wanted to kiss him and didn't know how to feel about him telling her no. By the time she spotted Daggart standing to the side, also watching everyone else, the men worked like a machine—unloading, driving up the incline, reloading, then moving the wagon for the next in line.

People milled around ahead of her as she waited, women searching for firewood, men wandering off to hunt, children playing or sitting in the shade. Beth took the horses along the dry creek bed while searching for new grass or hay. She scanned the ground for animal tracks, pretty stones, or anything else interesting as the animals ate. Every so often, upon hearing a holler, she peeked out from under her sunbonnet, knowing which man she wanted to see. Not Claude with his hairy face and neck, nor did she watch for Lawrence, his hat pulled low over his eyes and long white hair braided down his back.

Samuel caught her attention a couple of times; he looked enough like his brother. Her heart hadn't raced upon seeing him as it did when she merely thought of Nicholas though. Remembering how her name sounded in his voice sent shivers through her. He'd said no to her accidental request and recalling the sound left her hungry to hear a yes from him. Seeing the softening in his eyes even as he refused her, the affection there left her unable to think.

Once everyone had been pulled up the embankment, Nicholas, Samuel, Lawrence, and Claude came to her for their horses. Every man was polite as he took his mount and rode away, Samuel more so than Nicholas.

"Thank you, my dear. Nick told me you'd care for them well." He tilted his head to peer at her under the brim of her bonnet.

She smiled at Nicholas's name and at the compliment. "I don't know how much care I gave them. They're very self-sufficient."

"Nonsense, Mrs. Bartlett. Lawrence and I are to scout ahead for camp and needed our horses fresh for this afternoon and evening. You are a true angel of mercy for them."

Beth laughed. "A true angel would have given them water, apples, and sugar cubes."

"True. I'm sure if you had those items, they would not have wanted to see me coming."

"Probably not," she replied, hearing Lawrence whistle.

"Until we break for camp." He tipped his hat and rode toward the other man. Both gentlemen headed in tandem to the northwest, the lead wagon slowly following.

On the other side of the shallow canyon, the country grew hilly and the road roughened from prior wheel ruts. Nearly everyone who preferred riding to walking now strolled in the fresh air away from their wagon. Only the ill stayed under their oilcloth cover. Some canopies were raised to let in the cool breeze. Other women walked with her, herding the children as they ran and played among the spring flowers.

Beth listened with inattention to the conversations flowing in the air around her, shyness keeping her quiet. She didn't feel able to chat about anything. The farm she loved was gone and too painful to discuss, as was her family. She loathed even thinking about Daggart.

The wagons ahead slowed to a halt. The front wagon turned into the familiar circle. She wondered at their stopping for the day so soon. To the north grew a grove of trees with more scattered along a creek. People already unhitched horses, oxen, and mules, leading or riding them to the gully. She caught up with their wagon. Daggart had already taken the oxen, but only them. She grabbed the larger bucket and untied Erleen to take her for a drink.

Beth searched until she found a quiet, shallow part of the river where she could see the bottom. She soon tied Erleen to a tree close to the water, thrilled at the prospect of wading. After setting down the bucket for later, she pried off Lizzy's shoes with a curse under her breath. She threw them on the bank, lifted her skirt, and walked into the shallows. Beth sighed, raising her head heavenward in silent thanks.

Her feet stirred up silt in the cool water. A little choke of panic crawled up her throat until currents drew the clouds away, calming her. She wiggled her toes, not minding how they disturbed the creek bed and instead enjoyed freedom from the cramped leather. The blisters didn't sting anymore, the cold numbing them a little. Beth enjoyed watching crawfish scurry. Minnows darted around, some nibbling her toes and tickling them. She smiled from their touch. Wanting to rest, she searched for some sort of seat allowing her to still bathe her feet.

A little way down from the sand bank was a cliff cut into the earth. Beth waded over and sat, thinking this the perfect spot. She reclined on her elbows and let the sun shine on her face despite her husband's warning to keep her skin pale. Enjoying the icy comfort flowing over her feet, she laid down on the warm ground. Beth closed her eyes, listening to the birds chirp and rustle around her, smelling the fishy river, and soaking up the late afternoon warmth.

The birds must be fussing, she thought, hearing more of a rustle than usual. Beth hoped Daggart wasn't sneaking up on her to complain about something ridiculous. She only wanted a few moments to let her feet feel a little better before tending to chores. Better to be Nicholas sneaking up on her. She'd love him whispering her name in her ear. How wonderful if he were so near. She couldn't stop a small grin while wondering how much closer he'd have to be before she protested.

She heard a horse snort, and opening her eyes in surprise, Beth looked up into an Indian's face. Before she could scream a warning to everyone, the man clamped a hand tight over her mouth.

CHAPTER 6

Nick swung the hook out to the middle of the creek's eddy. He wanted to catch something for Beth to fry. When he'd found the fishing hole, he kept it quiet from the children and others in the camp, wanting to see what he'd catch before they scared away any fish. Once he'd casted out the hook, he sat, waiting for a nibble. The insects hummed around him as new leaves rustled in the breeze.

He held the cane pole, focused on the slightest movement. A different sound than the usual caught his attention, but not enough to cause him to look away from his fishing line. He frowned, thinking some children wandered nearby. They must be sneaking up on him, he thought, not hearing anything more. Then, he heard a couple of whimpers, then a hard slap and grunt. It sounded like a fight to him, so he stood, disgusted at the interruption, and went to find the cause.

Ducking through the brush, he picked his way to the sounds, now more frequent and louder. Nick glanced up from the log he stepped over to see Beth kicking and fighting with an Indian. The man sat on her, pinning her to the ground. He held her mouth with one hand and her right wrist with the other. She fought, kneeing his back and punching him with her left hand. Nick drew his gun and pulled back the trigger. "Stop what you're doing and get away from her." With each word, he took a step forward, close enough to press the barrel against the man's temple.

The Indian held up his hands, slowly standing. "I don't want to harm the lady. She needs me." Beth scrambled away from her captor and sat at a distance, staring at them both with big eyes.

"I doubt that." He didn't want to take his stare off the man, turning his head but not his eyes to ask, "Are you all right, Beth Ann?"

"Yes, I'm fine." She crossed her arms in a hug. "He didn't hurt me."

Smiling, the darker man said, "I wouldn't. I see the woman needs me and I came to trade."

Every time the stranger said Beth needed him, Nick wanted to shoot him. "Is that so?" What did this stranger know about her? he scoffed to himself. "Sneaking up on and fighting with her is a bad way to show it."

"Yes, you are correct. But I am Jack and I have my goods to trade. Let me show you." The Indian whistled. A little shaggy pony trotted into view, down into the creek and across to the man. "If you will allow?"

Nick kept the gun aimed at him. "No, I won't allow," he said even as the man dug around in a saddlebag. "You can't just come in here and attack a woman like that and expect to trade afterwards." He took a step back. "Why did you attack her?"

"I didn't attack but kept her from alarming others. No harm to her or me." He rolled up a sleeve and displayed a scar. "Women scream and I get shot, but not this time!" Jack gave them a prideful and toothy grin, and then went to the other saddlebag, still searching for something. "I see your woman walk in the water. I also see her feet and shoes." He pulled a pair of moccasins from the bag. "She will walk in these and smile." Like a salesman back east, he turned the shoes first one way, then the next. "My wife makes them for us. She is very good, everyone tells her so." The Indian held the moccasins with one hand and pointed with the other to Beth's shoes beside her. "If she takes these, I take those? Your woman will walk better today and be happy for you tonight."

Beth gasped before exclaiming, "I'm what? He can't have my shoes, not even for those."

Nick shook his head at her. This man hadn't been tracking them for very long, he knew, or he'd not have assumed Beth was his woman. He glanced at Beth's feet poking out from her skirt. Lines from where the leather pieces had been sewn together still left an imprint on her insteps and arches. He saw her blush, pulling her feet under her dress so he couldn't see.

"She has bad feet." Jack shrugged and had spread open his hands in a "See?" gesture.

"No, Nicholas, he cannot have those shoes." She limped a couple of steps over to scoop up the disputed property. "I'll be in trouble if I let them be traded."

He gave her a stern look. Beth's feet wouldn't last to the Platte River in what she currently wore. "I suggest you take his trade. It's best for you."

"No, it isn't." Anger flashed in her eyes. "What is best is I keep wearing these as Daggart prefers."

The Indian looked from one to the other, clearly confused. "I have other items to trade."

Nick shifted his weight from one foot to the other when Beth mentioned her husband. Every time she said his name, Nick hated Bartlett more. He spat, "He's a fool if he prefers you wear these. Does the man particularly want your feet amputated?"

"Of course he doesn't!" She frowned at him, hands on her hips. "He needs my help with getting to California."

Nick smiled to hide the cold hate he felt inside for Bartlett. Her first thought wasn't of being without feet or legs but of Daggart's inconvenience. Nick wanted her able to walk for the rest of the trip as well as the rest of her life. Keeping Beth safe and free from her husband's anger being a priority, he changed tactics. "What do you think will happen to his plan if those blisters get gangrene? If he does get to the gold fields, you'll be riding in the wagon the whole way, unable to ever walk again."

She bowed her head. "You're right, but I'm sorry, Nicholas. I can't let them go to this man. Daggart will notice and be furious with me."

He released the trigger, placing the gun in his holster, unable to believe what he'd heard. "Do you mean to say he'd rather keep the shoes than keep you?" Nick walked over to her and searched her face for a lie.

She lifted her chin and replied, "Yes, he'd rather. They're one of the few things he has left from the woman he loves."

Frowning, he didn't care for the riddle in her answer. Better to think about it later, when the camp was quiet and nothing needed doing. "Keep the shoes, then, and keep your feet in the water. This won't take long."

Nick turned to Jack. "I'll trade you something else for the moccasins. Come over to my supplies and let's talk." He walked with the man, the pony following them. Nick figured if everyone saw him with Jack, no one would suspect the Indian of attacking. Enough of the Kanza people lived near St. Joseph; the sight of a single native wouldn't cause a panic.

Some did stop to stare as he and Jack passed by, as they would have for any unfamiliar person. The Indian nodded to everyone, grinning. Nick smiled at his friendliness. Jack seemed to be a true trader, never offending anyone who might have something he wanted. Still, he wanted to keep an eye on the other man, just to be sure. They reached his wagon, and Nick gathered what he'd be willing to hand over to the man. "I have a lot of extra coffee, some tea, a lot of tobacco, beads, and hard crackers."

"Good, good." Jack leaned back, inspecting everything, touching nothing. Finally he said, "I'll take coffee and crackers for the moccasins." With a shrewd look he added, "And will tell you where to find fresh game for the beads. I want a present for my wife."

Nick laughed. "You're a good man. It's a deal." Nick handed over the string of beads, a small jar of coffee beans, and a tin of crackers.

"Before I find others to trade with, I'll tell you about the pond." Jack glanced around, checking for eavesdroppers before continuing, "Walk east to a pond alone, not far. There are no trees, but some hills to hide. At dusk, all sorts of game come to drink for the day."

Nick shook his head. "No tricks?"

He frowned and stomped his foot. "No! No tricks. I use this information for trade, not for trapping the whites."

Searching the man's face for deceit, Nick saw none and relented. "Thank you, Mr. Jack. I look forward to better meals tomorrow."

Bowing, he asked, "Is it all right if I talk with others about trading? Ladies besides yours might want moccasins."

He laughed, hoping no one overheard how Jack referred to Mrs. Bartlett as his. "Yes, it's all right if you do business here. Be fair or all trade stops and I warn everyone I see about Dishonest Jack."

Jack held up his hand as if to give an oath. "No need for warnings. I will deal fair."

He watched as Jack meandered away as if he couldn't decide which settler to target first. Nick looked at the moccasins and smiled. Beth might not want to wear something so primitive. He had another solution she might prefer. Nick went to the back of his wagon, getting his new boots. With those and the moccasins, he went to the Bartlett's campsite.

She saw him first and stood. Daggart lay sleeping against a wheel, hat pulled low to blot out the sun. "Hello, Mr. Granville.

I've told my husband you saved my life."

He grinned. "I don't think that's quite accurate. Jack is mostly harmless."

Daggart sat up and pushed back his hat. "He's an Indian, right?"

Nick nodded his assent. "Yes he is."

He threw him a disgusted look. "Then he's not mostly harmless. He's mostly a cold blooded killer who'd as soon scalp my wife as look at her. After that, they'd cook us up for dinner."

The comment felt like a kick to the gut. His Sally had been the warmest person he'd ever known. Nick ground out, "Is that so? I've met a few on the warpath, but none truly cold blooded."

Snorting, Bartlett retorted, "Thought you knew what you were doing out here. Everyone knows Indians roam around, preying on whites as if we were buffalo."

Nick struggled to keep the rage building up in him from spilling into his voice. "You have firsthand knowledge of this?"

"Not first hand." He shrugged. "The only people knowin' for sure are nothin' but bones."

To drive home the point, he asked, "So no one you've ever met has ever been shot or scalped by an Indian?"

Daggart cut his eyes to Beth and said as if Nick were a child, "No, I heard this from those who've seen the bones."

He knew what Bartlett meant. Wolves, coyotes, and feral dogs often dug up those who died along the way. In an effort to keep up with others in the journey, the family buried their dead in graves too shallow to elude predators. While the folks had good intentions, sun baked ground, rock, or simply not bringing a shovel or spade meant the dead lay above ground. Attempts to cover them with stone or branches often failed when faced with a hungry animal's determination. "Who, exactly, told you this, Bartlett?"

"It doesn't matter, Granville. I just know these things from people probably smarter than you." Daggart stood. "Damn! What does it take t' get some sleep around here?"

Nick let the man toddle off, knowing this was an argument he couldn't win. He wanted to convince Bartlett not all Indians wanted him dead. Maybe if Beth understood, Bartlett would fall in line too. He went to the front of the Bartlett's wagon for her. "Mrs. Bartlett, may I have a word with you?"

She kneeled on the ground, milking Erleen. "Yes, if you don't mind doing so while I finish here."

"I'll be glad to wait." Nick sat on his heels, happy to have the excuse to look at her. He hated her brown dress; the color muddied her eyes instead of showing off their deep green.

Beth looked up at him while continuing her work. "Good, I need to get this done. Daggart likes milk with his meals."

Nick caught her expression of dislike. "You don't care for fresh milk?"

She chuckled, "Not so much. I enjoy butter softening the bread and that's all." Beth stopped milking and tucked wisps of her hair escaping the braid behind her ear.

He grinned, noting she had new freckles across her nose and a bit of pink to her cheeks. Beth must not have worn her sunbonnet this afternoon when she rested beside the creek. "I enjoyed you cooking fish for Sam and me the other evening."

Laughing, she said, "I'm sure you did. We did, too. As long as you share the food, I'll be glad to cook for you."

"Sam will be pleased to hear it." He stood as she did, bucket in her hand. "I need to offer you something else."

She shifted the milk bucket from one hand to the other. "Oh?"

"The Indian you met today, Jack, found something he wanted other than your shoes."

Concern creased her face. "He's not angry? Daggart said he might be back to knife us all in our sleep."

He smiled in reassurance. "Not at all. He's very happy with the outcome. In fact, he's going through camp, seeing if anyone else wants to barter for his goods."

She fidgeted a little. "Do you trust him? I'm not sure we should."

Nick shrugged. "As much as I can trust anyone. He's not given me a reason to distrust just yet." He smiled at her still nibbling her lip, not reassured by his words. Leaning in a little closer, he quietly said, "Beth, nothing will happen to you on my watch."

She didn't look convinced. "Daggart said I was lucky he didn't slit my throat right there, or worse."

Worse? He knew what the man had meant, but nothing was worse than her death. She still seemed worried. Nick didn't blame her. Seeing her fight with the Indian had been scary for even him and he was armed. He suspected there was more to her fear than a native with bad judgement and believed he knew why. "That isn't all he said, is it?"

Beth pursed her lips at first as if she didn't want to say but then admitted, "He said if you, Mr. Granville, and your men had been doing your jobs properly, our lives wouldn't have been in danger."

Damn him. Nick didn't want to admit Bartlett was right but had to be fair. "Your husband raises a good point. The men and I are keeping a lookout all the time. Jack only wants to make a profit from us, but someone should have seen him before he confronted you. We need to make changes."

"What will you do?"

"Step up the guard, first. The people here are all friendly and comfortable with civilization. Attacks are no more frequent from here to Fort Bridger than they are back east."

Beth shook her head, blushing. "I'm hoping to be done with Indian attacks, Mr. Granville. Once was quite enough." She set down the bucket, peering into the wagon before reaching in.

"I agree, ma'am." The wind shifted, carrying a scent of warm cotton and her skin. He swallowed hard against the sudden interest in her spreading through him. Nick looked away from watching her rustle through her belongings. He needed to focus on Beth's true needs and not on how pretty she was. "First, I'd rather talk with you."

She stopped her search. "Oh, talk with me still? Why?"

He pulled the folded shoes from his back pocket, holding them out to her. "I traded for the moccasins because you need shoes better suited for your feet."

Beth examined them, tracking her finger along some of the beadwork. "Thank you for the offer. They are very lovely."

"They might save your life." He saw the yearning in her eyes for the shoes. "If you could, I'd like for you to wear these after your feet heal." Nick shifted from one foot to the other. "In fact, I have a favor to ask of you. I bought a pair of boots in town and can't wear them. They're too tight and I'd like it if you could break them in for me. Walk in them for a while, maybe with thick socks to help them fit better. Your skirt would make sure no one would have to see them."

Laughing a little, she asked, "My wearing them would loosen

them for you? I can't imagine."

He'd stretched the truth a little, sure, and needed to add more to convince her to take them. "You'd help me a lot, ma'am. I have these boots and they're good but I want to switch back and forth for rainy days." He held out the moccasins for her. "Take these for now and I'll go get my spare boots for you."

Shaking her head, Beth poured milk into a jar. "I don't think I'll be allowed to. Daggart prefers Lizzy's smaller shoes to my, um, he prefers my smaller shoes."

Her reference to herself puzzled him. She'd said something earlier about her shoes as if they'd not belonged to her but to some other woman named Lizzy. Nick asked, "What do you mean, exactly? Aren't they your smaller shoes and aren't you Lizzy to him?"

"Oh, yes, you're right." She glanced around. "I need to get water for dinner. Please excuse me."

He frowned, watching her make her way to the creek. In the back of his mind, he noticed how the sun edged closer to the horizon, bringing the day to an end. She'd run off and so far, no one seemed to take Beth's feet seriously. He'd seen gangrene before, watched as limbs had been amputated. Nick couldn't bear such a fate for her. Damn it, he had to do something. His only solution was a successful appeal to Bartlett. He glanced around the camp, seeing others busy with chores or enjoying the rest.

Nick went to the back of the couple's wagon. Bartlett lay on his bedroll, sleeping by an unlit fire. The way he treated Beth angered him, and the man's attitude toward Indians only served to infuriate him more.

"Mr. Bartlett?" he said, resisting the urge to nudge him with his foot. The man lay there, unresponsive. "Bartlett?" Nick repeated, a little louder.

Startled as if jabbed with a sharp stick, Daggart yelped, "What? What the hell's going on?"

The guy seemed hung over despite the lack of alcohol. Suppressing a chuckle at maybe causing him pain, Nick replied, "Nothing, I just needed to talk with you and wanted to do so before dark."

"Didn't we already talk?" Not bothering to open his eyes, Bartlett put his hands behind his head.

Nick felt foolish just standing there while the other man lay there as if asleep. "We did, but this is something serious."

Sitting up, Bartlett gave him a smug grin. "It's those damned Indians, isn't it?"

"No. It's about your wife's feet."

He squinted his eyes, shrugged, and laid back down as before. "So what about them?"

Nick wondered if his own eyes shot glares of hate as much as Bartlett's did. "Because her shoes are too small, she has difficulty walking."

Letting out a snort, Bartlett retorted, "Who doesn't except the lucky few on horses?"

Nick could take the jab at what the other man saw as a privileged status. He'd dealt with that all his life from a lot of people. What he didn't accept was Bartlett's lack of empathy for his own wife. He had half a mind to grab the man by his lapels and shake him. "Yes, most do, but hers have open sores with the potential of infection."

With a groan, he said, "I don't care as long as she can still walk to Fort Kearny. We can get some whisky to dab on there. By then she might be able to ride in the wagon, unless she wants to leave her stuff on the road before then."

Unacceptable, Nick thought, staring at the man. Sixteen to twenty days were a long time to walk with bad feet and he would not let Beth do such a thing. "You don't have whisky here to help her feet heal now? Wasn't that on the list we gave you of things to pack?"

"I bought some the day before we left." Bartlett sat up, still resting on his elbows behind him, not looking Nick in the eyes. "It just so happens, I got thirsty walking back from town." Having the grace to look ashamed, he added, "Next time I'll know to buy two bottles."

He had been and probably was still hung over from last night, Nick surmised, giving him a hard stare. "You do that. Until then, I think it best if she wears my boots or some moccasins until she's healed enough for her own shoes."

Standing, Bartlett pointed at Beth as she walked back to the camp. "No. My wife is not wearing a man's shoes or a dirty Indian's." He crossed his arms. "Lizzy will wear Lizzy's little shoes and have Lizzy's little feet."

The need to choke the life from Bartlett propelled Nick a step forward. To set aside his anger, he took a breath and instead of violence, he settled for being practical. "If she wears what I've suggested, we'll make better time." Gold seduced the man more than his wife, so Nick pushed that agenda. "I'd hate for you to be delayed on your way to California by a woman who is lame."

Bartlett shook his head. "We're dillydallying around too much as it is." He gestured in surrender. "I suppose she could wear the boots at least. We can keep Lizzy's shoes for when her feet heal up."

Nick smiled when seeing her peeking from around the wagon. He struggled to keep his expression more neutral than his heart felt. Also feeling Bartlett watching him, Nick said as though he accepted Bartlett's decision, "I'll make sure she gets them until then." If he had his way, Beth would never wear anything ill fitting again. He turned to her standing by the campfire. "Do you have a moment to retrieve the shoes?"

She looked at Bartlett who nodded then answered, "Yes, I'll go."

He handed her the moccasins, unable to resist flashing a triumphant grin. She made a face at him and put them in the wagon. Nick led the way and Beth followed. He slowed to let her stroll beside him. As they walked, he asked, "Do you have socks to wear with the boots?"

She laughed. "Yes, I have plenty. They're my favorite thing to knit."

"Hmm. I might have to commission a pair from you, then. I can't keep my own from wearing thin." At his wagon, Nick retrieved the boots, handing them to her.

Beth hugged them to her chest. "I'd be glad to knit you up a pair. Would you want them thinner for summer?"

He thought about what to ask for that would keep them talking longer than usual during the journey. "I'd like to pay you for a summer and a winter pair."

"Pay me?" She shook her head. "Oh no, you're doing enough getting us across the country."

"I've already been paid for doing so and will be glad to buy socks from you instead of purchasing them elsewhere." While Nick was sure he had ordinary feet, didn't he want perfect socks? He smiled, anticipating the need for fittings and several reasons to see her beyond the necessary.

She smiled back at him. "Very well, I'll charge you a fair price, same as you'd pay in St. Joe."

"Thank you." He saw Sam from the corner of his eyes. "Be sure to let me know how the boots fit. Even the slightest promise of a blister and we can find another solution for you." He tipped his hat.

"I will." Beth turned and went back to her camp.

Sam strolled up to their wagon with a bucket and jar of milk. "Did I hear your new friend refer to your woman while at the river?"

"Yes." Nick, not wanting an interrogation and the lecture sure to follow, derailed his brother's train of thought. "We need to keep a better watch on our party."

Sam stopped, raising an eyebrow. "Here?"

"Yes," he replied. "I've been given the order by Mr. Bartlett in no uncertain terms."

Laughing, Sam set down his things. He stopped after glancing at Nick's expression. "You're serious? The man is more likely to die from someone in camp than a Kanzas or Delaware."

He held his hands up in surrender. "Preaching to the choir. The man doesn't think much of the natives. He gave me an earful, all of it hearsay and none of it true. He also doesn't think much of us letting Jack run loose in the camp."

"Jack? I thought he looked familiar. He made the rounds on my last trip west. He'd barter with a tree for the joy of doing so."

"I believe it. He wanted Beth's shoes in the worst way this afternoon." Nick said before thinking then cursed himself for using her casual name.

Sam gave his brother a sharp glance, emphasizing her name, "Mrs. Bartlett is lucky Jack only wanted to exchange for shoes. He's offered several ponies for a woman, I've heard." Sam paused and then asked, "You didn't happen to trade for a squaw, did you?" he asked. "Although, if bartering for one helped you leave the Bartlett woman alone, I'd applaud your choice." He scooped salt into a cup.

Nick glared at him. "A what?" He caught the joke after seeing Sam's ornery expression and cooled a bit. "I don't trade for women, you know that."

"There is always a first time," Sam retorted, rummaging around in their belongings.

"Not for me." He knew his brother taunted him. Sam knew how Nick felt about Sally and now Beth. He wasn't going to rise to the bait.

"I think you have a soft spot for Mrs. Bartlett because she reminds you of how beneficial a wife can be." Sam climbed up into the wagon, still searching. "Have you seen the lid to this jar?"

"Do you have nothing better to do than goad me into a fight?" Nick went to the front, reached in for the lid, and handed it to Sam.

He laughed, putting the lid on the jar and shaking the contents. "Not at the moment."

Nick leaned against the wheel as his brother hopped off the wagon. "No fish to clean or cook, no horses to care for, or small animals to torture like you do me?"

"There is that. After you left, I found a fish at the end of your hook. Since then, I have been catching and cleaning." He grinned. "I've also taken the liberty of asking your woman for butter and her cooking skills while we fished. She caught some of these before running off to care for Erleen."

He sighed, hungry, irritated, and wanting the fish to be frying already. "She's not my woman."

"I know, but the Indian roaming the camp doesn't." Sam, still shaking the milk into butter, picked up the bucket full of fish and water. "You seem to forget who she belongs to every once in a while."

"I do not forget." He kicked a dirt clod, angry at his helpless feeling. "Even if I wanted to, her bruises and constant worry over what Bartlett wants of her continually reminds me she's married to him."

Sam shrugged his shoulders. "While I don't approve of a husband using fists to discipline his wife, I also don't approve of you being used as an accomplice to some woman's escape. And heaven help you if she has your bastard child while Bartlett's wife."

He whirled, grabbing the front of Sam's shirt. Water sloshed from the bucket and Sam stopped churning butter. "That's too far, Samuel. Beth isn't seducing me and you'll not speak of her like that."

Eyes narrowed to slits, Sam ground out between clenched teeth, "I'm glad you defend Mrs. Bartlett from my wit and hope you'll extend the guard of her to yourself."

Nick let him go with a slight shove. "Damn. Yes, I do try to guard her. Even from myself."

Sam put down everything he held. "Good, because the last thing we need is a half-crazed husband hunting for you with a rifle." He straightened his shirt, tucking what pulled loose back into his pants. "Did you get a trade on those moccasins for Mrs. Bartlett?"

"Yes." Nick handed the butter jar to him, and then took the bucket of fish.

He nodded. "I'm glad. She has limped for the past couple of days when no one's watching."

"You saw it too?" Nick was annoyed, wondering how many people noted her walking lame.

"Yes. I noticed when she took the cow to water and a few times since then." Sam began shaking the butter jar. "Others are sore from the march too, but when I see her, I'm very concerned."

Nick tried ignoring the sudden rush of jealously. Not wanting to, but unable to stop himself, he asked, "You watch her walk a lot?"

Sam followed his brother to the back of the wagon, watching and making butter while Nick cleaned the fish. "Not a lot, but yes, some. While, unlike you, I usually don't stare at the wives too closely, I do ensure they're healthy during the trip."

"Damn it, Sam! I don't stare at any other wives. I just watch out for Mrs. Bartlett." Nick raised his hat brim, scratching his forehead with the back of his hand. "I keep an eye on her since so far, she's the only one who's in camp with a black eye. Also, Bartlett has her in shoes too small. She has blisters bleeding and I don't want to see Elizabeth's feet amputated because her husband is dim or careless."

He whistled, saying, "Damn."

"Exactly." Nick cleaned with long practiced moves. "I've already explained to Mrs. Bartlett she could lose her feet if they become infected."

Sam held up the milk to see if any butter had formed yet. He frowned and resumed his work. "The moccasins won't keep her from limping if her soles are bruised and sore."

"I know." Nick hesitated for a moment, unwilling to admit to Sam he'd recommended something a little too intimate to Beth. "I've suggested she wear my new boots until she heals."

Sam's eyebrows rose. "I see."

"She's breaking them in for me." His justification sounded weak once said aloud. "I can barely get them on, they're so tight."

"Yes, that's as good an excuse as any," Sam nodded, smirking.

The other man's grin left Nick feeling defensive. He didn't look up from the fish. "It's not just an excuse."

"It is, and if it works, so much the better." He gave Nick a slight punch in the arm. "I don't want to see her lame any more than you do. She doesn't deserve that."

Done cleaning, he asked, "Is it settled?"

Sam shrugged. "It is to me. I think Mrs. Bartlett is waiting on our fish. If you want to hunt before dark, we need to get dinner eaten first."

His brother still shook their butter jar, compelling him to ask, "Didn't you say the Bartletts were to supply the butter?"

With a nod, Nick washed his hands in the leftover water and emptied the bucket. "Yes, but when I asked Mrs. Bartlett to cook for us, I'd not caught so much. She might need more." He put the fish in and followed Sam to the Bartlett's fire.

They strolled up to the couple's campsite, most of their hands already there. Nick greeted everyone, tipping his hat to Beth in particular. She grinned at him and lifted her skirt just a bit to show him the toe of his boots. He winked in approval and sat down around the low campfire with the others. As Beth readied their dinner, she was the only female in the group and the only one not deeply drinking of the whisky bottle being passed.

Chuck, the most jovial in the group, took advantage of the captive audience to tell a few jokes. Nick gave him minimal attention after the first line. He'd heard all of Chuck's best. Instead, he took a drink of whisky and passed it to Lawrence.

Once he heard the group's laughter, Chuck launched into another of his tall tales. Since he'd been there when the story happened, Nick covertly watched Beth fix their dinner. She'd already strained the butter from Sam's efforts and had it melting in a large iron pan. Now, she peeled a few small potatoes. He removed his knife strapped to his boot. When he caught her eye, Nick held up the knife and crooked his finger. Smiling, she held up the last potato to show him he was too late and began to peel it herself.

Lawrence nudged Nick for the whisky bottle, stopping him

from watching Beth. He tried to pay attention to stories the men told, each one wanting to outdo the man before him. Instead, Nick pretended to listen as he saw Beth place a sauce pan of sliced potatoes near the larger skillet.

When the whisky made its round yet again, he held up a hand in dismissal. "No more for me." Nick laughed when a chorus of disappointment rose from the group. "I have it on good authority there's a watering hole with plenty of game nearby."

Claude eyed the fish, watching as Beth gingerly laid each fillet in the pan. He spoke up, mesmerized by the food as he asked, "How far?"

"He didn't specify exactly, only that it is east of here," Nick answered.

While the others nodded, Daggart laughed, clapping his hands. "East? That could damn near be anywhere."

Nick gave the man a cold look. "I doubt it. It's within walking distance."

"Hell, the whole world is within walking distance if you go far enough." Bartlett held out his plate, addressing Beth. "Get a move on, woman. Food's gettin' cold. Get my milk, too."

He knew his face must have looked murderous when Sam shook his head. Nick gritted his teeth to keep his mouth shut. He forced a smile at Beth when she spooned his potatoes and placed a fillet on his plate. She smiled back, giving him a little extra potato. He started eating, pausing to add, "I'd like to go hunting tonight. I expect the watering hole is nearby since Jack said it isn't far from here."

"Jack?" Bartlett's head whipped to face Nick. "You're sayin' that old Indian told you where to hunt?"

Swallowing his bite before replying, Nick said, "He suggested a place to find game, yes."

"You go and you're walkin' into a trap, plain and simple." Daggart took a couple of long drinks of whisky.

Nick noticed Lawrence shifting with impatience beside him. It wouldn't hurt him to wait a little while more for the whisky. "Is that so?"

Bartlett pointed his fork at Nick. "Yeah, any fool can see that Indian is going to lure us over there one by one and pick us off like rabbits in a cage."

Sam cleared his throat. "I have a long-standing acquaintance with Jack and know for a fact he's a good man."

"Then you're a bigger fool than your brother." Bartlett waved Beth over to take his plate and refill his cup. "The 'man' as you call him, is an Indian. Indian and good don't go together. There's a reason they're called savages and animals."

Nick clenched his fists. He'd known many more women and children murdered by more savage whites than any red. All of his Sally's family were killed in one afternoon. He stood. Sam also standing caught his attention, stopping him from getting Bartlett in a headlock so strong he couldn't breathe. Nick's brother shot him a warning glare and nod. When glancing to where Sam indicated, he saw Beth staring at him with wide eyes.

Lucky fidgeted at the tension, took a huge drink of the whisky and passed on the bottle. "Y'all want to play cards tonight? We don't even have to bet for money if you're chicken about losing to me."

Beth stepped up to Nick while holding out her hand. "I'll take your things for washing."

"Take this too," Bartlett said, lifting up his cup.

She shyly smiled at the sudden attention from everyone as they followed Bartlett's lead. Taking their dishware as needed and glancing from Sam to Nick, she asked, "Would it be a good idea if you gentlemen went in a group to hunt instead of one by one?"

Nick swallowed his anger, not wanting to believe she thought of Indians as brutal animals. What he felt for Beth ran deep but couldn't last if she agreed with her husband. If so, any feelings for her would be like rain in the desert, gone before it hit the ground. "In case there is an ambush?"

Beth finished gathering dishes as she answered, "I suppose." Indicating her husband with a wave of her hand, she continued, "Daggart is expecting one, but I'm thinking more for strength in numbers." She paused when her husband snorted, adding, "You'll need help in bringing particularly big game back, won't you? I'm sure that's much more of a possibility."

Sam smiled at her and picked up the heavier of the pans. "She's right, gentlemen. The more of us going, the more we bring home. Chuck, Lawrence, help me spread the word. Claude, aren't you done eating yet?" The man nodded while handing over his dishes and Sam continued, "Lucky, we'll play cards when we get back. Nick, let's make sure we have enough cartridges for our rifles. Not the 50s, I doubt there will be buffalo there." Their men scattered to complete the tasks Sam set to them.

Bartlett lay back with his legs stretched in front of him and crossed at the ankle. "I'll just stay here and hold down the fort for you all. This party will need someone to protect them since this is a trap and you'll all be scalped and left for dead." He put his hands behind his head, looking very relaxed.

The lout's opinion left no impression on Nick, since he knew Beth didn't agree. His heart felt like he'd been drinking soda water at the thought. Unable to resist a glance before leaving, he took a quick look at her once more. He caught her glare at Bartlett whose eyes were closed. Seeing his hatred for the man reflected in her expression, he almost felt her anger as a physical thing. Nick cleared his throat, startling Beth into rattling the plates.

Bartlett opened one eye. "You two still here? I thought you had somethin' to do all important like. I know Lizzy Lou can't be standin' there gapin' all day."

Hunting required long stretches of sitting and waiting, giving him plenty of time to plan on how to get her for himself. "You're right. I have something very important to do. Good night, then." He smiled at her and she nodded, blushing. As they left together, Nick held Beth's gaze. "Thank you for dinner. The food was good and the company even better."

"You're welcome and I'm glad you think so." She indicated where the other men now gathered. "Good luck tonight. I'm sure Jack is right and you'll all do well."

Damn. He didn't want to leave her side, not even for fresh game. With a sigh, he tipped his hat and joined everyone else.

The Granvilles, their men, and a few others from the camp scattered out and walked to the watering hole. Jack had been right. They flushed out a few coveys of quail, which the men carrying smaller gauge guns shot.

All of them wanted fresh meat bad enough that whoever scared away tomorrow's meal might be shot themselves. This way of life was second nature to him on the trail, leaving his mind free to focus on Beth and how to get her away from Bartlett for good. He worked hard with the rest of them, and although loaded down with fresh meat, no one lagged behind. Everyone wanted to reach camp before the night grew too much darker. The men didn't chatter as much on the walk back as they did during dinner.

They made quick work of butchering the game, distributing it among themselves and those unable to hunt. Nick set up as much of his own as he could to dry. There was an unsaid agreement to leave the Bartletts out of the division. Nick hated leaving Beth out of the spoils. Doing so strengthened his resolve to rid her of Bartlett, if she desired.

Nick went to Beth's campsite to retrieve his and his men's dishes for the morning. Knowing his reasoning as an excuse to see her, he found her knitting as she had done the first day they met. She sat by the fire, cross legged. He grinned when she looked up at him with a smile, and he asked, "Is that mine?"

"I'm thinking so." She motioned him to her. "If you'll come closer, I'll check your foot to make sure this fits."

He went over and sat, putting his foot near her knee and pulling up his pant leg at the same time. "Do I need to take off my boot?"

She put her hand over her nose and mouth. Through her fingers, she said, "Heavens no. Not until you have clean socks."

He laughed. "You're a very smart woman."

Beth put her hand on his boot, squeezing first the instep, the arch, and then his ankle. "Thank you. I don't hear how smart I am very often."

As she compared the sock with his foot, Nick enjoyed the chance to watch her work. He liked seeing her long eyelashes against her cheek when she looked down. The sky reflected colors from the setting sun on her, giving Beth a warm glow. "You should be told at least once a day."

She blushed, the pink in her cheeks visible even in the waning light of evening. "I have a good idea of how big your foot is, so this'll fit."

Nick couldn't resist teasing her. "Sounds like you need to see my legs to be sure. I can take off my boots and roll up my pants if you like. Or just take them off entirely in case you'd like to knit me long underwear."

Beth pressed on his knee as if to push him away. "You tease me. I can't say such things to you!" She picked up the knitting, making a show of focusing on each little stitch and ignoring him.

He wanted to laugh as she tried to concentrate with him watching. Nick found he enjoyed taunting her. "Sure you can say you need to see my naked legs. I don't mind hearing that at all."

She gasped and said, "Not your 'naked' legs!"

"Yes, my very naked legs. Do you need to?" He leaned in to whisper. "Or just want to see them?" He loved watching Beth's feelings show on her face. A little closer, Nick thought, and they could kiss.

A hunger in her eyes matched his own, making it difficult to resist giving her what she asked from him. She paused and looked up at him. "It might be both want and need. If you don't want these to sag around your ankles, I'll need to check your calves."

He frowned at her calling his bluff. She laughed at his expression as he sat back, arms folded. Nick thought it just as well; he'd been pushing the intimacy a little too much. "Where's Bartlett? Why isn't he here protecting you from bad-mannered men like me?"

After giving him a disgusted glance, she stared into the waning fire. "Mr. Lucky's talk of cards incited him to find a game. He's hoping to win whisky, if not money. I'm not sure when he'll be back."

He caught her disgust like the weak catch a cold. Nick couldn't keep the sarcasm from his voice, asking, "He's nowhere around and you're alone? What if Jack scalps you tonight?"

Beth laughed, and giving him a wry smile retorted, "I'd rather Jack didn't return without warning. His holding me down scared me today more than him being Kanzas ever would."

"Why, Mrs. Bartlett, you don't hold the same opinion as your husband?" He nodded at a passing Chuck on his evening watch.

She matched Nick's sarcasm with a mocking stare. "No. I rarely ever do." Beth glanced around and leaned in closer to him as if to share a secret. In a quiet voice, she said, "Since we're alone, you do have permission to call me anything but Lizzy Lou or Mrs. Bartlett."

His gaze swept her face. They weren't truly alone; he couldn't do anything he wanted, but he could say anything he wanted. Fighting the urge to kiss her until they both surrendered, he instead said, "I'll be sure to remember that, Beth."

She closed her eyes and shuddered. "You should go."

"I should, before I embarrass us both." He paused, not wanting to leave, saying "Goodnight, Elizabeth Ann."

Taking his hand and giving him a squeeze, she replied, "Goodnight, Nicholas."

He stood and went to his own bedroll, seeing Sam already there and pretending to sleep. Nick grinned. His brother had never been able to fool him even once. "We're on second watch?"

With a sigh, the younger man replied, "Yes. And how is your woman?"

"Sam," he warned, laying out the blankets.

"Exactly. I'm as tired of saying it as you are of hearing it." His eyes open and glaring at him, Sam went on, "She isn't available and if Bartlett catches on how you're sniffing around her, he won't be happy."

Nick settled into bed and closed his eyes. "I don't care how he feels."

"Nor do I, but if you accidently or intentionally kill him, the others might let you swing."

Grinning because he already knew his brother's reaction, Nick retorted, "Fine. I'll wait until we're on the prairie before letting him have a fatal accident."

"Pardon?" Sam propped himself up on one elbow. "His death isn't a subject for you to plan. If something does happen to the cretin after you've courted his widow, you're the guilty party and the facts won't matter out here."

Pausing, hesitant to say aloud a thought from the meanest part of him, he said in a quieter tone, "Even if it's an accident?"

"Nick, don't even pull somebody's leg by saying that."

Unable to help smiling at his brother's warning, Nick said, "You know me better than to think I'd kill a man in cold blood."

"I do and know you wouldn't." Sam settled in for sleep with a rustle, adding, "It's the hot blood I'm more concerned about."

"You have a point." He paused for a second before confessing, "All joking aside, I want her, but not at anyone else's expense, not even Bartlett's."

A few moments passed before Sam replied to the admission. "I understand. I had the most difficult time not boxing him in the nose after his comment about Indians. If he'd known Sally, she might have changed his opinion."

The words felt like salve to Nick's broken heart. Not a day passed yet that he didn't think of his wife and child. Wanting to hear more, he asked, "Think so? Men like him have closed minds the truth can't pry open."

"Everyone loved Sally. They couldn't help themselves," Sam

murmured in the quiet. "Even our mother accepted her after a while."

The lump in Nick's throat ached and he swallowed. Four years of forced existence without her hadn't healed his wound entirely. His heart hurt when he wondered how different his life would be if she and their son still lived.

He'd rather distract himself with thoughts of Beth. With her, he felt like a dormant tree in the spring, as if life held possibilities unimagined before meeting her. Nick grinned. She seemed so shy and quiet until flashing a bit of wicked humor. Beth surprised him every time they talked, and every night since they'd met, he fell asleep thinking of her.

He woke with a start to Sam shaking him. "Second watch. Let's get going."

"Ug. I'm there." Nick shook the slumber from his head. He and Sam relieved Lawrence and Claude from their watch, taking the same circular path around the wagons as the prior two men had walked. He hated second watch, preferring first or third's opportunity for unbroken sleep. Once awake, he had a difficult time napping until dawn.

This late in the night, everyone slept except for the nocturnal animals creeping up to the camp due to curiosity or scraps. Some people snored while even the most ornery of sleeping children appeared like angels wrapped in blankets. The late rising moon gave a ghostly glow to everything. Nick hesitated as he and Sam drew near Beth's wagon. He wanted to make sure Bartlett kept some sort of protection over her.

They cleared the back of the wagon to where the couple's fire was. When he saw Bartlett on Beth, her skirt hiked up to her waist, Nick felt as if shot in the chest and gut. In the back of his mind, he'd known they had to be intimate, but when faced with reality, his stomach roiled in protest.

"Damn," Sam whispered. "Let's go." They stepped back to where the wagon lay between them and the couple.

The crack of a palm against skin captured both men's attention. Nick heard Beth's voice growl, "I said no, damn you!" Another smack sounded.

He glanced at Sam. "If that's Beth being hit, we have to—"

His brother grabbed his arm, shaking him quiet, and called

out, "Ma'am, are you all right?"

After a long minute, Nick couldn't resist asking for himself, "Ma'am?"

"Oh heavens." She walked to them, smoothing her skirts and carrying a thin blanket. "You two weren't—you didn't see…?"

Sam spoke first. "I saw you slap him. Nick, however, missed the pleasure."

"This is very humiliating." She put her hands over her eyes.

"You two aren't the first married couple to have relations on the trail," Nick said more to himself than her, wanting to reinforce the idea that she belonged to Bartlett. "It happens."

"He's right," Sam added. "It's a long way to California and a long time for a couple to wait for privacy."

Beth took her blanket, wrapping it around her and giving them a glare. "You're very kind to reassure me. I could wait for privacy easily." She went toward the wagon's front.

Nick cleared his throat. "Um, ma'am?"

"Yes?" Her muffled voice sounded from the cart's other side and he followed her, his brother close behind him.

He rounded the corner, stunned into silence. Nick fought against laughing when seeing Bartlett by the fire face down, his butt bared. He indicated the man's undress to Sam with a gesture. His brother chuckled and told Beth, "Well, ma'am, your husband isn't quite covered."

She faced them, hands on her hips. Each word dripped venom as she said, "He's too drunk to care and can stay that way."

With a sigh and a glance heavenward, Sam said, "I'm more concerned with women and children seeing him in this state."

"Very well. I shall take care of it." She grabbed the back of his trousers and gave several sharp pulls until the pants covered his behind. Beth then took his blanket and flipped it over him. Without another word, she went back to her seat at the front of the wagon.

As if it were their own mother angry at them, Sam gave Nick a "Should we talk to her?" look. He shook his head at his little brother, unwilling to say anything and give Beth another focus for her anger. Sam made a let's-go motion with his chin and Nick nodded, ready to continue their guard.

Walking on around the wagons, he couldn't remember the last time jealousy consumed him so much as now. The idea of Bartlett making love to Beth angered him. He took a deep, calming breath. She didn't seem to care for the man tonight, either.

Nick wondered, was only her husband's drunkenness repulsive to her, or was it Bartlett in general? He wanted to think Beth desired him too and now pushed away her husband. Would he do the same if Sally still lived? Lost in thought, he shook his head. Even though he adored and wanted Beth now, Nick still considered Sally his true love. Had she survived, they'd be at home in Oregon raising their children.

The next two days passed in a blur of routine for Nick. Beth avoided him, not meeting his gaze. When their paths did cross, she gave him a quick greeting before finding a justification to start or finish a task. He brushed off the thought of how she only treated him this way. After two exhausting days of traveling twenty miles or more, he didn't want to ponder their feelings so much as have her in his arms at night as they slept. Still, he'd see her chatting with various people in the camp more than she did with him. Her distance bothered him, but he understood her embarrassment.

At day's end, he'd broached the subject of Beth with his brother. Sam found her as difficult to talk with as Nick did, barely able to share some of the game hunted around the watering hole. She tried to decline, saying they'd not earned it. Sam pressed her to take some, saying the meat would spoil if she didn't. He convinced her, but wasn't able to charm her into anything more than a distant politeness.

The shallow Wolf River ran swift and clear. People took advantage of this by scrubbing themselves and their clothes. He went through his things and gathered up his worn shirts and pants. Every time Nick ran across the material he had bought in St. Joseph, it nagged at him. Running across the fabric frustrated him because he'd not yet invented a reason to give it to her. He hated how each day passed without him inventing a good excuse to give her such a gift. It bothered him to see how other ladies dressed in their Sunday best as their everyday clothes dried. Beth wore her freshly cleaned everyday clothes damp. The day warmed as the sun hit noon, yet Nick knew she had to be chilled. She sorely needed a new dress, even as impractical as the white print was. He regretted the color choice but knew she loved what he'd purchased.

He went to the river, intent on washing his own body and

clothes. A soft breeze blew, carrying the hum of insects and chirps of nesting birds.

Sam was already there and almost done and met him at the bank. "Nick, I noticed how Mrs. Bartlett never received her material for a new dress."

At first, the coincidence that Sam should bring up the very source of his frustration even as he pondered it himself startled him, but then an odd sense of shame crept in that Nick knew he had no right to feel. It hurt him to see Beth's need so plain that others noticed it too, particularly when such a simple thing as giving her fabric for a dress would help her. His own need to step in warred inside him, like he'd failed her somehow, but the job of providing for her belonged to her husband, bitter as it was for him to admit. He pretended indifference for Sam's benefit. Shrugging, he said, "I've not found a reason to give her something so personal just yet." He pulled off his boots and socks, placing them in separate places.

"I see." The younger man buttoned his crisp shirt before asking, "Do you mind if I make sure Mrs. Bartlett has the fabric today?"

Nick removed his suspenders and his own grubby shirt. He attracted dirt as much as Sam repelled the stuff. "Not at all. It'd be a relief if you did."

"Great, I'll be glad to do so." Sam gave him a carefree salute and went off in their wagons' direction.

Nick continued to strip down to his long underwear, wanting to get done before the day grew much older. He washed his clothes first, using a plain bar of soap, and then laid them to dry on the grass. The river too shallow to truly bathe in, Nick regretted not having the foresight to bring a bucket or water pitcher to pour over his head. He glanced at the camp, wondering whether anyone would see him in his underwear if he ran and found a container of some sort.

He saw a young woman walk toward the stream, her own bucket in hand. Quickly, he searched for bushes, a tree, anything to cover his lower half at least, but nothing around could hide him. Nick sat in the mid-calf deep water. He smiled at the woman as she stepped to the river.

"Hello, Mr. Granville," she greeted.

"Hello." He pretended to wash, just wanting her to leave.

Nick watched her out of the corner of his eye as she scooped up water for her family.

She looked around at his belongings and then grinned at him. "Did you forget something?"

The woman knew he had. Still in shock from almost being naked in front of her, Nick couldn't remember her name. He had to admit after a few moments, "I'm afraid so."

Laughing, she said, "How about I lend you our bucket and you bring it back full of water? Not soapy, please."

He grinned. She had a kind heart. "Thank you, ma'am. I do appreciate it."

"You're welcome. I'll leave it here on the bank for you." She returned his smile and backed away to the wagon circle.

Since someone now waited on him, Nick made short work of cleaning up. He finished, folded the wet clothes and grabbed the bucket to return to Amelia Chatillon, Robert Chatillon's daughter. He remembered her more now not having to hide his underclothes from her. She and her family traveled to Oregon hoping to help farmstead the eldest son's land.

Beth smiled at him as she walked toward him and the river. Nick smiled back. She said, "Mr. Granville said you'd be here but to be cautious. You might still be filthy."

Showing off his clothes, Nick retorted, "He's actually wrong. I'm nearly as clean as he is."

She laughed, continuing, "I've already thanked him and now I'm here to thank you as well."

He knew by seeing what Beth held why she sought him out. But after several days of not hearing her voice, Nick wanted to do everything possible to keep her talking with him. "For?" he asked.

"Oh honestly!" She laughed, "For this." Beth held out the fabric. "Sam told me you'd bought this at Henry's, thinking it might come in handy later for some woman on the trip."

"And it has, hasn't it?" He hid a grin at her reference to "some woman."

"It will, as soon as I cut and sew a dress from it." She ran her fingertips down the material as he'd seen her do the first day they met. "It's the most beautiful I've ever seen. I'm so happy you picked it out of the others."

Nick decided his new vocation had to be making Beth happy. Seeing her joy brightened his day, if not his entire life. Her approval felt like the machine moving the blood in his body. Struggling to maintain a distance, he said, "I'm glad you like the color. I thought it the prettiest there too."

A slight blush stained her cheeks as she replied, "I tried to refuse the gift. It's too extravagant for me."

"I don't think so. It's perfect for you." He leaned in closer to speak softly. "I'm also glad Sam turned down your refusal."

Beth smiled up at him. "Secretly, I am too."

CHAPTER 7

"Mr. Granville?" A young woman walked up to Nicholas, asking, "You'll have dinner with us tonight?" She clasped her hands together, her forget-me-not blue eyes pleading. "I'm so anxious to begin learning French from you. Say you will, please?"

Beth smiled at the other woman—Amelia, she'd heard her name was. She looked so much like Lizzy, Beth had to force herself to adopt a pleasant expression instead of scowling. She excused herself with, "I need to start our own supper." While Amelia went on about French being the perfect language, Nick waved a distracted goodbye at Beth. She nodded and went to her own wagon.

She busied herself with cooking, unable to think of anything but Amelia and Nicholas together this evening. Amelia, like Lizzy, had every physical feature Beth didn't. She stood much shorter than Beth and was pleasantly round in all the ways men liked best. She also had no freckles while Beth was sure many dotted her own nose. The girl also wore a new Sunday dress of blue paisley matching her everyday dark blue dress and sunbonnet. If she'd not possessed the sweetest disposition, Beth was sure she'd dislike her.

So far during the trip, Amelia seemed much kinder than Lizzy had been. Beth had often seen Daggart gawk at Amelia when she walked or rode by on her horse. She had such a porcelain doll face with sunshine gold hair. Maybe if he'd married her instead, Daggart would be much more agreeable.

Beth already missed the tasty stew of beans and rice she and Daggart had eaten at noon. The meal overshadowed the biscuits and bacon dinner now facing her. She glanced up and noticed Lawrence standing nearby. The man must be part snake, the way he silently glided to wherever he needed to go.

His light blond hair kept its mashed down shape when Lawrence removed his worn hat. He twisted the hat in his hands, adding creases. Most days he bristled with friendly energy, but now his dark eyes didn't meet hers. "Ma'am?"

She smiled at his shyness. "Yes, Mr. Lawrence? How are you

today?"

"Fine ma'am." He shuffled from one foot to the other. "Ma'am, if I'd caught a couple of fish, would you cook them up as you did the other night? I've got a bit of a hankerin' for them."

To save his hat from certain destruction in his nervous hands, she reassured him. "Certainly, I'd be glad to."

"Would you let me share with you too? As a sort of trade for the cornmeal and all? I mean, I got cornmeal in the wagon to trade with you." He sighed as if realizing he needed to breathe. "So you ain't workin' for free and all."

Making a show of it, she scratched the back of her head and squinted. "Hm, goodness. I'd have to have fish instead of the usual bacon." Beth sighed as if giving in to a demand. "I suppose so, since you're forcing me and all." She almost laughed at his anxious expression, but instead patted the ground nearby her. "Please, Mr. Lawrence, have a seat and I'll fix up your dinner."

He gave her a shy smile and sat a little way from the fire. Lawrence watched as if memorizing the motions as Beth dunked the fillets in a plate of milk. She rolled each in cornmeal before laying the fillet in the bacon grease.

Lawrence stood. "I'll rinse those, ma'am, while you watch dinner." He took both plates and headed toward the river. A little later, he returned and wordlessly handed clean dishes to her.

Beth smiled at him. "Have you been to Oregon or California before now, Mr. Lawrence?"

Nodding, he replied, "Each once, ma'am."

She hoped he'd continue with a story or two. Finally, she asked, "Which of the destinations do you like best?"

He pondered for so long, Beth flipped over each fillet while wondering if he'd forgotten the question. "Hard to say, ma'am."

"It's just as well. Dinner is ready." Beth dished him up a full plate and handed it to him. Pausing, she asked, "Are you sure you don't mind sharing? The fish should all be yours."

"I don't mind, ma'am." He cleared his throat. "You don't need to save some for Mr. Bartlett. The hands are sharing venison with him."

"I see." Smiling away her irritation, she said, "That means extra for us, then."

They ate in silence as the dusk grew darker. Beth hated how fast night came, giving her no time to cut a new dress from the material. She marveled at how Nicholas knew exactly what to buy, and then remembered he'd seen her at the store fawning over the print. First the night he and Samuel saw Daggart all over her, now this. Did he think her a charity case? She felt her face burn in mortification. Maybe she was, but she didn't want pity from anyone.

Beth poked at her food with a fork. Samuel did say she'd earned a new dress with her cooking. She glanced at Lawrence eating as if this meal were his last. If she ended up cooking for any hired hand with freshly gathered food, Beth supposed she should be paid in any goods the Granvilles gave them. She liked that idea much better than being someone's cross to bear.

"You are a very good cook, ma'am. Thank you," Lawrence said.

"You're welcome. I'm glad you liked it." She stood, taking his dishes, and added them to the washbasin. Beth watched as he tipped his hat and walked off, presumably towards his own campfire. He seemed like a very nice man, although much more shy than her. She went to the river to wash up and get water for tomorrow morning.

Once done, Beth put the water on to boil with the water jar nearby. She retrieved her knitting from the wagon, sat by the firelight and continued work on Nicholas's socks. Although, she thought with a sneer, maybe she should let Amelia do this, since Nicholas seemed to prefer her company.

Beth knew she was being unfair to the unmarried and lovely girl. A man would be a fool to not have his eye turned by such a beauty and even crazier to prefer Beth instead of her. She scowled, doubting even if she were also unmarried that any man preferred a tall, string bean with dark hair and eyes the color of muddy water. Daggart didn't like her appearance, and until meeting the Granvilles, she had been glad every man agreed with him.

She bound off the top cuff, finishing Nicholas's first sock. Beth absentmindedly broke the wool and wove in the loose end. She gathered up everything, placing the items back in the little fabric bag. Staring into the fire, she wondered not for the first time how much the Granvilles had seen of Daggart's attempt at lovemaking. She squeezed her eyes shut at the mortification, knowing her skirt had been pushed up around her waist.

Daggart's growl startled her. "If you're that tired, go to bed, woman."

"Oh! Good idea." She liked the suggestion and hiding under covers would give her time to decide how embarrassed she should be around the Granvilles tomorrow. She pretended to yawn while retrieving the bedrolls and wool stuffed pillows. "It's been a long day."

He poked at the waning fire. "I've heard tomorrow will be longer. Everyone's anxious to get to Fort Kearny for supplies."

Beth worried about how much she'd rationed for each day so far. Had she been wasteful and not known? They didn't have money left for much more. Plus, rumor held that prices only increased as the trail continued. "Are people running out already?"

"Some are, most aren't." He reclined on his blankets. "Since the Granvilles and their men like me so much, they take care of us."

She hated his smug grin and thought they more pitied than liked him. "I'm glad. Are you putting up our tent tonight?"

"Nah, there were no storm clouds to the west. We'll be all right."

She set up her blankets on the opposite side of the fire from Daggart, hoping he was too lazy to attempt lovemaking. He'd not found any whisky tonight, so she doubted he'd bother. It took him being dead drunk to forget she wasn't Lizzy.

He'd had good information. The next day, Beth was sure they'd traveled at least twenty-five miles, passing a great number of good camping places only to halt next to the trail instead of near water and grass. She had to lead first the oxen, then Erleen nearly a mile for their drink and meal. Daggart again didn't eat at their wagon, instead swapping stories with other men in the group.

Beth ate cornbread left over from lunch and started cutting her dress. Each movement of the scissors both excited and scared her. A wrong snip could waste precious material. Holding her breath during each cut, Beth had to stop every so often. After a while, she glanced around in surprise. The sun had slipped just under the horizon without her noticing. She folded the pieces separately from the uncut material and placed everything back in her keepsake trunk.

Beth decided against starting a fire on such a warm night. Not knowing when her husband would return, she set up their tent and bedrolls. At least tonight if he returned drunk, they'd have privacy.

She paused, sick to her stomach. If he wanted to do that disgusting thing most people called making love, Beth didn't know if she could let him ever again. After Nicholas carried her over the creek on horseback, she'd realized a man could feel quite good while against her. She shivered as if chilled. If Nicholas tried to pull up her skirt like Daggart... Beth stopped herself from imagining anything further. She crawled into her cold bedroll, too tired to endure thinking about either man.

Another couple days of travel passed like the prior two. The activities were the same, but at a slower pace. Those with horses left the road in search of better grass or water. Finding none, the group stayed with the shallow, muddy creeks they crossed. Beth filled the water jar and let the silt settle overnight. In the morning, she'd boil the water in the cleaned out jar for the day's use. Fortunately, neither the oxen nor Erleen were as picky about grit as she and Daggart.

The third day after leaving Wolf River, they found better water and fishing. The mood around camp brightened when word reached the last wagon of the large stream lying ahead of them. Everyone agreed to cross now instead of leaving the work for tomorrow.

Beth tapped her foot as she and her husband waited their turn. Had they camped on this side, she'd have her dress ready for sewing. Beth peered around people and vehicles at the stream to see how close they were to crossing. The longer the wait, the more likely she could start sewing.

From what she could see, the wagons made good progress across the river, too much for her to sit and sew a spell. She watched as high-spirited horses splashed over, while the steady oxen lumbered across. Mules dug in their heels, unwilling to walk over anything different from the usual dirt and grass. Never mind the animals had crossed water before this; every creek was a new experience for the stubborn creatures. She shook her head, certain only a fool would want a mule.

A disturbance to the right caught everyone's attention. Six oxen pulling a Conestoga spooked, the ruckus drowning out many other sounds. Beth watched as the driver tried to calm the animals in mid-stream before the team broke away. The wagon tongue tore off with the oxen as they pulled left, overturning the wagon. People scrambled to gather items before they vanished in the currents. Other animals weren't as affected as the horses, most of whom stayed calm, while only a few reared in displeasure.

Several men hauled the wagon upright as the driver and others retrieved the wayward team. Beth noticed Daggart standing close to their oxen, acting as if he needed to calm the already placid pair. She stifled a chuckle at his pretense, walking forward to see if the couple needed help reloading their items.

She stopped at the water's edge. The river reached one of the taller men's knees, and Beth chewed her lip from worry. Not only was the water cloudy, it rapidly swirled around people and things, causing definite ripples. A little shiver of fear went through her, and she stepped back a couple of paces.

"Mrs. Bartlett," Nicholas addressed her. "We have things well in hand; get on to your place. You'll be up here soon enough." He rode off into the stream with a splash.

Feeling a bit rebuked, she nodded and moved out of the way for the next wagon. Amelia rode past Beth on her bay. The girl waved at her and joined Nicholas as he helped lead on individual wagons. Beth walked back to where Daggart waited, knowing she had no right to any sort of jealousy. Not for the first time in the past week did she think Nicholas deserved someone like Amelia.

She reached her husband, looking in the same direction he stared. Upon seeing his target, Beth gave him a sharp glance. "She thinks you're married."

"So do I," he retorted, not taking his gaze from Amelia. He spat on the ground near her and then led the team up to the water.

She shook her head at his meanness and blinked back tears. Seeing him and their belongings enter the stream, she didn't have time for crying. Beth took a deep breath and grabbed hold of the backboard of their wagon. She'd devised a plan on how to approach rushing water the day Nicholas had to carry her across. While she enjoyed being so close to him, Beth knew she couldn't rely on him for crossing every river or creek. She figured the man had a job to do that didn't include playing her knight in shining armor at a moment's notice.

Beth held onto the wagon until her fingers grew numb. She ignored the water rushing into the boots she wore and stared only at her sunbonnet's brim. She consciously inhaled and exhaled while hoping she didn't appear too foolish to others. Only after reaching solid ground did she let go her fierce grip of the backboard. Her hands ached and Beth just knew she left indentions from her grip. She shivered despite the afternoon's warmth.

Nicholas rode up to her, a concerned expression on his face. "Are you doing well?"

She nodded, "I think so." Beth pulled off a boot, upended it and let the water run out. "I didn't catch any fish, though."

He laughed, tipped his hat, and rode on to the next family to cross. Beth didn't spend any time watching him ride away; instead she emptied the other boot and hurried to catch up to Daggart.

In a rare good mood, Dag set up camp for them once they joined the wagon circle. All Beth had to do was make sure the animals had plenty to eat and drink. Her husband staked up their tent and scrounged for firewood, planning to join others at a fishing hole further down the stream. As she led Erleen around for grass, Beth also picked up any tinder for future fires. The further they traveled into the prairie, the less she saw of forests or even solitary trees. Despite assurances to the contrary, she felt sure burning buffalo chips would result in foul-smelling food.

After milking Erleen, she wanted to know if Daggart had any fish for dinner. She took the milk jar for him and brought a pail to the fishing hole for the evening and tomorrow's water. Beth found Daggart sitting alongside several others, including Nicholas and Amelia.

"For me?" he asked, taking the jar and bucket.

"Of course." She watched as he poured milk into the jar. "You're probably thirsty, dinner time or not."

He drank deeply of the milk, wiping his mouth on his sleeve afterward. "I was, thank you." Daggart lifted the pail for her to take, keeping the jar.

"You're welcome." She looked out over the pond, seeing if anyone else pulled in a catch. "Any luck?"

He shrugged. "A couple of the boys caught some five pounders."

"Hopefully, their friends will find your hook too."

"Yeah, I'm gettin' tired of bacon, no matter how you fix it." Daggart shifted around, getting comfortable for a long wait.

Someone waving to her left caught Beth's eye. She looked to see Nicholas walking with Amelia as the younger woman called out to her, "Bon jour!"

Beth waved back. "Hello."

"Comment allez-vous?" she asked. To Beth, it sounded like Amelia had asked her "Come on, tall ay voo." She understood the first part but not the second, and so responded with a shrug and a smile.

Daggart whistled. "What a fine woman. I'll bet she speaks French and a lot of other languages. Probably reads them too. Dang."

To her chagrin, after Amelia said something quietly to Nicholas, he and the girl laughed. He murmured in her ear and waving, the girl added, "Bonn chance et au revoir!"

Beth waved, having the feeling she'd been dismissed for the second time that day. Daggart was right. Amelia was a fine woman, much finer than she. Beth forced a bright smile at her husband, who wasn't looking at her but at the retreating pair. "I'll let you continue fishing, then."

"I liked the milk. You don't need some for butter?" he asked.

Beth shrugged. "No. Not unless you catch something."

Dag cleared his throat as if getting ready to say something difficult. "I liked that bacon grease you used with the cornmeal and grass stuff like last time."

She smiled at his somewhat accurate description. "Do you mean rosemary?"

Giving her a skeptical look, the same one she received when doing something stupid, he chided her. "You call it rosemary like some gal's name?"

"Yes, and so does everyone else because that happens to be its name." She eased down to the water's edge, rinsing the jar of milk and filling it with fresh water. "Since you approve, I'll use it when you bring back something for me to fry."

He grinned, giving her a salute. "You got a deal, woman."

Beth smiled as she carried the pail up to the campfire, pleased there'd been no fight or argument with her husband. She started the fire, put the pail on for boiling, and started bacon frying. While the heat did its job, Beth picked a couple pieces of her dress to sew. Working with the fabric was a joy. She took care, making each stitch small and even, although she'd rather go faster, impatient to wear such a lovely garment.

"Hello, Mrs. Bartlett."

She looked up to see Nicholas with a stringer of fish, Amelia beside him. Beth stood, a little flustered at having been so engrossed in her work that she'd not heard them approach. "Hello, Mr. Granville, Miss Chatillon. It's nice to see you both."

"Merci beaucoup!" Amelia replied.

Nicholas smiled at the young woman next to him, saying, "I need to give Mrs. Bartlett a message from her husband. Je vous verrai au dîner, mon cheri?"

"Oh!" She cleared her throat then replied, "Mais oui, mon chere."

"Good. I'll see you then." He didn't watch her walk away, instead addressing Beth, "I see you're making progress."

"Yes, I am. This is so lovely I wish I could sew while walking."

He raised an eyebrow, asking, "Should I ask how my socks are coming along?"

"Um," Beth put the fabric behind her back. "I'd prefer you didn't."

Chuckling, Nicholas reassured her, "I'd rather see you out of your old dress first." He grinned like a little boy caught eating a stolen apple. "And in your new one too, that is."

Beth felt the blush all the way to her toes. Surely he couldn't be courting Miss Chatillon while being so ornery to her. "Lucky for you, I can knit and walk at the same time if the ground is somewhat level. You'll get your socks before my dress is finished, I promise."

"No need to fret, Beth." He winked at her. "As long as they are done by the Rockies, I'll be happy. I truly would prefer your dress finished first."

"Honestly? Because I agree even though I shouldn't. You needed new socks or wouldn't have asked me to make you a pair." Beth brought the pieces of fabric up front for him to see. "But this is so beautiful and wonderful, I couldn't resist. It has been a dream to sew."

"I'm glad." He glanced toward the fishing pond. "I need to get these started cooking. Your husband wanted me to tell you he's caught a couple for you to have for supper."

She smiled, knowing Daggart's hunger had won out over his jealousy over another man talking to her. "In that case, we're having cornmeal fish with rosemary." She turned to the side casually as if Erleen had caught her interest, trying to keep her request informal. "Would you like to join us? I could add your catch to ours."

Nicholas hesitated, staring into her eyes. "You're very tempting, but I have plans already this evening."

She looked away on the pretext of checking the boiling water to keep him from seeing her resentment. Before Beth could stop herself, she asked, "I'm assuming with Miss Chatillon?"

"Yes, Sam and I are having dinner with both her and her father. I'm helping her cook for the hands."

"That's very nice." Beth forced lightness to her voice she didn't feel and smiled up at him. "I won't keep you then, and thank you for the message."

He opened his mouth to say something then stopped, tipping his hat instead. Beth knew she imagined it, but with him gone, the night seemed darker than usual. She sewed until Daggart returned. He arrived not long after Nicholas left, with three fish for them. Whistling, he cleaned the catch, handing them over to her for cooking. Neither talked much; she didn't know his reasons, and wanted to ignore hers. Both settled into their bedrolls expecting tomorrow to be somewhat the same as today.

Little spatters of drizzle on the tent woke her the next morning. "Daggart! It's raining!" Water seeped in under the tent, soaking their blankets and them. She shook him awake, knowing he'd join her in having a bad mood over the rain. The day had yet to fully dawn, clouds darkening the sky. Crawling out, the chilly rain drenched her. She looked around, watching as others folded up their shelters, loaded them, and hitched their animals to the wagons or carts.

As the sky lightened, the faces of those traveling did not. Everyone, it seemed, missed their morning coffee very much. Some were able to ride in their wagons, others preferred walking in the chill to the rough bounce of the roads. As the morning wore on into noon, the trail became mushy and difficult to ride over. They didn't stop for noontime; instead, everyone ate their cold lunch. Beth rode in their wagon, handing Daggart a biscuit bacon sandwich of sorts, wishing she'd had fresh vegetables from the garden to add. Any sort of a different taste would be wonderful, she thought, trying to chew the dry bread.

The steady drizzle continued into the late evening, never ending. Large, shallow pools stood on parts of the flattest land.

The train couldn't travel far today, the animals unable to take pulling their load through soggy dirt. Yesterday's hot dinners were a fond memory when facing a cold evening meal. Daggart led the oxen around, searching for grass. After Beth did the milking, she looked for the cow something to eat as well. The land here had been too dry for too long. The tufts of grass had dried into crisps. A hungry Erleen pulled at the shriveled blades. Beth patted the cow on the neck, hoping for better grass ahead. She figured the nearer the Platte they were, the better the vegetation. Beth made a mental note to ask one of the Granvilles or hands when the grazing would improve.

As she staked the cow near the wagon, the rain pelted down harder. A blinding flash of lighting too quickly followed by booming thunder led more than one lady to cry out in shock. Beth clambered into the wagon, moving aside to let in Daggart.

"Help me pull down the flaps," he ordered.

She took the back flap while he took the front. They tied them off, making the wagon less likely to leak. In the flash of lighting, she saw men running past, chasing errant animals. Several more loud thunderclaps sounded along with horse shrieks. The rain almost drowned out the sound of a stampede. Daggart hopped out to check on their cow. Beth peeked from under the flap to see Erleen's broken rope. Heaven knew where or if they'd ever find her. After a while, they all straggled past, lightning illuminating the distant landscape without the deafening thunder. Daggart appeared at the back of the wagon where she looked out, startling Beth.

"Did you find Erleen?" she asked him. "How is she?"

He shook his head and hoisted himself into the wagon. "I don't know." Settling in beside her to look out also, he added, "I'm hopin' we'll be able to find her and the rest. They could be anywhere by now at full run." Daggart began unbuttoning his shirt.

She turned away to get out the bedrolls. As many hooves as she'd heard, Beth had to ask, "Was anyone trampled?"

"Naw," he shook his head and pulled a dry shirt over his head. "But I heard someone was struck. Killed them."

Beth paused while setting up their bedding. Another person dead so soon? She took a deep, calming breath. Keeping her tone indifferent, she inquired in an offhand manner, "You don't know who?"

"No one knew for sure which one of us it was." He grunted,

struggling out of his wet pants, then putting on a dry pair. After a slight tussle to get dressed, he added, "Weather's so bad out there, most won't know what's gone until mornin'."

Beth laid down on her blankets. She placed the back of her hand on her forehead, forcing her voice to sound calm. "Morning sounds good. Since everything is wet, we might as well sleep here for the night."

Dag stretched out for the night, yawning. "We'll do that. I'm bushed."

Soon, she heard his slight snore. Beth couldn't sleep, wondering who'd been hit by lightning. She prayed Nicholas wasn't out there, dead. Tears leaked from the corners of her eyes. She also couldn't bear it if Samuel or the Misters Lucky, Chuck, Lawrence, or Claude had been killed, either. All of them, at one time or another, enjoyed her cooking for them. She suspected it was them missing a wife or mother more than her way with spices. Still, their company made mealtimes enjoyable. The possibility any of them suddenly gone broke her heart.

Beth paid for her restless night the next morning. Her mind foggy, she desperately wanted coffee. The whole camp shared the same foul mood, the men especially so. They'd all left to search the countryside since Erleen and a couple of other cows were the only livestock still in camp. Beth hugged her and fixed her a new tether. She dug around for a small potato to give Erleen, who gobbled it up and rooted around Beth for more. She laughed at the animal's enthusiasm and scouted around for fresh grass to feed her.

Water stood a couple of inches in places, more in others. The rain saturated the ground into muck, leading everyone to duck walk to avoid sticking in the clay. Listening to the chatter, Beth learned Jackson Watts had been killed in the storm. He was one of the card players Daggart liked chatting with in the evening. She didn't relish the idea of telling her husband his friend had died and hoped he learned the news before coming back.

She saw Daggart leading their oxen to the wagon. "Did you hear?"

"Yeah." He walked past her to hitch up the animals.

Beth looked at his face. "I'm sorry. It's such a shame."

Still busy checking the yokes, he muttered, "Doesn't matter, he didn't owe me money."

She stepped back to let him pass. Not often, but sometimes Daggart surprised her with his lack of concern for other people. Amazed at his apathy, she asked, "Is whether he owed you anything all you care about?"

He came around the front. "Yeah, after walkin' four miles to get our team, I don't care about much except you gettin' our water for coffee."

"Water?" Beth had gone earlier and retreated after seeing how the dirty brown water rushed past, bending saplings. Debris from further upstream drifted down, damming up in some places where rocks outcropped. "I don't want to. I can't." She didn't see the furious glint in his eyes until too late.

He grabbed her by the arm, took a pail, and drug her to the stream overflowing its banks. "You'll get me my damned water, Lizzy, how and when I tell you to." Daggart pulled her closer and closer, each step leaving her more paralyzed with fear. Beth's knees wouldn't bend as he hauled her behind him.

At three feet from torrent's edge, she dug in her heels and leaned back. "No, no!" At her cry, Daggart turned to glare at her, his jaw set. He pulled Beth's arm and shoved her toward the torrent, tearing her sleeve loose from her dress. She stumbled down the embankment, grabbing onto a bolder half submerged. The roar of the river filled her ears. Too terrified to scream, Beth clung to the rock. She couldn't open her eyes, instead pressing her face against the stone.

Daggart yelled at her over the noise. "I want my damn coffee! Don't come back until you have water!"

Beth turned her head a little, peeking through her lashes. He'd set down the pail and now walked up the slight incline, not seeing her in the rising water. She shivered in the cold and looked down where she held onto the rock. Her heart skipped, alarmed at how water now came up to her waist. Was the creek getting higher? she wondered, lifting her head and looking west. Angry dark clouds rushed toward her, full of more rain. Heaven help her, the faster and higher water wasn't her imagination. The boulder was her own island and soon to be submerged. Dizzy from fear, she hugged the stone with all her might. She couldn't let go and be swept away like the last time. Beth started crying, hot tears creating warm tracks down her cold face. Burying her face in her left shoulder to hide from the water, she only now noticed the sleeve torn away.

"Elizabeth! Please, sweetheart, grab hold of me!"

She heard Nicholas first and then felt his hands on her waist. He pulled at her, leaving her no choice but to grip tighter. If she let go, they'd both be swept downstream, just like before with Lizzy. "No! I can't!"

He worked his arms between her waist and the cold rock, his warm body thawing the fear from hers. "Elizabeth," he said in her ear, "I have you. I'm not letting go."

"No," she sobbed. "You won't be able to hold me. The current is too strong."

"Please, Elizabeth, sweetheart. You have to trust me. I've got you." He squeezed her even tighter. "I've got you and won't let go."

The river splashed her face, causing her to sputter. "You can't hold on to me like this. We'll die!"

"No, we won't. Let me get you out of here. Turn around and hold me. I'll get you back on ground." He pressed his lips against her ear, saying, "Please, trust me to keep you safe."

With a deep breath, she loosened her grip on the rock. He wrapped his arms more securely around her waist as the gap between her and the stone increased. She asked, "Let go completely?"

His arms tightened around her. "Yes, I'll get you back to shore."

Beth pushed away from the boulder and onto Nicholas. They tumbled in the current as he kept them above the surface. She turned to him, pressing her face into his neck. The swept away sensation stopped as if they were snagged by a large fishhook, and Beth opened her eyes.

Nicholas held onto a handful of river marsh. He'd wrapped the blades around his hand and had them in a white knuckled grip. "When you make your mind up to let go, you let go more than I expected. I'll try to remember that the next time I pry you from a rock."

Feeling his slight chuckle, she also reached out to the vegetation he held. "I didn't mean to fall in, I promise."

"I know, sweetheart." He kissed the top of her head. "How about we get back on shore?" When she nodded, he said, "Keep your arms around me, I'll do the pulling." Once her hands were locked around his chest, Nicholas reached for his other hand. He hauled them both out of the water and onto the bank.

Although safe, she held him, still hearing the torrents. "I had to get water." Beth shivered, his warmth contrasting with her cold. "I was so scared and I'm sorry to be such trouble."

"You could never be trouble and everyone is afraid of something. In fact, I'm afraid of letting you go." He loosened his hold on her. "But if I don't, your husband will call me out."

"Oh! Oh my husband, of course." Beth drew away from him, a little. "Again, I'm sorry."

"Again, sweetheart, don't be," he whispered near her ear. Nicholas pulled her sleeve from where it draped on her elbow up to her shoulder. "Why were you so close to the creek? It's not like you with the water so high."

"Daggart insisted and had to make me, I'm afraid." She saw the anger in his expression and trembled, not wanting to upset him but not wanting to lie. "I couldn't make myself go."

"I see." His eyes were almost as dark as the storm clouds overhead.

She swallowed and tried to salvage the situation. "Falling in was my fault for being such a goose. I overreact to floods, muddy water, rapids, and those sorts of things. Daggart was probably trying to help me get over my fear, and here I've caused fuss and bother for you." Beth stood, unsteady on her feet still. "If I promise to never act so foolish again, will you please forgive me for my thoughtless behavior?"

"Tell me if I understand this correctly." He stood also, saying through gritted teeth, "You are terrified of floods. Despite this, your husband forces you to gather water from an overflowing creek. Now, you beg me to forgive your panic?"

"Yes, if you don't mind." She picked up the pail and gave him her best smile. "Let's forget all this and it'll never happen again."

Nicholas held out his hand in a give me gesture and took the bucket from her. "What I want you to do is go back uphill to where you feel safe. I'll be up in a minute, no debate."

She nodded, too intimidated by his stern tone to argue. Beth struggled up the incline, her legs still unsteady. Nicholas soon caught up to her, his strides solid from determination.

He glanced at her from the corner of his eye. "Your husband will have his water, filthy though it may be."

She followed him to the camp without a reply. Beth bit her lip when she saw Daggart waiting for her by the wagon. He looked as angry as Nicholas.

"Mr. Bartlett, your water." Nicholas handed him the pail.

Daggart addressed Beth, "What happened to you getting this for me?"

She started an answer, but before Beth could speak, Nicholas interjected, "She was unable to, having fallen into a flooding stream." He indicated their appearance. "Neither of us are exactly dry at the moment."

"A good excuse to force your work on others." Her husband still spoke to Beth as if only the two of them were there.

Nicholas stepped in between them, facing Daggart. "No. It is fact." He went forward, forcing the taller man back a step. "For some reason, she was clinging to a rock as the creek rose. If she'd been there much longer, Mrs. Bartlett would have been swept away."

He scoffed, "As useless as Beth is around here, you should have let her. Saved us all a lot of trouble."

CHAPTER 8

Beth glanced in stunned silence from one man to the other. Daggart hadn't used her own name since her father died. Both men glowered at each other, locked in a wordless fight. In an effort to diffuse the situation, she began, "Um, now that we have the water..." She trailed off when they turned to her, fury evident in both their faces. All that anger left her speechless.

His tone clipped, Nicholas acknowledged, "Yes, we need to get started." He tipped his hat to both of them. "Mrs. Bartlett, Bartlett."

After the man walked far enough away, Daggart threw down the pail with such force the side bent. He turned to her and grabbed the front of her dress under her throat. "You're always hoping a man will save you from drowning or other accidents."

"I hope someone would, yes," she whispered.

He shook her a little with every few words. "One day, and I hope it's soon, no one's gonna be there to save you 'n even if I am there, I'm not helpin' you one bit."

Before she could stop herself, Beth snapped, "Like you didn't help Lizzy?"

Dag released her with a shove. "No, damn it all, I wanted to save her." He followed her as she stumbled, adding, "I wasn't there to help her like you were." Once close, pressing her against the wagon, he reached back and grabbed her braid. Daggart dug his fingers in, nails scraping her scalp. "You let her die and are doin' a real bad job of bein' her. Your daddy wouldn't like that, would he?"

Beth nodded as much as possible, wishing she'd never promised to be anything to this man. "I suppose not."

He leaned in close, whispering, "You'd best be thinkin' more of how Lizzy would behave on this trip and less as to how you would, or else."

She doubted he'd have ever uprooted Lizzy from their home, even for gold. Beth hated his using threats and guilt. She hissed, "Or else what? Are you threatening to kill me? I thought you wanted Lizzy even if I had to pretend."

As he grinned, she could see the remnants of his prior meal still in his teeth. "That's the thing, Lizzy Lou. There are a lot of miles and a lot of accidents between here and California." He looked up, tapping a finger against his chin in mock sorrow, "I'd hate to lose another wife. Such a pain, havin' to dig your grave." Daggart shrugged. "But if you're not her, no sense in sharin' my gold with the likes of you. Wouldn't hurt me to get in practice with a shovel, either."

Beth's hairs on the back of her neck rose. He'd hit her, made her do things she'd thought awful, even threatened to leave her behind without anything, but Daggart had never spoke of murder when he was sober. Seeing the man's determined face, she felt certain he'd carry out his threat. The Granvilles wouldn't allow him to harm her, they couldn't. She clasped her hands to keep them from shaking so Daggart wouldn't see and use her fear against her. "I'll do my best to be a better Lizzy."

He laughed, "That's what I want to hear. Do what I want when I want and nothing bad has to happen to you." Letting go of her, he added, "Get goin' on chores. I want my breakfast."

For the rest of the morning, Beth did whatever possible to avoid Daggart. Heavy clouds blew in overhead, blasting everyone with hard, cold gusts. She couldn't work on any stitching, instead concentrating on following the trail. In view of Daggart's destructive mood, he'd likely use the new material for traction to get them out of the mud instead of anything else. While they stopped for noon, she sewed up her ripped sleeve. She considered herself lucky the left arm torn and easier to fix without having to take off her dress entirely. The stitches weren't neat, but served a purpose until she could change into other clothes.

Very few had fires built for dinner, having found small amounts of wood in the distance between the morning and evening camps. She'd hoped this far in the prairie, buffalo chips weren't so rare. Even if the chips were plentiful, they'd be soaked and useless. She and Daggart had their milk and yesterday's bacon without a word. He smiled and chatted when others strolled by their campsite. After they passed by, he returned to a sullen silence. Beth enjoyed the quiet, but not the damp chill.

The wagon circle was far from any proper water, but heavy rains had left large puddles. The stock drank from them while the people used collected rainwater. Those who tried to raise tents soon found them flattened in the wind. She saw Daggart shrug and walk away as a nearby family's blew down. Beth went over to help, folding, and making sure all the stakes were found.

The sky darkened with evening. Tired, cold, and still very wet, Beth decided against sewing or knitting, instead wanting to sleep. Her body still ached from the earlier fall in the creek and Daggart's resulting temper. Despite hanging up the bedding to dry during the day, the humid air kept them damp. She felt more than saw Daggart come in under the blankets. He snuggled against her, waking her a little with his cold body. Not smelling the stink of whisky, Beth relaxed and fell back to sleep.

Beth both enjoyed and wondered about Daggart's absence at breakfast. She'd soon fastened the blankets to the canopy, letting them hang outside again all day or at least until it rained. Beth followed their wagon at a distance. Her healing feet and other aches slowed her pace. The train continued through noon, stopping upon reaching Dry Creek. The stream lived up to its name by allowing everyone to cross easily but forcing the animals to go without a drink.

Samuel and Mr. Lucky caused a fuss when they rode back to the train. In the gossip, Beth learned they'd left a few days ago to scout ahead. She saw them in the camp later, but didn't hear where they'd searched. Talk drifted back to her and the others walking with her that they'd stop at Wood Creek for the night.

The ten miles passed quickly. The breeze, still chilly, didn't blow as hard as the prior two days. She smiled, thinking of how nice a dry bed would feel tonight. The sky stayed cloudless, keeping the day cool but dry. Daggart, along with the others, drove their team into the now familiar wagon circle. He continued to ignore her, something she found refreshing. Better to be ignored than scolded.

Beth had spent the day thinking of how scary rushing water was and how twice she'd needed Nicholas's rescue. While she enjoyed how close he held her then, she'd rather be near him for other reasons. Determined to conquer some of the fear, Beth took Erleen down to the stream. The creek rushed by, higher than any she'd seen so far. Even the rivers hadn't flowed with such voracity. The water escaped far out of its banks, judging by the trees lining a narrow strip down its middle. Erleen trotted down the bank and stopped for a drink. Her heart pounding, Beth stayed a safe distance away. She wanted to have no chance of falling in while holding onto the cow's rope.

When Erleen finished drinking and started munching at the grass along the bank, Beth led her back to the wagon. She tied the animal off at the greenest part of their cart and went to get water for the evening meal. She took a deep breath and released it, hoping to calm her racing heartbeat. The pounding hurt against her sore ribs. She reassured her fears by thinking that they only needed a little water. Erleen's milk could supplement, Beth admitted to herself, and she didn't have to do this tonight. Nervous and biting her lip, she fixed her gaze on the opposite side.

She lifted her chin and took a step toward the creek. Beth gripped the pail so hard the handle dug into her palm. One step at a time, she slowly neared the bank. People around her went up to the churning creek, scooped up the water and left. Bending at the knees, Beth leaned over, skimming the surface and filling the bucket half full.

After straightening, she stepped back and took a couple of calming breaths. She walked toward the circle, thrilled at the small task she'd accomplished. Beth saw Nicholas walk toward her, carrying his own bucket. She couldn't help grinning and pointing out her success. As he neared she blurted, "Look! It's silly, I know, but I have water!" Her sore arm trembled with the effort as she lifted the pail.

Dutifully, he peered inside the bucket then looked at her with a smile. "Are you doing better, then?"

Beth's face grew warm as she returned his grin. He didn't need to know about Daggart's abuse. "Yes, and I have something to drink now if I'm not."

He laughed, "I'm very proud of you trying, never mind doing."

"Thank you! I'm proud of me too." She sighed, somewhat embarrassed at admitting, "You've already twice played hero to my childish phobia. I couldn't let you waste your time with a third incident."

"There's to be no third time?" He glanced around them then gave her an ornery smile. "Then I'll have to find another reason to hold you close to me, sweetheart."

He'd called her by the endearment before now, but always

while she felt in danger. Hearing such an endearment in his voice, and directed at her no less, left her breathless. "You will, hmm?"

Nicholas, not breaking his gaze, took Beth's hand and raised it to his lips. "I will."

She tingled from the back of her hand to her heart. "That's very comforting, thank you." She couldn't look away from his eyes, the grey in them catching and reflecting the gold and red of the setting sun.

"What's going on, here?"

Samuel's voice startled her. Even though he smiled at them, Beth jerked away her hand, tucking it behind her back in shame. Fright left her mind unable to think and she couldn't answer.

Nicholas chuckled and shrugging said, "Come on, Sam. You're not the only charmer around here. I think I'm allowed to congratulate a woman on a supreme accomplishment."

Samuel shook his head at Beth in mock disbelief, "Supreme? It must have been to warrant holding hands. Please, my dear, tell me I'm truly the only appealing man in the entire group."

She smiled, forcing herself to think fast and be witty. "You might not be the only one, sir. I think Mr. Nicholas has been learning from your fine example."

"You break my heart with such confessions!" Samuel went to stand next to her, taking her arm in a protective way. "You'll have to let me walk you back to your camp, telling me how I may regain my place as the most eligible one of us two."

Glad she held the pail with her sore arm in case Samuel grew angry and pulled her along, Beth said, "I don't think you have any reason to fret. Your brother may give you a close race, but you certainly win any contest."

"She wounds me." Nicholas put a hand to his heart, mocking, "How will I survive?"

She shook her head, not thinking he was serious by the way he smiled at her. "Just fine, I think. You already have one adoring admirer. Isn't that all a man needs?" Nicholas spent so much time with Miss Amelia and the girl clearly preferred him, too. Beth could and must pretend she didn't care.

A warning glance went between the brothers. Nicholas narrowed his eyes as if angry while Samuel cleared his throat, saying "I'm sure Nick has things to do while I see you safely back to your hold. Nick, later?"

The older brother gave a mock salute, and went to the creek to fill the pail. Beth resisted the urge to look back at him, instead falling in pace with Samuel.

They walked a little way before Samuel said, "My brother is a good man."

Nodding, she agreed, "I've found him to be so."

Samuel stared at her, eyes narrowed. "I would expect you to be a good woman."

His frown unnerved her, but she shrugged off the worry. From his prior treatment of her and the other ladies, he'd been stern but never truly angry with anyone. Did Mr. Granville see through her? Did he see how much she felt for his brother already? Samuel had to know Beth only felt an infatuation for Nicholas and tried to deny herself even that little bit. She swallowed, replying, "I try to be a lady at all times."

He patted her arm. "Good. I would hate to think of a married woman leading Nick on to discard him when he's served his purpose."

She stopped and chuckled at the idea. "Me discarding him?" Beth felt sure trading Daggart for Nicholas had to be an improvement. If she ever had the chance at a relationship with him, she'd never let Nicolas go. "Are you sure the reverse wouldn't be true?"

"Not of him, he's not the play around type. Nick cares too much about people." Samuel started toward the circle again. "He's been a hermit by choice for the past few years. He had his reasons, but I'm glad he's out in polite society again." They drew close to the Bartlett camp. Samuel continued, but in a quieter voice, "Don't entertain yourself with his affections or I will not be happy with you. Do you understand?"

Beth felt sick. She now had two threats from two men in less than a week. Maybe she should be the one to leave polite society if threats were all anyone gave her. Pulling away from him, she answered, "I understand."

"Good." He released her arm and smiled as if nothing were amiss. As Daggart strolled up to them, Samuel hollered, "Bartlett! Will you be at tonight's games?"

Dag grinned, replying, "Lookin' forward to it already. If I can get my lazy woman to fix dinner, I'll be there before mornin'."

"Excellent! We'll see you there." Turning to leave, he tipped his hat at her. "Mrs. Bartlett."

"Mr. Granville," Beth nodded in reply. She sighed, considering herself warned. Would Samuel be as physical as Daggart? She watched her husband start a fire. Beth supposed, by Daggart's continued silence, he still punished her. She smiled, thinking how his idea of punishment didn't match her own. After peeling a couple of potatoes for dinner, she cooked them with bacon and made flat bread. They ate without conversation, Daggart leaving as soon as he took the last bite.

Beth gathered up their dishes, unwilling to go to the creek. A task achievable in daylight proved impossible in the dark. The thought of stumbling in the blackness terrified her. She settled for stacking everything in the bucket, promising a better wash during daylight.

Alone at last, she smiled while retrieving her sewing. First Dag beat her, then Samuel threatened her. Would Nicholas hurt her, too? She didn't believe him capable, but wouldn't have believed it of Daggart when they first met either. Despite the unease she felt when thinking of the Granvilles, Beth loved nearing the finish of her dress. She didn't want to imagine any more meanness. Instead, she counted the stitches as she sewed.

The fire and dry place to rest was a blessing, allowing her to get several large pieces sewn together. Beth couldn't help working faster on the hem. Once done, she tied a small knot, hiding the thread's end in the fabric. Standing and stiff-legged from sitting so long, she held the dress up for inspection, loving how beautiful it looked. After folding and placing the garment in the wagon, she stoked the fire into a roaring brightness. Unable to wait any longer, Beth scrambled up into the wagon. She worked fast, changing from Lizzy's old dress to her new one.

She hopped out into the firelight and spun around so the skirt flared. The waist hugged Beth's waist. The bodice rose up enough for modesty's sake, and yet she'd made a neckline low enough to be stylish. She hugged herself, thrilled with her efforts.

"I hope I enjoy my socks as much," Nicholas said, walking into the firelight.

She started. "Oh my! I didn't see you there." Beth put a hand to her clavicle, surprised at touching skin. Lizzy's dress had unfashionably gone up to her throat's hollow, and she'd grown so accustomed to it over time that now a normal fitting dress seemed odd.

"Sorry if I startled you."

Beth returned his smile, "I was enjoying my new dress too much to notice anything else." His admiration warmed her more than the fire.

"It's beautiful." He stepped closer. "Turn around, let's see if it fits in the back as well as it does the front."

Her cheeks burned with bashfulness under his scrutiny. If Samuel saw how his brother stared at her, he'd be angry. She needed to shoo Nicholas away. "Sir, I think you're enjoying this far too much."

"You're right, I am enjoying this." He went to her. "If you knit better than you sew, I'm one lucky man."

"Then, you're lucky. I do knit far better than I sew." She smoothed imaginary wrinkles in her skirt, shy from her boasting.

He folded his arms. "Seeing you in such a dress? I'll only believe it when I get my socks, and that will be when, again?"

"Oh, you!" She smiled at his apparent strategy. "If you're trying to get me to knit faster, it's working."

"Good!" Nicholas leaned toward her, saying with a sly grin, "I want something you made hugging my feet."

Beth laughed at him. "You mock me far too much! To think, Samuel warned me not to tease you. He should be warning you about teasing me instead." She stopped smiling when he frowned. "Is something wrong?"

"Sam warned you not to tease me?" His friendliness cooled to a hard anger.

Beth didn't want yet another person livid with her, so she countered with, "I think I should set up the tent. Aren't you tired?"

"No, I'm not at all." Nicholas stepped closer to her, frowning. "Did Sam warn you about me?"

"A little, yes." Nervous, she laced her fingers together, adding, "He pointed out, and rightly so, my status as a married lady."

"Something we're both very aware of."

"Yes." Beth wished she held something to worry with like men had their hats. Making a sunbonnet from the remaining fabric would help. He still watched her, as if waiting for Beth to say more. "Also, I'm not to amuse myself with you."

Nicholas raised an eyebrow. "Amuse?" He chuckled. "He said that?"

She nodded. "Almost exactly."

Laughing, he said, "I can imagine how he must have sounded. He's far too protective for a younger brother."

His amusement reassured Beth. Nicholas's anger didn't scare her as much as Daggart's, but it still worried her. "Maybe so, but in this case I think he's correct." She glanced around, checking for eavesdroppers. "I find myself forgetting about Daggart when you're near." In a quiet voice, she added, "And sometimes when you aren't near, I want to forget him."

Nicholas started to say something to her but stopped. After a moment of staring off into the distance, he said, "Sam was right, shielding me from you." He gave her a wry smile not reaching his eyes. "I need to go tell him to protect you from me."

Panic surged through her. "Oh no, no, don't do that. He'll know I've spoken to you about this and I shouldn't have." She stepped up to him, willing to grab his suspenders to stop Nicholas if necessary. "He's already not happy with me. Please don't make it worse." Beth bit her lip, saying, "I warned you about me, you warned me about you and everything is fine." She smiled, patting him on the arm. "And now we've both been warned, so Samuel doesn't need to be told anything, right?"

"He doesn't," Nicholas repeated, arms crossed again.

"Good." The dangerous look returned to his face but not as intense as before. She put her hand on her hips, exasperated. "I can't imagine why I mentioned his and my conversation to you. Once I'm near you, I start telling secrets. You are a dangerous man, Mr. Granville."

As if liking the idea, he nodded, saying, "I am, and I'll tell you a secret of my own."

She took a step back. "I don't know if I want to hear one from you. The other Mr. Granville wouldn't approve."

Giving her a sardonic look, he said, "It's simply this: tomorrow will be here too soon. Your dress is done, so get some sleep. We still have the creek to cross, and I'm sure you won't like doing so."

"Oh dear." She stared heavenward, wondering whether to get over her fears or just go back and try to find a new life.

He took her hand, gave it a reassuring squeeze. "You'll be fine, good night and sleep well." Nicholas said and left for his own bedroll.

"Good night, Nicholas," she whispered. "I miss you already."

In the morning, Beth gathered as much wood after breakfast as she could before travel started. The wagons crossed a wider portion of the creek bed laying a little north of camp. She rode across in the wagon, uncomfortable with wading across. Even though the water level was lower here, she'd still be in more than knee deep. She shuddered, thinking of what stumbling over a rock might do.

As the other teams drove over, a few mules resisted, balking and spooking the other animals, but no one was hurt. On the opposite side, the land flattened with slight hills on either side. They followed the wide valley, giving Beth a chance to knit as she walked. During lunch, Beth fervently wished the men found game of some sort. Cooking the same food day after day grew monotonous and eating it was worse.

The pace today seemed faster than usual to her. Not that anyone moved in a rush, but more as if the group's rhythm moved quicker than in the prior days. They continued far into the evening, past the usual time for dinner. Word passed around the captains wanted them to gain as much ground as possible during the fine weather.

She agreed, liking the late spring air. Word was passed down to stop for the night just before dark. With no water source nearby, the men took turns digging a hole in the damp sand of a dry creek. Muddy water filled the temporary well as they dug. Women and some men scooped out what they needed then led animals for their drinks before night. Beth strained the liquid and set it aside for the silt to settle. Tomorrow, she planned on pouring the clearest layer from the top into the water jar and coffee pot.

Without being asked, Daggart set up their tent. She smiled at him, "Thank you, I appreciate this."

He scowled, looking at his feet. "Aw, yer welcome. We're about a couple days to the Platte. I'm goin' to stop at Fort Kearny for supplies."

The fort meant a chance to wear her new dress. Beth still didn't relish the crowds, but did like the idea of wearing something pretty. "Good! I'd like to go, if possible."

Daggart shuffled from one foot to the other. "One of us needs to watch our property here. You could tell me what you're needin'." He kicked an imaginary rock.

She gritted her teeth, wanting to yell at him. Beth instead forced herself to maintain an even tone, saying, "I'd prefer you not buy whisky there."

In one swift move, Daggart grabbed her arm, pulling her close. He sneered, "You're not tellin' me what to do, are ya?"

Unable to look him in the eyes, she admitted, "No, but you hurt me when you're drunk."

He let her go with a little shove. After a few seconds, Daggart put his hands in his pants pockets. "I wouldn't if you'd do your duty."

"We both know the truth." She clenched her teeth to keep calm. "It's not my duty."

Like a petulant child, he retorted, "As long as you're my wife, it is."

Beth didn't want to argue, didn't want to be reminded of their arrangement. She went to Erleen as if the cow needed attention. "Very well."

He left without a word. Beth watched him walk away, glad Daggart had found other amusements. She'd heard enough gossip to know he played cards with the other men, or chatted with Mr. Chatillon. While Daggart was away this evening, Beth finished Nicholas's socks. She wanted to find him, but suddenly felt shy. Beth put her sewing trunk back in the wagon instead, ready for sleep.

Sometime during the night, Daggart came back to their camp. He slept through the hustle of morning. She gently shook him awake. "Dag, it's time for us to round up and go."

He mumbled something about being tired and turned over for more sleep. Resigned to his sluggishness, Beth took down the tent around him. She loaded the canvas, pegs, and center pole as he slept.

Only after she hitched the oxen did he come around to the front of the wagon still rubbing his eyes. "I appreciate you pulling up stakes for me."

She smiled at the first nice thing he'd said to her in a while. "You're welcome. You set it up, the least I could do is pull it down." He nodded, dismissing her. Beth patted Erleen as they followed the lurching wagon.

Beth watched for Nicholas all day, hoping to give him his new socks. She didn't want a fuss, or anyone to consider her brash in making clothing for a man. She'd thought of him with every stitch, longing to spend hours alone with him. She loved talking with Nicholas as herself, not as some parody of Lizzy as Daggart preferred.

The wagon train ground to a halt as a large, sandy expanse stretched before them. Instructions spread through the group. Each wagon was to follow the one before as Chuck and Lawrence found a solid way through the sand. Drivers were encouraged to keep rolling, no matter how slow, to keep from sinking. Fine grains whirled in the hot afternoon air, choking everyone on two or four legs. After ten miles of blinding dust, both people and animals' eyes burned. Beth's own eyes held tears as if she cried in earnest.

Looking like bandits with bandanas covering their nose and mouths, Nicholas, Claude, and Mr. Lucky rode by her with only Nicholas stopping. He dismounted and went to Beth. "Mrs. Bartlett. We're checking on everyone. Are you well enough to continue to Blue River for tonight?"

"Yes," she replied through the cloth tied around her face.

He tipped his hat. "Good. See you this evening."

The next nine miles passed by quickly for Beth. The harder grassland was so much easier to traverse than the desert. Plus, the promise of seeing Nicholas tonight kept her in high spirits. They'd not talked in a few days and she missed him. Catching sight of him once in a great while as he worked wasn't enough to satisfy her.

Upon stopping, Beth did all her usual chores. The closest anyone came to clear water was a muddy stream, barely a trickle. The men again took turns digging in the soaked earth for water. At the shallow well, she gathered their portion and saw Sam, who nodded.

He walked up to her. "Mrs. Bartlett."

"Mr. Granville." She turned toward the camp.

"If you don't mind, ma'am, we'd like you and your husband to join us for dinner tonight."

Beth wondered, after his warning, why did he ask this? She saw nothing suspicious in his expression. "I'd like to, but can't speak for my husband. He's lately had his meals with whoever is playing cards that evening."

His eyes narrowed. "I see. I hope you can attend, even if he chooses to dine elsewhere again."

"Thank you." She asked, "Should I bring anything?"

"No, you'll be our guest this evening." Samuel gave her an inscrutable smile and went to the camp.

By the time Erleen was fed and milked, the sky glowed amber. Not seeing Daggart anywhere, Beth went on to stake out the oxen, making sure they also had a long drink at the well. While leading the animals around for their refreshment, she saw various couples walk along the embankment, pretending to look for a spring. She smiled to herself at how the young adults flirted under their elders' watch. If Lizzy still lived, Beth might have her own husband by now.

Beth forced the thought out of her mind. She didn't want to dwell on her situation. Anything near the subject led to her brooding, and that would leave her unable to enjoy the evening. Once the animals were settled in, she took Nicholas's socks from her trunk to make sure he received them.

She went to the Granville's camp and saw all their hands circled around the fire. Nicholas and Samuel sat there too, taking turns tending to the food. Beth chewed on her lip, not wanting to call attention by boldly stepping into the light. Samuel saw her and waved, causing Nicholas to see her too. Beth smiled and walked over, her face warm from the greeting everyone gave. The men all stood and talked at once.

"Good evening," she said when the fuss quieted. "Thank you for inviting me. I've not seen Mr. Bartlett this evening, or I'm sure he'd be here too."

Mr. Lucky piped up, "I saw him at the Chatillon's. He and the old man play a lot of poker."

Chuck nudged him quiet, and he added, "Not for keeps, though. Mr. B says he's saving up for his stake."

The others snickered at this. Beth glanced around at them. Each one noticed her gaze and lowered his eyes. "I'm sure he is," she responded. She knew their opinions because they echoed her own. Any gold in California had already been claimed by '49ers, or by those with money to buy huge tracts of land. Lizzy had refused to go when alive, so Daggart didn't argue. If not for the two good years of farming and his bullying, they'd not be going now.

Chuck asked her, "Ma'am, if you don't mind me wondering, what's in your hand?"

She glanced at Nicholas talking to Claude. "This?" Beth held up the items. "Mr. Granville requested a pair of socks after seeing me knit my own pair."

Samuel cut his eyes over to his brother, while Chuck, Mr. Lucky, and Lawrence made catcalls. After Nicholas said something inaudible to Claude, he too joined in on the taunts. Beth felt certain she blushed to her toes.

Standing, Nicholas quieted them. "Now, now, gentlemen. The lady has been kind enough to make me something that not only warms my heart, but my toes as well."

"Oh goodness!" she gasped, entirely mortified. "I enjoy knitting, and you needed something less holey. Nothing more than this, certainly."

He went to Beth, holding out his hand for his socks. She gave them to him and he examined them, grinning. "These are perfect, thank you very much."

Nicholas went to his place in the circle. While Claude and Samuel watched, he took off his boots and socks. At that, everyone, including Beth, acted as if they smelled how foul his feet were. He gave them all a withering glare before pulling on his new socks. The men laughed as he wiggled his toes, except Claude until Samuel translated. He joined in and said something to Nicholas Beth couldn't understand at all.

Nicholas put on his boots and stood, saying, "Gentlemen, Monsieur Claude wants a pair of his own. I'd like to suggest he find some other charming woman to knit him socks, someone sweet and lovely like Miss Amelia." This earned him more good humored jeers.

"However, if Mrs. Bartlett is asked nicely and would want to waste her time on the likes of all of you," he paused for their snide comments to end before continuing. "Then, I'm sure she'll consider knitting anyone interested a pair of their own."

As one, the men looked at her. Shy, she looked at her hands then up at them. "If you wanted, I might." They all nodded, including Nicholas. "The only thing I ask is when we reach Fort Kearny, you see if there's any wool. I used the last of what I had on Mr. Granville's request. If you choose what color you prefer, I'll knit socks for you too." She tilted her head, smiling at them. "Unless, of course, there's a beautiful girl you want to knit for you instead."

"I can't imagine anyone more lovely than you, my dear," Samuel said. "I also can't imagine how waiting for dinner will make us any hungrier than we already are." He dished up a tin cup of food, passing it to her with a spoon.

She waited until everyone had food before taking a bite. It was delicious, a much welcome change from the usual. "What is this?"

"Rabbit stew," Chuck replied. He took a quick look up at her from his dinner, adding, "Mr. Lucky shot a big hare, not like those little brown rabbits back in Missouri."

Taking another bite, she was grateful for his assurance that no sweet little rabbits had died for her dinner. Her dismay must have shown on her face, Beth figured. She ate all of it, enjoying every spoonful. They had carrots and potatoes in the stew. She missed her garden more after every mouthful. Beth noticed Nicholas finishing just after she did and then putting his dishes in a bucket.

"If you don't mind, gentlemen, I'll walk Mrs. Bartlett back to her camp." He took her dishes amid their protests, placing them with his own. "Her husband might be done winning all of Chatillon's money and wondering where she is."

Beth told them, "Thank you for a wonderful dinner." She addressed Samuel, "Thank you too for inviting me. I had a pleasant evening."

"You're welcome, Mrs. Bartlett," he replied, putting up his things as well.

She followed Nicholas out of the camp. They walked along the outer edge of the wagon circle. Now alone with him, Beth realized everything she wanted to say were things Samuel had warned her against. She sighed in frustration.

Nick gave her a sidelong glance. "Let's step a little bit away from the wagons."

Biting her lip to hide a smile, she asked, "Is that safe?"

He leaned close to her, whispering, "No."

She laughed and nodded. "Oh? I like an honest man."

"Then you'll love me." He stopped walking and she also halted. "I'm honest to a fault, which can be bad in some cases."

"I could see that," she acknowledged with a grin. "Especially if a woman wants to know how a dress fits her or if you think another girl is prettier than her."

Holding his hands up in surrender then taking one of hers, Nicholas said, "Exactly so."

As he led her on to her camp, Beth added, "So, now I know not to ask you questions if I don't want to hear the answer."

"Do you think so?" Nicholas guided her a little ways out from the circle where the light faded. "If you asked how your dress fits, I'd have to say perfectly. It accents every beautiful curve. If you asked me if any woman could be prettier than you, I'd have to say no, never."

She chuckled a little, unsure of how to react in a sophisticated way to such language. "I think you've been taking sweet talk lessons from Samuel."

He faced her, tilting her chin up to him. "The talk may be sweet, but it's also honest."

Beth tried to think of her promise but Nicholas stood too close to her, his scent affecting her too much. "You can't really feel such things. Not about me."

"I do feel such things about you, all the time." He caressed her cheek.

"You can't, anymore than I can. When I'm around you, I want to forget all the agreements I've ever made to anyone else." Beth put her hand to his chest, more to push her away than him. His eyes were so dark in the dim light. A shadow of whiskers dusted his cheeks and chin.

"You agreed to something you don't want anymore?" He cupped the back of her neck in an embrace.

"Anymore? No, never." She shuddered with revulsion, taking her hand from his chest and holding one of his suspenders. "I was forced into accepting something I never wanted."

Nicholas pulled her closer to him with one hand on her arm as his other hand caressed her tense neck muscles. "Do you know you're speaking in riddles?"

"Yes, and I'm sorry." She ran her fingertips slowly up and down his suspenders. "Part of the promise is to never tell anyone what truly happened."

"If you asked, would they release you from this?" Nicholas rested his lips against her forehead.

Beth paused. She wanted to tell him everything but couldn't. Then too, she couldn't lie to him. Maybe he'd be satisfied with some of the story for now. Beth closed her eyes before telling him more. "I made a promise to my father and Daggart. My father's gone, so I'd be disrespecting the dead. And, Daggart wouldn't ever release me, not while," she paused. Unable to think of a fitting reason, Beth continued, "Well, never." She felt his smile against her skin.

Each word he said felt like a kiss as Nicholas countered with, "Never is a very long time. I've said never again then recanted far sooner than I expected."

Seeing a chance to divert him from her own history, Beth asked, "Did it have something to do with you being a hermit?"

He pulled away, giving her a stern glare. "Sam told you?"

She nodded. "It was when he warned me away from you. He also said you'd have to tell me yourself if I wanted to know any more about you."

Nicholas took her hand, leading her further into the dark. "Come with me."

His brother's warning came to her mind as the light behind them faded. She shuddered, whispering, "I can't. I promised Samuel."

He took her other hand and walking backward, said, "You can and will. I give you permission."

"But if Sam..." she protested as they went deeper into the darkness.

"He isn't invited," he said, drawing her close to him.

Chest to chest, his arms around her, Beth panicked, thinking of Samuel's warning. Only, with the smell and feel of Nicholas, what had he said? Don't something? "Nicholas, we can't..."

His mouth covered hers, tender at first, then insistent, hungry. Beth tried to resist, keeping her own lips still under his caress. When he drew away, his mouth still touching her own, the sudden absence increased her desire a hundredfold. Wrapping her arms around his neck, she pulled him into a deeper kiss as he held her to his waist. Their bodies were pressed so close, she couldn't tell which one of them moaned first.

The ferocity in his kisses both scared and thrilled Beth because she felt the same driving need for him. The thought of her and Nicholas accomplishing what Daggart drunkenly tried to do occurred to her. Upon imagining she and Nicholas undressed together, she felt his tongue touch her own. Beth whispered, "Please, Nicholas, please. I want more of you. All of you."

He kissed down her neck to Beth's shoulder. "You don't know what you're asking, sweetheart."

She wanted to argue her meaning, but as his lips traveled down her cleavage, she couldn't speak. Such pleasure now seemed worth any price Beth would later pay. Nicholas leaned her back in his arms. He nipped at the swells above the bodice. She gasped as he did so, the first time she'd ever felt such a thing. He braced her weight against his hips. When Nicholas pressed something hard against her, she suspected he was aroused. "Are you wearing a gun?" Beth asked, and then felt his smile against her breast.

"No, that's not my gun." He pulled down a shoulder of her dress, lips pressing against the warm flesh exposed to the cool air. He kissed his way from one of her shoulders to the others, pausing at her cleavage.

Every touch, every breath she heard increased this craving for all of him. Beth tried to control the hunger her body had for his. She must stop herself, must stop his lovemaking. "Nicholas, they'll start looking for us if we don't..." Beth ran her hand through the hair at the back of his head, pressing him closer to her. "I need to care if they see us like this."

He kissed his way up to her lips, back where he started and less intense than earlier. After replacing her dress's shoulder where it belonged, he ran his hand down her spine. Resting in the small of her back, his hand pressed her nearer to him. "I want you, Elizabeth, but not yet. Not until everything's ideal for us," he murmured against her mouth.

She wanted to argue with him, tell him everything was ideal right now. The hardness of his desire pressed against her, causing Beth to say, "That can't all be you."

He quietly laughed. "If not, something's different from last time I checked."

Beth chuckled, pressing a hand against his chest as if pushing him away from her. "You're so terrible! Manly too, but mostly terrible."

Nicholas kissed the tip of her nose. "I think it's a little soon for you to be so sure I'm terrible at this."

"You tease!" She pretended to pull away, but his arms held her fast. "Nicholas, I really must tell you something."

He groaned, saying, "Sounds serious and I don't want to be. Tell me tomorrow."

Smiling at his petulance, she went on, "It is serious. You should know Samuel frequently reminds me of my marital status."

He loosened his hold on her a little. "I see."

"He's very charming about it, mostly." She bit her lip. "And he's right. I'm supposed to be married. We shouldn't be alone in the dark." Beth swallowed the lump in her throat. "He seems to think I have no morals concerning you."

Nicholas sighed as if hearing the worst news. He shook his head, saying, "We can't have Sam being right. He's full enough of himself as it is. You need to get these morals as soon as possible."

Beth's jaw dropped until she realized he was joking. She held his suspenders out, then let go, laughing at their snap on his chest. "You're a wicked man."

"I am, when it comes to you." He stepped back, releasing her from his arms. "And you're correct too. As long as you have promises to keep to others, we can't be alone again."

Beth crossed her arms, chilled from his absence, and nodded. Not wanting to agree, she said, "I'll do what I can to avoid us being together."

"Damn it all. I don't want that. I want you." He ran a hand through his hair. "Fine. Let's return. It's getting late and I need a plan for us."

CHAPTER 9

The next day found Beth grateful she had enough wood for breakfast and dinner. Daggart's bedroll appeared slept in; he must have been there and gone without waking her. Coffee stayed hot on their campfire embers. She drank deeply, wanting the boost of energy. Her stomach tensed inside. Had she kissed Nicholas last night? Had he kissed her? Beth held on to the warmth of her coffee cup. She wanted him with a lust unknown to her before now. Was this what Daggart and Lizzy felt for each other? If so, little wonder he couldn't let go of her memory.

Beth drained the coffee and readied to decamp. The air smelled of rain and river, a combination unnerving her. She didn't look forward to today, crossing a flooded Platte. They'd survive only to reach Fort Kearny where Daggart would end up drunk. She heard the signal to leave, and yet her husband didn't appear. After packing the tent, Beth hitched up the oxen. She stood by, ready to lead them on while keeping a look out for Daggart. Although a relief, his absences meant more work for her. She thought it a shame he didn't just get another horse and ride on to California, letting her do as she pleased.

Her breath caught, thinking of going to a different destination from Daggart. Would he let her go to Oregon alone? The idea sparkled in her mind like snow on a sunny day. She didn't want to live underground, digging for phantom gold. Beth couldn't even bear the idea of mining for real gold. Living without the sun and fresh air wasn't a life at all. Her husband might be happy as a mole, but not her. The best part of traveling proved so far to be finding new flowers, seeing butterflies, and spotting various birds and animals. She looked up at the puffy clouds, outlined in sunset's brilliance.

She longed for her garden, certainly, and all the fresh vegetables grown there. Making bread, growing herbs, and gathering eggs were high on her list of desires. Beth imagined all the yarn she'd be able to spin if she could have had her own sheep again. Everyone would have blankets, a nice coat, and socks of course. Did anyone in the California hills have sheep to shear? Maybe only farmers in the Oregon Territory had them and Beth would have to go there for any wool.

She led the animals on, following others up the Platte River bottom. Although the course curled and twisted, the train hadn't needed to cross yet. Everyone stopped for a cold lunch and fresh water. Another group of wagons, twice their number, camped on the other side. Beth watched across as those on horseback worked a large herd of cattle, keeping them with the wagons. She liked the tranquility of their smaller group. Only a few head of cattle traveled with them, keeping stampedes low.

They continued along the Platte until noon. Daggart walked up while she ate lunch and greeted her. "Good day."

"Hello. Are you hungry?" She went to get him some dried meat, flat bread, and a pickle.

"Yea." He sat and ate, saying in between bites, "We're crossin' to Kearny late today. The Platte is about three foot deep, and there's no ferry."

Now nauseous, she put down her food. "Three foot? That's pretty deep."

Daggart gave her a withering glare. "Only you and children would think so."

She ignored his jibe, searching for a solution to being in water herself. "The animals won't need walking across, so I could ride in the wagon, couldn't I?"

"Yea, you can." He stood and brushed off the crumbs. "I'll take the team this afternoon. You didn't tear up anythin' this mornin' while leadin', so that's good."

His near praise surprised Beth. Whatever he'd been up to this morning helped his mood. Maybe Daggart had learned of a cheap claim in California. Whatever the reason for the lack of ill-treatment, she wouldn't complain. Best of all, she had permission to ride over and not walk in the river.

She followed the teams as they kept on the south bank. Shallow pools dotted the wide bed, most of them foul smelling and green. As they went, the Platte's level rose. With storm clouds in the distance, word passed around they'd stop for the night near Fort Kearny, but not cross the river. Beth agreed with the decision when informed, not willing to risk anyone in a flash flood.

For the first time during the trip, she saw wagons rolling east.

Some traveled on the north side, fewer on the south. The people walking and riding appeared beaten by the elements. Beth wondered if those in her group would be in the same condition at their journey's end. No one going back joined them when the train camped that night.

Even with the smell of rain blowing in from the west, the Platte kept its smooth currents. Beth didn't fear washing up supper dishes, nor scooping water for tomorrow. She'd found a fresh flowing part, away from the stagnant ponds. While heading back to camp, she saw Nicholas and Claude walking toward her. As they passed, both men nodded in greeting but didn't halt their conversation in French. She loved hearing anyone speak the language. Maybe some intrepid schoolteacher thought to bring a book on French to California or Oregon territories. If they let her copy a few pages at a time or even borrow the book, Beth could learn the language on her own.

"Ma'am?" Lawrence sought her attention. "The captains say to prepare for a storm."

"Oh dear. Will it be bad?" She chewed on her bottom lip.

"Yes ma'am. There are gusts right there." He pointed up to a bow of clouds rapidly moving out from the towering thunderhead.

"Thank you, Mr. Lawrence. I'll prepare everything." Beth smiled at him. She didn't see Daggart anywhere, so she tied the oxen to the far side from the wind and Erleen to the back, facing east. When the storm front hit, the wagon shuddered with the force. No lightning flashed, but the rain beat down like hailstones. She'd fastened the flaps, making the wagon as watertight as possible. Even then, rain seeped in, soaking the bottom few inches of everything. Beth made a mental note to rinse the damp food for tomorrow's meals. After the gust front, the rain settled into a steady drip, lulling her to sleep.

The day started much too early for her. She kept waking up from fretting about the animals and Daggart. Considering how much he liked his comfort, she was sure he'd found a warm place. Beth changed into her new dress, the only clothes dry. She took care of the animals while eating some dried fruit for breakfast.

Firewood in the wagon was soaked, making coffee impossible. Even without the luxury of hot drinks, atmosphere in the camp seemed extra lively. When the captains decided to stay put for a day, getting supplies at the fort was the only topic of conversation. She shared in the anticipation but also had feelings of dread. Beth wondered how much money Daggart allocated for whisky. He'd not been drunk since the men stopped playing poker for rotgut, no one willing to part with enough to intoxicate him.

With the Platte River at almost four feet instead of the estimated three, only those on horseback bothered crossing to the store. Most people sent a family member or two over while others remained behind to dry out possessions. Beth also stayed, hoping Daggart did too. She emptied the wet beans and rice into a pan for cooking, and added some bacon and spices for flavor. Beth wished the wood was already dry. The mix would keep until evening when she could cook.

She was busy cleaning out the wagon when Claude peeked inside. Beth squeaked, startled, and he laughed, showing her his hands in surrender.

"Bonjour, madam."

"Bonjour?" She asked, thinking he might be saying hello.

"Oui. Pour vous." He held out a skein of yarn in a light grey.

"Oh! All right." Beth climbed out of the wagon and took the yarn. "Hm." She pointed to his feet. "For you?"

"Oui, pour moi, s'il vous plait." Claude smiled, gave her a wave, and went on to his next task.

She ran the back of her hand across the wool, liking the softness. Beth smiled to herself. The man had good taste. This would be a joy to knit. No sooner than she'd placed Claude's future socks in her knitting bag, Beth was surrounded by the other hands in the Granvilles' company.

The three dismounted, each greeting her with a tip of the hat and a "ma'am."

"I don't suppose you all have a request?" Mr. Lucky and Lawrence each held a ball of yarn, while Chuck held two. Beth laughed, asking, "I didn't notice you having extra large feet, Mr. Chuck."

"I don't so much, ma'am. This here's from Mr. Sam. He said he didn't want Mr. Nick getting ahead of him in the favors."

"Ah, I see. Very well, I'll get started on these sometime today." She gathered the wool, every man having picked a different natural color. They each thanked her as she took the yarns, afterward getting back on their horses. Beth smiled as they rode off to duty, happy to have such lovely yarn to knit. She'd take more pleasure in working with their choices than they'd enjoy wearing the product.

Beth ate a quick lunch then organized her knitting. Whose socks to start first? All the wools tempted her. She chose the grey, almost black, from Mr. Lucky. She cast on and knitted a couple of rows to establish the cuff. A shadow darkened her work, causing Beth to look up at the source. She noticed with a start Amelia stood in front of her.

"Good afternoon, Mrs. Bartlett."

"Hello, Miss Chatillon." She stood. Even in a new dress, Beth felt dowdy next to the younger and more stylish girl. "It's a pleasure to see you."

"Likewise." Amelia smiled. "I would like you to join us this afternoon. A group of ladies are getting together, working on various projects while we're resting."

"Thank you, I'd love to, but…" Her face warmed when she thought of all the women looking at her knitting. They were all possibly far beyond her in skill and would later laugh at her.

"No, you must join us. Don't be shy." Amelia made a little gesture. "Don't think about it, just come along."

After shrugging in mock defeat, Beth said, "How can I say no, now?" She followed Amelia to the hen party where everyone seemed welcoming. Being observed by so many pairs of eyes made her shy and unfocused. She listened to the women chatter about the personalities of the others, some biting, others amusing. She paid particular attention to various clever solutions to problems caused by the travel.

As she picked up stitches along the heel flap of Mr. Lucky's sock, Daggart and Mr. Chatillon walked up to them.

"There's my girl!" Daggart said.

Hearing his voice, Beth looked up to see him addressing Amelia. An embarrassed hush fell over the group as the ladies waited for Beth's reaction. Daggart's cheeks reddened. She wanted to laugh at his discomfort, humiliating himself instead of her for a welcome change. Standing, her sense of empathy won over orneriness. "You're right, here I am. I'd not realized it grew so late. You must be starved." To Amelia, she said, "Thank you for including me this afternoon. I had a lovely time. Ladies."

He glanced around at all the people staring at him. "Uh, yea, I am hungry." He went to her, taking Beth by the elbow in a gentlemanly fashion. "Tell me about your day, and I'll tell you everythin' about Fort Kearny."

Letting him lead her away, she said, "I had a grand time. Dinner won't take long either. That's all so now may I hear about the Fort?"

"It's bigger than I imagined with more people." He glanced back. "Thank you, Beth. I really put my foot in it over there."

She wanted to reassure him, but couldn't. "Yes, you did."

He gave her a wary look. "You must be angry."

"I should be, don't you think?" She shook her head. "But I'm not."

"Yea." Daggart gave a forced chuckle. "I didn't mean she was my girl, not like Lizzy."

Didn't she want him to like Amelia enough to let her go? Beth asked herself, did she want to play matchmaker? "She can't be yours, not while you're married to me."

"I'm married to Lizzy."

She glanced over to see that stubborn set of his jaw. Maybe planting a seed of an idea would take root in that sparse field of a brain he had. "And I'm supposed to be her, unless you'd prefer me not to be."

Shrugging, he said, "I don't know what I want."

She watched as he walked away, out of the wagon circle. Her eyes narrowed. Pushing him toward Amelia was like shoving the girl under a wagon wheel. Unless Daggart treated her as he had her sister. Beth tried ignoring a sudden fury. Lizzy received all his love and care, while Beth received his resentment and hate. She dumped the beans and rice mixture into a cooking pot with an angry shake. Her father and Daggart may have thought differently, but Beth wanted to be a man's first love. She didn't deserve to be a consolation prize. Not only that, he'd not noticed her dress. A childish thing, to be sure, but if Daggart was the only one allowed to notice her, then he needed to do his job.

Adding water to the pot, she stirred dinner. She'd not paid attention to the quantities and made too much for just the two of them. Beth straightened. Instead of throwing out the excess, maybe the Granvilles and their men would help them eat all of it this evening. They'd shared their food last night, after all, and so offering to return the favor was only right. Nervous at the possible refusal, she looked at the beans and rice. It already smelled too good to waste. Beth took a deep breath. If she didn't have to ask Samuel himself, she could do this.

Beth went to the Granvilles' wagons. All of them sat around a campfire, Lawrence playing a banjo while Claude sang. Her heart beat faster, anticipating interrupting their fun. She leaned against the wagon, enjoying the song.

Once done, Claude waved her over to them. "Bonjour, madam!"

"Bonjour, Mr. Claude," she greeted, pleased to understand this much at least.

"Monsieur Claude, s'il vous plait."

Nicholas and the others laughed. "Aren't we so proper? Mrs. Bartlett, he would like to be called Monsieur Claude, if you please."

"Ah, Monsieur Claude, then, and gentlemen, it seems I've made way too much dinner for us two tonight." She wrung her hands at so many people seated and staring at her. "In fact, I would be grateful if everyone helped me by having dinner with me. Us." Beth made sure she glanced at each man, but not too long for fear they would think her forward.

Samuel spoke first. "A lovely woman wants to serve us dinner, men. Do we need to be asked twice?" They all grinned like cats in the cream and spoke over each other.

Claude stood, stretching. "Non!"

"Not me," Chuck replied, taking Claude's banjo and putting it away.

Mr. Lucky bounded to the front of the group. "I'm in! Let's go!"

Lawrence shook his head, following Claude.

"I can't say no." Nicholas grinned, bringing up the rear with Beth.

As with the afternoon, Beth contented herself with listening to the news and gossip from her guests as they ate. Daggart stumbled over halfway through the meal. He dished up some dinner, which seemed to sober him a bit. She appreciated everyone's efforts to ignore his drunkenness. Claude made an effort to sit by her when seeing her get his sock to work on in the firelight.

During a lull in the conversation, he pointed to her work. "C'est pour moi."

She looked to Nicholas for a translation when Samuel said, "For you? What about us?"

"Oh! Yes, this one is for him." She held up what little she'd done so Monsieur Claude could see. "Don't worry. I plan to make sure all of them are done by the time we reach cold weather."

"But why is he first?" Samuel asked.

Beth laughed at how much he resembled a petulant child. "Because he's special."

Claude winked. "Et Monsieur Nick?"

She felt her face burn, knowing what he meant. Beth stared at her knitting for a moment and glanced up at him. "Monsieur Nick may be special, too, but was also the first to request."

Mr. Lucky quickly translated for Claude, who laughed and clapped, saying, "Bonn, bonn."

"Yea," Daggart interjected. "He's not special, or first. I am. She made me socks before I married Lizzy." He rose, unsteady on his feet. "I'm sick of all of you having fun and laughin'. 'M goin' t' bed."

Everyone stood, parting so Daggart had a path to the wagon. Her husband reached in, fumbling for his bedroll. Finding what he needed, he hugged the side of the wagon, groping around to the darker side to sleep.

Beth snapped out of her shock at Daggart referring to Lizzy and her in the same sentence. He'd slipped up before, but every time continued to surprise her. Heart still beating hard in her chest, she said, "Thank you, gentlemen, for coming to dinner." She grabbed a bucket by the wagon. "Put your dishes in here and I'll have them ready for breakfast tomorrow."

Nicholas stepped forward. "I can wash these up for you tonight."

"Excuse me, Mr. Granville?" She shook her head. "I think not, since you were my guest this evening."

"Let's compromise," Samuel said. "Nick, you can see to our bedrolls while I help Mrs. Bartlett clean up."

She didn't want to hear a possible lecture from him. "No need, I can do this myself," Beth argued.

Samuel smiled at her. "Nonsense. With the two of us, it'll be short work."

"I'll leave you two to it, then." Nicholas nodded to her. "Thank you again, and goodnight."

None of the plates had so much as a grain of rice remaining, leaving them easy to wash. The pot also had been scraped empty. She let him lead her to the water's edge and settled in beside him. Not wanting to say anything, she washed as Samuel rinsed.

"I've noticed you and Nicholas aren't as cozy as usual," he quietly stated.

"No," Beth replied.

"I dislike saying this, but maybe that's for the best."

She pursed her lips, trying to remain neutral in tone. "I'm happy to please."

"I'm not pleased. I'd rather Nick found a woman to love, even if it's you." Samuel took the plate she handed him.

Even if, she thought, trying not to be offended. He didn't need to reiterate her second choice status. "Oh? I appreciate your approval, such as it is."

"Now, don't misunderstand me." He dried the dish with a cup towel she handed him. "You're very lovely and I'm glad you're able to be a good friend for my brother."

"Despite Daggart, of course."

Raising an eyebrow, Samuel said, "He is an obstacle."

Beth clamped a wet hand over her mouth to stifle giggles. She restrained herself enough to say, "He always has been."

Samuel paused before asking, "This is very forward of me, but I want to ask, why did you marry him?"

She bit her lip, wanting to be honest, but afraid to be. "I made a promise to my father to take Daggart as a husband and let him take care of me."

"I assume your father passed away?"

Nodding, she said, "Yes, soon after I made the promise."

"It seems he made things difficult for you with his death."

"He did, not knowing how much I'd..." she paused to hand him the last fork, then changed the subject. "Um, we're all done."

Samuel took the utensil. "Mrs. Bartlett, tell me. Not knowing how much you'd what?"

She swallowed a lump in her throat. "How much I'd regret making that particular promise to him. Both Daggart and I deserve much better."

"Interesting." He dried his hands. "Your secret is still yours to tell Nick." Samuel handed her his towel. "My concern for him in this hasn't changed. I'd prefer you remember your marriage before befriending him too much."

"The other Mr. Granville and I are acquaintances, not friends, we've decided." She stood when he did and headed back to camp. Before they parted, she added, "A friendship would be very improper, considering."

"Considering, yes," he said. "I'll bid you good night, Mrs. Bartlett. Sleep well."

"Thank you." Beth wanted to throw a plate or something in sadness and frustration. Nicholas seemed to seek her out, not her catting around for him. She needed to stay far away from both Granvilles. Otherwise, she'd tell them everything about her and Lizzy despite her husband's orders. Daggart staggered from around the wagon, startling her. Beth knew the drink usually changed him to meanness, not to weakness. "Dag, are you all right?"

He rubbed his eyes like a child. "No, I'm not," he replied, his voice small.

"What's wrong? Will a little sleep help you? Maybe some coffee?"

Daggart shook his head and went to her. He hugged her close, sobbing. "I miss her, Beth. I miss Lizzy so much." Burying his face in her neck, he mumbled, "She can't be back, can she?"

"No, dear, I'm sorry." She patted his back, stunned that he showed true grief at last. He'd not cried at Lizzy's funeral. Daggart had spent the last two years clinging to Beth as a replacement for her sister as if she were a sturdy oak in a storm. She didn't know what to say to him to help, so she just let him hold her.

"You can't be her, can you?" he asked in a wavering voice.

Beth assured him as gently as she could manage, "No matter how hard I try, I can't." She began to feel a little hope for them both. Maybe he could see reason and release her from the chafing vow they'd made.

"Miss Chatillon is so much like her."

Continuing to pat his back, she replied, "I know."

Daggart sniffled, saying, "I don't think she cares for me like Lizzy did."

She made shushing sounds, saying, "No one could. Lizzy loved you so much."

He started bawling in earnest, his sobs louder. "She, she likes that Granville, Nick." Daggart hiccupped. "They're always together, talking that French stuff. I hate him."

Beth paused, suddenly not too fond of Amelia, herself. She took a deep breath, knowing jealousy colored her feelings. "Daggart, you only hate him because you care for her. Isn't that right?"

"Yea." He sniffled. "I love her. She's so pretty."

"She is, I agree." Beth stepped back, saying, "How about we go to sleep so you'll look good tomorrow, in case you see her."

Daggart wiped his nose on a sleeve. "All right." He let her lead them to his bedroll, letting go of her arm to slide into his blankets. She retrieved hers, setting up to sleep a little ways away. Beth worried he could change his mind about preferring Amelia. In that case, he would try to make love to her as Lizzy. She shuddered with revulsion, unable to bear him touching her again.

Her brother-in-law turned husband had cried for his wife. She lay on her side and stared at the dying fire. He also found another woman appealing. He'd promised to take care of her while she was Lizzy. But now, she'd see to her own care if it meant no more pretending. For the first time since her sister's death, Beth hoped they could both walk away from each other.

The next morning, while doing both sets of chores, she saw Daggart helping the Chatillon's with their large tent. She snorted, her sympathy for him evaporating. Of course he helped them. Amelia resembled Lizzy so much, Daggart had to play gentleman to her. Let him play the hero to her, she quietly seethed, but only after he did his own work.

While getting water for their coffee, Beth overheard someone say buffalo were nearby. Plans for a hunt were in progress, and they'd start traveling in the herd's direction soon. She cut her eyes at Daggart. He'd go hunting for fresh meat if it meant impressing Amelia. First, she needed to convince him that being manly in front of her by hunting was a good idea.

Strolling up to him with his gun, Beth smiled at Daggart. "Did you know? The men have seen buffalo over the next ridge and are going hunting late this morning. Only the best shots and strongest are going, so I'm assuming that includes you?"

He glanced at Amelia and winked at Beth. "Sure am, Lizzy. I'll bring back the biggest, and we'll share with the Chatillons."

She smiled and looked modestly at the ground. "Good, I'll make sure everything is ready for traveling this morning while you go with the men."

Her husband tipped his hat, and gun in hand, swaggered off to the group of hunters. When he was out of earshot, Amelia asked her, "Have you seen Nicholas and Mr. Claude today?"

"Not today, but it's early yet," Beth replied, forcing a smile.

"Hm." The girl put hands to hips, exasperated. "Too bad, because I wanted to chat with Nicholas before we started today."

Their first name familiarity grated on Beth's nerves. She bit back a sharp retort. "Should I tell Mr. Granville you are looking for him if I see him this morning?"

Amelia blushed. "No, please don't. I would rather ask Nicholas myself."

"Very well, I'll keep mum," she said. "If you'll excuse me, I need to finish." Beth went back to their wagon. She tried to ignore the lingering envy over the other girl's calling Nicholas by his given name. It was such a little thing, but she wanted to be as open with her affections as Amelia could be toward him.

Despite her best efforts, Beth's musings stayed on Nicholas and Amelia the entire day. The trail went on forever, as did the land. Rock bluffs ran low alongside the river's bottoms, the sandy soil in between the cliffs had been worn flat by the Platte's flow. She'd heard news about Daggart hunting a buffalo and how he'd stayed behind rendering the kills. The men, loaded down, caught up to the wagon circle at dusk. Everyone had already settled in, their chores done, and ready to cook and dry the fresh meat.

Daggart was in the best mood she'd seen in years. He chatted about the hunt, the other men, how the Chatillons appreciated him sharing with them. "We have more than enough for us. It's the right thing to do, since Miss Amelia's father is lame."

She listened, enjoying the buffalo as he went on to tell her how Mr. Chatillon was injured, why they came west, about the deceased Mrs. Chatillon, and what Amelia thought of the journey so far. Beth let him go on and on about the two, not wanting to disrupt his disposition.

"It sounds like they are very nice." She gathered their dishes. "Is this where you are, usually, visiting them?"

He nodded a little shamefully. "Yea, usually. Sometimes at a card game, if there's room." Daggart leaned back, watching her. "What about you? What do you do when I'm not at camp? I ain't never seen that dress before. It wasn't Lizzy's, was it?"

His question surprised her. He'd not expressed interest in Beth's activities nor had he caught her working on her clothes. How did he go through life so obtuse? "I keep busy with Erleen some, but mostly sew or knit." Feeling guilty at the near condescending tone in her answer, she added, "Rarely, I'm asked to cook for the hired hands and maybe the Granvilles."

"Sounds interestin'." He yawned, glanced around them, and stood, stretching. "Well, I suppose I'll get tomorrow's water for you then hit the hay."

She watched a little while as he left, glad he'd not pressed about her new clothes. Beth laid out their bedrolls, leaving it to him to put up a tent cloth if he wanted. After the fire died down too low to see her knitting, she went to bed.

The wagon train traveled the river valley for five almost identical days. Sometimes they saw hundreds of buffalo on the bluffs above, other days, forty or fifty. To her surprise and delight, Beth found buffalo chips burned clean. None of her food smelled like manure, not even when accidently burned. She loved the buffalo meat, encouraging Daggart to hunt. He went out with the rest of the men often, hoping to impress Miss Amelia with his shooting skill.

Beth saw little of Nicholas or Samuel. The other hired hands greeted her, too busy to talk much. Mr. Lucky wore the socks she made and bragged to everyone else. When giving him his new socks, she'd understood Mr. Claude's "Marvelous." He surprised Beth by giving her a kiss on the cheek. She was certain her face glowed with a blush from his actions.

The Saturday's travel, though light, exhausted everyone. The sandy road seemed to suck in the wheels, hampering progress and annoying the draft animals. A family up ahead delayed almost everyone, digging their way out of a deeply sandy portion of the trail. Palpable relief swept through the group when they stopped mid afternoon at the north and south forks of the Platte for the night. The sun shone high over the horizon, lending a festive atmosphere. Plus, other trains stopped here to camp too. Beth looked forward to hearing news from back east.

The few hours of light gave her lots of glorious knitting time. She meandered over to the other ladies in the sewing circle. Beth smiled at their warm welcome. Women from other camps were there too. Listening to the stories of their travels since they left Omaha interested her. She completed a lot of work on Mr. Chuck's socks. They also exchanged new ways for cooking the same old food stores. After hearing all the new ideas, Beth was impatient for a chance to try enhancing dinner.

Evening mealtime approached and everyone disbanded. She went to their camp, seeing Daggart there, napping. He'd started a campsite, but not a fire. She agreed the day was already warm enough. Him being asleep disappointed her. She couldn't start dinner without waking him, and she'd rather kick a bear awake. Beth decided against any fire and ate a cold meal before turning in for the night.

The next day, Sabbath dawned bright and cold. A steady wind lifted the loose ends of their tent, keeping them from dozing late. Beth took care of Erleen while Daggart started the fire. When it was ready to drink, both held onto their hot cups of coffee. They ate a quick breakfast, eager, like everyone else, to warm up by continuing on the trail.

The train trekked three days, each just a little warmer than the one before. After a morning jaunt of six miles, they reached the South Fork crossing. News went around from wagons heading east about how easy South Fork was to cross. Sharp gusts rattled everyone's canopies as the train approached. Some of the children rode in their wagons, unable to stand in the harsher winds.

She and Daggart traveled close to the front. Before their turn, the mules ahead balked at the water. They reared as much as they could while rigged up and bolted, dragging their wagon on its side until the rigging jerked free. The mules' panic rippled back to the other teams. The Bartlett's oxen ran as if whipped, through the river and onto the other side. Daggart tried to stop them, being towed a little way before letting go. Beth ran up to him to see if he was injured.

He shrugged off her concern, giving her a little shove. "I'm fine, woman. Stay out of the way!"

Beth stumbled over a clump of grass, falling on her rump. To her right, another wagon headed in her direction, the team running amok while managing to stay upright through the river. She scrambled out of the way. Keeping a watch behind her, Beth went to the water, hoping to help retrieve items without having to actually get her feet wet.

Mr. Lucky rode up to her. "Are you fine, Ma'am?"

She looked down at her muddy but not bloody dress, nodded, and at her "Yes," he rode north. Watching, Beth saw another runaway set of oxen, the driver holding on with determination. In the water, the wheels slowed, causing the team to lunge. As they did, the driver lost his grip, falling into the river and under the wheels. Beth cried out in horror as first one wheel and then the other rolled over the man's legs.

Running, she arrived at the bank near Mr. Watts just as Nicholas and Samuel did. Mr. Watts lay almost underwater, his face barely above the surface. He screamed with the pain, howling and yelling for help. Beth squelched a shudder of fear and gathered her skirts in one hand. She entered the river and lifted Mr. Watts' head, keeping it above water while the men dismounted. Blood from the injury flowed toward her in the current. She looked up into Nicholas's pale face and shouted above Mr. Watts' cries of distress, "We need to get him out of here. This isn't safe."

Samuel stood to the side of the man and held him by the torso, asking, "Can you hold him by his shoulders, Beth?" Nicholas went to Mr. Watts' feet, his expression fierce.

"Yes, I can." She let go of her skirt, concentrating on Mr. Watts more than the current. Beth took a deep breath as she lifted his shoulders. The water only came up to her knees, she reassured herself. Not enough to sweep anyone downstream.

"No," Nicholas said. "You do it, Sam, and I'll get his feet."

Sam went to Beth's side, taking hold of where she held the man as she let go of him. "Go get a blanket and a medicine kit from the lead wagons."

She hurried as much as possible, concentrating on the items instead of the river. Mr. Lucky had anticipated the need and she met him halfway between. As the two of them went back with the medical supplies, the three men carried Mr. Watts to the bank.

Samuel took the kit, opening it and giving Mr. Watts the whiskey. He stopped his bawling enough to drink down the flask like water. After draining the contents, he moaned, "I'm gonna die. It hurts so much," over and over until the alcohol eased his pain.

Nicholas rolled up the bloody pant leg to the knee, revealing a compound fracture on the back of Mr. Watts' calf. He put the back of his hand up to his mouth before ordering, "Hold him down

Sam, this'll hurt." He waited until Samuel held onto both shoulders.

Beth saw his reaction and how Nicholas's face grew paler. "Nicholas? Are you all right?"

He lowered his hand and glanced up at her. "I'll have to set his leg." By now, a crowd of those already across the river had gathered, watching.

Samuel stared at his brother, "Will you be able to do this?"

"Yes, I can. It's not surgery. I've seen much worse," he snapped. "Keep his good leg still so he doesn't hurt himself or us." Mr. Lucky braced the patient while Nicholas set the fracture. Mr. Watts yelled as the bone slipped back past his calf muscles.

Even in the cool air of the day, beads of sweat rolled down Nicholas's face. He addressed Beth, "I'll need two splints. Have Mr. Claude help you, and tell him bois deux pour la jambe."

She repeated phonetically, "Bwahduh poorla shawmb."

He waved her off as he would a mosquito. "Good enough. Go tell him."

Beth ran to where Mr. Claude led others across the river. "Monsieur! Nick—Mr. Granville wants bwahduh poorla sha, um, shasha?"

Claude looked where Beth pointed. "Il besoin bois deux pour la jambe?"

"Yes! Poorla shawmb!"

He removed his foot from the stirrup and slid down from his horse. "Allons, ma cheri!"

She wasn't sure what he wanted, but followed as he led his horse to the Granvilles' wagons. Mr. Claude quickly tied off the animal to the wheel and hopped into the wagon. Beth peeked in as he found two thin planks of wood purposely made for broken bones, and some thick bandages as well. He hopped down from the tailgate, giving her the bandages, and motioned for her to follow him. They wove a path through the crowd of onlookers to Mr. Watts.

Watts moaned. Samuel and Mr. Lucky had released him while Nicholas retained his feet. He nodded his thanks then went to work binding up the injury.

Beth watched, fascinated at how quickly and gently he worked. Nicholas made binding a leg look easy. She said, "You should be a doctor. You're very good."

Finishing, he glared at her. "You don't know what you're talking about." He gathered the medical kit and stood. "Let's get Watts in his wagon. We'll need to make a bed for him in there." Mr. Lucky and Claude supported the man, walking him to his family. Nicholas took the blanket and supplies to the Granvilles' wagon, leaving her behind.

She blinked, astonished by his sudden hostility. Beth bit her lip to stay the tears threatening to fill her eyes. Samuel stepped beside her, catching her attention. She turned to leave without a word to him.

"Mrs. Bartlett?"

Beth faced him, giving what she hoped was a glare, "Yes Mr. Granville?"

"You did well in helping us just now." Samuel held his hat like an errant schoolboy. "Later, Nick won't like how he spoke to you."

"Oh?" She didn't want a discussion or lecture. Beth needed to hide before the tears began falling.

"No." Samuel stepped closer to her. "He'll have to apologize, after thinking on how harsh he sounded."

"Mr. Granville need say nothing to me. He's correct, ask my husband. I often don't know what I'm talking about." Concentrating on not stomping in anger, she left him to find her wagon. Beth couldn't see Daggart or the animals, and hoped the oxen hadn't run completely across the country.

Others in the train had obscured her husband's tracks. She found Erleen a quarter mile away, happily munching on some grass. A little dot in the distance west of them neared as the train spent noontime on the South Fork's bank. Beth walked to the dot, recognizing it as her husband and their wagon once she was closer. "How are you?" she asked when she reached him.

He slapped an ox on the back. "I'm angry as hell, but there's nothin' I can do about it."

She responded, "I understand," sympathizing with what must have been a difficult trek.

Daggart stopped in his tracks. "No you don't." Staring at her in contempt, he said, "I'm the one who had to run down these bastards. You got to play around the water."

Rage hit her full strength. She glowered at him, furious. "I don't play around water."

"You should more often," he sneered.

Furious, she yelled at him, "Maybe I will, then! I wish it had been me who drowned instead of Lizzy. Then, all of us would be blissfully happy instead of so miserable."

All through the afternoon, Beth used her anger to carry her onward. She ignored everyone, only responding out of politeness. The train rolled into the usual circle in a clear area. They found no wood but plenty of buffalo chips. A handful of the men went to hunt for the few deer spotted, later coming back empty handed.

Though loath to do so, Beth went to their wagon. Daggart wasn't there, neither were their animals. She pursed her lips, unable to believe he did her chores for her. Beth took out her knitting, hoping the soothing activity would calm her temper. She leaned against the wheel in the shade, working on the last sock for Mr. Chuck. The past few days of steady wind kept her from knitting as much as she'd have liked. With luck, she'd be able to cast on for Mr. Lawrence's first sock.

"Hello." Her husband walked up beside her, leading Erleen. He tied the cow to the other side and went to Beth. "I'm sorry about this afternoon. I was angry at the oxen, not you."

She didn't want to discuss anything with him. "I see."

He kicked at a rock. "I didn't mean you should drown or anythin'. I know what I said before about wanting you dead, but I don't. I hate that you're not Lizzy, but I don't hate you."

Refraining from making a rude remark, she instead said, "That's nice to hear."

"It's true." Daggart cleared his throat. "You, uh, don't hate me, do you?"

Beth stopped knitting, glaring at him. "Not too much, no." She gave up on Mr. Chuck's sock for the moment, putting it back in her knit bag. "I hate having to be Lizzy for you more than I hate you."

Daggart stared at her. "You don't like bein' Lizzy? She was an angel, Beth. Better'n any woman ever born."

"Yes, I know. You and my father have told me how perfect she was. I'll never live long enough to be half as good as her or our mother." Beth put her knitting back in the wagon, rummaging for her cooking supplies. "But, since she isn't here to fix you her manna from heaven, I'll have to. So if you'll pardon me, I'm busy."

"Yea, you do your best. Thank you."

Beth grit her teeth and headed for the South Fork. She wanted to put the pail over his head and tap it with a spoon until his ears rang. He considered her inadequate, yet he didn't catch on to her sarcasm about Lizzy. She used all her frustrations to speed through cooking dinner.

Daggart tried talking with her, ignoring Beth's monosyllabic replies. When done eating, he handed her his plate and fork. "Good meal. I might go see if Mr. Chatillon needs help with their tent or team."

Taking his dishes, she looked at him in surprise. He didn't inform her of his whereabouts often. "Very well. Most likely, I'll be here or washing something." She gave a little wave as she watched him walk away. Once Daggart was out of sight, she put their dishes in the larger pail to take to the river.

She took her time, enjoying the flowers. Beth chuckled at the frogs startled by her strolling past. The North Fork ran slow and shallow, the cool water inviting to her sore feet. She saw the bottom of the river through the clear water and set down the pail, removing her boots and socks. Gingerly walking across the sand to the stream, she stepped in and enjoyed the squish between her toes.

"Good evening, Beth."

At the sound of a familiar voice, she turned, seeing Nicholas approach. She gave him a tight smile, responding, "Good evening."

He sat as she had, removing his own boots and socks, and rolled up his pant legs. "I like this idea."

"I'm glad you approve." Beth walked away, up the river.

"Wait," he hurried to her, the water slowing him down a little. "I owe you an apology. I was rude this morning. Sam told me I should talk to you about my outburst."

She stopped, kicking a small splash with her toes. "How nice of him to say so, but he needn't have forced you to act contrite."

"He's not forcing me. I spoke out of turn." Walking downstream with her, Nicholas kept quiet. After a few more moments, he sighed, stepping in front of her to stop her. "Not everyone knows this, but I was a doctor at one time."

Still unhappy, she looked up at him. "So I might have known what I was talking about?"

He laughed, "Yes, you did, more than you were aware of at the time."

His amusement rankled her. Beth didn't want to forgive him so soon. A growling attitude tolerable from Daggart was instead unbearable from Nicholas. She wanted a little more remorse from him. "I appreciate that admission and almost accept your apology."

He stared down at the water like a little boy getting a reprimand from a teacher. "Almost?"

A little of her heart melted. Still, considering the hermit she'd first met and the professional he'd been this morning, Beth wanted to learn more. "Well, I'd like to know why you aren't a doctor now. Your skills are valuable out here."

"Yes, they would be." He paused, watching the water drift sand over his toes. Finally, he said, "I was a doctor in the west and central part of the Oregon territory. A couple of patients of mine died in my care. I quit after that."

Nicholas looked so sad she wanted to cheer him a little and said, "Only a couple of them? The doctor in my town should be so lucky. I'll bet he loses several in a year."

Looking up at her, he asked, "Was his wife and baby among those he lost?"

CHAPTER 10

Goosebumps raised on Beth's arms as she understood. "I'm so sorry. The loss, how very sad."

Nicholas didn't say anything for a while. He watched the sun set, adding, "It drove me insane. She was the love of my life. To lose her and our son in the same day tore out my heart."

"I understand."

With a smile not reaching his eyes, he asked, "Do you? Have you lost a spouse and a child in the same day from your own incompetence?"

She heard the sarcasm in his voice, angering her. "Not me, no, but I understand how the loss of a wife drives a man mad. When Daggart lost Lizzy, he was silent and inconsolable for months. He'd not lost a child too, so I suppose you're right that I have no idea of how you might have reacted."

"Excuse me?" His expression changed as if finding one key out of many for a stubborn lock. "I'd been wondering if Lizzy was a completely different person. Who was she, other than Bartlett's first wife?"

Beth crossed her arms, turning away from him. She felt childish doing so, but couldn't answer his question. "I don't want to talk about it."

"I didn't want to talk about my failing as a doctor, either." He stepped up behind her, putting his hands on her shoulders. "I know you want to tell someone, and I'm good at not spreading gossip."

She laughed at his attempt to sway her. "You're right. I do want to tell someone, but can't."

Nicholas hugged Beth, saying in her ear, "You made yet another promise?"

His breath tickled in a way she liked. "Of course, and I don't care for this one either." Beth tilted her head to look at him with reproach. "I shouldn't tell you anything."

"But you will because I want you to and because you trust me." His smile fading, he added, "I don't care for how Bartlett treats you, and I don't care for how much time he spends at Miss Amelia's camp. He's pretending to befriend her father, but anyone who sees them together suspects otherwise."

She shrugged as much as his embrace allowed. "I'm not surprised. The ladies in the sewing circle hinted as much. I let it pass." Beth paused, wanting to keep any envy from her tone. "Since she looks so much like Lizzy, I knew he'd make a pest of himself with her."

Nicholas turned her around, examining her features. "You look nothing like Miss Amelia. Why are you pretending to be this Lizzy of Bartlett's?"

The assessment stung a little and she gave him a bit of a glare. "Oh, I'm well aware of my looks. While I'm not the porcelain doll like her, I knew Lizzy best of anyone. She and I were twins."

His face crumpled a little before he blurted, "Beth, I'm so sorry."

"What? Why?"

"She may have been Bartlett's wife, but she was your sister too. Did you get a chance to mourn Lizzy at all before becoming her for him?"

His observation surprised her and she swallowed the sudden lump in her throat. Beth stared at the middle of his chest, biting the inside of her lip, willing herself to not start sobbing like a baby. Nicholas put a hand to her cheek as a caress, leading her to look up at him and say, "My goodness, you're the first person to ever ask such a thing. Both my father and Daggart were so distraught over Lizzy's death. I had to take care of them." She stared at her feet, shy from seeing the warmth in his eyes. "It's getting dark. I'd like to go back to the bank. I need my, ok, I suppose, your shoes on."

"All right, I'll walk with you." He took her arm. "Are you cold? You're shivering."

"I am, a little. Mostly from fear at how dark it is. Silly me, I like being able to see where I'm stepping." She smiled, not liking to fib, but not wanting to tell him the truth just yet.

He helped her up to the grassy bank where their footwear was. "Can you tell me how Lizzy died?"

Already ashamed at how much she'd said to him and how emotional she'd been, Beth asked, "Are we going back to that again? Daggart is not going to like me talking about all this with you. If he knew, he'd be worse than furious."

Grinning, he said, "We can discuss him and how I don't care what he likes later. For me, I'd like to know what happened to your sister."

She sat, pulling on her socks, then the boots. Once done, Beth glanced at Nicholas, still standing, waiting for her answer. "You are so stubborn, aren't you? Very well, have a seat and I'll give you the quick version." He joined her, also putting on his footwear. She smiled at him doing little more than nothing in order to keep her talking. "The story explains a lot of oddities about me, and you'll understand about poor Daggart."

He snorted a laugh before sitting beside her. "You're stalling and I doubt Mr. Bartlett is to be pitied in this. Please continue."

Taking a calming breath, Beth picked at the tough blades of grass. "Lizzy drowned. She and I were washing clothes one day and a flash flood caught us both unaware. By the time either of us looked, a wall of water overtook us. We clung to each other, grabbing at anything solid. After hitting something underwater, we split apart. I made it to shore, she didn't." She hoped he understood her brother in law's anger a little better now.

Nicholas paused before pulling on his second boot. "I see."

Beth shook her head, not wanting to say more, but like a weakened beaver dam, her words flowed before she could stop. "Lizzy's death devastated our father. She'd always been his favorite, since she looked like our mother. I was his buddy, his shadow, while she was the sun. Pap was ill from grief. He died from it six months after Lizzy."

He watched as she picked and tore the grass's seed stalks. In a quiet voice, he asked, "How long have you and Bartlett been married?"

She chuckled and pushed at his shoulder. "Oh now, haven't you asked me enough questions?" Beth wondered how to distract him from this entire conversation. In an effort to focus on Nicolas instead of her, she chided him, "If I didn't know better, I'd say you worked for a newspaper instead of as a healer."

"Let me guess, you've been married less than two years."

"Of course. We're not polygamists. Besides, I've had to share enough with Lizzy as it is." Beth felt sick at the very idea of being herself and still married to Daggart. "I didn't want to share a husband too. He's a brother-in-law, or had been."

He hugged his knees, gaze fixed on the horizon. "Why did

you allow all this? My bet is on you were asked or forced."

She glared at him. "You're determined to learn everything, aren't you?"

"I am," he smiled. "Asked or forced, Beth?"

For a moment, she stared up at the faint stars appearing as the night darkened. The cool of evening brought the scent of wildflowers and creek water. She inhaled, almost enjoying the wet smell for a change. "Does it matter?"

"Forced, then."

Repressed anger in his voice made her smile. She liked him being outraged on her behalf. "Yes, but not physically. My father made Daggart promise to take care of me. He agreed as long as I did my best to replace Lizzy. I think all of us weren't in our right minds. Pa and Daggart missed Lizzy." Beth couldn't admit her feelings to him, about how it should have been her who died. Not her sister.

Nicholas exhaled a whistle. "It's obvious to me his grief did drive Bartlett crazy, because no one could ever take my Sally's place." After a pause, he shook his head, adding, "I'd have to be insane to ask a woman to do so."

"Even if you did ask, the woman couldn't do well. I'm doing a lousy job of taking Lizzy's place. I don't look like her at all. I can't act like her." At his raised eyebrows, she explained, "I'm too shy. She loved being in town and crowds. I find all those people around me exhausting. I'd rather be home, and Lizzy hated staying on the farm."

He leaned against her a little, their shoulders touching. "You'd told me once your name was Elizabeth Ann. What was her name, other than Elizabeth?"

"Elizabeth Louise. Our mother died before knowing she had twins, so Lizzy got Louise and I got Ann, a form of And." Beth saw his incredulous expression. "I know, but it's better than Two as a name. Pap wasn't as creative as I'd hoped, but I rather like being Beth Ann."

"I like Beth Ann better, myself."

Beth paused, wondering if she should correct him. In for a penny, in for a pound, her father had always said. She took a deep breath and smiled at him. "Then you'd be wrong, Nicholas. I'm Beth Ann Roberts. Or I was, until I promised my father and Daggart I'd take Lizzy's place."

He stared at her through narrowed eyes, his brows almost meeting above his nose. "You never legally married him?"

His taking her into his confidence had led her to trust him. She needed to end this entire confessional. "I made a vow to be Lizzy for the rest of my life and that's what I must resume." She gasped when Nicholas gripped her by the arms.

"But Beth, it's not what you should do. You should never have promised such a thing."

"I can't be Beth any more. Not to you or anyone else." She couldn't think while so near to him.

Nicholas held her closer. "I can't agree. If you're not Lizzy, you can't be married to Bartlett."

"This was mine and Daggart's choice, not yours, and it's done." She tried to wrestle from his grip, his energy and ardor proving difficult for her to resist. She'd had enough sips of whisky on the sly to know what intoxication felt like, and it felt exactly the way Nicholas's touch made her feel now. Reason left her when he arrived, every time. "Please address me by Lizzy, preferably by Mrs. Bartlett."

"The man doesn't love you, Beth." He lifted her chin, forcing her to meet his gaze. "He loves Lizzy."

She bit her lip, tears welling in her eyes and blurring her vision. "I know," she choked. "He loves her more dead than anyone loves me alive."

Nicholas pulled her against him, kissing her with a fury that took her breath. He hugged her tight, his arms feeling like steel. She didn't struggle, wanting to abandon herself to the heady feeling of loving him. His hands caressed her back, molding her hips to his. He opened his mouth as they kissed, raking his tongue over Beth's teeth and lips.

The sick flutter in her stomach from confessing gave way to a ticklish craving. "Nicholas," she sighed against his lips.

"I'm not Daggart and I don't want Lizzy. I want you, Beth." Nicholas said in a whisper touching her mouth. He gently released her to arm's distance. "When you decide to be my Beth Ann, then I'm yours and this can continue. Until then, you're Mrs. Bartlett. That's all you can be to me."

Goosebumps raised on her arms. He said his Beth Ann? She shuddered with longing at the idea of being his. "I want to be myself, but can't promise anything."

"Of course not, you're all sworn away with ridiculous promises. Once you decide those pledges are absurd and end them, you'll be able to promise me anything you desire." He gave her a quick, soft kiss. "Assuming you do desire me."

She laughed at his suggestion. How many times had she let him kiss her? Making love to him sounded like a splendid suggestion. She exclaimed, "Ha! I want you far more than you fancy me."

Nicholas gave her a wicked smile, "Somehow, I doubt it." He grabbed up her pail of dishes, letting his shoulder brush against her stomach as he bend down. "Let's go, sweetheart, before your brother in law notices you're missing."

Beth tried to deny the flush of need racing through her body even now. "He's my husband and I can't be your sweetheart," she hissed.

"No, he's not and not now, but later you can be." he hissed back. When they reached the Bartlett's camp, Nicholas handed her the pail. He swept up her hand, kissing it.

She watched him in shock. "You can't say and do such things; they invite trouble."

"I'll see you tomorrow." He squeezed her hand before letting go. "Oh goodness, run and find someone else to tease before I become angry."

He tipped an imaginary hat brim. "You win, for now."

As Nicholas left her camp, Beth felt distressed. He was the only one, other than her and Daggart, who knew about her taking Lizzy's place. No one in St. Joseph had known. Daggart and she had stopped going to Kansas City for supplies just to allay suspicions.

She wanted to cry. She'd done so well in the past year and a half, tolerating Daggart and replacing her sister for him. Her father had also forced her to agree, in a way, since Beth couldn't deny his final wish. If she'd known men like Nicholas existed, she'd have run away before giving Pap her oath.

Used to the mindless routine, she set up the tent, laid out their bedrolls and tried to sleep. Snippets of her conversation with Nicholas stayed in her mind. He'd lost a wife too, and his voice softened when he mentioned her. Beth turned to her side, curling to hug her knees. He loved his Sally as much as Daggart still loved Lizzy. Tears slipped down, one to the side of her eye, the other across the bridge of her nose, and plopped onto the pillow. Beth couldn't stop her feelings for him and knew she'd forever be his second choice. She wasn't sure she loved anyone enough to accept life as a substitute yet again.

The train made good time the next morning, traveling sixteen miles. The Granvilles decided to camp near an Indian village. Beth wasn't afraid of them thanks to meeting Jack, but still shy. While she'd seen plenty in St. Joe, there were so many of them here, she kept close to the wagon. She took out her knitting and sat in the shade, facing away from the village. Mr. Lawrence's wool was tighter spun than the others. For him to have a well-fitting sock, Beth needed to knit up a test piece of fabric.

Concentrating on her work, Beth shrieked when she saw a little face peering at her from around the wheel. The little Indian girl giggled, and Beth laughed, too. The child came out to look at what she held. Beth showed her the knitted swatch of wool, letting her take it to hold. She smiled, her small round face beaming. Her dark eyes twinkled. Beth couldn't help but notice how her skin looked like beige satin.

Beth made a little give-me movement, and the young lady handed back the swatch. Once she had the wool and needles, Beth quickly knitted a lace border and bound off. She picked up stitches along one side, knitted another lace border, and bound off, doing this for each of the remaining three sides of the square while her audience of one watched. After weaving in the tail, Beth gave the girl the knitted swatch.

Giving her a toothy grin, she skipped away, braids dancing. Beth watched her go while getting to her feet. She shook the dust from her skirt.

"What the hell did you just do, Lizzy?" Daggart yelled, grabbing her arm.

"Nothing," she ground out from between gritted teeth. Beth worked to keep from yelping in pain. That arm stayed continually sore, thanks to him.

"Nothin'?" He shook her. "I saw you give that Indian something."

Her teeth rattled and she tried to pull free. "I just gave her a little bit of wool. Please stop hurting me!"

"You gave something to that dirty little Indian? Why the hell for?" He shoved her against the wagon but didn't let go of her.

"Now she and every last one of them are goin' to come over here, beggin' for handouts."

He seemed so certain. She struggled to say, "No they won't."

"Goddamn it, they sure as hell will." He hit a fist against his open palm. "All of them will be here, expectin' you to feed them with my food." Daggart gripped her arm again, squeezing harder this time. "I don't have money to buy more at Fort Laramie, and you're not giving my supplies to a bunch of animals."

She sucked in air, trying to ignore how his fingers dug into her skin. "Please, Daggart. It was just a little bit of wool, nothing of yours."

"It'll be something of mine next time." His voice grew louder with each word. "Whatever you don't give them today; they'll steal from us tonight." He grabbed the back of her hair with his left hand, fingernails digging into her. Despite her cry, he continued, yanking back on her hair with each word, "We're goin' to be scalped and killed tonight, ever last one of us, thanks to you."

Out of the corner of her eye, Beth saw Nicholas holding the little girl's hand. He led her away with a grim expression. She pleaded with Daggart. "Please don't do this. You know you don't mean any of it."

He let go of her arm to grab her chin. He squeezed her face, sneering, "You've not seen the bones of white men scattered across the plains."

Beth whimpered from the pain but was compelled to reply, "You've not seen it either." He squeezed even harder, fingers digging into her jaw and she cried, "Stop, please stop! You're hurting me."

"Not as bad as you've hurt all of us."

Samuel interrupted him with a cold, "What is going on here?"

Standing taller and still gripping Beth's face, Daggart retorted, "None of your business. This is between me and my wife."

Grabbing him by the shoulder, Samuel swung her husband around to face him. At such force, Daggart let go of Beth. "As loud as you were yelling, sir, it's between you two and everyone else. This makes it my business." Releasing the man, Samuel asked, "Do you need help in resolving this issue quietly?"

Daggart shifted from one foot to the other. "No, I'm just mad. My idiot wife gave an Indian runt something without a trade."

"Daggart!" she gasped and stepped from his arm's reach when

he glared at her.

Clearing his throat, Samuel stated, "I don't understand how this warrants a riot."

Enunciating each word as if to a child, Daggart told him, "She's goin' to give away all my supplies before I find a single gold nugget."

Nicholas walked up, holding the little girl's hand. "Did I hear him yell something about Mrs. Bartlett causing the tribe to scalp and kill us tonight?"

Samuel laughed, shaking his head, "I think the whole country heard."

"I'm glad you think this is funny," Daggart sneered.

The younger brother sobered up fast. "I find it ridiculous. No wonder Chuck sent me over here. I'll see to it no one from the tribe bothers you today or tonight."

"You can't promise me they'll not hack us into little bits to eat." He gave one of his mean little laughs. "They ain't called savages for no reason."

Nicholas stepped up to him, the girl hiding behind and clinging to him. "I'm more likely to do such a thing to you right now than they ever will be. Consider this a promise."

Daggart took a staggering step backward as if propelled by the force of Nicholas's fury. "Fair enough, then, I'll take your word there's no problem from savages tonight."

Beth saw people, both whites and Indians, gathered around them. Embarrassed, tears filled her eyes and she wiped them away with a sleeve. Daggart stomped off, and as he walked away, Beth glanced at those assembled. She saw pity in everyone's face and shame filled her. She ignored their stares and gave a wavering smile to the little girl hiding behind Nicholas, clinging to his leg. Her voice broke the tension. "Hello again, sweetie."

Samuel asked, "Are you well, Mrs. Bartlett?"

The argument now ended with Daggart's departure, Beth sighed in relief after glancing around the crowd. All the bystanders each moved on with better things to do. "Yes, I'm fine." She gave him a small grin as if she meant her response. "It seems I have a guest from the village, though."

Nicholas smiled at her, although his expression was still grim. "This young lady would like me to thank you for her gift. Her mother insisted on Sunny giving you something as trade until I explained this was a gift."

"Sunny? What a perfect name for her!" Beth nodded, "Yes, her wool is a gift. I wouldn't want anything in return."

"I thought as much." He knelt, said a few words to the girl, who laughed and ran back to her family. Nicholas straightened. "Despite what Bartlett thinks, these people don't take what isn't theirs."

"I'm sure they don't," Beth replied.

"Your husband seems convinced all red men are savages," Samuel said. "I would like for him to reverse his opinion before his words cause harmful action."

She nodded slightly. "I would like that too." Especially since their captains had such strong feelings. What if Daggart offended them enough to be left behind, Beth wondered. She wanted to believe Nicholas wouldn't do such a thing, but didn't trust her own judgment of him.

Nicholas's eyes narrowed as he stared at her. "You have never stated your opinion. Do you agree with him concerning the natives?"

Beth bit her lip, thinking of how to answer honestly. "As his wife, I shou—"

"But you're not—" Nicholas broke off at her warning glare.

She smoothed her skirt of possible wrinkles. "As his wife, I should agree." Looking up at both men, she added, "As a human being, I have difficulty doing so."

Samuel smiled. "Mr. Bartlett is fortunate to have a wife so loyal to him."

"Sam, she isn't his—" Nicholas kicked the ground, cursing, "Damn it all to hell! I've got things to do."

His anger scared Beth. She watched him walk away and held her hands from nervousness. Rattled, she jumped a little when Samuel's voice startled her.

"Mrs. Bartlett, I apologize for my brother's rudeness. He's been in a foul mood since yesterday sometime." He smiled at her. "My brother also dislikes anyone disparaging Indians. He's very protective of them."

"I understand," Beth said, although she didn't. The man cosseted such an aggressive group of people. Surely they didn't need his defense. She could think of only one reason why Nicholas would be so caring. "He must have friends in the tribe."

"Ah. Something like that, yes." Samuel tipped his hat. "If Mr. Bartlett needs calming, do let me know. I have a talent for making hotheads see reason."

"Thank you, I will," she lied. Beth feared the humiliation from her asking for another man's help would kick off Daggart's terrible temper. Beth sighed in relief as Samuel left.

Everyone seemed cranky without warmth, coffee, or tea. A drizzle gusted from the north, chilling Beth to the bone. The downpour darkened the day too early, and no one wanted to stop long for noon. She agreed with the other ladies, better to keep warm by moving. Later that evening and through the next morning the temperature remained too cold to even talk. The wind pushed rain into wherever they tried to sleep. Chimney Rock appeared in the west after almost twenty miles, giving everyone the reassurance of progress.

Beth kept on the south side of their wagon with Erleen, the sunbonnet's brim keeping her face somewhat dry. The blowing rain made seeing anything impossible. She avoided Daggart, going to sleep just before dark. Even when around her, he'd kept to himself. For most of the day, their oxen needed his attention more than her mistakes did.

The next two days stayed cold and less windy. Warm food and hot coffee lifted spirits as did dry clothes. The air seemed to sparkle with the party's improved mood. Beth hoped to see Nicholas a little. The days seemed long without him. She didn't have the nerve to ask anyone where he was, but did notice Mr. Lucky wasn't around either. The men rotated as scouts, she knew, and speculated this was his turn.

Just before nightfall, everyone took the opportunity to enjoy drinking from Scott's Spring at Devil's Gap. Abundant vegetation grew around the sweet, clear water, a welcome change from the muddy North Platte. A few tried climbing the bluffs to see from the top, but the loose soil at the bottom carried them back down each time. Beth gave socks to a grateful Chuck and Lawrence, with Samuel playfully unhappy at not receiving his.

Once all the cattle, oxen, and horses gathered the next morning, the wagon train moved through Devil's Gap. The sandstone underfoot bore deep ruts from other emigrants. A couple of wagons were able to fit side by side between the two tall chimney-like bluffs on either side, but most needed to pass through in single file. Past the bluffs, the land stretched out in front with no trees and no wood for noontime meals. A few had found driftwood by the river, but most of the timber still grew behind them on sandbars carved out by the North Platte.

After traveling an easy thirteen miles, the group continued to a place called Horse Creek. Each took a drink from the water jar filled at the bluffs. Beth and Daggart went about their evening chores as usual. Near dusk, she leaned against Erleen as the cow tugged at the dried grass. She relaxed and closed her eyes, enjoying the animal's warmth and comforting bulk.

Erleen shifted her weight in search of a new supply of food, startling Beth into opening her eyes. She saw a couple emerge from the willows around the creek. Amelia and Nicholas walked along the bank, arm in arm. Beth didn't want to watch, in case she saw an intimacy she'd not like. But, just as a disaster draws in gawkers, she couldn't look away from them. The laughing girl whirled to face Nicholas, hugged him, and kissed both cheeks in a European fashion. She saw him grin and return her kisses. Beth turned towards Erleen, ignoring the sudden stinging in her eyes.

CHAPTER 11

"Do you want me to have a word with him?" Nick asked Amelia Chatillon. They walked a deer trail that hugged the creek's bank.

"No, my goodness, Daddy can take care of him. He enjoys Mr. Bartlett's company," she replied.

"Mr. Chatillon is in the minority." He held up a tree's branch for her to walk under. "I dislike the man more each time we meet."

Amelia playfully slapped his arm. "Oh, phooey! That's only because you have designs on his wife."

Feeling as if his thoughts had been written on his forehead, Nick choked out an, "Excuse me? I have no designs on any woman in our group, married or not."

She waved away his protests. "Don't be coy. I've seen the way you look at each other. Considering how little time Mr. Bartlett spends with his wife, it's no wonder she seeks, how shall I put it? Comfort, somewhere else."

Anger filled him. Beth never initiated their kisses and he considered her a lady, not a courtesan. "Comfort? I don't appreciate what you're insinuating. Mrs. Bartlett doesn't seek anything from anyone here, not like that."

She laughed, shaking her head. "My, you do have a bad case of it, don't you?"

Nick put his hands in his pockets, still a little angry and a lot more shamed. "It doesn't matter what I think or feel. She's a nice woman with a good-for-nothing of a husband. I do nothing more for her than for any other lady in the group." He stared ahead, uncomfortable with the lie. Nick hadn't let anyone, not even Sam, know the extent of his feelings for Beth, never mind the kisses.

The girl stepped over a fallen log after him, holding Nick's hand. "If you say so..."

He'd heard the skepticism in her tone and had to correct her. "Yes, I do say so, since I've been teaching you French, helping Mrs. Watts with hitching their animals, and have carried a lot of water for the ladies."

At a wider part of the path, Amelia took his arm. "Especially the single ones, it seems."

Nick frowned, now aware of the married women not needing as much help. "I've not noticed until just now."

She laughed, "Don't you find it odd how one minute they're capable, but the next minute when you're nearby, they're helpless?"

He cut his gaze to her. "Those girls are flirting with me, aren't they?"

Laughing at him, she turned Nick to face her. "Yes, they are. Now I know to not bother Mr. Claude with fetching things for me, since he won't have a clue I'm flirting with him."

Holding back willow branches so she could pass, Nick retorted, "He's a romantic Frenchman. He'll know."

They paused once clear of the woods. Amelia turned to him, "Speaking of the French, thank you." She kissed one of his cheeks and then the other. "And this is for teaching me how to flirt with Monsieur Claude in his native tongue. I hope he appreciates my effort."

Nick returned her kisses in the same way, replying, "You're welcome, and I don't see how he couldn't like a young woman who's gone to such effort for him."

"You are too kind." She smiled at him. "Remember to send Monsieur Claude in my direction a few times, if you please?"

Nick shook his head, resigned to a reluctant role of matchmaker. "I'll send him but the rest is up to you."

"Not to worry. He won't be able to resist." She nodded to her left. "Speaking of irresistible, there's Mrs. Bartlett."

He glanced over and saw Beth leading Erleen around for greener grass. She wasn't facing them. Had she seen Amelia kiss him? The thought of Beth thinking him taken by the younger girl bothered Nick and he didn't know why. Although wanting to think about the odd emotion, he first needed to reassure Beth of his... Nick stopped. Affections? He shook his head, unwilling to admit so much for her. Feeling his companion's stare, Nick said, "I need to visit with her for a moment. Will you excuse me?"

"Certainly!" Amelia put on her sunbonnet and winked at him, "Have fun, but not too much lest her husband catches you."

Nick mock glared at her teasing and then crossed the field to Beth. She'd made the perfect dress for her figure. The color, cut, everything enhanced her slender curves. He smiled, knowing she wore his clunky boots under such a womanly skirt. Nick supposed he should ask for them back but liked the idea of her wearing them.

What would he say past the first hello? He stopped in his tracks, knowing he had no real reason to speak to her. Anything the Bartletts needed to know could be told to Bartlett himself. Nick veered away from her, toward his own camp. He stopped by the Watts's, then the Chatillons'. Seeing Bartlett seated between Amelia and her father angered Nick. The man had a wife already, one kept shackled to him by an inane reason. Yet, he sat here, sparking another girl before releasing Beth. Instead of dragging Bartlett away by the scruff of his neck, Nick smiled at the trio. He tipped his hat and went to check on everyone else in the group.

He found time to talk with the hands as they settled in for the evening. Spirits were high, knowing they'd be carousing at Laramie this time tomorrow. He passed on singing with them. Instead, he yearned to go to Beth, to talk and pass the time with her. His scouting the trail kept him from seeing her with any sort of regularity. Had she missed him as much as he had missed her? Nick hated the constant craving he felt, always wanting what he couldn't have. To hell with this, he thought. He had every right to check on one of the party's status and wellbeing. Nick went around the wagon circle first, making himself be patient in seeing her. Once done, he eased his way over to where Beth camped.

He saw her sitting by the fire, concentrating on what he assumed to be Sam's sock. The warm light flickered across her heart shaped face, lending an extra glow to her skin. While she looked down, her long eyelashes seemed to rest against her cheeks. Nick leaned against the wagon, enjoying this chance to stare as much as he wanted. She smiled, lost in thought, and he smiled with her.

Nick noticed she'd lost a little weight since making her new dress. The waist didn't fit as snug, nor did the neckline. He caressed the dipping neckline with his gaze, lingering over the shadow of her cleavage. He'd been wise to avoid her, the memory of how Beth's lips and neck tasted still strong in his mind. Shifting his position a little, he looked away from her. He didn't want to grow any more interested in Beth physically at the moment. If he let his imagination have free reign, he'd not be able to walk back to his camp.

Instead, Nick imagined Bartlett's reaction to him visiting with his wife. The man might be sniffing at Miss Chatillon's skirts, but could still be a dog in the manger over his own woman. The reaction of such a mutt kept Nick's desires in check.

Before common sense stopped him, Nick strode over to her. "Mrs. Bartlett?"

She glanced up while getting to her feet. "Yes, Mr. Granville?"

He smiled, ignoring how much a kiss from her could help, instead saying, "I'm here to see what you might need. I'm sure you're aware Fort Laramie is our next stop and a chance to restock on supplies. They'll be at mountain prices, always a premium, but worth the cost to some."

"My husband might, but I'd prefer not to go tomorrow." She tucked the wool into her cloth bag.

Nick shook his head. Didn't all women want to catch up on the latest news? He'd bet she needed supplies. "Is your husband getting fresh stores for you two?"

Beth stood to face him. Focused on the fire and not him, she replied in a small voice, "I hope so."

Nick stared at her close up, entirely forgetting his purpose for speaking to her. Beth's eyes were a little red, and she sniffed. She'd been crying. He took a couple of steps forward, ready to beat the innards out of whoever caused her tears. "How are you today, really?"

"Fine, thank you for asking, and you?" She looked everywhere but at him.

"I'm fine too. Although, I am tired of hearing my hands brag about how warm their feet are. Also, Sam's been sulking because he's the only one left out, so if you could somehow hurry on his socks, we'd all be grateful."

Beth gave a choked laugh and sniffed again. "I'll step up the pace, then."

"Thank you." Waving in the slight breeze, tendrils of hair framed her face. Nick wanted to let one of the curls wrap around his finger as he kissed her. She must have taken advantage of the Platte being up. Beth smelled a little of flowers, leading him to believe she washed clothes with the rest of the women.

She put away her cloth sack, getting the pail. "Mr. Granville? I do have a request of you. Would you mind walking with me for water? I don't mean to be a 'fraidy cat, but rumors of the Sioux are more alarming when it's dusk."

He grinned, pleased she'd asked something of him at last. Nick knew and dismissed the rumors, knowing they had nothing to fear. Still, he jumped at the chance to be alone with her in the dark and with a real reason to do so. "I'm here to help."

"Thank you, I appreciate your coming along with me. I'll get the pail." She went to the wagon, discovering she already had the bucket in hand. A blush colored her cheeks. "Oh! Yes, let's go, then."

Nick suppressed a smile at her distraction. He wanted to believe he affected Beth as much as she did him. They walked beyond the firelight's reach, the gold replaced by a full moon's silver. When Beth stumbled on a shadowed tuft of grass, he grabbed her hand to steady her. Her skin felt soft and sweet against his, despite her slight calluses. He couldn't let her go and searched her face, hoping she mirrored his desire. "Why don't I hold your hand, just in case?"

"That might be a good idea. I wouldn't want to fall and ruin my bucket." She intertwined her fingers with his.

"Is that what you ladies are calling it, now?" He leaned back, looking at her bottom.

Laughing, she reproached, "For shame! You know what I mean."

Nick was pleased with himself for brightening her mood. He walked with her, enjoying her touch. Once at the bank of the North Platte, he said, "If you do choose to visit the fort tomorrow, let me or Sam know. There's a ferry taking people across." He liked the idea of escorting her, telling her the history and about the ghost haunting the place. Maybe Beth'd cling to him, partly in fright, partly because she adored him. He took her pail, though reluctant to let go of her hand. "Let me get this for you."

"You don't have to." She smiled at him, shaking her head. "I'm not quite as afraid of water as I used to be."

He fought the urge to cup her face in his hands. "I'm glad you aren't, but let me help. It's my good deed for the day." Nick bent, careful to get the upmost layer of water. Runoff from the mountains churned the river, turning it muddier the closer to the bottom.

With a full bucket, he straightened, saying "You might enjoy visiting the fort. If you're interested, I'm here tomorrow to help in case the crossing is rough."

She bit her lip, glancing west as if seeing the fort on the horizon. "I might like going after all. Is it very crowded?"

Nick grinned at her nervousness, remembering when he first saw her at St. Joseph. He'd recognized a kindred spirit in her face when within a bustling town. "The place has a lot of various types of people, all either going one way or another. A good number are soldiers."

Her eyes narrowed as she appeared to study the distant bluffs. "With that many men in one place, there is probably a saloon or two."

Every town he knew had a watering hole of some sort for men. "Yes, a couple, maybe more by now."

She crossed her arms as if a surly child. "My bet is there are many taverns of one sort or another. I'd prefer we not go anywhere near the place."

Nick understood her irritation, remembering how Bartlett had started the trip drunk. "Are you afraid your husband will spend too much time in the saloon?"

Giving him a smirk, she replied, "Of course I am. How silly you are to ask. What wife wants her husband to come home drunk and penniless?"

Her bruises seemed a lot more distant in the past than two months and Nick regretted mentioning her husband's abuse. He wanted to reassure her that not all men were as violent towards women, saying "I'd never put Sally in such a position and can't imagine a woman who would want that from her man."

She shook her head. "You can't imagine any because there are none." Beth paused and looked around them, then took a step towards him to softly say, "I have to admit, Daggart's not himself when he drinks. He's bearable until then."

With her close, the smell of soap and flowers hit him full force. She stood so near to him, Nick felt her warmth. His throat suddenly dry, he swallowed. "Most men aren't themselves when drunk," he managed to croak. If Beth could see his eyes in the dark, he knew she'd notice his desire. He wanted to kiss her lips with such a passion that she'd beg him to make love to her.

"When he's drunk, he's horrible." She glanced up at him, into his eyes, and weakly smiled. "But, that's not something needing a discussion."

His free hand clenched into a fist. He barely tolerated her acting in this farce of a marriage. If Bartlett was still beating Beth, Nick would kill him. "I've seen what he does to you. It's not my place to interfere, but I will if he's continuing to hurt you."

She turned away from him. "You needn't be concerned. He's not so much hurting me as something else."

"As what else?" He took her arm, pulling her gently toward him. "I want to know."

"I couldn't tell you. It's too humiliating." She pressed her lips together.

He set down the water and cupped her chin in his hand. "I can imagine a lot of bad things a man could do to a woman, sweetheart. Sam and I take protecting the people in our train seriously, and you're included. If he's causing a problem, I need to know."

Beth was quiet for a moment then admitted, "Daggart will be drunk and forget I'm not Lizzy, entirely, and doesn't listen when I say no." She bit her lip then continued, "You and Mr. Granville have seen what happens, once. I dread such a thing occurring again."

Nick released her arm and stepped back. He loathed thinking of her under Bartlett. Running a hand through his hair in irritated frustration, he didn't want to acknowledge Beth's continued role as the man's wife. And yet, how could he fault the man in taking what Nick also desired? "I see. And it's not my place to interfere no matter how much I'd like to do so." As long as Beth approved the sham, she accepted the cost, and disgusted Nick with her compliance. "It is a part of what you agreed to, I assume."

"I know. This is so awful." She put the back of her hand up to her mouth. "I've tried to be accepting, but I hate him, hate leaving home, and hate everything about this place." Beth's eyes watered and in between sobs, she said, "I try to be a good wife, I do, but I despise the love part of marriage. He's always drunk, always forces me, and I always hate him afterward."

Her tears rolling down her cheeks broke his heart. He pulled Beth into his arms, holding her close, trying to be gentle. "Come on, sweetheart, please don't cry." Nick kissed the top of her head. "I'm sorry I've asked. Of course it's not something a lady talks about with anyone. I was wrong to even broach the subject."

"No, you asked what was wrong and deserved an answer."

Beth clung to Nick, saying, "I spoke far out of turn, but appreciate you letting me do so."

Her body fit so well against him he couldn't breathe. Feeling her and smelling her scent increased his tender feelings and his lust. His body responding too much, Nick eased his hips away from hers. The woman had just told him how she felt about intimacy. He didn't want Beth thinking of him the same as she did her husband. His heart pounded so hard Nick wondered if she heard. He pushed his focus back on to her distress and off his own. "Does Bartlett always force you when he's drunk?" Nick asked.

"Not always." She sniffed, snuggling a little against him. "He acted odd after Fort Kearny."

Holding her in the moonlight, Nick's every nerve ending hummed with hunger. His lips against her hair, he ignored his body's need and asked, "Odd? Can you give an example?"

She pulled from his embrace. "Yes, this time, he didn't want, um, the intimacy when drunk. Daggart was more upset over Lizzy's death and about how much Amelia looks like her." Beth wiped her eyes with a sleeve.

Nick cooled with her absence from his arms. "That would explain why he's always at their camp instead of his own."

"It does," she agreed. "Lizzy was always so beautiful, everyone loved her. A lot of the women in our church in Kansas City disliked how their husbands looked at Lizzy."

He laughed, "I'll bet. Miss Chatillon's a lovely girl."

"The men were always polite and always ready to help her into a wagon as the men do now for Miss Amelia." Her voice sounded sharper than usual. "They seem to prefer her over any other woman."

"They do?" He wanted to smile but instead kept his countenance somber. If he didn't know better, Nick could swear Beth was jealous. He wanted to test his theory with a few remarks. He liked the idea of her being possessive toward him and his time. "Miss Amelia is a charming woman, I'll agree. She and I have walked together a lot more in the past month or so."

She started toward the wagon circle. "Well, that's to be expected. She's a very pretty girl."

Her frosty tone amused him as her latter comment surprised him. "You noticed that, huh?"

"Of course I have. Who hasn't?" Beth shrugged with

something looking like forced casualness to Nick. "Daggart is foolish to follow her skirts when you're our group captain. She's beautiful and you're handsome. You're both single and healthy, perfect together. Anyone can see that."

Nick felt sure her voice cracked on the word "perfect." When seeing her chin tremble, he stopped wanting to tease Beth. He hadn't counted on her caring if Daggart found Miss Chatillon charming. Maybe her husband chasing the woman upset Beth more than Nick chasing her. "The girl is pretty, Mrs. Bartlett. She's a kind person too."

She snorted, "Of course. Amelia looks like a china doll. She's beyond beautiful. Plus, she has a good heart. It's easy to see why every man who meets her has met his match."

He lifted her downturned chin and stared deep into her eyes, hoping to drive home his meaning. "She's not my match." He leaned nearer Beth as if to kiss her. Nick wanted her to stop pretending a marriage with Bartlett and whispered against her mouth, "I'd met my own, once, lost her, and never thought to find another. I might have met her, though. And if the lady I want most in the world chose me, I'd claim her as my own in a second."

"Oh my," she replied, her lips parted. "I so wish I had the choice to make." She shook her head, saying, "But then, I'm assuming you mean me." Beth's smile didn't reach her eyes. "How silly I am, you're probably thinking of someone else entirely."

He kissed her with just a brush of his lips, withdrawing just long enough to say, "I do mean you and it's your choice to continue or not," before leaning in to kiss her again.

"It's not," she whispered against his mouth. "I promised my father."

"You made a bad promise, surely meant to be broken. You're not Bartlett's wife and he's forcing you." Nick slid his hand down her spine to the small of her back and lower. He wanted her to admit her preference for him. Goading her into a confession, he squeezed her buttock. "Is it force, though? Or do you secretly enjoy his attentions?"

She gasped from his intimate touch. "Never!" She put her hands on his chest to push him away. "He'll always be my brother-in-law, never my— my goodness, you're warm." Her hands slid up his suspenders and she wrapped her arms around his neck. "You're not feverish, but still very warm."

"He'll never be your what?" He held her closer against him.

"Heavens! I've lost my thoughts." Beth buried her fingers in the hair at his nape and fiercely kissed him. She stopped only to moan, "I enjoy this, you. I want you."

He bent his knees, easing them both to the ground and pulled Beth on top of him so she straddled his hips. Nick deepened his kiss, tracing her teeth with his tongue. When she gasped, he said, "I'm yours only if you're not his."

"I'm not. Never his." She shuddered.

Nibbling his way down to the hollow of her throat, Nick chuckled. "I don't know about that. I hear him call you Lizzy more than I like. If you truly aren't his, you'll have to convince me you're not." Kissing down her neck, he paused at her cleavage. Nick breathed in deep her fragrance, needing to pleasure her into a confession and not give in to his demanding body. He slid a hand down her spine to the small of her back and lifted his hips to meet hers.

Beth's body tensed and she gasped, "No! We can't do this."

"Yes we can," he said against her skin. Her thighs still straddled his, but above enough to not touch him. He didn't move, instead demanding of her, "I'm yours and you're mine, Beth. Tell me I'm right."

"You're right." She pressed her hips to his. She eased down, kissing his forehead, his mouth, and finally the hollow in his throat as he had hers. She continued on lower, and as her lips touched his chest, Beth said, "We belong together, more together than this, even."

He didn't want to move a muscle and risk disturbing her as she lay on him, her ear against his heart. When seeing where the full moon hung in the sky, he almost cursed aloud. Instead, Nick said, "Sweetheart, we need to get back before we're missed."

"You're right." She sat up on her knees, still against his hips, then stood, shaking out her skirt. "I don't want anyone learning of this."

He rolled to his side, suppressing a groan. Nick stood despite being stiff in every way. He straightened his clothes, agreeing, "Me neither." He took her water and leaned in to whisper. "Before we go back, I want to know if you're ending this ridiculous charade tomorrow. I'm not making love to another man's wife, even if she's you."

Beth took a couple steps away from him. "We can't talk about this now. We have to return to camp."

He didn't want to let her escape just yet. "You and I are dressed and merely walking together. If we're seen by anyone else, we greet them as usual. Therefore, we can talk about this now and will do so before going back to camp."

Her jaw clenched, she said, "Fine, let's talk and walk in that direction at the same time."

Letting her lead by half a step, he blurted, "You're going to be Lizzy Bartlett tomorrow morning, aren't you?"

They nearly reached her wagon before she replied, "I have to, Nicholas."

He held his breath, suppressing the urge to yell she didn't have to do be Lizzy ever again. With an exhale, he instead told her, "Before I say goodnight, I need to know why you won't inform Bartlett you can't be your sister anymore."

Beth replied in just above a whisper, "All right, since you can't let it go. My father was ill and fading fast. A few months before he died, Pap made me promise to take Lizzy's place since I let her die."

Nick had a tough time in believing Beth's brother in law as an innocent bystander in all this. What was in it for the man to allow such a farce? "You did not let her die, Beth Ann. I can't believe Bartlett would agree to such a foolish idea," he said, giving her the water bucket.

"Dag uses the promise I'd made against me, reminding me of how unlike Lizzy I am. He is always telling me how unhappy my father would be if he knew. It worked because I wanted to honor Pa's request and because I didn't save Lizzy."

"Beth, sweetheart, you're the type of woman who'd die to save her sister." Her surprised glance at him said he'd surmised correctly. Beth had understated everything earlier. He imagined her body in the water and took her by the shoulders to face him. "I know you, and am positive you did everything possible for Lizzy that day. Sometimes things just happen and no one can stop them. Being your sister isn't the answer."

She put a hand on his arm. "I must admit, since meeting you, all this playacting has become unbearable."

"Good, because every time I see you, it's unbearable to me too." He squeezed her shoulders, fighting the urge to hold her close. "Despite my actions since meeting you, I don't seduce other men's wives. That is not the sort of man I am. I've been trying to seduce Beth Roberts, but she doesn't exist, I guess."

"She can't. I promised her away."

He wanted to talk, if not shake, the absurdity out of her. If despite his arguments, Beth wanted to continue the pretense, Nick decided to play along and help her change her mind. "I'm sorry, Mrs. Bartlett, but I may be too busy to help you out much in the future. I wouldn't want to cause any gossip for you."

"I understand."

Nick paused at the sadness in her face. He hated seeing her anything but happy. Still, she needed to reconsider her life with Bartlett. This second episode of kissing cemented his feelings for her and Beth needed to see reason as well. "I hope so. Good night." He turned on a heel toward his camp, hating the upset he saw in her eyes. Damn it, hurting her was the last thing he'd ever want to do.

"Nicholas?"

At her saying his given name, he halted. One word from her to stay and he'd never leave. "Yes?"

"I had a nice time walking with you this evening."

His back to her, he said, "Mrs. Bartlett, you'd do well to call me Mr. Granville. You also need to remember there was nothing 'nice' about our time together this evening."

Nick made it to his camp, Sam and their hired hands sitting around the fire. He resented their chatting, singing, and laughing as if without a care in the world. Chuck and Lawrence were out on watch. He'd not seen them while in the tall grass with Beth. Even so, Nick could count on their discretion. Before he found a place to sit, he saw Sam motioning to him.

"We'll need to review the supply list before reaching the fort tomorrow. Let's go and check for certain."

He knew Sam's expressions and wasn't in the mood for a lecture. "This won't wait until tomorrow?"

"No, this needs doing now." The younger brother left the camp, heading out into the night.

Nick followed, but only after giving whatever cooked in the Dutch oven a wistful glance. The sooner they did this, the sooner he could eat. "We couldn't wait until after—"

Sam turned, facing him. "What in the hell were you doing

with that woman?"

The sudden wrath surprised him. "What?"

"Never mind, I'm sure I already know." Sam glanced around before continuing, "Even if you don't have shame now, Bartlett is sure to beat it into you."

What had his brother seen in the dark? Nick wondered. Too much, he suspected, and tried an offence response instead of defense. "Wait just a minute! We did nothing shameful."

"No? Why does your guilty face tell me you two did more than the kissing I saw?"

"You saw more than the kissing?" He winced, knowing his voice squeaked an octave higher than usual.

"Damn it all. You're such a jackass!"

Nick tried a feeble smile, hoping to calm his unusually angry brother. "You're right, I crossed a line."

"Crossed? No, you jumped on, spit at, and rubbed out the line, Nicholas." Looking at the sky, Sam went on, "You know she's married. I'd already told Mrs. Bartlett to leave you alone, and—"

"Let's talk about that." Nick could almost pinpoint when, and asked, "You said what to her, exactly?"

"I said to leave you alone, she had no business seducing you. Exactly."

He laughed at the idea of Beth being so forward. Her kissing him this evening still amazed him. Nick taunted his younger brother, "Ever consider I was seducing her?"

Sam crossed his arms. "Since you're more moral than the usual cur, I never imagined it. I suppose I was wrong."

"But, you imagined her seducing me?" Nick paused. "She is, but not intentionally."

"Oh, well, that solves everything," he retorted, sarcasm laced through Sam's words. "Hopefully the beating you deserve from Bartlett isn't meant as well."

His sarcasm and anger infected Nick like a common cold. Despite working to keep the tone light, he became more irritated at his brother. "You're not being fair and don't know everything in this case like you think you do."

Sam was silent for a moment, as if mulling over his next words before speaking. In a calm voice, he said, "I know you've missed Sally. We all do and your loss must pain you still. Mrs. Bartlett is a fine woman, but if you need a lay—"

Nick interrupted him, his hands in fists, his body ready for a fight. "Choose your next words carefully."

"As I was saying…if you need a lady to court, there are quite a few in the group less encumbered with a husband."

He wanted to confide in Sam, but his stomach chose that moment to growl. "After I eat and before we sleep, there's a lot I need to tell you."

CHAPTER 12

The sun shone, birds sang, and Beth's favorite flowers bloomed in profusion. Even Erleen seemed happy on a farm too bright and colorful to be real. Beth snuggled into the bedroll, trying to block out sounds of a camp waking for the day. She didn't want to leave her subconscious, especially since Nicholas, not Daggart, was her husband. Like trying to hold fog, she grasped at the last bit of an idyllic life before giving up the fight. A bit angry at having to leave such a dream, she rubbed her eyes and wiggled out of bed.

Fort Laramie loomed so close, no one hurried breakfast. She wanted to snap at everyone else's lighthearted mood. Most looked forward to some sign of civilized life, but she fretted over Daggart's potential drunkenness. Beth dreaded his touch before last night, but after the shared intimacy with Nicholas, she felt ill at the thought of Daggart making love to her.

While she fixed the same old breakfast, her husband sat opposite Beth with a plop, asking, "Where were you last night?"

"Here, mostly." She made coffee, not wanting to indulge in small talk with her husband.

He watched her every move. "I stopped by and you weren't here. No one was guardin' the wagon. I checked, no one stole anything. Lucky for you."

A pang of guilt hit her as to why he'd not found her last night. "You're right, I should have been here, watching our things." Beth lifted the coffee pot and Daggart lifted his cup in response.

He slurped the coffee, stopping to say, "I hope you weren't out cattin' around for that one Granville."

Beth tasted fear in the back of her throat. She forced herself to remain calm. While handing him his breakfast, she willed her hands to be steady. He couldn't really know anything. If Daggart knew for certain what had happened between her and Nicholas, he'd have done something by now. "I wasn't out cattin' around, not for anyone." Which was the truth, she reassured her conscience. She'd not planned on a simple chore to be so thrilling. "I had to get water for this morning's coffee."

In between bites, he said, "Good, because you promised your Pa to replace Lizzy, not chase after men not interested in you."

"Not interested in me?" Did Daggart see something in Nicholas she'd missed in her bias, Beth wondered.

He laughed, "Granville couldn't be. I've seen him more and more with Miss Amelia this week."

Beth stood, taking his dishes and empty cup. "Since she's so much like Lizzy, of course every man loves her. Including you, I suppose?"

His face flushed. "I dunno. Probably. Even the gals love her."

"She is nice," she agreed and added, "Do you think she'd be a better wife than me?"

Not looking at her directly, he replied, "Hadn't thought about it."

The idea of releasing her had played out in his mind, judging by his guilty face. "Of course not. But, since you and I aren't really married, I suppose there's nothing stopping you from courting her."

"Nothin'? I promised your pa I'd take care of you as I'd have done for Lizzy for the rest of our days." He stood, crumbs clinging to him. "That ain't nothin', Lizzy. That's a promise and whatever else I've done, I've not gone back on a promise."

She didn't want to cause an argument but had to press home her point. "But are you happy? I think Pap would want both of us to be happy in our lives."

He pointed a finger at her, not bothering to walk over and poke her in the chest like usual. "I'm not going back on a deathbed promise, Lizzy, and I'm not allowing you to either. It's wrong." He stomped away from her, yelling at the oxen as he hitched them to the wagon.

She put the back of her hand to her mouth, fighting the tears burning in her eyes. Beth didn't want to go back on a promise either, but surely if her father had known about Nicholas, he'd allow her to stop playing as Lizzy. No, she admitted dismally, Pap would have held Beth to her promise. He'd appreciated her, but cherished Lizzy more. Tears leaked out from under her lashes. She'd always known it, and so had Lizzy. Her sister tried to make up the inequality, but it remained between them. She knew he had her best interests at heart, making Daggart swear to take care of her. Beth would never understand how he thought she could ever replace Lizzy.

The wagon lurched forward and she hurried to put away their belongings. To break up the monotony, she tried to engage Daggart in conversation. Beth pointed out the spring green valleys with Laramie Peak far away and snow capped. She knew he didn't comprehend the beauty. He nodded but his eyes remained blank as if unable to focus on the distance. She started knitting mittens, not quite believing they'd be useful before winter. Someone with a thermometer said the high temperature hit the 90s. As drenched with sweat as her hat was, Beth believed it.

The train lunched just south of Fort Laramie along the banks of the Platte. A few men swam their horses across to the Fort while others jumped in a wagon and split the ferry cost.

"Hey Lizzy, is there anythin' we need at Laramie?" Daggart swayed from one foot to the other.

"I'd prefer you not go," she replied.

"And I'd prefer you to stop yappin' if you don't have anythin' useful to say." He took off a dirty shirt and climbed into the wagon. "We need whisky, maybe some pickles." After putting on a clean shirt and vest, he jumped out of the wagon.

She crossed her arms, bracing for an argument. "We do need pickles, but don't need the whisky."

"Doesn't matter what we need, I want whisky." He put a hat on his head, his expression one of defiance.

"I'm sure you'll get what you want. Something we do need is more wool. I have half of what we need for the higher elevations. The ladies were talking about how cold it is past South Pass. We'll need warmer things and I don't have the materials."

"Wool and pickles, got it," he said, staring past her. "Hello, Mr. Granville! Are you all ready to go?"

"I am," Nicolas replied. "I think a few of the others ferrying over with us aren't gathered yet." He nodded to Beth without a smile. "The ladies want to wear their Sunday best."

Beth's face grew warm. His steel grey eyes looked through rather than at her. Her cheeks burned as she remembered last night's pleasure. How could he be so cool after such a heated encounter? She still tingled when thinking of how he'd felt against her. Unnerved by his presence, she squeaked "So would I."

Nicholas looked her up and down, stating, "I'm assuming you're not visiting the Fort."

Since Beth wore her sister's brown dress, she felt the need to explain. "I'm taking advantage of the wind and water for clothes washing." Indicating the skirt, she added, "This isn't my best, obviously."

"Obviously not." He turned back to Daggart. "We'll see you there. Some of us are swimming our horses over. If you'll excuse me." He left, with Daggart trailing after him.

She wasn't surprised neither said anything before leaving. Although, she recalled, Nicholas had excused himself and there was no excuse for Daggart. Beth snickered then felt guilty for her uncharitable thoughts.

While carting buckets of water for the washbasin, Beth dwelled on Nicholas. She didn't blame him for being angry with her. If their situation were reversed, Beth felt sure she'd argue with him over a sham marriage.

She washed clothes and gave the wagon a good cleaning. All the while, Beth argued with herself over her promise to Pap. The good side of her honored the vow to her father, while the bad wanted to forget ever uttering a word of consent. The inner war raged as she sorted her trunk of belongings. She took out and stacked the three books the others left behind on the farm. Lizzy's shoes, cleaned earlier, she put on the bottom, placing a couple of quilts over them. She left out the sewing box, wanting to sort through it as well. The works of Shakespeare and their school primer went back into the trunk, but she kept out the Bible, tracing a finger on the cover's gilted lettering.

Sad and knowing the family events recorded within, Beth hugged the Bible as she sat in the shaded wagon bed, missing her sister. Most days, her resentment of having to pretend to be Lizzy kept Beth's feelings busy. She'd forget how much she missed her sister until having a quiet moment like this. She knew what her twin would think of the situation with Pap and Daggart. Lizzy would have told them both where to go long before now. Beth shook her head and placed the Bible back in her trunk. In this case, she wished she were identical to her sister.

A few of the group had returned to camp by evening, giving those who stayed behind a chance to visit civilization. With Daggart not being among those who came back to camp, Beth went ahead and did his part of the chores. Drink must be cheap there, she thought, knowing whisky kept him so long. Beth ate a quick dinner, cleaned up, and settled in to work on Samuel's socks until bedtime.

Later, raucous laughter from Daggart woke her from a dozy sleep. She sat up as he crawled into their tent. He slumped halfway on the threshold, his eyes closed. Beth heard Samuel outside, shaking Daggart's legs.

"Come on, Bartlett, let's go."

Her husband woke a little, looked around through half-closed eyes, and crawled into his bedroll.

She didn't move until she heard his snores. Once sure he slept, Beth left the tent. Samuel stood there as if knowing she'd wake and thank whoever dragged her husband back to camp.

He nodded in greeting. "Mrs. Bartlett."

"Mr. Granville." Beth joined him beside their wagon. "I'm glad you brought back Daggart in one piece."

Chuckling, Samuel replied, "You make my task sound easier than it was." Going to his horse, he quietly said, "I'm glad you're awake. I was ordered to bring you a couple of things." Samuel retrieved two items from his saddlebags. "You requested pickles, I heard, and wool." He handed over a jar, and a middling sized flour sack.

She set the pickles in their wagon then opened the sack. "Oh my!" Beth couldn't help but exclaim. She clamped a hand over her mouth, certain she'd been loud enough to wake everyone. He'd given her a sack full of spun wool, just waiting to be knitted into hats, mitts, and socks for the mountain traveling. She examined the various yarns, tilting the sack to where dimming firelight showed her the colors. "These are beautiful! They'll be fun to work." Beth smiled at him. "I don't think Daggart picked these out, and whoever did has my eternal gratitude."

"I'll be sure to let Nick know he chose well. He fretted for a good half hour before deciding on one of everything."

"Nicholas did this?" His thinking of her thrilled Beth. In front of his brother, however, she kept her tone even and impartial. "How very nice of him. I'll have to ask him how much we owe."

"I think he has enough of Bartlett's money to pay for that and then some."

Her happiness evaporated like dew on a dry day. "Uh oh," she sighed.

"I'm afraid so. Nick won most of the hands at the saloon with one of the soldiers winning the rest."

Wanting to keep Samuel talking, she asked, "Did you lose a lot as well?"

"No, I know better than to bet against my brother. He wins most hands he plays. What Nick lacks in a poker face, he makes up for in luck."

Beth knew the hour grew later, but she didn't want to face Daggart, even if he slept. She put the wool in the wagon and retrieved his socks. "These are done and I hope they fit."

He took them. "They're perfect and just in time."

"I'm glad."

"Thank you, my dear." He held out his hand and she placed hers in his.

She knew she blushed when he kissed the back of her hand in a courtly manner. "You're very welcome. I enjoyed making them."

Samuel let her hand fall. "Are you next in the queue?"

"Not quite." Beth paused, not wanting to wake Daggart by saying his name. Then, too, she didn't want to refer to him at all. Despite her reluctance, she replied, "First my husband, then me."

His eyebrows rose as Samuel crossed his arms. "Your husband, hm?"

"Yes." She sighed, disgusted at having to classify their relationship as such. "My husband."

He nodded, uncrossing his arms. "Goodnight, Mrs. Bartlett. I'll give Nick your regards."

"Please do." She went back into the tent and crawled into her bedroll. Beth heard the soft sounds of him walking past them. Lying there, thinking of Nicholas and smelling Daggart's sick drunkenness, Beth tried imagining how different circumstances would be if her family still lived. She fell asleep imagining meeting Nicolas in town as Beth, not as Lizzy.

Next morning, she tried not to laugh at every wince of Daggart's. He grimaced at every clang of metal, bellow of the hands, and beam of sunlight. "Too bad you didn't think to save a hair of the dog that bit you," she said, trying to keep a sympathetic tone. He replied with only a grumble she barely heard. "Would you want breakfast? Or maybe just coffee?"

"Only coffee, please." He shielded his eyes from the morning sun. "I need my hat too."

Beth tried to feel sorry for him. She shouldn't even smile at his pain, much less want to laugh at the groaning and whining he did. If he'd not spent most of last evening drinking until sick, she might have more pity.

"Here," she handed him a fresh poured cup. "Speaking of a need, thank you for remembering to send back pickles and wool. You'll be glad we have both in a month or two." Beth meant her thanks since snow fell in August in the higher elevations. He had last year's winter wear; hers needed more replacing than mending.

"No, no pickles. They make me sick."

She couldn't help a smirk at how green his skin appeared. "I'm sure everything is making you ill at the moment."

He hugged his coffee as if to never let go. With closed eyes, Daggart added, "The wool ain't makin' me sick. Nick reminded me you'd asked about it."

"Oh?" Beth concentrated on drinking, trying to be calm. "That was nice of him."

"I guess." He held his cup out to her. "Any more coffee?"

"Certainly." She poured more for him, wanting to ask more about Nicholas. More drink meant more chances to hear about the elder Granville. "He didn't pay for our purchases, did he?"

Back to hugging his coffee in a worshipful way, he replied, "I don't remember. All I know is whatever the man spent at the fort, he and Jon won at the Hog Farm Saloon."

Sick dread filled her. If he'd not brought home more whisky last night, they might be out of money entirely. "You lost money at cards to Mr. Granville and some person named Jon last night?"

Giving Beth a red-eyed glare, he snapped, "Are you goin' to ask me to repeat myself every time I say something?" Daggart blinked from the sun and went back to keeping his eyes closed.

"No, of course not." His evasiveness and mood said everything. Beth considered learning how to play cards. If nothing else, she'd win her money back from either Nicholas or Daggart.

"Good." He drank, slurping, and afterward said, "Nick and this Lieutenant Stiles, Jon, first won everyone else's money. Then, they spent the time I knew of winnin' and losin' to each other. I don't know for how long. Most of the night is a blur."

Beth knew the answer before asking, but wanted to hear it from him. "Did you happen to bring back any whisky for the trip?"

He had the grace to look ashamed before replying, "Not so much."

She shook her head. "I didn't think so."

"I just figured a small bottle would do. Then, we walked a long way from the fort and I got real thirsty." He drained the last of his cup as if to emphasize his point. "After losin' some at the tables, we can't afford any more liquor until we're past most of the ferries." He shrugged. "So I couldn't turn around and buy more, now could I?"

Beth began packing up their breakfast and camping supplies. He followed, moving at a quarter of her speed, so she worked around him. "You do know there'll likely be ferries all the way to California."

He glanced up at her sideways and then turned away from her. "Probably so."

She watched as he left their campsite. At least now he had the idea to save some of the money for future water crossings. They'd been lucky so far. She'd heard of entire families drowning in an attempt to save ferry fees. Beth shuddered. She didn't want to die like Lizzy had, struggling against a relentless current.

With breakfast dishes in her medium pail, Beth led Erleen to the river. Children played in the water, splashing each other while under their mothers' watchful eyes. She nodded, smiling a greeting in return to several of the ladies. Glancing around the riverbank, Beth saw the bare ground along the water's edge. An island in the Platte grew new grass. A lot of others swam their stock over to run loose on the isle. Many of the men chatted while grazing their stock. With the rumor of lean grazing, she had to find the best for her animal to eat.

She walked with Erleen a little way along the shore. The clearer water revealed the bottom of the shallow flowing river. Reassured, she led Erleen into the water. Beth didn't glance down; instead, she focused on her destination. Once across, she smiled at the men who greeted her with nods. They didn't know how great a victory she'd experienced. Not wanting to appear a bigger baby than the playing children, she kept to herself and didn't brag either. She rather wished Nicholas had seen her success.

Beth looked at her cow eating instead of dwelling on the past week. She focused on the blue sky, green grass, and fishy smell of the water. She couldn't decide which was more pungent, her animal's dusty hide or the brackish river. If only a tree grew nearby, she could tie off Erleen and wash the dishes. She needed help, but didn't want to trouble anyone. Instead, Beth looped the end of the rope around her wrist, knelt, and began cleaning plates. She scrubbed off the stubborn food with the river bottom sand. Grease from the morning's bacon floated to the top, carried away by the current.

One task of the morning chores done, Beth stood, her body stiff. Despite the warm sun, she shivered with a sudden chill. The air held a crisp coolness. She rather liked the feeling of warm days and crisp breezes. Yet, Beth shuddered with another wave of a clammy cold. Maybe this wasn't her favorite after all. She scooped up her pail and clicked a couple times at Erleen. The cow stopped eating at the signal, ready to follow Beth wherever she led. Still flushed with her success, she crossed to the south bank without hesitation.

Those who camped nearby had already added fuel to their fires for the noon meal. Beth walked through the faint smoke. The dirty air must be why her eyes watered so, she figured, tying Erleen to the wagon. Beth wiped away the tears. She glanced around, glad no one saw and questioned why she cried. She couldn't muster the gumption to coax embers into a fire for the next meal, never mind explaining her sniffles and irritated eyes.

She yawned and shook her head in an effort to push away the laziness. Her husband would want his food. As if her thoughts magically summoned him, he strolled around the corner. She smiled a greeting, which he ignored. Such a shame the same powers didn't work on Mr. Granville, she mused. Even impersonal, she much preferred his easy company over Daggart's sullen one. She glanced over at him as he sat down with a thud. "Do you have any plans for today?" Beth asked. "Or are we able to cross the Platte before nightfall?"

He sighed, throwing rocks into the fire. "No. I don't have any plans. Can't cross yet. The line's too long. Can't go to the fort. Need the money for later." Daggart picked up another handful of gravel. "Talk around here is to leave behind what you can. Ain't no use in pullin' a heavy wagon up and down mountains."

She sat down beside him, hoping to learn more about their journey. "From what I've seen, nothing looks all that steep."

"That's what I said, but the hands just laughed. Said all we'd seen so far is foothills." He watched a couple walk by, adding, "The hands last night said a few wagons headed to Oregon lost all their oxen before reaching Fort Bridger. They'd been trying to bring the whole farmstead to the Territory in one wagon."

She'd seen various foodstuffs strewn about older campsites. "I though about salvaging some of the flour but figured everything edible left out had spoiled somehow."

"Naw, everything I saw was picked over. One family I saw leavin' behind all sorts of things had been told to trade if they could, leave it if they couldn't." He leaned forward, resting his elbows on his knees. "Of course no one left me any whisky or seed money for my gold mine."

Chuckling, Beth asked, "You did check, though?" She smiled at him. At least now his eyes weren't red from drinking.

"Yeah," he yawned. "Thought about not botherin', but sure as I didn't, some fool would have dropped both thinkin' he didn't need them." Daggart went on, "There's a lot more belongin's the closer you get to the ferry site. Like, the nearer they got, the heavier the load got."

"Is there a difference in cost to get across the river when a wagon is heavy?"

He whistled. "I didn't notice. They go more by the space they take up on the ferry. A man on a horse, even with loaded saddlebags, don't pay nothin'. There was one family, two wagons, all these oxen, and three of the men had horses. They paid more than we had at the beginnin' of the trail." He shrugged. "They shoulda left behind a wagon. When those ox start dyin' off, they won't need it anyway." He stood as if kicked in the butt. "We need to dump everythin' we don't need to dig gold."

Beth stood also, the sudden movement making her lightheaded. She took a couple of deep breaths while Daggart climbed into the wagon. After recovering a little, she went through a quick inventory of what they carried. She followed him. "I don't know what we could leave behind and still live."

He had the lid open to her trunk, peering inside. "We don't need any of this. Maybe the Bible, but I don't expect to have time for much churchin' when we should be prospectin'. Maybe your wool for cold weather clothes, but not these fancy blankets." Daggart held up one to examine. "Did Lizzy make this?"

His referring to her sister directly surprised Beth and she

blurted, "No, our mother and grandmother did. I will not leave it behind." As an added incentive, she thought to add, "It was Lizzy's favorite."

"Oh." With a reverence she'd not seen often in him, he folded the blanket. Daggart put it back in the trunk and closed the lid. "Maybe over here is something I can take out."

Another wave of weakness went through Beth. "I'm not feeling very well." She held on to the wagon for support. Maybe her monthlies had left her more puny than usual, she reckoned. Beth retrieved her bedroll. "I might need to lie down for a while until this passes. We have leftover biscuits from earlier and jam next to them for your lunch." At his grunt of a reply, she settled for a nap in the wagon's shadow.

Beth slept the entire afternoon, only rousing at unfamiliar or loud noises. Even then, she never reached full consciousness. She woke up only after Daggart wouldn't stop shaking her. Seeing the sun inching lower, the shadows long, she sat up with a start. "Dinner! Oh my! I need to get started."

"Yeah, I'm hungry," Daggart said as if to an idiot.

His sharp tone pushed past her reluctance. He rarely hit her while sober. She didn't want to tempt him into doing so again. Beth began the motions of cooking, her stomach rebelling at the aroma of others' campfires. The food smelled good for the most part, but nothing quelled the sharp pangs of nausea at the thought of eating. Her mouth watered with the threat of illness and she paused until the feeling passed. Had she eaten something, Beth wondered, or did the water have poison already? She had seen a place called Poison Springs on Mr. Lawrence's map and knew it to be close.

She rushed through fixing his food, focusing on getting done and getting away from the smell. Handing him his plate, she said, "Excuse me, I have some chores to do." At his shrug, Beth left for anywhere away from the intense odors. She didn't want to go near the water, of course, so she went to look at all the items discarded by others. As she walked among the graveyard of junk, Beth shook her head at the waste. Some of the wagons, nicer than any her family had ever owned, lay in pieces, pulled apart for firewood. Children's toys, books, clothes, all scattered as if thrown there in a hurry.

Wondering how many of the former owners died of a sickness

kept Beth from claiming anything. She turned back to camp, leaving everything behind. If smallpox could be used in blankets to kill Indians, it could kill her now. The faint feeling returned and she wanted to lie down for the evening.

The fire burned low, Daggart was gone, and the dishes, still dirty, lay stacked in the pail. She needed to give Erleen and the oxen water and food, but felt too weak. Beth put the back of her hand to her forehead. She promised herself to give the dishes a lick and a promise in the stream, bringing back water for the livestock. Once done with the abbreviated chores, she shook her bedroll for critters, and settled in for sleep.

Late that night, wolves howling in the distance woke her. She shivered, drenched in sweat, and feeling far too vulnerable out in the open. Beth shook Daggart awake. "I hear wolves outside."

He grunted. When she shook him again, he groaned, saying, "The watch knows. Go back to sleep."

Another howl, this one sounding very close, startled her. She fretted about Erleen. "What if they attack our animals?"

"It's their problem tonight and my shooting practice tomorrow." He turned over away from her in a huff. "Leave me alone."

She lay back down, still worried. Beth knew Daggart's accuracy. If a betting person, she'd place odds on the wolves over him any day. Hopefully whoever patrolled tonight shot straighter than her brother-in-law ever did.

Morning noises woke her from a dream of singing wolves. She smiled at the foolishness and opened her eyes a little. Daggart gone, she closed her eyes again as a wave of dizziness swept her. Maybe he was off getting breakfast somewhere else. She rather liked him not pestering her for food. The spinning world feeling subsided, even if the sick feeling in her stomach didn't. She rested for a moment longer.

The quiet in the camp worried her a little. Beth struggled to sit. Once upright, she waited until the dizziness subsided, saw the empty camp and fainted.

CHAPTER 13

Day three and Nick had hoped for better than this. The time spent waiting to cross the ferry passed by as if the clock ran backward. He wanted to spend every second with Beth, not avoiding her like a typhoid carrier. Picking at a breakfast he didn't want to eat, Nick sighed. The crew kept him entertained, and he liked most of the people in his care. Yet, they weren't her.

Sam swallowed a bite of pancake. "Too bad you never found an elixir for lovesickness. It might improve your horrible mood."

On edge from his younger brother's chipper behavior and a lack of seeing Beth, Nick retorted, "So sue me, jackass."

"Oh ho ho! Such a bad example for your younger, innocent brother!" He held out his hand. "Give me, if you're not going to eat that."

"Fine." Nick passed Sam his plate. "This is all slop anyway."

With his mouth full, Sam said, "If so, I blame the cook."

He stood, retorting, "Thank you. Noon and dinner are yours, then." He went to the animals, getting them ready for crossing later this morning. Nick planned to let them graze once on the other side. With only one group in front of them, the Granville party didn't have long to wait. He counted on Sam to clean up while he hitched up the oxen. Each animal got a scratch between the ears as Nick worked.

They didn't have a lot of cattle to swim across the river. Most families had at least one, but no more than five. He wanted to go see Beth, make sure she knew how safe the ferry was. He paused in his chores. Staying away from her had been his idea. Nick needed the time to cool his feelings. If he couldn't keep his own ardor in check, how could he ask her to do so? As long as she stayed with Bartlett, Beth had to know Nick wouldn't see her as anything more than a client.

"Nicky!"

He returned her greeting, "Amellie!" and smiled at her laugh.

"We're next!" She clapped her hands in a cheer. "Monsieur Claude told me of how difficult the remaining journey will be. I'm ready to get started and be done with it. How about you?"

Grinning at her exuberance, he nodded. "I have to admit, the next week or so will be tough on everyone."

"Once we're done with that part of the journey, we'll be fine, won't we?"

Exhaling, he wondered how much to tell her about the land ahead. Two thirds of the trail remained, with most of the flattest part behind them. He'd spent the prior days' delay encouraging families with four or fewer oxen to trade or leave the less essential belongings. Animals pulling heavy loads sickened faster than those with easier work. A land with alkali water, if any, ensured disease and death among the dehydrated stock. Nick smiled to reassure her as much as himself. "We'll be fine. Sam and I have traveled this route. While there'll be unexpected events, I'm sure everyone will be fine."

She toyed with her collapsible fan, a slight shake of her hands betraying her nerves. "I'm not sure I like the type of surprises a wilderness could provide."

In a hope to reassure her, he said, "A few are good, but most can be bad."

Playfully hitting him with her fan, Amelia asked, "How about we think of the good? What are they again?"

Nick shrugged, enjoying teasing her. "Monsieur Claude may have something special for you and will tan my hide if I ruin it for him."

Amelia stepped up to him, putting her hand on his chest and pleaded, "You have to tell me."

"And ruin his surprise for you?" He took a step back as if to escape. Plus, Nick didn't want Beth to see the girl touching him and thus think he was interested. "Monsieur may have nothing planned anyway."

"You rotten man."

"Better you think so than him. He's meaner." A whistle caught his attention. Nick looked over to see Mr. Lucky give a signal. Turning to Amelia, he said, "They're ready for us. Let your family know."

She gave a little cheer and hurried to her own camp. Nick watched her go for a moment, smiling. If Mr. Bartlett's wife had truly resembled her, he could see why the man still mourned. His own Sally lacked Amelia's effervescence, but he'd loved her calm quiet in chaotic circumstances. Beth had the same trait most times, he'd observed, but not in all. He grinned when thinking of how she'd lost her temper when they first met. He'd loved how such a sweet looking woman held such a fiery interior. Nick had expected familiarity would breed contempt. With another man's wife, he'd hoped for it. He'd not counted on falling a little more in love with her each day.

The family in front of him rolled onto the ferry, shaking Nick from his daydream. Seated on Buck, he clicked at the oxen and they snapped to attention. Another two clicks when the ferry returned and they followed him. Sam paid the fare while Nick made sure both of their wagons loaded without trouble.

Once across, he lead his group on out of the way of others disembarking. When looking for Beth, he noticed how the Bartlett wagon lagged behind as usual. Nick watched from a slight hill as Daggart paid the man and loaded their wagon. From this distance, he couldn't see Beth. Something seemed wrong, he thought, causing a tightness in his chest. He'd feel better after catching some glimpse of her, even from so far away. The Bartlett wagon reached the other bank and he still didn't see her. Nick imagined she must have ridden inside.

Upon seeing Lawrence's signal, he knew everyone ferried over just fine. He breathed a sigh of relief. No stock lost this time, and even better, no people. Now, on to the task of getting them through the waiting desert. When Sam rode up to him, Nick knew what he was going to say and asked, "Camp for the night at noon?"

"Yes, and you're the last person I had left to tell."

"Very well." Sam and his mount didn't continue on and instead fell into step with him and Buck. "We're not going to talk, are we?"

Sam tipped up his hat, replying, "We don't have to, no."

"Good." Nick wondered how long the easy silence would last.

After a mile or so, the younger brother said, "You don't have to tell me what you'll do at Fort Bridger."

He shrugged. "I hadn't planned on doing anything."

"Nothing when she heads south instead of west?"

Nick heard the disbelief in his voice. "That's her decision."

"You'll let her go?"

"It's not my choice unless I want to kidnap her."

"Hm. That's a thought."

If he didn't know better, Nick could consider his brother's

tone as encouraging. "Not a legal one, or have you suddenly forgotten everything from university?"

"No, I still remember a few things," he said. "A law about kidnapping still being illegal is one of them."

"Legality doesn't matter." He continued despite Sam's beginning of a protest, "I want her only if she wants me. She has this displaced loyalty to her brother-in-law and a deathbed promise to a man who clearly did not have her best interests in mind. Add in a lot of guilt over her sister's death and it's a problem I'd like to solve for her." Nick wanted to give Beth a better life than Bartlett offered and had to at least convince Sam he could do so. "Have you seen her smile?"

"Yes, a few times."

"She's beautiful when she's happy and she's happy being Beth, not Lizzy. You should have seen the first time I accidently called her by her real name." Nick grinned. "She looked shocked, of course, but smiled at me. A man would do a lot to receive a smile like that from her."

"Um hm."

Sam's lack of a reply discouraged Nick from saying anything else. He'd rather think of how to see Beth this evening or next anyway. After several minutes, none of the excuses to talk with her seemed plausible. He sighed. Maybe just waiting for an opening to see her would be best. He'd find a reason to search for her when the group reached the far off foothills ahead.

While the distant blue mountains never neared, an approaching thundercloud darkened the western sky. Nick said, "I think we have another half mile before stopping."

Sam also looked at the storm. "Maybe as much as a mile, but I wouldn't count on it."

Hearing the siren song of opportunity, he said, "I'll go to the back and tell the stragglers. You can take the lead."

"Impressive try. I'll tell the Bartletts. You tell the leaders when to halt." Both left to carry out their duties before the storm hit. They unhitched their animals, tying them on the sheltered side of their wagons. When done, they checked on everyone else. The gust front hit and the day darkened to twilight hues. A strong smell of rain felt like a physical touch due to the thick air. Huge splats of drops, then the pings of hail hit their wagon's canopy. Nick peered out to check on their animals. The wind blew horizontally hard enough so the wagon sheltered them. He sat back, relieved.

Instead of attempting conversation, Sam dealt his brother a hand of cards. Frequent gaming together lent such familiarity they didn't need words. Gestures worked fine. When a hard gust shook the wagon, both winced and laughed at themselves for reacting in the same way. The storm and afternoon both passed in a hurry. Once the rain eased, Nick opened the canopy. "Think there's enough daylight?"

Sam pushed his way over to see the sky too. "Not to go as far as we'd like."

"True." He edged his way past the young man, hopping down to the squishy ground.

Following, Sam asked, "The creeks will be up. Will you be helping Mrs. Bartlett over them?"

Nick knew a trap when he heard it. "No. She has a husband who can help her." He patted Buck and got in the saddle.

"Good," the other man said, also riding.

Letting Sam take the back end of their group, Nick went to the front. He helped those who needed him, chatted with the others. The wagons made their usual circle to keep in the stock, with some building campfires on the outside. He cooked up an early supper of ham and beans for them and their hands. One by one, Chuck, Lawrence, Claude, and Lucky came in and sat. They talked about the storm, passed around gossip like old hens. Nick grinned when Claude talked about Amelia, glad the attraction was mutual.

When Claude mentioned seeing Bartlett at the Chatillon's campsite that evening, Nick remained quiet. Instead, he listened to the man detail how Daggart made sure he sat by Amelia, how courteous he was to the girl. Nick wondered how Beth liked doing chores by herself. He might be able to help her with the animals and such. Though sitting cross legged, he leaned forward as if to stand. Catching Sam's wry look at him, he returned an "I know" expression and sat back. This disgusted him, the inability to think without Sam interfering and censoring. He listened to his hands' chatter, struggling to use the gossip and laughter as a distraction. Every time he wondered what and how she was doing, Nick refocused his attention back to the dwindling campfire.

The next morning, Nick took inventory of the small amount

of dry wood they carried in their wagon. Low, but not critical enough to skip coffee. He grinned. The day, still fresh, had a crisp feeling from the recent rain. He led the stock to the creek, two by two. The vegetation glowed with sparkling green, the dust washed away in the storm.

He completed morning chores, saddled up, and led the way through the Black Hills. Even this late in June, Laramie Peak had snow. Nick enjoyed the green valleys and darker knolls in this part of the country. The scrubby evergreens broke up the grassy hills. Craggy, slate grey cliffs dotted the landscape, with outlying blue foothills behind them. The wheels and hooves of so many crushed the sage and prairie grass, giving the air an added scent. An even deeper blue line of clouds moved over the western sky. Seeing no advancing wind, he knew they might have a light shower after noon.

The party bounced over the rocky trail, up sharp inclines and down steep declines. Their wheels traced over ruts from prior travelers cut deep in the limestone and sandstone. He smiled at how the children walked over the embankments on either side of the parents' wagons. Most removed their canopies this morning. Between the fresh air and warm sun, clothing hung on the exposed ribs dried before noon.

Nick gave the signal to stop for midday's meal at Warm Springs. The rich smell of damp earth reached them there as well. Used to the routines, no one needed telling to replace canopies or search around for dry wood after eating. Once replenished and ready, they continued. He wanted to reach a certain place among the Black Hills. The abundant wood, fresh water, and thick grass enhanced the natural beauty of the place. They pressed on despite the light showers expected.

Upon reaching the intended camp, he anticipated Sam's protest at the decision and readied his argument for spending the night here. Sixteen miles seemed too short a distance to go in a day, especially when more scenery to discover lay around the next bend or over the next hill. Yet, Nick knew his group required this place. People and animals both needed a rest from the many loose rocks walked over today.

Nick dismounted, beginning his evening schedule. Halfway through his chores, Sam interrupted by trotting over to him. Nick said, "I know."

Sam slid from his horse. "All right." He leaned against their wagon, watching his brother. "I'm glad we didn't reach here earlier, at least."

"We wouldn't have stopped if we had."

"Pardon me if I don't believe you." Sam took the flint kit held out to him.

Nick grinned. "You don't have to; the truth is the truth."

Every other word more forceful with the effort of striking a fire, he said, "It is a lovely place and good for the animals."

"Which reminds me, how are the Bartletts today?"

Sam laughed, saying, "Fine, I suppose. Bartlett is his usual obnoxious self, while I've not seen Mrs. Bartlett."

The flames took hold of the smaller twigs, spreading to the sticks. Had no one spotted Beth among the group, he wondered. "Not today?"

Pausing before getting the cook pot, Sam said, "No. Come to think of it, not at all since Fort Laramie." He tapped the bottom of the pan like a drum, lost in thought. "I've not been looking for her, though. I might have seen her today and just not noticed." He made a motion for his brother to follow as they went to the Platte.

He went along, not liking how low a profile Beth had. Even if he kept his distance, Nick needed to know about her. He nodded at a couple greeting him while walking by on the way to Register Cliff. They'd passed the milestone a few miles back and some missed the chance to carve their own names in the soft rock. He watched as they strolled east to take part in the activity. Once out of earshot, he admitted to Sam, "I can't help but look for her every moment we're apart. But until she ends this farce between her and Bartlett, I'm staying away so Beth will see she cares for me as well."

"That's a first rate attitude." The young man eased down the embankment and scooped water for dinner. "You'll gain less buckshot in your hide for doing so."

They went back to camp and Nick added, "I do think if you or I don't see Beth before we leave tomorrow, one of us might have to ask Bartlett her whereabouts."

"I agree."

Nick looked at his often-contrary brother, surprised. "You do?"

Sam frowned before continuing on to start dinner. "Absolutely I do. She's a member of our party we've not seen in a few days. Her husband's not known to lie about Mrs. Bartlett." He paused at a glare from Nick. "Er, Beth, I mean. But if he's done away with her, I'd like to know before too much further."

Nick stopped short. "Sam, if he's hurt her in any way, I want to know this instant so I can kill him inch by inch."

"I'm sure he didn't." He knelt at the fire, placing the pan on the embers. "Have you not heard the man at dinner time? If nothing else, he needs her as a pack mule for his gold mine."

Retrieving the usual staples from their wagon, Nick muttered, "I would like to do away with him for that alone, myself."

"Me, too." Sam looked up while taking the food for cooking. "She's his property, and until she's agreed to be your property instead..." He threw ingredients into the cook pot.

"I know." He crossed his arms, angry, "No need to remind me."

"Onion?" asked Sam. "This could use a little flavor."

"Let me chop one up right quick." He found the least moldy root and cut it so the pieces fell into the soup. The aroma of food soon filled the air. With the signal, their hands gathered around the fire. Nick didn't feel comfortable continuing the discussion about Beth in front of his employees, so he took care of the animals. He caught sight of the sun just dipping below the high horizon. As good as dinner smelled now, Nick looked forward to passing Fort Bridger. So many people heading west thinned out the wildlife. The reduced populations meant scarce fresh meat and beans for dinner every night until hunting improved. As the rays spread gold among the clouds, he wondered if Beth enjoyed such a sight from her camp. Tomorrow, he promised himself, he'd check on her.

Before opening his eyes, Nick smiled. He'd see her today, whatever it took. Sitting up, he saw Sam still slept. Light struggled to brighten the eastern sky. Could he go on over to the Barlett's camp now? he wondered. No one stirred, all still asleep. He lay back down on his bedroll with a sigh. Each minute passing made the wait more unbearable.

Disgusted with how slow the day dawned, Nick sat. He wanted a reason to visit Beth, but thinking without coffee was difficult. What reason, he wondered, could he concoct for seeing her? He settled on neither Granvilles having caught sight of her for several days. Checking on someone in their group, even at this early hour, was his duty. He glanced over at Sam. No one had seen her, and he wanted only to make sure she slept without impediment. Nick got to his feet and headed to the Bartlett's wagon.

Once there, he stopped cold. Daggart slept, snoring, no campfire nearby. The lack of a fire concerned him. Everyone cooked last night and he knew Beth would have as well. Nick tasted fear in the back of his throat. Swallowing the metallic sensation, he reassured his concerns. She had to be resting in their wagon. He didn't want to be rude and peek inside but had to check.

At almost a tiptoe, he went to the wagon, to the back where the canopy opened. Nick saw nothing amiss when peeking inside. Her sewing bag sat on Beth's trunk, and from what he remembered, everything else remained in place.

"What the hell are you doing in my wagon?"

Daggart's bellow startled Nick, and he turned to see Bartlett still seated in his bedroll. "I'm not in your wagon. I'm just looking for Mrs. Bartlett."

He frowned. "What for at this time of mornin'?"

Nick kept his face expressionless as if he held a bad hand of cards and didn't want the other man to know. "I woke up early, remembered talk of how no one had seen Mrs. Bartlett in a couple of days, then came over to check on you and her, simple as that."

With a sigh, Daggart stood, hands on hips. "Fine. I might as well tell ya now. You were goin' to find out sooner or later. Beth's gone."

"Gone?" he said, fear replacing the blood in his veins. "What the hell do you mean, gone?"

"What else does that mean?" Daggart turned away from him and walked away a few steps. "I don't see her 'cus she ain't here 'cus I left her at Fort Laramie. That's what that means."

Nick's heart stopped. They'd gone three days now from the fort, leaving Beth alone in the world. Blind fury shoved out his panic. He went to the man, grabbing him by the front of his shirt. Engulfed in a haze of anger, he gripped Daggart by the neck, "Why did you leave her behind? Why would you do that to her?"

Pawing at the hand squeezing his throat, he choked out, "Leggo!"

"Answer me! Why did you?" He saw Chuck out of the corner

of his eye. Some part of his rational mind noticed how the young man stared for a moment and ran off in his other boss's direction. Nick didn't care who saw him manhandle Bartlett. He needed answers.

"She was sick and wouldn't wake up the next day," he squeaked, not looking Nick in the eyes.

Stunned, he released Bartlett. "Wouldn't wake up? No, I can't believe you." Not wanting to know but needing an answer, he asked, "Did you ever see her wake up?"

He looked ashamed. "No. Not really. I thought she was dead from being' sick and I was sad. But I wasn't sure and everyone was leavin', so I let her be."

"Let her be?" She'd been ill and he'd not known? Nick exhaled, feeling like lead shot filled his gut. "You left her there, possibly..." He swallowed, unable to say the word aloud. "Left her there alone, out in the open?"

"Not so much alone. There'd be others goin' by to the territories." He shrugged. "If she was alive, she could always go to the fort and work."

"If alive and to the fort?" Nick thought of the fear Beth would have at being alone, her panic at how she needed to cross the Platte to Laramie. He struggled to keep his voice lower than a yell. "But you don't know. All you're sure about is she's not here and must be there." A resurgence of rage hit him like a horse's hoof. As if by reflex, he punched Daggart in the face. The man reeled and before he recovered, Nick punched him again. Bartlett stumbled back from the two right hits but not far enough to evade a left hook. Before he could throw another punch, Nick felt himself pinned from behind.

"Stop it, Nick!" Sam held him. "Chuck told me Mrs. Bartlett is gone?"

Nick struggled. "Let go of me and I'll tell—" just then, Daggart stepped up and struck him across the jaw.

Sam released his brother with a shove to get him out of the way. Fists clenched, he raised one, saying, "Do something like that again, and you'll contend with both of us right now." The man seemed to wither in on himself at the promise. Sam added, "Find something to do for a while that takes you out of my sight." While Daggart slithered away, Sam turned to Nick. "Tell me."

He thought for a couple of seconds before replying, "I don't know if I can."

The younger brother put his hands on his hips, staring at the sky. His voice quiet, he asked, "Is it as bad as Sally?"

Taking in a wavering breath, Nick acknowledged, "Maybe not as bad, but close."

"Fine." Sam looked at him. "I'll just come out with it, is she alive?"

Men don't cry, Nick thought to himself and ignored how his nose stung. "Bartlett doesn't know for sure." He forced himself to add, "Beth wouldn't wake up and had been sick. He didn't want us to leave him behind, so he left her behind instead."

Sam stared in the direction of the rising sun. After a moment, he said, "There's something more to his story than this. We don't leave anyone unless they've passed, and even then only after a service. He knows that and is making excuses." He looked at Nick's face. "How's your eye?"

"I don't care about that and you're right. We don't leave people behind." Nick's nose still hurt with the ache of tears and he coughed to keep back the pain. "Sam, if she's dead…"

"That's not for certain." He paused before continuing, "You'll have to make sure she's cared for no matter what her condition." He patted Nick on the back. "Bartlett's an idiot who wouldn't know a corpse from a copse." Taking his brother's upper arm, he led him to Buck. "Get ready and go back. You can catch up to us later."

The bossy manner of the young man amused him as the comment gave Nick hope. "Thank you for permission, because I was going to go, anyway."

"I had no choice, I know. Let me have my delusions. Don't worry about anything here, just pack enough provisions for you both."

Nick took his hand and gave him a bear hug. "I owe you."

"Bring her back to us safe and that's enough." He backed out of the embrace. "Have some coffee and saddle up Buck while I make you and the rest of us breakfast."

He watched Sam go to the wagon and campfire. Their hands all sat around, drinking their morning brew, silent. Judging by the somber expressions, they knew. He took an offered cup without a word. Nick wanted to keep his worry to himself.

"Uh, Mr. Granville?"

He knew Chuck well enough to hear the concern in his voice and looked up at the man. "Yes?"

Twisting the hat he held, the employee said, "We all hope you find her just fine. She's a very kind woman."

Unable to trust his voice, Nick tried to smile and nodded. He finished up his cup, packing it for the rescue. While gathering things, he forced himself to focus on sustenance and possibly medicines Beth might need. Bartlett hadn't mentioned symptoms, now that he thought back. Nick didn't trust himself to go and ask the man about her condition. Holding his medical bag, his hand trembled and eyes watered. Likely she'd had some sort of stomach bug, he thought, steeling himself even now for what he might find. The sickness most likely had passed, he reckoned, and she wondered when he'd come back for her. Three days now and another two or three until he found her, she'd be very hungry. He needed to pack filling foods, easy to carry. But then, he'd need room for any belongings Bartlett left with her. If Beth was alive, and Sam seemed to think so, he'd buy whatever she needed at Fort Laramie.

One of his saddlebags stuffed full for him, the other empty for her, Nick carried them to his horse. Seeing Sam, he asked, "You don't need help with morning chores before I leave, do you?"

"You've not left, yet? You're keeping a lady waiting and should hope I don't tell our mother." Handing over breakfast wrapped in a cloth, Sam watched as Nick tied the bags onto his horse. "I hope you find her well."

"So do I." Nick mounted his horse. He turned, nudging Buck into a gallop back to Fort Laramie. Despite his desire to travel fast, he slacked the pace every so often for his horse's sake. All morning the need to find Beth alive consumed him. His stomach growled. When hearing the noise, he noticed how the afternoon shadows stretched along the ground. Nick felt bad for his animal. "Sorry, boy, we'll stop for a while."

He settled for a rest along the Platte with decent water and grass. Not as good as the place he'd stopped a couple of days ago, but acceptable. Nick dismounted, wincing at how stiff and sore his legs felt. He led the horse to a flat spot on the river's bank and let him drink his fill. As Buck grazed, Nick dug around in his bag for something to eat. He'd be no use to Beth if he were weak. Fear for her safety distracted him so much that he didn't taste the jerky. He drank from a canteen, once done, emptying it. Since his horse continued to nibble at the new grass, Nick refilled his canteen for the miles until nightfall.

Landscape he admired before didn't register with him now as he continued. Nick pushed thoughts of her being dead from his mind. He wouldn't allow for the possibility until seeing for himself. He had to believe Beth was a strong young lady. Just like Sally, a mean little voice of his conscience said to him. A wave of hurt spread through his chest at the thought. He squinted his eyes to keep the sting of unshed tears at bay. Sally died from his negligence. He wondered if not keeping a closer watch on Beth meant he'd neglected her as well.

No, he pushed away the idea. Nick had watched for her with every step since the ferry crossing. She'd made her choice to stay with Bartlett and he'd honored her decision at the time. The beginning of sunset brightened the eastern sky with gold. He nudged his horse into a gallop, wanting to go a mile or two more before dark.

The day raced to an end like he raced to Beth. Nick stopped when the last bit of twilight remained. He made camp in the open. Not his favorite place to sleep, but one guaranteeing to wake him at first light. He didn't want to stumble around looking for water, so he built a fire first. Being near a dry creek bed didn't help his horse's thirst, so Nick drank first, then let his animal drink from his hand until the canteen emptied. Tired as he was, Nick still unsaddled and brushed his horse for the night. He'd not seen a campfire nearby and hadn't passed anyone since dusk. Even though Nick felt safe, he kept his rifle close in case of predators. He had a quick bite to eat and lay down on his bedroll. For the first time in a long time, he was alone again.

As planned, the morning sun woke him with its new rays peeking over the hills. He sat, seeing his horse thirty feet away, grazing. He now needed to find water for both of them. Nick stood and packed what little he'd taken out for the night. Coffee sounded good, but that meant starting a fire, boiling the beans, and even more of a delay in finding Beth. And if he didn't find her? Nick paused in saddling his horse, and then shook his head. He swung up into the saddle and signaled gallop to his ride. He slowed when finding the first clean water in miles and stopped for his horse. Nick took the time to fill his canteen while the animal drank. Not wanting to bother with food, he continued on at a rapid pace, rushing past camps just now awakening.

His fear of discovering her grave increased with every mile closer he rode to Fort Laramie. Nick swallowed, wondering how he would know her resting place. Unless the persons that dug her grave still waited to cross the river, he wouldn't. His eyes watered at the thought of her in the ground. He wiped the tears before they could fall, glad no one would ever know. He sat up straight and nudged Buck into a slow gallop. She had to be alive, he reassured himself.

He topped the hill and saw the ferry below carrying people across. Riding down, the distance seemed shorter from higher up than it was. He waited, once there, to pay his fare.

The ferryman took the five dollars, grinning. "Not much call for folks to go back."

Nick returned the smile, albeit with more teeth. "I'll bet not."

The stout man stood next to him still. "Ah course, some folks balk at poisoned water."

"Don't blame them." He didn't want to chat about the obvious. He wanted to reach the other side in an instant.

"Then others don't believe the Territory to be any better."

Nick suppressed an impatient grunt, instead using his manners, saying, "Probably not." His mother would hear about this. He'd expect her approval for remaining so calm and civilized.

Leaning closer, he said, "Still, not much call for folks to go back."

Nick nodded his assent, not giving in to the open ended statement. The idea hit him like lightning to ask the ferryman about Beth. The man had seen everyone crossing and had to remember her. "Tell me, have you seen a young woman going west by herself? She's about yay high." He held a hand up near his neck. "She has brown hair and green eyes, and was wearing a white dress with flowers on it."

"Oh, well, I reckon I see a lot of young ladies cross." He put a hand to his chin and scratched, thinking. "No, none of them were alone. There were some pretty gals matching your description, though."

Damn. He'd hoped to hear a yes and the man point to exactly

where Beth waited for him. As it was, he couldn't get to the other side fast enough. They soon reached the opposite bank, answering his prayers. He glanced over and saw how the ferryman was busy with other customers. Nick took his chance to escape the chatter and look for Beth.

He resisted the urge to gallop around, calling her name. Instead, he went to their last campsite. Once where the Bartlett's camp had been, he swung off the horse. Nick recognized her bedroll, now neatly folded with the pillow on top. Others discarded their belonging in this area too. So many items lay around, he couldn't tell if Beth might still camp in this spot. He knelt, taking her pillow. Had the rainstorms reached here, and if so, had they washed away her scent? He smelled the fabric, too distracted with fear to detect any trace of her soap. Replacing her pillow, he stood and looked around at the people with their own groups. Nick tried to think of where else she might be, but his mind blanked. He needed to pick the first place to search. The fort, the river, Missouri, or worse, California? Had she tried to follow Bartlett and he'd not seen her in another group on the trail? The outcome Nick worked hard to ignore sprung to mind. Maybe she lay under his feet even now, or under the wheel ruts to where wild animals wouldn't find and dig her up for food. He fought against a rising panic. "No, not that," he whispered, unwilling to let her go.

Nick looked over at Fort Laramie, the safest place for a single woman to be. He wanted to search the fort first. Going to Buck's left side, he put a foot in the stirrup.

"Nicholas?"

CHAPTER 14

"Elizabeth!" He freed his boot just as she reached him, hugging him with all her strength. "You're here!"

She loved the feel of him. "I am! So are you!" They seemed to melt together. She wondered if he shared her relief.

He still held her in a bear hug. "Always, I'd always come back for you, sweetheart."

"I wasn't sure if you could." Beth rather liked holding him this way, even in the open where anyone could see. "Mr. Granville might not have let you backtrack."

Nick laughed at the idea. "Sam knew from the moment Bartlett said you'd been left here. No one had a choice over my returning, even if it were for the worst."

Beth leaned back, unsure of what he meant. "The worst?"

"Yes." He brushed a stray lock of hair from her face. "Your brother-in-law implied you passed away or was close to it when we left."

"You thought I was dead and came back anyway? Why do that?"

"Because I care for you." He kissed her forehead. "I needed to make sure I knew what happened to you, and Bartlett had been too vague for my liking."

She took a deep breath, giving voice to the suspicions she'd had these past few days. "I'm sure he was. Daggart left me behind intentionally. My illness gave him the excuse."

Nicholas laughed and said, "No one would do that. I can't imagine leaving you behind in such a way, ill or not."

"He would." Before he could protest, Beth continued, "The night before you all left, he'd been talking about how expensive wagons were to ferry. A lone rider needed less fees to cross."

"Why would he bring the wagon and leave you, then?" Nicholas loosened his hold on her. "Wagons and oxen are easier to replace than you ever will be."

Her eyes filled with tears. Did he not see how expendable she was? "I'd like to think he'd intended to sell the wagon later.

Otherwise…." Huge sobs escaped her and Nick pulled Beth closer. With her face pressed into his neck, she couldn't stop crying. Relief of no longer being alone mixed with her assessment of her brother-in-law's callous intentions. Nick held her, his body comforting as an old oak tree in a storm.

"What have you had to eat?"

"A few things." She loosened her hold, but didn't let go of him, needing the reassurance of his touch. "I found preserves still good. Plus, someone discarded flour, moldy in some spots but not others."

He kissed her forehead. "I'll fix you a decent dinner this evening." Keeping his lips against her skin, Nick asked, "I'd prefer you not be alone again. Would you like to go to the shop with me?"

Beth shivered, "Across the river?"

"It's not deep and you'll be with me the entire time and mostly dry." He leaned back, looking at her face. "Does that help?"

She returned his smile. "Yes, very much."

Nick hugged her again, so hard her breath left her in a whoosh. He laughed, letting her go. "Sorry, I'm just so very glad to have found you."

"I am too." She let him slide from her arms, resisting the urge to cling.

He took her hand, leading Beth to Buck, grazing several feet away. "I also want to get you fed and rested." Once at his horse, he added, "We can leave at first light tomorrow, maybe later if you're still feeling ill." He got up on his mount, took his foot out of the stirrup for her and held out his hand.

She placed her right foot in the left side stirrup, using his help to sit sidesaddle behind him. Wrapping her arms around his waist, clasping them together at the front, she said, "I do feel a lot better and have for a couple of days. I'd found a lot of discarded food, not all of it spoiled. Coffee was scarce, but I managed to boil a few beans. Even drinking the hot water helped me."

He turned to look at her. "I'm glad," he said and kissed her cheek.

Her face burned from all the blushing caused by his tenderness. Nearing the water distracted her from Nick's affections, and she asked, "Are you sure it's safe?" Before he replied, she interrupted, "Of course you are, how silly of me. If it weren't, you'd not risk your life like this."

"Oh, I'd risk mine, but I'd never risk yours."

Before Beth could reply, he nudged the horse into the river. She held on as they crossed, the water high enough to reach the bottom of their shoes. She swallowed against the rising feeling of nausea and fear. "I don't like this."

"I know, and it'll be over soon. There's an oxbow bend in the river here, and it'd be too far to go around instead of crossing twice." He placed a hand over hers clasped around his waist. "Plus one more time across and we're done with the Platte. Next time is by ferry, all right?"

"I'm glad." She held onto him, focused on the warmth of him through his shirt. Her face rested against his back, and she felt his muscles move as he controlled the horse. Water leaked inside her boots. Beth yelped at the sensation then laughed at herself.

"Cold, isn't it? I'm sorry about not warning you."

Hearing the smile in his voice, she grinned. "Don't fret. It just took me by surprise. As long as this is the only water I touch, I'll be fine."

"We're more than halfway across," he said, squeezing her hands.

"Good." She snuggled into him a little more, grateful for his strength. He smelled like dust and leather.

Nicholas glanced back at her. "Don't breathe in too deep. I can't remember the last time I washed."

Beth exhaled in a laugh, his quip catching her by surprise. "You're not bad at all. I miss my soap, or I'd smell better than you."

"Soap or no, you'd always be fragrant in a way I like."

"Hm, yes, fragrant would be a word for it, certainly." With a start, Beth realized they'd reached the opposite bank already. She'd forgotten to be afraid of the water. Their chatting kept her mind occupied.

He grinned and held onto her hands covering his stomach. The horse climbed up the bank and Nick reassured her, "We can retrieve your belongings once we reach everyone else. In the meantime, we can buy a few things for us at the post store."

"We?" Before thinking, she blurted, "Unless there's a mouse in your pocket with money, I won't be able to shop until Daggart gives me something worth trading with you."

"Your former husband is a topic for discussion after dinner this evening."

"Oh?" The hard tone of his voice bothered her. Had she offended him by hinting he'd have to pay for her expenses? She'd not meant to be even more of a burden to him.

"Yes. We're going to discuss your life without Mr. Bartlett and where you go from here."

"I see." She didn't feel able to guarantee Daggart's future actions enough to call him a former husband. "His abandoning me is rather surprising. He'd always valued Lizzy more than anything else in the world. Now, it seems gold is his true love."

Nicholas didn't reply, instead halting the horse in front of the store. When he held out his hand and removed his foot from the stirrup, she used him for support and slid off the mount. She stepped out of the way, brushing against another horse tethered to the hitching post. Already she dreaded going inside the crowded building. People turned sideways to get past each other through the door. "I don't need to go inside and can wait out here."

Done tying off his horse, Nicholas took her hand. "I'm here to keep you safe, ma'am, and you'll do fine in there."

His authoritative tone made her smile. "I'm sure I will." He led her in, the cheese and pickled herring aroma strong and the air heavy with tobacco smoke. The crush and noise seemed less oppressive with him so close. She gave him a squeeze as a silent thank you and he squeezed hers as well.

At the counter, he brought her around to his left to be at his side. He put a hand at the middle of Beth's back, a subtle, steadying touch she appreciated. When a shopkeeper addressed him, Nicholas said, "We'd like a pound each of flour, corn, rice, and coffee. Also, a half-pound of sugar and soda, and a quarter pound of your freshest cheddar."

Beth took in her surroundings. While she didn't care for the close quarters, all the sights and sounds interested her. Customers bought goods from shelves behind the counter. Others, soldiers and women she supposed were wives, sometimes placed orders for finer things. Like the general store at her home, this place stocked fabrics. However, the bolts lay behind the counter. She sighed at her foolishness. Wearing a new dress and yet she yearned for more. Once they reached the others and her belongings, she'd have enough clothes.

"If we were still in Independence," Nicholas said, leaning into her, "I'd have Henry repeat my fabric and sundries order."

"You wouldn't!" Looking at his profile, Beth realized he'd bought her dress's fabric just for her. Nicholas had noticed after all, she thought, and knew how much she'd wanted the material. "I can't let you buy me so much."

"You're right. I don't have the room to carry much else. I'll have to find you a horse of your own." He turned to the clerk, "How much for what we have so far?"

The man answered and Beth gasped at the amount given. She'd been keeping a running total of the items in her mind and Henry never charged so much.

"Very well." Nicholas handed over the money. "As I was saying, I wouldn't repeat the order entirely either. You'd have to pick another fabric." He nudged her shoulder with his. "Unless, of course, you needed two identical dresses."

"Oh no," she smiled at the thought. "I wouldn't want that!"

"Didn't think so, sweetheart." He led her out of the store.

Her face heated from his endearment. "I couldn't let you do so anyway. Once for necessity's sake is fine, but not twice." Following him, she added, "Especially if the second is only because you enjoy taunting me."

"Taunting?" He divided the packages among his saddlebags. "No, I enjoy seeing you wearing clothes and shoes that fit. You deserve that much, at least."

Beth didn't agree but smiled instead, not wanting to argue with him. "Are we ready to endure another round of wet feet and then no more water for a while?"

"That's right." He readied to help her astride. "Not until the ferry tomorrow or until you decide I need a dunking."

She hopped on Buck and wrapped her arms around Nicholas as before. "We both could use one, I'm sure."

He turned back to look at her. "I agree. I'll even let you scrub the dirt from me."

The gleam in his eyes warmed her through. Her palm felt the pulse in his stomach. "Washing my dress at the same time I wash me might be beneficial too."

He grinned. That's something I'd like to see."

She shook her head. "Don't expect to do anything of the kind, mister," she said as he straightened and urged the horse onward.

Beth leaned against Nicholas as the animal picked his way down the river bank and into the water. Prior experience helped ease her fears about going back to camp. Water filling her boots no longer alarmed her. She breathed in, slow and steady. The waves sloshing when others passed them at a faster pace unnerved her a little. Buck's amble helped to calm her.

"I'm glad you're not as fearful."

"I am too." She gave him a reassuring hug. "I don't like being such a baby about this. It's made the journey more difficult for everyone around me."

Nicholas exhaled, seeming frustrated. "As difficult as you say you've been for everyone else, your fears are what bothers me most. There are more turbulent waters ahead. Or, at least, there is on the way to Oregon Territory."

Beth needed to ask what he knew about the trail to California but only cared about Oregon. Closing her eyes, she wanted to pretend Daggart didn't exist. If he didn't give Beth her few remaining belongings willingly, she might be forced to accompany him just to keep her heirlooms. She shuddered at the possibility of ever seeing him again. What if he'd already left the Granville party? Would Nicholas go with her to retrieve her things, or would she be on her own? She asked, "Have you ever been to California?"

"Going to the gold fields may be different." He shrugged, adding, "Mr. Lucky and possibly Chuck might know. They've been down that way." The horse began climbing onto the bank, stumbling a little. Nicholas placed his hand over hers on his stomach. "Hang on."

The way up jounced her so she did as he said and held onto him. When the horse had a solid footing, Beth said, "Thank you for seeing me safely over and back."

Squeezing her hands, he replied, "My pleasure, ma'am."

She let go of his waist. "I suppose there's no need to hold you so tight."

"Then I must find another excuse." He held out a hand as support for her to dismount. When she gripped him, he turned her palm up to kiss.

Tickles ran down her spine and she bit back a saucy comment. Instead, Beth held onto Nicholas and slid down from her perch. "I'm rather hungry. The shop smelled very good too."

He dismounted. "I'm starving as well." Unpacking his

saddlebags, Nicholas knelt, placing the purchases next to the campfire. "Do we need to wash up these?" he asked, indicating the cooking utensils Beth had gathered while alone.

"No, I scrubbed them before and after using." She picked up the cooking pan. "This one has dust in it now. I can get water to rinse everything." Beth filled the bucket with all the dishes she'd found.

"When you take the pan, fill it half full too, please."

Beth nodded, taking both a leaky pail and the pan to the river's edge. She rinsed and half filled the pan. Each dish and utensil received a quick wash, and after she tried to bring back a full pail. By the time she reached Nicholas, a quarter of the contents had leaked through a hole in the side. Showing him the results, she said, "I'm sorry about the water. This was the best I could find."

"Don't fret. No one throws out a solid bucket." He'd cut up a ham into chunks. Adding the meat, a handful of rice, beans, and corn into the cook pot, he said, "I brought some bacon with me, hoping I'd be able to share with you."

"I'm glad you did." Beth loved how he'd returned just for her. She watched as he stirred the food then sat back when done. "As soon as I woke up and saw everyone gone, I became afraid." She picked up a flat rock to worry with, keeping her hands occupied. "I went to the ferry but couldn't cross. No one leaves money behind here at camp. Just household goods and the occasional wagon."

"If people did leave behind their money, this place would be a lot more crowded." Nicholas patted her knee. "Did the storm hit here that first day too?"

"Yes, and it was horrible." She saw how he stared into the fire instead of at her. His expression seemed angry, and Beth heard her voice waver. "The hailstones hurt until I found an old wagon to hide under until the storm passed. A few others huddled under with me."

"Handcart Mormons?" He looked up at her, his face still grim.

She hesitated, wondering what he thought of them and of how much to say. Honesty being the best, Beth admitted, "Yes, I shared because they didn't have shelter. We didn't have any problems. I'd heard a lot of stories about them in town, and they're a far nicer people than most say."

Nicholas nodded and stirred the food. "I think that's true of a lot of people in this world. What is gossiped about them is far removed from the reality."

"Like the natives? I noticed quite a few of them in the store, all in various stages of undress." She couldn't help her curiosity. He'd been married to a native. Had his wife been near naked so much, she wondered. And had he? She bit her lip at the thought of him dressed like a savage. Her face began its heated blush from embarrassment. Still, Beth felt the need to ask, "Are they all so unclothed? Is it just in front of whites that they even bother with dressing?"

Nicholas laughed outright. "The colder the weather, the more they wear, no matter who is around them." He glanced at her, grinning. "Most cover the more, um, vital parts."

"That explains a lot," she said, relieved at his amusement. "It's rather hot here, so undressed seems best at the moment."

He mixed flour, water, a little bit of soda, and some sugar to form a sticky dough and pressed it into biscuit shapes. "Did anyone harass you the past couple of days?"

The question, abrupt, took her by surprise. "No, a few came by, being nosy. I shooed them away, saying my husband was out hunting. I might have added I hoped he shot something because coming back empty handed always angered him."

He grinned at her lie. "Very good."

"The threat of a returning husband kept all but one away. He came back, but when I begged and pleaded for laudanum, he left."

Pausing, his expression puzzled, Nicholas asked, "You wanted medicine from him? Why?"

"After he called me out, saying I was lying and he could do what he wanted with me, I agreed he could. I told him my husband had died of something too horrible to describe." She folded her hands in her lap, looking down at them as if a modest young woman. "After he laughed at me, I said a lady doesn't talk about her husband when he eliminates blood instead of urine." She looked up at him through her lashes, smirking. "His jaw gaped open, so I added I was just starting my husband's symptoms. He could have his way with me, but first, I needed medicine before I died too."

Nicholas snorted, "He backed away, didn't he?"

"More like ran away." She paused her story until he quit laughing. "Word must have spread, because I was in something like a quarantine for the first day."

He handed her a dish of food, saying, "Until they moved on, of course."

"Of course." Nicholas fixed his own plate, soon joining her.

"This meal is heavenly." She paused before taking the last bite. "Why ever do you let me cook when you're such an expert?"

"Because hunger makes a good sauce for me." He pointed a shortbread biscuit at her, "You, however, are a great cook no matter how hungry I am."

Nicholas's beard was grown the most she'd seen since they'd first met. Dark circles colored the skin under his eyes, adding to the air of weariness Beth saw in him. "Nicholas, how far were you when you came back for me?"

"Not far, thirty miles or so." He sighed, putting his dishes in the water pail. "If I had not been so keen on resisting you, I'd have left sooner and we would be caught up with the others by now." He reached out his hand to her

She gave him her dishes. "The blame is mine too. I avoided you as well, despite my wishes."

Nicholas stared at her for a moment. "We feel the same?"

His looking into her eyes in such an intense way caused her heart to thud. "It seems so."

"I'll wash up for us."

"I can help." She stood.

"No need. Stay here, keep an eye on our camp, and I'll be back before you notice I'm gone."

"Very well." Beth watched him for a moment before turning to store their foodstuffs. When opening a saddlebag, she paused. Nicholas had a small Bible there, and she hesitated putting edibles in with it. Instead, she opened the other bag. She found a coffee pot with the beans inside, so placed the items in the second bag.

Nicholas walked up to her, dishes dripping still. "Thank you for putting away everything."

"You're welcome. One of your saddlebags is still empty."

"I did that in case you needed the space for your belongings." He walked Buck out a little ways to better grass and staked him with a discarded peg. "A woman can be left in the middle of a desert and in an hour find enough things to fill a saddlebag."

She blushed knowing he spoke the truth about her at least. "That's very thoughtful, thank you again."

Nicholas walked up to her. "Stop thanking me and apologizing for everything."

"I…all right."

"I know, not easy, but it's good you're trying. I'm not your husband. There's no need to be on tender hooks around me."

"I'm not." As he readied his bedroll, she caught his disbelieving glance and ignored it. What he thought didn't matter. She trusted his kindness but couldn't help her politeness habit. He'd have to learn tolerance, she decided, readying her own bedding next to his.

"Elizabeth, we need to talk about what will happen when we reach the others." He pulled off his boots, flexing his toes.

Nicholas still wore the socks she made him. Beth smiled, saying, "I have been thinking already." She pulled off her boots and socks, dismayed to find another hole in the toes. She'd seen wool in the store but not thought to say anything. Seeing Nicholas had distracted her beyond all reason.

"And have you reached any conclusions?"

"I need to go with them, since I have nowhere else to go." She settled into her blankets, tired all of a sudden. Beth had to confess to him, "Although, I'd prefer to never see Daggart again. He left me here on purpose, breaking our vow to Pap." She glanced over at him to see Nicholas laying back, staring up at the stars.

He shook his head. "You are in no way, shape, or form married to that man. And even if, in your convoluted mind you are or were, the union is over because the contract goes until 'death do us part.'" Settling back into bed, he added, "You died and he parted, so whichever Elizabeth you decide to be, you're not married anymore."

She lay back down as well, nestled under the covers. Beth knew Nicholas was right. Daggart had no obligation to provide for her. His leaving her behind gave proof of this. Tears welled in her eyes, running down her temples and into her ears. "Then I have no one and nothing."

"I think my feelings are hurt." He reached over and brushed away her tears. "You have me for sure, and I'm certain you have Sam, plus all the men who work for us. We all care very much about you, some more than others."

Beth sniffled, wanting to believe him. "Some do more than

others?"

He chuckled as if catching her hint. "Yes, I do, more so than any other."

Smiling at his admission, she said, "I'm glad, because I'd hate for this between us to be one sided or unequal."

"Do you care more for me than anyone else?" He sat up a little and leaned closer.

She looked into his eyes as they reflected the campfire's embers. "Very much so."

"I'm not sure I believe you. You'll have to prove it with a kiss."

Putting both hands on his stubbly beard, she teased, "I don't know if I want to kiss such a porcupine. If only there was a way to miss your quills."

"Let's try." He gave her a gentle kiss, brushing her lips. "Is that nice?"

"Very," she murmured, pressing her lips against his too. "But nothing more until your beard is all out or all in, I think."

He smiled, closing his eyes, and she kissed his forehead, wanting him to rest. Nicholas unconsciously complied, his breathing slowed. Beth smiled, never having seen him asleep before now. He seemed younger, less serious. She wanted to hold him close, but resisted, not wanting to wake him. Before long, she fell asleep too.

Awake after dawn, she saw Nicholas's empty bed next to her. Fear of being abandoned again hit her until she thought of how he wouldn't have left behind his bedroll. She rubbed the sleep from her eyes and looked around for his horse. The animal grazed nearby, still unsaddled. Relieved, she stood, looking toward the river. He walked toward her, carrying their water bucket. The container leaked a steady drip and she smiled. He'd shaved, held his wet shirt in his other hand, but still hadn't fixed the bucket. "I slept far too late," she admitted as he approached

He filled the cook pot with what remained of the water. "Don't fret, we both needed the rest."

"I've had enough and am ready to leave whenever you are." She handed him the coffee beans.

Nodding a thank you, he asked, "Before breakfast?"

"After dinner last night, I may not be hungry for a good

while."

Nicholas grinned. "Once the food starts cooking, you might change your mind. I'll take care of coffee. I'd suggest cleaning yourself up and gathering whatever you'd like to bring."

Looking at her bedroll, Beth shrugged. "I don't have a lot."

"Good, because I'm having a difficult time finding a horse for you."

She gathered up her bedding, asserting, "I can walk. I have so far."

Shaking his head, he argued, "No. You'll not walk while I'm astride. You'll ride my horse on the way back."

"No, you'll not walk while I'm astride either."

He laughed, folding up his own bed into a seat of sorts. "Do you think we'll ever say yes to each other?"

She blushed at the desire she saw in his expression. "At some point, I hope so."

"So do I." He nodded and went back to the campfire.

Beth went to the river as she had the prior mornings. Enough times and she had a system. She wanted a full bath but settled for washing her feet and the hemline of her dress. Later, when alone, she might be able to find a place safe enough to bathe. She needed to ask Nicholas if the Sweetwater River offered such a luxury. Once done cleaning, she wrung the water from her skirt and socks. Beth picked up her boots and made her way back to camp. Nicholas had been correct. The smell of coffee and bacon whetted her appetite as she approached. "Could we have preserves with our biscuits again this morning, or should we save them?"

He glanced up from cooking. "I think saving them is a good idea, maybe a little for flavor later."

Wanting to help, she offered, "I could rummage through the discards for more food."

He stood, glaring at her. "Absolutely not. You are your own person, but I forbid you to do such a thing ever again."

She swallowed a rising lump in her throat from his harsh tone. "Oh? I don't mind doing so if it's necessary."

His face softened into a sad smile. "We aren't discussing this. You did what you had to while left here. But as long as I am anywhere near you and can provide, digging through rubbish for food is not an option."

She nodded and took the biscuit and bacon he offered. A part of her felt offended by his bossiness. Another enjoyed him being so protective, something Daggart had never done. "I see."

"Do you?" He ran a hand through his hair. "Because I don't think you do. I care for you very much. When I think of you here alone, foraging through discards for food..." Nicholas looked up at the clouds. "When I think of how scared you must have been, then to learn of how you might have been attacked." He looked at her, concern evident in his expression. "When I thought you were dead and likely left out in the open, I prayed some kind soul took the time to bury you. Then, I thought of you buried and how would I know where you rested?"

Beth smiled to reassure him and keep the catch she heard in his voice at bay. "Nothing happened and everything is fine now. You're here to get me back home, I suppose. I'm feeling better now with some solid food in me. Coffee, too, has been beneficial."

"You're right, I'm being foolish about imagined events." He drank the last of his coffee and indicated his horse. "I'll try to find you an animal I can afford."

She brushed the crumbs from her dress, worried about the cost. "I don't know if I could repay you for such a thing."

"Consider this a loan, and it's only if I have the money to cover the cost." Nicholas stood, taking her cup, adding it to his and the cook pot. "I didn't bring everything I had, just enough to get me back to the others after I found you."

Beth stood, making a give-me motion for the dishes. "I'm glad you came back for me, even so."

He grinned, handing over the dishes for her to wash. "Me too. Now, providing you're able to travel, I'll get started on finding you a mount." He saddled up, double checking the bit in his horse's mouth and patting the animal's nose.

She nodded, wanting to argue, instead. How could she ever repay the cost of such an animal? Even if she sold everything after catching up to Daggart, she couldn't afford to pay him back. She watched as he crossed to the fort. Maybe she didn't have money to return his kindness, but she could do everything else. Beth took the dish pail to the river's edge. Staring into the water, she thought of how attractive he'd looked without a shirt. If they shared a horse and he rode without such a covering? Beth shivered with desire at the thought. She scrubbed at the plate. She rather liked the kiss last night. Shaking the water from everything, Beth had to admit she enjoyed every kiss with Nicholas.

She wondered if she should suggest riding in tandem on the same horse. What might be pleasurable for a few miles might not be so after tens of miles. Beth shrugged off the worry, knowing she could always walk if riding became difficult.

Nicholas returned with a stormy expression. "I couldn't find anything resembling a horse for you." He dismounted, still frowning. "And what they did have, they wanted an entire gold mine for in exchange."

"Goodness!"

He smiled a little. "Yes, I know you want to protest but I'd rather just share my horse all the way there than have you walk since you're too stubborn to let me walk while you ride."

She grinned at him. "I'm glad you know that now."

Nicholas checked what few belongings they had and nodded. "You've packed up everything. Very good! I might make a trail hand of you yet." He picked up his saddlebags, placing them astride the horse's shoulders instead of his rump.

His acceptance without anger felt wonderful. Beth rather liked life with someone not finding fault in everything she did. "I couldn't fit the blankets into your bags, so I rolled them as you and the other men do. Is that what you needed?"

"It's just right." He made certain the ties keeping them in a cylinder held. "We can put these between us to keep the cantle from bruising your stomach. You might also be more comfortable sitting astride from here on in."

His thoughtfulness appeased her heart. She waited until he sat in the saddle before taking his hand and joining him. She placed the bedrolls between them as he'd suggested. "What happens if the horse gets scared and gallops? Will I fall off and break my neck?"

He clicked the animal to go, chuckling. "It takes a lot for this guy to spook. Falling asleep and topping over is more of a worry for you than him bolting."

Teasing him, she asked, "Should I untie one of these and tie myself to you?"

He turned, giving her an ornery look. "I wouldn't complain about that if you did."

"Maybe I will if the trail becomes steep."

Nicholas laughed outright. "I can make that happen in a hurry so you might as well prepare now."

Her cheeks heated at the thought. "I don't know, tying myself to you seems extreme." She could see how he still grinned.

Leaning back, he bumped into her, returning her teasing. "If you feel the need, you have my full cooperation, sweetheart."

"Thank you, I think." She returned his smile as he again faced ahead and nudged Buck into a faster walk.

Riding the ferry, they'd not needed to dismount, paying from horseback. The day grew warm, almost hot. The bedrolls did protect her from the cantle's jostles. She liked riding. The speedier travel let her see more of the mountains and landscape. Showers tracked north and east, missing them but giving a rain scented breeze. She looked at the back of Nicholas's neck. A sheen of perspiration shone there, the black curls damp with moisture. She felt a trickle of sweat down her cleavage and resisted the urge to scratch. "How far do you intend to go today?"

"As far as possible without causing you injury. Maybe fifteen miles since we had a late start."

Beth sighed. "The country is lovely here. It's a wonder more people haven't settled."

"They forget, I suppose, that Oregon isn't the only place to live."

"I'm sure." She fell silent again, wanting to ask him a myriad of questions. Yet, Beth didn't want to be intrusive. Instead, she kept to a safe subject more interesting than the weather. "Will we stop for midday?"

"I'd like to noon at Warm Springs."

She bit her lip, unsure of how best to tell him. "I might need to answer nature's call before then."

He laughed. "I blame the coffee."

"Even so, may we stop before noon?"

Grinning back at her, Nicholas said, "Very well, we can stop here. There's not much grass, but the water looks good for the three of us."

When he pulled the horse to a halt, she put her foot in the empty stirrup. Beth tried to lift her right leg to jump off, but couldn't. "Nicholas, I think I'm stuck somehow."

He laughed a guffaw. "I'll bet you are. Have you ever ridden a horse before now?"

"Don't be mean. I have a few times." She bypassed his

offered hand and held on to his shoulder. With that, she managed to drag her leg over the horse's rump and down with her left leg. "Just not so much all at once."

"Take it easy dropping to the ground." He kept his hand out, waiting for her to hold it.

Beth slid her grip from his shoulder to his hand. She eased her foot down, her legs almost numb. "This is more difficult than I'd anticipated."

"I'm sure." He leaned over to let her reach dirt without falling in a heap. "It'll take a while, but you'll be used to horseback by the time we reach the others."

"Just in time to continue walking." She stepped back, a little unsteady, to let him off the horse as well. "Maybe I should go ahead and walk anyway. You could scout ahead for safety and ride back to me when done."

He took food from his bag. "No. We'll make better time with you on horseback, and I refuse to be the only rider." He handed her a biscuit and broke the seal on the jar.

They ate, Beth feeling rushed by Nicholas's hurried tasks. He let Buck get a drink and graze a little while she found a private place. Once finished, she found him, watching the animal eat. "I think I'm ready, if I can get back onto the seat."

He grinned. "I'll see that you do." He swung up, bringing her with him once settled. Their movements flowed better this time.

She kept the bedrolls between them after a bump jabbed the cantle into her. It stung a little, fading after a few minutes. The initial soreness from the morning's ride also eased. The horse's quick walk lulled her to sleep until feeling a few sprinkles of rain. A cold wind brought the heavy smell of wet to them. "We're getting a bath in a moment," she said when seeing the wall of showers drifting their way.

"Yep, and I'd feel better if we were lower." He turned the horse a little to the south. They rode alongside a cliff so lighting might find a higher target. "Let me know if you need to stop. Otherwise, I want to camp at Good Springs tonight."

The rain increased, chilling her. "Is it far?"

Taking her arms, he wrapped them around his waist. "That'll keep you warmer. It's eleven miles ahead. Not bad, but a lot to get in before sundown."

"I suppose the springs will be worth the effort, being good

and all." The rain pelted them, drenching them in a moment. "Do we have any soap?"

He nodded. "We do. I bought a bar at the post."

She squeezed around his torso in appreciation. "Thank you, assuming I may use some too."

"You're welcome. It's been rough being downwind from you."

"What?" Beth leaned away, horrified she might have offended him. "Oh no."

Nicholas laughed, saying, "I'm joking with you. I like your scent, even if a little scrubbing would help."

Making a show of sniffing, she retorted, "You're not exactly the best smelling thing around here either."

He turned, giving her head a teasing bump with his. "So that leaves Buck as the most attractive animal here?"

"I suppose it does."

They rode on for a while before Nicholas said, "Your scent resembles wildflowers, and sometimes clean cotton. Other times, you'll remind me of campfire smoke and bacon."

His admission took her by surprise, and she laughed loud enough to embarrass herself. "I suppose I should be glad to be so appetizing."

"You should."

"Now it's your turn. I think you smell like leather, sun warmed linen, and sometimes sweat, but not in a bad way. Isn't that odd? Then, in the morning, you'll have a campfire and bacon perfume too."

Nicholas chuckled. "Perfume, huh?" He looked back at her. "We pay entirely too much attention to each other, don't we?"

"I think so, considering Daggart and Pap," Beth replied, looking at him. The storm clouds mirrored his gray eyes. When he faced her like he did, Nicholas's lips were close enough for her to kiss. A lean forward and lifting her chin helped her reach him. When their lips touched, he paused, and she felt him breathe in sharp. He broke their contact, turning his torso to her.

While standing a little in the saddle, Nicholas pulled Beth closer. He kissed her with an intensity she felt to her toes. His slight stubble scratched just enough to remind her of how manly he was, but not enough to hurt. She caressed his face, enjoying the rough feel against her palm. He groaned when she did so and kissed down to the underside of her chin.

When he said, "I'd have to be a contortionist to take any further liberties," she laughed. He kissed her once more and faced forward. "I will absolutely smell better than my horse when we bed down tonight."

She thought of sleeping with him and Beth felt her cheeks burn. If they both bathed, would they share more than sleep by the morning? She shivered.

"I'm chilled, too. We're already out of the rain shower's path. We're sure to find sage or wood to burn at camp this evening."

They made good time, covering ground until the shadows lengthened. With the western sun in her eyes, Beth leaned her cheek against his shoulder. His hat brim blocked the sun for him. She lowered and rested her hands around Nicholas's hips. A slight sweat beaded her upper lip as she thought about how strong he felt. In the quiet, her stomach growled loud enough to catch his attention. She felt his quiet chuckle and said, "Sorry, it has a mind of its own."

"Mine does too and happens to agree. Another mile and we're stopping for the night. But then, I see others are here already." Nicholas indicated ahead with a nod of his head.

She straightened. "Do you know them?"

"No, I don't think so."

"I'd prefer to not socialize if you don't mind."

"I don't mind at all." He patted her leg as if to reassure her. "We can pretend we're newly married and want our privacy."

She raised an eyebrow at this and bit her lip. "Won't they know we're not honest? Especially when I blush at every word?"

Letting her slide down first, he said, "Maybe that's normal for a new bride."

"I suppose." Beth stepped back to give him room. "Lizzy did blush a lot."

He pulled the reins over Buck's head and waved to one of the men looking at them. "Stay here and set up camp for us, please. I'll visit with them some, saying I have a new wife to attend to and leave in a short while."

"Very well." Her face burned as he walked over and began chatting. She envied him his easy way with strangers. The women may be fanning themselves over his brother, but everyone else who met Nicholas seemed to respect him. She pulled the saddlebags from the horse, laying them a few feet away. More unwieldy than heavy, she pulled off the saddle with an awkward tug. She set it on the ground, pommel down so the horse's sweat could dry.

Raucous laughter caught her attention and she looked up at the noise. Nicholas stood with his back to her, the men around him laughing. He must have told them of their pretend marriage, she surmised. They made hoots and catcalls like the people at Lizzy's and Daggart's wedding. Ignoring her embarrassment at the attention, Beth focused instead on removing the bit from Buck's mouth to help him eat better. Once done, she led him to a ravine a little south of the others. They'd not stopped often and she lingered a while to let him get his fill.

Strolling up to her, he put his arm around Beth. "Well, wife, we're on our own tonight. They're going to let us have our ongoing honeymoon."

His bold move flustered her. "Nicholas, are you sure..."

"I told them we've been married for a few months, but the new hasn't worn off of either of us."

She laughed at his triumphant grin. "Very well, I'll try to act like you're still irresistible after all these months."

"I'll help." He slid his arm around her waist and brought her to him. Nicholas tipped her back a little and kissed her in a long smooch. She held onto his arms to keep from falling backward.

As he eased back upright, she put both hands on either side of his face and returned his kiss. He paused, still as stone. "We need to stop or we'll give them more of a show than you intend."

She glanced at the onlookers, her face hot from shame. "I'm sorry. I became carried away by the ruse."

"I'm not complaining, I'd just rather wait until there's no audience." Nicholas took her chin, lifting up her face to give her another kiss.

Beth turned from him, shy and still holding the reins to his horse. "How about you start a fire while he eats? Then I can cook supper if you like. You'd mentioned getting cleaned up while it rained." She took his hand, leading him and Buck back to their planned campsite. "Now I have my heart set on smelling like something other than old socks."

"I'd like to smell a little better myself." Taking his saddlebags, he said, "I'll make a decent fire and start the food. When you're done, come eat with me, and it'll be my turn to wash before bedtime." He glanced at the horizon. "We don't have too long before dark."

"I'll get started, then." She smiled and turned to lead the horse to some scrub brush near the creek. Beth walked a little south, looking for even a tiny basin of clear water. She found a decent sized swimming hole a few yards from camp and walked up to it. She almost cheered upon spying sand at the bottom of three foot deep water and went back to camp.

"Were you successful, wife?"

Beth laughed at his comment, thinking him silly to say such a thing. ""Yes! It's wonderful and I can see the bottom." She saw the concerned expression on his face. "Of course I need to get over my fears, but until then, it's a nice place to wash."

"All right." He dug around in a bag, "Here you go. Leave the horse here and I'll hold supper until you're done."

She almost hopped with glee. "Thank you so much!" She smelled the soap. "What a lovely fragrance! Are you sure you'd want to use this though?"

He gave her an intense look. "In an instant if it meant I smelled like you."

The warm tickly feeling in her stomach began, and Beth's face grew hot yet again. "Very well. I'll be sure to save some for you." Beth turned, going back to the small bathing spot she'd found.

Since the ravine concealed her from anyone else, she pulled off her dress. Dirt turned the hem to brown and Beth sighed. Both she and Nicholas knew better than white with flowers, but the fabric had been so lovely. Maybe the new soap would remove most of the dirt. Confident her undergarments kept her covered should anyone happen by, she lathered and scrubbed the dress's skirt. The white remained a slightly creamy color before she went on to wash and rinse the rest of the garment. She laid the dress on some nearby brush to begin washing herself.

Beth undid her braid, running her fingers through the waist length hair. She needed a good cleaning as much as her clothes did, and her chemise needed mending. Beth sighed, wondering when or how to ever get the materials to fix everything. Everything would have to wait until reaching the others. Instead, she focused on washing her body. The chemise made the task more difficult, but she didn't want to be nude with others so nearby.

Once the stream carried the suds from her, she worked up a

thin lather in her hair. She rinsed her scalp by bending over the water. The expensive soap Nicholas purchased wasn't as strong as the lye she made and Beth enjoyed it. Mosquito bites were bad enough without adding lye to the irritation. Beth flung her sodden hair up and behind her. The wet hair slapped her back and she grinned. Thought it may not dry until morning, at least the dirt and grime from the trail no longer clung to it.

"Is it my turn?"

Beth saw Nicholas standing at the bank, hands in his pockets. The way he looked at her, she felt like prey in front of a predator. "Yes, of course. Do I need to finish cooking dinner for us?"

"No, it's done and waiting for you." Nicholas went to her, holding her upper arms. "Do you need my help?" He leaned in toward her.

Aware of how thin her chemise was and how close he stood, Beth shivered a little. "I'm done, but...." She leaned forward, wanting to feel the same tingles as when they'd kissed on horseback. Their lips touched and her insides turned to oatmeal mush. He wrapped his arms around her and she moaned an "Um hmm," in appreciation. Beth loved how he held her as if needing her even closer. She returned every nip and lick he gave her.

He broke away first. "You need to eat and I need to get cleaned up." Nicholas set her back at arm's length. "Go and I'll be there when I'm done."

"I can't help you here instead?"

He laughed, "No, not like you'd think. Go eat."

"Very well." She climbed the ravine to their campfire, scooping up her dress as she went. Turning her back to him, she pulled her damp dress over her head. She used the fabric as a cover to slip off the chemise before putting her arms through the sleeves. As it pooled around her feet, she put her clothes on completely. He had the food kept warm and ready for Beth at the campsite. She ate the dinner, plain but filling.

Nicholas joined her, shirtless and in wet pants. The fabric clung to him, she saw before looking away as her morals fought her desires.

"Have you had enough?" Nicholas asked, scooping some beans and rice onto a plate.

"Yes, thank you." Beth sighed, wanting something to do so her hands kept busy.

He ate, focused on his food. "Don't worry, as soon as I'm done, we're going to bed." He took another bite, saying while chewing, "We have a long day of travel tomorrow."

"All right, I'm pretty tired already."

"So am I." He set his plate on top of hers. "We should wash up, but I'm exhausted and just want to bunk down for the night."

"The dishes could wait until morning, while the bacon cooks and the coffee boils."

"I agree." He settled into his bed. "Are you going to be warm enough tonight?"

"I should be. I've slept like this the entire way here."

Sitting up on an elbow, he said, "Wet? I doubt it. Your dress is still dripping. If my shirt wasn't still drying, I'd let you have that to wear." He thought for a moment. "Tonight is going to be cold and I have an idea. Take off your dress and leave off your undergarments. Let them dry tonight, and wrap up in your blanket."

She gave him a stern look. "Is that safe?"

Nicolas laughed. "Probably not, but I'm not wanting you sick, either."

"I won't be."

"Sam said the same thing when we were kids. Just before he caught pneumonia, of course."

"Very well. If it will stop your fussing, I'll undress." Beth faced the fire, knowing how what she did might lead to more. She eased down to sit on her bed. "Could you hold up my blanket, just so no one will see." Nicholas sat up and held the blanket out like a screen, blocking everyone's view of her, including his own. She glanced behind her to be sure and lifted the dress over her head and off. In almost the same motion, she wrapped up in the blanket. "Thank you."

"You're welcome. Move your bedroll over here and I'll keep you warm."

An oafish snort escaped her. "I'm sure you will." Still, Beth pulled her bedding adjacent to his and let him under the covers to snuggle his stomach against her back. She lay still, feeling his breath in her hair. He put an arm around her, his hand rested on her stomach. She wanted more from him, but didn't know quite what. "Nicholas? I don't know if we should be so close. This feels dangerous."

"It does, but I don't want to let you go."

She turned to face him. "I don't want you to, either." Beth accepted his kiss, even when his tongue raked her teeth. Combing her fingers through his hair, she squeezed him tighter.

He broke away to ask, "Should we continue, or say goodnight?"

"I want more, Nicholas," she replied, feeling an emptiness only he could fill.

He groaned while kissing her again and nipping to the base of her neck, not stopping until his face nestled into her cleavage. His touch led her to the edge of a cliff and she didn't want him to stop. Beth had never experienced such intimate touching before, and she shuddered at how good his lips felt there. When she ran her hands down his back, he moaned. She smiled at his reaction, asking, "Do you mind?"

"No, please continue."

She felt his firm muscles tense under her caress and felt the same anticipation in her own body. "I'm not sure what else to do with you."

"It's all instinct, or should be." He looked into her eyes. "I'm no different from any other man." Nicholas kissed her chin, sliding up so their lips met.

She gasped, feeling the hardest part of him between her legs, and forgot to argue how exceptional he felt to her. Beth held on to his shoulders, both afraid of the building hunger in her, yet needing more from him. She paused to give herself one last chance to refuse anything increasingly intimate. His insistent point so close to completing her tempted her sorely. His kisses, his touch, and the feel of his skin against hers all intoxicated her into letting him have whatever he desired. She reached under the waistband of his pants and at the same time lifted her hips so he pressed a little more at her opening. The sensation sent a ripple of lust through her. "Nicholas? Would you please take me now?"

"Oh God yes, Elizabeth," he whispered against her ear.

She felt him slide into her, easy at first and more than halfway. He didn't stop or even pause, instead pressing through until she felt a slight resistance. Beth gasped at the discomfort, which ended almost as soon as it began.

Nicholas stopped, being very still. "Have you never done this before?"

His question called to mind all the other times, events she never wanted to remember again. "Nick, I, I'd thought so, but not like this, not with so much of a man."

His body relaxed as if boneless and then shook with silent laughter. "You flatter me."

"I don't mean to, but this is something else." She pressed her face against his neck. Feeling his heartbeat, his breath, the salty clean smell of him, Beth wanted tonight to wash away every prior bad experience her body had ever had. "Could you continue?"

"If you insist...."

Hearing the amusement in his voice, she kissed his neck. "I liked how easily you entered me."

Nicholas exhaled, hard, as if needing strength. "God, so did I." He withdrew a little and slid in again, this time a little further than before. "This doesn't hurt?"

"No." She wrapped her arms around him, his body hard against hers. Beth understood and shared his tension, even if she wasn't quite sure what to do about it. She wiggled her hips, surprised at how pleasant being pinned down by him felt. "Maybe move again, please?"

He gasped out a strangled, "Yes, ma'am." He continued moving, slowly at first, then faster.

She looked at him, and seeing his face pained, wondered if this now hurt him instead of her. "Is this all right for you?"

"Yes." Nicholas slid his hands under her back, holding Beth tight against him. "Better than I ever imagined."

"Good." She enjoyed how he filled her too much and then withdrew. "Oh, very good." Just as she longed for him again, he entered her yet again. Each time, he built a hunger within Beth she didn't understand. She ran her hands up and down his back as if that could give her relief. His thrusts slowed and a little cry of protest left her. "No! I'm so close, you can't stop."

He turned his face away with a growl. "I'll do what I can." He continued to stay up on his elbows but kept his eyes closed while he thrust into her.

The feel of his bare skin against her thighs thrilled Beth. Nicholas's teasing movements built up a pressure she wanted eased. To help, she lifted her hips each time he pushed forward. "Yes, Nick, more." She shuddered, fearing the increasing strain would never end.

When he said, "Let go, Beth, let me...." she responded in an instant. Every muscle, every pulse in her body throbbed in pleasure radiating from his center to hers. She cried out a little before biting his shoulder so others couldn't hear. He continued to move, beyond the point where her tremors eased. His pace increased and when he stopped, Beth held him as his body echoed hers in relief. He cried out into her neck, every muscle tight with the long held release. Now relaxed, she enjoyed feeling him experience the same pleasure she'd felt.

Nicholas lifted his chin, looked into her eyes, and said, "You've honored me far more than I'll ever deserve."

She smiled at him, still in her. "Whew! No wonder the Murphy's have so many children. This is very enjoyable."

"I agree." He chuckled and nuzzled along the side of her face. "You're amazing." Nicholas turned away and yawned. "You've done me in, sweetheart."

Turning Beth to where her back faced him, he pulled her close, his arm wrapped around her waist. She didn't mind, enjoying the feel of him against her. Lulled by her body's relaxed state and his warmth, Beth fell asleep.

Beth reached consciousness in short stages. The cold seeped into her bones first. The dawn so new, the sun's light didn't yet touch the frozen dew. She didn't feel Nicholas at all and sat up in a hurry. Had something happened to him, she wondered while looking for his horse. Beth didn't see Buck anywhere, so had he left her? His blanket still covered her, while his bedding also lay on the ground. He had to be nearby. A movement to the south caught her eye. Nicholas approached carrying a few pieces of firewood.

"You're awake," he said, putting the wood on the dead embers. "Good. Let's get started on the day already." He looked up from starting a fire and indicated her dress. "You'll want to be wearing clothes, since the other camp is still here."

Her eyebrows rose at the suggestion. She'd not been unclothed in front of anyone in such a way. "Of course." Beth wore her blanket as a wrap and kept it to cover her as she shrugged into her dress. "There, crisis averted."

He gave her a stare and shook his head. "We'll need water."

Without a word, she took the cook pot and headed for the river. She made her way back to see the fire going well.

Before Beth could ask, Nicholas anticipated her question and answered, "Yes, I need you to start the coffee while I mix the dough."

"Very well." She started the coffee and sat on the bedroll, still half asleep.

"You could fold up our bedding while I cook our breakfast," he said, concentrating on his task.

"I could, after a cup of coffee."

"You could now while we're waiting."

"You can stop giving me orders since I know what to do. The sun is barely up, I can be sleepy if I want."

"I can order Miss Roberts around like she's one of my hands," he replied. "I had no say so when you were Mrs. Bartlett, but now? I can tell you exactly what to do for the benefit of our party." Nicholas handed her his pocketknife and the preserves from his saddlebag.

She took them in a huff, retorting, "How kind of you to treat me as one of your men. Do I get pay for this?"

He grinned. "Your payment is time spent with me."

"My goodness, I'm underwhelmed."

"Good, I hoped so." Nicholas sealed up the jar. "Seriously, though, I'd prefer if you did as I say most times. Not because I want to be your boss, but because your welfare is important to me."

She tried to still be angry, but couldn't in light of his obvious concern. "I appreciate that and will do as you say."

"Not entirely, I hope." Nicholas kissed her cheek on his way to get Buck. "I don't like when you give in to Bartlett and wouldn't like you giving in to me so easily."

"You are so impossible. Like trying to catch a chicken in the open field. Just as I'm close, you run away, cackling."

Once on the horse, he asked, "Like a chicken, eh?"

"Yes, but not afraid like one, just wily." She gave him a droll stare and he laughed.

He held out his hand to help her up. "As much fun as you are to bother, we need to saddle up again."

"Very well." She washed while he folded and packed, ready to leave when he was.

The day passed in a hurry. She'd make comments to him on the land, noting the mountains to the north and west. Nicholas replied in single words. At early afternoon, they stopped for a little while. Beth took the opportunity to walk around while the horse grazed at the sparse grass. "Are we going to eat too?"

He shrugged, saying, "I'd prefer not to at the moment."

Beth tried and failed to keep a hungry edge from her voice. "Didn't you make extra at breakfast?"

"I did." He sighed. "All right, eat one or two biscuits now, and I'll fix a good sized dinner this evening."

She went to his saddlebag for food. "Did you want one also, and the preserves?"

"I suppose so, and hold off on the preserves for now."

Beth made a face while turned away from him. Too bad he couldn't suppose himself a better mood, she thought. Hadn't last night been a momentous event, one to give a person a brighter outlook on life? She handed a biscuit to him and bit into her own. Sullenly, Beth knew jam would have made the small meal taste better.

He glanced at her. "I don't want to hear your argument. No telling how far ahead the others are, and I have nothing to trade when that runs out."

"I didn't say anything."

"You didn't have to, your face shows your thoughts." He got up on his horse and held out his hand for her to follow. "Let's get started."

Wordless, she let him help her. His bad mood had affected her too, despite her struggle to prevent it. When placing a bedroll between them, she was glad to soften the cantle as well as keep her distance.

They rode for miles. Only the horse's hooves on the rocks and dry ground along with the hum of insects sounded. Tired and still unhappy with Nicholas's attitude, Beth concentrated on what to say to Daggart when she faced him. All she wanted from him was her trunk, some food, and an ox to pull whatever discarded wagon she could find. She'd gladly be dead to him once more, after he met her conditions.

"We're still a ways from Horseshoe Creek. It's a decent place to camp, and I'd like to get there before dark." Nicholas looked back at her. "Would you like to stop here and stretch your legs?"

She squeezed his shoulder, grateful for the suggestion. "Yes, that sounds lovely."

"All right." Holding out his hand, she took it, sliding off due to being sore. As she landed with a grunt, he said, "We can't stay too long."

"Of course." She walked down to the bottom of an almost dry creek bed with him as he led the horse to the thin stream of water. "Will we have dinner before dark?"

"I'll see that we do." They both watched as Buck nosed around for grass. "I know you're hungry, Beth. I am too." He reached up and brushed a stray lock of hair from her face. "Tonight's meal will make up for noon's lack."

"Thank you." She smiled, her mood softening from his warmth. "I'm trying to not be difficult."

"You have a couple of days alone and hungry to catch up from and I need to remember that. So do say when you need to stop or when you want more to eat." He got on Buck, scanning the horizon. "I don't know there's much here to hunt, but I'll do my best."

"I'm sure you will." She took his hand and joined him on the horse. "You've been a true hero so far."

"Not quite." He brought her hand to his mouth. "What I've done isn't so much heroic as necessary for my sanity." Nicholas kissed her before letting go. "I couldn't live with myself without knowing what truly happened to you."

She looked down at the saddle, wanting to hide a smile. Although wanting to ask, wanting to know more about his thoughts and feelings, she hesitated. Beth bit her lip, thinking. What if, like Daggart, Nicholas loved his first wife so much he couldn't love another woman? She'd felt like he loved her last night. However, he'd not said as much then or today. After their intimacy, she understood how both men pined for their first loves.

"We'll be there soon. Are you doing all right?" He looked back at her.

His question shook her from her thoughts. "Yes, thank you."

Grinning, he said, "You're the politest woman."

Not knowing what to say in reply, she instead examined his face. Nicholas would be difficult to resist if he'd shave as he'd done last night. "I try to always be mannerly." Beth noticed how his gaze softened when she glanced into his eyes. She saw the same longing she'd seen in him last night, fireside.

"You do very well." He turned, facing ahead. They rode on

for a while, him silent and her wondering what he thought. He broke the quiet first. "When Sam hauled me to Independence, I went along to help. Begrudgingly, of course." He glanced back at her chuckle. "I didn't have plans, didn't want them. Then, there's this woman sitting on a bench in town, minding her own business. She glanced up from her knitting, and when I saw the color of her eyes, she'd hooked me like a fish. I've not been my own man since."

"Oh." Beth smiled. Clouds in the west covered the sun, the shade cooling her warm face. She didn't know what to say to him in return. Daggart's rash actions had so distracted her then and since. "I remember your smell, sadly, but also know the next day you looked quite handsome. Enough to almost rival Samuel."

He laughed, "Almost? I'll settle for that."

The late afternoon inched into dusk as they rode on. Just when the brightest stars began to shine, Nicholas pulled Buck up short. "All right, ma'am, we're here for the night." Now a habit, he helped her dismount and soon followed. "We'll have a decent sized dinner and make enough for a couple of quick meals tomorrow." She helped with the saddlebags while he stripped his horse of everything else. "Hand me the cook pot and I'll get water while caring for Buck."

She handed him the pot. He did his chores while she built a small fire from the surrounding sagebrush and rolled out their bedding. She did a quick check of their supplies. They still had some beans and rice, the bacon just enough to flavor one meal. Flour, sugar, and soda remained plenty, and Nicholas had been correct about the preserves. They'd both been using too much on each biscuit. When he brought up the water, she put in a couple of handfuls of rice and beans to cook.

Nicholas rummaged around in his personal saddlebag. "The creek is full, if you'd like to wash. I might take this chance to shave and skip tomorrow."

She nodded, having noticed the alternating scruffy days. "I wouldn't mind washing my feet, if the water is clear and cool."

"Go on ahead and I'll be there in a moment."

Taking his advice, Beth went ahead to the creek. She sat, unlacing her boots and peeling off her sweaty socks. The bank sloped to an easy walk into the water. She stepped in and gave a little yelp at the icy temperature.

"Is it so cold?"

She turned to see him shirtless, his pants rolled up to his knees. "Very!" The sandy bed felt good to her toes.

"Maybe I won't shave after all." He stroked stubble growing into a beard. "This cocklebur stage lasts only a few days."

She smiled at his apt description. "You will have a beard by the time we reach the others then. I rather liked your face smooth but can see how much easier a beard might be."

He returned her smile. "Did you need the soap?"

"Yes, please. I'd like to wash today's dust from my face." She carefully took the soap and rubbed it in her hands before giving the bar back to Nicholas. She dipped fingers into the water and used the water to work up a lather. Rubbing her hands together, Beth warmed her palms and washed her face. Eyes closed from the suds, she panicked a little, remembering where she stood. She yelped when she felt a hand on her upper arm.

"It's all right. I have you. Go ahead and rinse, I'll stay here until you're done." He touched her back, leaving his hand there even as she bent to splash her face clean.

When done, Beth used her upper sleeve to wipe the water from her eyes. She looked up at him and saw the last rays of twilight's golden glow illuminating his face. The tension hovered between them like the humidity in a Missouri summer. "I should check on our dinner."

He caressed her arm before letting her go. "You should, it might be ready or burnt by now." As she turned to the bank he added, "I'll be along in a while."

Beth went to the campfire, now glowing embers. The consistency seemed fine to her as she stirred the beans and rice. The mush most likely needed salt. She looked for the spice in a saddlebag. Finding it, the two plates, and forks, Beth set them aside. She heard a rustle behind her and looked to see Nicholas approach. As he neared the firelight, Beth noticed he'd shaved his face after all. He went and put up his razor and soap before joining her. "You're just in time, dinner is ready."

"It smells good."

She took a bite and added a sprinkle of salt. Swallowing, Beth said, "This makes me miss home and my garden."

"I'd have you tell me all about the vegetables you grew."

"And my fruit trees."

"Those, too. I'm missing everything that isn't beans, bacon, and biscuits." He shook his head. "The variety on this trip is far less than any other. So many have passed through here, taking everything and leaving nothing."

"It isn't all bad." She gave him an ornery grin. "They've left us furniture and bacon."

He laughed. "There is that." Sober, he added, "Besides the wild fruits and berries eaten to nothing, the animals have been hunted until gone."

Beth considered the Indians she'd seen so far. "What will the native people live on when everyone is finished emigrating to the west?" She smiled at him when he paused, fork in mid air, to look at her. "It just makes sense that a people who live as nomads might need food wherever they go for the season."

He placed the fork back onto his plate. "Exactly right. The land has been changed by the whites crossing it. I've seen animals shot for sport during one trip. When the next group passed, they starved for lack of fresh meat."

Beth ate, quiet at this. If he'd not found her, Nicholas might have had more for himself. She saw how much money he carried while purchasing items at the fort. "I've not given you much time to hunt, have I? If you hadn't found me, you'd be able to live a little bit better." She set her dish and utensil aside, near the fire. "When you're done, I'll wash."

He scraped out the last few bites from the cook pan. "Will you share this with me?"

"I'm full, thank you."

"If you're sure?" When she nodded, he said, "I'll eat this up and rinse these for tomorrow." Nicholas stood, adding, "Be back in a moment."

He left before she could squeak out a protest to do the work herself. Instead of remaining idle, Beth spread out their bedrolls. She looked up from arranging the blankets to see him enter the ring of light and set down the pan with dishes. "I have a plan for breakfast tomorrow and lunch. I can make up biscuits with a little sugar in them for more taste."

His eyebrows lifted in surprise as he sat beside her. "Good! I look forward to breakfast already."

"So do I." She settled in under the covers.

Nicholas glanced between her and his own bed. Getting up to

a kneel, he moved his bed to touch hers. "Just in case you get cold tonight, you can use me to warm yourself."

She smiled as he slid under his covers, turning to face her. "How very thoughtful of you."

Returning her grin, he looked at her while they both lay down on the blankets. "I try."

"You do well." She reached out and caressed his smooth face. "I appreciate you very much."

He took her wrist, bringing her palm to his lips. "I appreciate you as well."

He smelled good, his face clean. His proximity drew her closer. He put an arm around her shoulder and pulled her close, kissing her. He paused long enough to ask, "Shall we?"

Instead of answering, she pressed her lips against his. He shuddered. Beth melted into him, tired of resisting. Now aware of how lovemaking with him unfolded, her anticipation almost hurt. She wanted to be wild, but still felt shy.

Nicholas murmured against her ear, "I liked feeling every inch of your skin against mine." He pulled the shoulder of her dress down to expose more of her chest.

He kissed lower, nipping at the upper swell of her breast and she gasped. She asked, "Could we undress now? I wouldn't mind."

Her neckline prevented him from dropping her other shoulder and sleeve. With a quick move, he rolled onto Beth. "I don't want to take the time." He rested his weight on hands and knees, pulling up her skirt. "I want you now."

Tingles of desire danced along her skin. When his hand slid up her thigh, she bent her knee, needing him. "I want you too."

"Why don't you undo my pants, then?"

Though nervous at doing such a thing, Beth reached for his belt and buttons. Her hands shook while unfastening them. He groaned when she touched his hardness. "Is this good?"

"Very." He lowered to rest on an elbow, widening his legs to spread hers apart. Brushing a hand between her thighs, he asked, "Is this good too?"

"Yes!" The feel of him, the possibility his fingertips might reach inside her caused Beth's stomach muscles to tense. "I want you, Nicholas. Please, let's start."

"Since you ask so nicely, how can I refuse?" He positioned himself, pressed and slid in as if she were made of warm butter.

She let out a wavering "Oh!" at the same time he panted her name. "Last time," Beth gasped as he rocked back and forth. "Now this time, and my goodness!"

His lips rested against her ear as he murmured, "It's better now, isn't it?"

"Oh yes, so much. We have to do the same as last night."

He kept a steady rhythm for a few minutes, the tension building like a steel spring. "Beth, wrap your legs around my hips." He moaned when her ankles locked behind him. "Maybe not, I can't last...."

The position drove him deeper into her. "Yes! This is better!" The steady pace he kept pushed her ever closer to the cliff she knew waited for her. "Don't stop, Nicholas, please."

"I might have to," he ground out, his voice harsh with restraint.

"No, faster. Give me more!" Her hunger shocked Beth, as did her crude language. However, the way he kept driving at her sent such tendrils of pleasure through her body. Each rush of passion led her to urge him further. Each liberty she took with her words increased the need for release.

"You've wanted this, haven't you?" He exhaled in her ear. "I've needed you under me, warm and willing." He ran a hand down to her breast, fingertips raking her nipple. "Every day, I've fallen a little more in love with you and longed to feel you this way, all sweet and hot and soft."

Her climax hit Beth like a cannon shot, all consuming and too much to ignore. "Yes!" she gasped and held onto him, the rush of pleasure so intense her toes curled and her hands clenched. She knew he'd been waiting for her and when he stopped moving, Beth knew he'd found heaven too.

He pressed his lips against her forehead, giving a groan at each throb of his body. He put his arms around her, lifting her up to do so. "You're an amazing woman, Elizabeth Roberts."

"As you are an amazing man, Nicholas Granville." She sighed. Even her bones felt too relaxed to be solid. "I thought of last night as the best of everything good. But you proved me wrong just now."

"I agree." He yawned and went to the side. Turning her as last night, Nicholas snuggled her as if spoons. A few moments passed before he said, "Beth, before I fall asleep, I need to tell you something."

"Sounds ominous. What is it?"

With lips still pressed against her skin, he said, "I've acted terrible today." He paused before continuing, "Last night, and then this morning, I kept thinking of Sally and wondered if I'd been betraying her memory by loving you."

She worked to keep her tone even. "I see." Her heart hurt at how he shared the pain Daggart had felt. She dreaded the moment Nicholas would confirm her worst fears and tell her that she would never be first in his heart anymore than she had been first in Daggart's.

"I don't know that you can." He intertwined his fingers with hers. "I thought I would be ready for you when the opportunity occurred, and at first, I was."

Beth bit her lip to stop the sob threatening to escape her. "But then you remembered your late wife and how she was and is your first love?"

He sighed as if in relief. "Exactly."

"Very well, Nicholas, I understand." Her nose stung with the need to cry, and she turned so he couldn't see her face. No matter what happened between them, Nicholas had just admitted he loved Sally like Daggart loved Lizzy. Not trusting her voice, she managed to croak, "I'm also very tired. May we talk more in the morning?"

"Good night, Beth." He wrapped his arm around her waist.

"Good night," she replied, eyes squeezed shut to prevent tears from falling. She loved Nicholas. He was her first love. He'd always be her first, and now Beth knew she'd always be his second. The warmth of him against her almost burned with how good he felt. Tears slipped and rolled from the corners of her eyes. Even with him being so different from her brother-in-law, she just couldn't be yet another widower's consolation prize. How could she ever be the only woman he loved?

CHAPTER 15

Nick breathed in deeply, enjoying the smell of early morning mixed with the scent of Beth's hair. She lay in his arms, head resting on his now numb shoulder. He grinned, wondering how to get started on the day. She'd been such a heavy sleeper so far. He might get away without waking her. The guilt of two nights ago didn't haunt him anymore. Not after he'd told Beth how conflicted he'd been. He leaned forward a bit and kissed her. Admitting he still loved Sally hurt to say, and yet Beth seemed to understand. Nick felt her heart beat under his hand. He'd never wanted to move on from Sally's death, but the woman he held gave his heart no choice.

Thinking of how passionate she'd been with him last night, his body awakened against her. He stifled a chuckle and eased his arm out from under Beth. While he'd like to wake her with kisses and more, they needed to reach the wagon train soon. He'd bought as much as they could carry back, and yet it might not be enough. He didn't want to take the chance on having to let her go hungry. They'd either need to find some game animals, or he'd need to give her his rations. Nick shrugged at his thoughts. There'd been plenty of days he'd been too distracted by sorrow to eat. He didn't want that for Beth though.

By the time he'd walked Buck to water and let him graze at the sparse grass, she had woken up. Beth held the cook pot and a cup. "Good morning. I'll get water for the coffee and breakfast if you'll build the fire. I'd also like to wash up for the day."

She walked by him as he said, "All right." He watched after her, puzzled by her expression. She didn't seem as happy on the outside as he felt on the inside. He turned, going back to their small camp. She'd probably just had a bad dream, he figured.

He secured Buck, stoked the fire, and rolled up their bedding. After setting them aside, he dug out the foodstuffs for the meal. Nick looked at his personal saddlebag. He'd brought his Bible and retrieved the little book. Opening it in the middle, he found his drawing of Sally. He heard a sound at his side. Beth stood beside him, looking at the sketch. "This is my Sally. We'd not been married long, so I just wanted to have some sort of portrait of her. I tried to capture the laughter in her eyes." He took the paper and held it up for Beth to see.

She took the depiction, saying, "Oh, Nicholas, this is beautiful, she's beautiful." Tears welled in her eyes. "You drew this yourself, then?" He nodded and she continued, "I had no idea you were such an artist."

Her praise embarrassed him a little. Nick held out his hand to replace the picture in the Bible. "I'm not sure drawing anatomy in medical school made me an artist."

"Yes," she gave him the picture. "Yes, it did. You have an amazing talent." She sniffed, wiping the tears with a sleeve. "I'm sorry to be so emotional. This took me by surprise, how lovely she was and how much of her personality you've shown."

"Do you think so?" He enjoyed her praise. Nick liked hearing his opinion of Sally echoed by someone else.

"Absolutely. I think it's amazing how a few lines in charcoal can say so much with no words." She picked up the cook pot, checking the coffee. "I wish you'd met Lizzy. I should think Daggart would like a drawing of her as well. At least, I would like one." Beth poured their drinks.

He took the cup she offered. "I'm not inclined to do anything for him, especially now. And yet, if Lizzy still lived, I might never have met you."

"Maybe." She took a drink. "I might have found my own husband by now, instead of being a spinster. My father might still be alive, and I might have my own farm with my husband or stay at the family place." Beth shrugged. "A lot of mights that never happened, I suppose."

Nick also drank his coffee, thinking of how close they'd been to never meeting. He didn't like the idea of her married to anyone else now that Daggart had been dealt with. "Spinster, hmm? Did you ever have a husband in mind?"

"A few. Henry at the general store seemed nice, but wanting him was selfish on my part."

He'd met the man and remembered very little about him. Other than the obvious as a successful business owner, Nick didn't think Henry had much to offer Beth. Not as much as he himself did. "How were you selfish?"

"I wanted him for all that fabric and wool he'd order for me."

Nick laughed, relieved she'd not lost her heart to the man. "You know at some point you'd have too much to ever use."

"Nevertheless, I'd have liked to try having too much." Standing and smoothing her skirt, she added, "But he'd never live on the farm, and I wasn't resigned to living in town."

"I suppose my family's place being at the edge of both is in my favor?" he blurted before realizing how much like a proposal his words could sound to her. Self-conscious, he walked a few feet away to dump out the coffee grounds.

"Very much in your favor." Beth helped him pack the cups and bedding. "Or at least for me it would be if I were in the market for a farm. The best of both worlds."

He smiled, nodding, "I think so, too." A little glimpse of sadness on her face puzzled him. "I don't suppose any other man appealed, or you'd have refused the request your father and Daggart made."

"Some suitors did seem like good husbands, most did not." She followed him to where Buck stood. "When I did see a man I rather liked, I couldn't speak to him."

He reflected back, wondering if she'd ever been shy with him. "So maybe being married at first helped you talk with me? Assuming you rather liked me and all."

"It's pretty clear I do like you. I was so angry at Daggart when you and I met." Beth hopped up onto the horse, sitting behind Nick. "I forgot my shyness and later, speaking with you stayed easy."

"I'm glad, hope it always does." He settled in, ready to ride for at least ten miles before noon. The way he figured it, they had a good five days of riding before reaching the others. Maybe fewer if illness, death, or weather delayed the train. Nick reviewed the supplies they had on hand. Beth might be a marvel with catching fish, but he'd been in too much of a hurry to pack a hook. "If I see a deer, I'm taking the shot."

"Venison sounds good right now." She patted his shoulder. "I'll help watch."

"We should be finding more as we go." He looked back at her and saw Beth nod. Facing forward, he breathed in, the cool air feeling good in his lungs. Nick enjoyed how mountains hugged the horizon, some distant and blue, others closer and brighter colored.

Buck's hooves sounded a steady beat as they continued covering the dry, rocky land. Whenever the animal nudged sagebrush, the spicy scent surrounded them.

Nick had time to consider two choices in how they reached the group. One way they skirted the Platte for an extra couple of days. Most travelers took that route in the trail's first few years. With the detailed guidebooks published since, folks began cutting across some hostile country in an effort to save time.

They crossed a murky creek. He could smell the stagnant water from horseback. "Next time we stop, let's make sure to drink our fill. This might be fine, but as long as the canteen is full and we're this close to the Platte, I'd rather wait." He turned to her, adding, "We can always cut across to the river, if you'd prefer."

Beth bit her lip. "Which would add a few days to our travel time."

"Exactly." He liked how she'd drawn the same conclusion, and loved how she looked when pondering a problem.

"I can wait until later too. We'll make what we have last."

He faced front and nudged Buck to a faster walk. "Very well." He loved the sound of her voice, but didn't want to chatter. Yet, Nick wanted to learn more about her. Had she given any thought to life after Bartlett, he wondered. Curiosity chewed at him, so he asked, "No suitors, none serious, so you can go anywhere you choose. I suppose, even Independence is a possibility."

"I suppose so."

He stifled a sigh, now knowing how she must have felt yesterday with his short answers. After waiting to see if she said anything more, Nick added, "Or, there's Oregon Territory. Men outnumber women, still."

"I can imagine. It's probably why so many men marry Indian women there."

"Hm. I suppose that's true for some." Nick felt her hands on his shoulders.

"You'd mentioned both a wife and a child, and losing them."

He searched his memories with her for such a statement, asking, "I did?"

"Yes, after the accident where…."

"I remember now." He'd forgotten, upset from the man's injuries and the sight of so much blood in one place again. Nick tried to find the words to tell Beth what happened to his family.

She interrupted his thoughts, saying, "I suppose not telling anyone you're a doctor is beneficial. People wouldn't be asking for cures night and day."

Smiling at her concern for him, he replied, "It's not that, so much. Although, that's a good reason to stay quiet." Nick shook his head. "It's more serious than inconvenience." He breathed in deep for the nerve to tell her what happened without becoming maudlin. "I worked hard to save my wife and child. When Sally bled to death, I tried a cesarean but not in time to save our son." He sighed, still disgusted at his incompetence. "So, I cut her open for no reason. The two patients I'd give my life to save and I lost both in the same hour."

"Oh no. I'm sorry, Nicholas, truly I am. Is that why you'd looked so unkempt back in Independence?"

He squeezed her hand. "Pretty much. I didn't care anymore. I'd been at my cabin, alone, when Sam pulled me with him to Independence. Out of spite, I didn't shave and bathed only when I couldn't stand myself anymore."

"I could tell."

Nick laughed at her sardonic tone. "I did my best to get him to leave me alone, hoping he'd tell me to turn tail and leave already."

"Was it just you and him?"

"No, all our hands were there too. We'd met up with them after helping you and Bartlett. They threatened me with a dunking, and I'm still sure Lawrence could have thrown me in himself."

"Would he have?"

"I'd like to think they were joking."

"Not as bad as you smelled."

"What was that?" Nick laughed before she could reply. "You thought so too?"

"I'm so sorry, but yes," she laughed. "You smelled horrible. Your horse smelled better except where you'd touched him."

"You hid your disgust really well. Thank you for that."

"Thank you for bathing at last." She wrapped her arms around him, leaning against him. "I'm glad Mr. Granville insisted you accompany him. I like having you as a friend."

The action comforted Nick, and her soft admission made him feel like mashed potatoes inside. Eloquent speeches escaped him, and all he could say was, "I feel the same."

He enjoyed the feeling of contentment within him, having done without it for far too long. They rode on with her arms around him for the rest of the morning and into the afternoon. Around midday, he asked, "Do we need to stop?"

"I'd like to stretch my legs and maybe have some privacy," Beth said as if just awakened.

"We can do that." He directed Buck closer to some scrub brush, pulled the reins to stop, and held out his hand for her. When both of them were on the ground he added, "If you need to, I'll keep my back turned."

"Thank you," she murmured. "We could have the biscuits and maybe a drink of water?"

"I'll have them ready by the time you've returned." He watched as she nodded and laughed when she made a turnaround gesture to him. He obliged and found their luncheon, even breaking out the preserves in case she'd ask. Beth returned and they ate without talking. After a final drink, they both returned to the trail. He rather wished she'd put her arms around him again. Nick also wanted to hear more of her life on the farm. A few abortive attempts to start a conversation later, he decided to wait until her mood improved. Her sweet, quiet, but short answers let him know her feelings.

The sun inched ever closer to the horizon. When the light dipped behind the mountains, he had to admit they'd not find water this evening. "I hate to say this, but tomorrow is our best bet for refilling the canteen."

"I was wondering if we'd ever reach a spring of some sort." She patted his shoulder. "There's still water left and if we reach a creek by tomorrow noon, we should be fine, right?"

"We should. We'll rejoin the Platte River tomorrow." He looked back at her, stopping the horse at a dry gulch. "Would you mind sharing with Buck? Not much, but some?"

"Of course we'll share." She took his offered hand and dismounted. "There's not a lot of anything for him to eat either, so he'll need the moisture."

Nick smiled at her consideration for his animal. "I'm sure he'd appreciate that." He began the now familiar ritual of bunking down for the night and she helped. With nothing liquid to spare, he didn't bother with a fire. "How about you and I share what's left of the bread, and tomorrow, when we stop for noon we'll have a big meal."

Beth shrugged, hands on her hips. "I don't see how we have much of a choice."

He didn't want her feeling trapped. "There's always a choice. We could cut across to the Platte. It would take an extra few days…."

"No, I can make do until tomorrow, certainly." She took the jam and biscuit he offered. She ate in a hurry and took a quick drink before holding the water out to him. "Too bad you didn't bring whisky."

The idea amused him and he retorted, "A big enough bottle and as thirsty as we are, who knows where we'd be?" Her grin felt like a reward to him. He accepted the canteen from her and drank. A quarter remained, and while he loathed using all of it right now, Buck needed water as well. He let the horse drink straight from his palm so little was wasted.

"I'm rather tired," said Beth. "May we just sleep after I have a little privacy, first?"

"Sure," he stopped himself short of calling her sweetheart. "It's late, we're tired and hungry. I don't mind getting a head start toward tomorrow." He watched for a moment as she walked up the ravine. Wanting to respect her wishes, he focused on getting ready for the night. Nick unsaddled Buck and staked him out to a tall sagebrush. He got into bed, struggling to stay awake until Beth returned. Only after she settled in could he sleep.

The next day began cold. Neither wanted to wake, or at least Nick didn't, but the lure of food and water motivated him. He shook Beth, saying, "Rise and shine, dearest. We get to gallop for our supper today."

"Ummm," she groaned, turning to face away from him. "I'm tired."

"I know, and probably hungry too. The sooner we get started the sooner we're finished." He patted her on the arm, resisting the urge to kiss her awake. "There's some critter out there needing to wear our cook pot for lunch." He heard her stomach growl and chuckled.

Beth sat up, giving him a sleepy smile. "I suppose there's no denying that."

"Can you be ready in a few minutes?" Seeing her nod, he

continued, "All right, I'll get Buck saddled up and we'll get going."

She nodded again before packing their beds. They kept to the new routine, except without refreshment, and continued on for sixteen miles or so. Tired and hungry, neither said much. He kept an eye out for anything to hunt, seeing eagles at times, but not much else. As they drew closer to water, he'd hoped to see something substantial for maybe lunch and dinner. The green haze of vegetation in the distance gave him hope.

He felt Beth lean against his back, falling asleep. Nick smiled at her touch. After an hour or so, he spotted a herd of pronghorn grazing. He waited until the last possible moment to rouse her, not wanting to scare her with shooting an animal. "Beth, sweetheart? It's time to wake."

"Hm?" She lifted her head. "Oh! I drifted off. Please excuse me. I didn't mean to use you as a pillow."

"I didn't mind at all." He looked back at her. "I might get a chance to hunt and didn't want to scare you."

She stared past him at the foothills. "Are those deer?"

"Of a sort. More like pronghorn antelope. See the antlers?" He faced the front. "Smaller than deer."

"How do they taste?"

"Good. Not as good as bison but better than deer, I think."

"Should I be ready for a gunshot the closer we get?"

"Yes, and so should Buck. He knows what to expect when I pull my rifle. Nick stayed quiet as they approached the herd. Some of the animals started, looking at them. The more wary eased away while others went back to grazing. Nick kept an eye out for a healthy male. He slid the rife into position against his right shoulder. A perfect animal stood off at a slight distance, unconcerned about being a meal. The pronghorn foraged as Nick raised his weapon and aimed.

Buck snorted, a quiet sound but enough to catch the prey's attention. Nick tapped the horse with his right toe, warning him of the impending noise. Holding his breath, he brought the sight up in line. The animal remained still as if a lack of motion rendered him invisible. Once the small male continued eating, Nick held the aim and pulled the trigger. He felt Beth start at the noise as the animal fell to his knees.

"You got him," she said.

He grinned back at her, "You're acting as if wanting a feast."

"I do! Shall we get started?"

Nick nudged his horse forward. "Let's do. Just over that next rise is the Platte."

Both dismounted when they reached the animal's side. Nick took out a hand cloth and knife to butcher the pronghorn. "I'm not happy at having to waste so much. The bobcats and coyotes will eat well with no effort. If I'd paid more attention to what my wife did with our kills, we'd use every bit." He laid out the cloth beside the dead animal, using the knife to cut into the legs.

At first, Beth remained quiet while he stripped away the meatier parts. "Your wife hunted too?"

He laid out the slabs of antelope on the cloth. "Not often, but when she did, she was an excellent shot."

"Hm," Beth replied, lips pursed.

He glanced up at her, seeing her face and the sour expression she wore. Nick didn't want to take Beth's silent reaction as a criticism of Sally and said, "I know, it's not what a lady does, but I'm glad she had the skill."

"Of course. I'm sure her abilities were a great asset."

Her voice had an even tone now. So maybe, Nick thought, she'd just been reacting to him slicing the kill. "I agree. Hunting is something we did together and I miss it." He sat back on his heels. He'd cut almost too much for them, and yet, so much remained. He wrapped up the meat, holding it away from him as he climbed onto Buck. She followed him up to ride a quick half mile to the Platte River.

As they neared the water, the scent of damp and fish grew stronger. Their horse kept trying to trot the rest of the way there. Holding back on the reins, Nick said to Beth, "If you'll start this cooking, I can get Buck staked out. The sooner we all eat something, the better."

She slid off, taking the saddlebags and meat he handed her. Beth gave him their cooking pot from one of the bags. "Could you bring this back half full of water, please?"

"Sure." He took the offered pan and allowed Buck to gallop the short distance to the riverbank. Nick did as requested only after the animal finished drinking. He left him tethered to a sage brush, grazing, and went back to camp.

Beth still struggled to cut the meat. A bead of sweat dripped from her nose and he saw how she'd not started the fire. He both didn't want to wait to eat and didn't want to see her use so much effort. In his sternest voice, he said, "Why don't you get a drink and freshen up? I can finish this and start cooking." She nodded, standing with difficulty, he noticed, and went to the water.

Years of practice helped, and soon their food cooked over the open flame. Stretching, he went to find Beth. Nick walked down to the bank, looking both ways up and downstream. When he spotted her, Nick halted, knowing she'd not seen him approach. Beth stood beside the water, bent over, looking at the river's bed. He smiled, supposing she watched the minnows dart or maybe a crayfish scurrying across the bottom, but couldn't be sure at this distance.

The bun she kept her hair in had loosened and a French curl of a sort fell down against her shoulder. He wanted her hair to wrap around his forearm and to his elbow. The lock resembled a rich wood sanded to a silky texture. He shook his head. The woman didn't know he found her beautiful inside and out. Had he ever told her? Nick couldn't remember and resolved to fix this at the best time. A breeze carried the aroma of food and his stomach growled in response.

Not wanting to be sneaky, he took a few scuffling steps forward, intending to cause a ruckus. The water birds cried a warning, causing Beth to look up at him. She smiled a greeting at first, which faded. Something bothered her, Nick suspected, but he didn't quite know how to ask what it was. He instead decided to keep the topics safe and see if she told him on her own. "See anything down there bigger than a frog?"

"No, not really." She let her hem fall. "I like how the water is so clear."

"Figured you might." Nick watched as she stepped back.

"I suppose you have our dinner started?"

He held out his hand for her. "You figure correctly."

"I'm sorry I couldn't do more." She accepted his help up the riverbank.

"Don't be. I'm sorry I didn't send you for a drink first." Nick saw the sadness in her eyes. He needed to brighten her mood. "You've been a good traveling companion through all this and I'm grateful."

"You are?" She smiled at him as they neared their camp. "I'm the one who's been rescued. You could have gone on and left me to my own devices."

"Ha! No, I couldn't have." He sat, glancing over at Buck while Beth dished up the meals. The horse still grazed, not as intense now. Taking the plate she handed him, "Thank you. I hope it's as good as it smells."

"You're welcome." She took a bite, chewing. "Very good, but then, hunger makes a good sauce."

He laughed, "I've heard it does." They continued to eat until nothing remained. By facing the east, they didn't see the rainclouds. Not until showers began did Nick notice the approaching thunderstorms. "Hope you're in the mood for a washing."

She held out a hand to catch the drops. "I don't mind. The rain is warmer than the Platte." They cleaned the dishes in the river while the storm drenched them. When the drizzle eased, Beth said, "The water is still rather clear. But I'm not sure I want to wash so soon."

"I understand," he replied. "I'll take the chance to get cleaned up instead." He went to the saddlebags and retrieved his soap, razor, and washcloth. While walking back to the river, he saw her lead the horse to a fresh patch of grass. She must be tired, he thought, thinking he saw her eyes water. He was too, and wanted to get settled in, despite the sun still being so far above the horizon.

At the river, he stripped down to his pants. The water wasn't high enough for him to feel comfortable being nude. At least not yet. Nick would feel more secure with a lookout posted. He shaved the stubble from his face and considered what to do once reaching the group. A lot depended on what the Beth wanted. But then, he admitted, he had wants of his own. He knelt to sit in the water and paused when catching movement out of the corner of his eyes. Beth approached, gaze lowered for his modesty, he supposed. "Hello, care for a swim?"

"I should. Is it safe?"

"It is with me here." She kicked off her boots and sat to remove her socks. He watched her walk as if on a tightrope. She made her way through the brambles to the water. He almost stood to help, but she reached the riverbed before Nick could do anything. As she neared him, he said, "You could have gotten closer to the water like you did before."

Beth shook her head. "Flash floods. I don't want to lose my boots, just in case."

He watched her as she stood on the bank and scanned the

horizon. He loved everything about her. Her moss green eyes drew him in like nothing else, and he loved burying his nose in her beautiful hair at the nape of her neck. "You're beautiful, did you know?"

Startled, she stared down at him. "Oh! No, I didn't know because I'm not, but appreciate you thinking such a thing." She smiled, her chin trembling, "You're quite handsome too."

"Thank you, I'm glad you think so." He got to his feet and held out the soap. "Your turn?"

"Very well." She took the bar, just holding it.

"What is bothering you?" he asked after a moment of watching her remain motionless. "Don't tell me it's nothing because I won't believe you."

"If you want me to be honest..." At his nod, she continued, "I don't know what will happen when I see Daggart next. I'm afraid he'll think I've betrayed him." Before he could protest, she added, "He will. He'll think I've betrayed him and now can't go back to being Lizzy. I don't know what he'll do when I tell him we won't continue."

His heart broke when seeing her eyes fill with tears. "Whatever he does, I'll be there to help you. He will never hurt you again, not while I'm alive."

"I appreciate that." She sniffled, eyes still downcast. "I also ask for time to think about how I want to tell him to go on to California without me. I don't want to be a burden to anyone. If he'll let me take only what's mine, maybe I could travel with another family to Oregon Territory."

Nick saw the glow of late afternoon reflected onto her sweet face. Another family, he thought. Like pulling the hammer back on a pistol, something clicked in him. His family. He wanted her as his own, and needed to belong to her as well. He went over and stepped up onto the bank. "Whatever you need, I'm here for you."

She smiled and sobbed at the same time. "Thank you." As he wrapped his arms around her, she continued to cry, saying, "You're such a good friend. I don't know how..."

"I don't want to be a friend, Elizabeth." Nick said the words as he felt them in his soul, "I want to be your husband."

CHAPTER 16

Beth's mind and heart felt split in two. How else to describe her desire to say yes and her need to say no? "I can't marry you."

He chuckled before saying, "Yes, you can."

His amusement annoyed her. She stepped back, intending to press home her seriousness. "No, I can't and won't. Accepting your proposal is not an option."

"The hell it isn't!" He took a step closer to her, keeping his voice low and insistent. "Your marrying me is more than an option, it's a necessity."

If this had been Daggart who argued with her in such a stern manner, Beth would have been terrified of being hit. Instead, she smiled at him, glad to have him as a friend. "I don't see how."

Nicholas frowned at first before returning her smile. "Because I love you, and I think you love me."

Her insides squirmed like tadpoles in a jar because he'd said the words. She had to be honest with him. "Yes, that's true, but love isn't enough in this case."

His jaw dropped a little before he recovered to say, "Beth, there's nothing else. We make a good team in a lot of ways." Nicholas crossed his arms. "Bartlett's not an issue, or won't be once I'm done with him, and marrying you is the practical thing to do."

"Practical?" Beth narrowed her eyes at him, wondering why the love talk was over.

"Of course. We've been out here long enough. People will suspect what's happened, and it did, so I might as well make an honest woman of you and marry."

"What about Sally?" She saw the flash of pain cross his face and knew the answer. Sally held his heart. Beth never would.

"She...is gone. I've mourned her for a long time and always will." He shrugged, "But that doesn't mean I can't or don't love you."

Beth crossed her arms for warmth in the cooling air.

Considering how easily he claimed to care for her, she wanted to believe his words as much as he did. Yet, fear held her back from accepting his proposal. "I love you as well. Give me time to consider what I want for my future, and I'll give you an answer when we reach the others."

"Fair enough. I can wait." He went to where his shirt draped over some brush.

Nicholas's bare torso distracted her as did his damp pants clinging to his legs. She looked out into the fading light and suppressed a sigh. To go a lifetime without love seemed unbearable, but the notion of being with any other man felt intolerable to her as well. She glanced at him as he rifled through the saddlebag. Had he felt the same the first time they lay together? That he'd betrayed Sally and sullied their love?

He interrupted her thoughts by holding out blankets to her, asking, "I'm wondering if we should bother with a fire tonight."

She unwrapped her bedding from him, checking for damp. "Maybe not. The bedrolls are mostly dry."

"Sounds like we're set." He smiled at her, his eyes sad. "Let's bunk down and see what tomorrow brings."

"Maybe I'll come to my senses?" she teased.

"I can only hope."

The next morning progressed as usual. She knew enough about bears to consider Nicholas behaving as one today. He didn't say much at breakfast and even less as they traveled. The food and water refreshing her must have done little for him. A few attempts at lightening his mood later, Beth decided to let him have his demeanor.

A line of rocks buried like a monster's backbone loomed ahead for most of the morning and behind them in the early afternoon. They skirted Emigrant Pass and passed so many springs, she couldn't keep the names straight. They saw a large crowd camping at Willow Springs but Nicholas never slowed, letting the horse walk past everyone. She wanted to hug him in gratitude. Other men might have made her go along into the middle of everything, exactly what she hated. "Thank you," she said close to his shoulder.

He looked back at her, lips near hers. "You're welcome. I'd like to go a little further than usual for midday. If we get to

Independence Rock before dark, I can guess where Sam and the men are by now."

Beth didn't know what else to say. Lingering behind the group all the way to Oregon, having Nicholas to herself sounded like heaven. Not, however, if she shared him with Sally's memory. He'd not mentioned much of her before rescuing Beth. Maybe them being alone and intimate had reminded him of how much he loved his former wife. "How close are we to them?"

"That's tough to call. Everything depends on how long they spent stopped at any one place. Most stay at Independence Rock a few days if they get there before July 4th."

"We're close to the rock ourselves though?"

"Yes, very. Keeping our noontime short and riding into the late evening, we can reach there just before dark." He paused before asking, "Did you want to press on or hang back a little?"

"Press on, please," she replied and saw him nod as he nudged the horse into a faster walk. A couple of hours later, her stomach growled and he laughed. He slowed Buck's pace and dug around for leftovers. She ate the sweet biscuit he offered and used canteen water to wash it down.

"There it is. If you need to, we can stop before we get there." She shook her head and he pointed toward the southeast. "There's always a lot of people there. I wouldn't ask you to go with me except I'd prefer to not leave you alone. Plus, I need to check when Sam and our company passed by here. With any luck, the group stayed a few days knowing we'd be right behind."

"Don't worry, I can go. It's nice you thought of me." She looked up at the late afternoon sky. She'd worked hard today to resist asking him about Sally. Enough time for thought had passed that Beth didn't want to hear how wonderful the other woman had been. Daggart gave enough lectures about Lizzy since her death. Nicholas was sure to do the same. The sadness in Nicholas's eyes at the mention of his wife reminded Beth of why she must refuse his offer. Better for her to marry any other widower than him. Accepting Nicholas's proposal meant longing for a man who'd never give her all his heart. At least if she married another widower, they'd be each other's second choice.

Independence Rock appeared to be a lot closer than it was. The time seemed slow and their destination more distant than when they'd first noticed the landmark. "Does it usually take so long to reach the camp there?"

Nicholas laughed. "Yes, always. I'm anxious too."

She rested her forehead against his back in frustration. "If I could be certain of staying seated, I'd ask to gallop."

"We'll be there before too much longer." He patted her leg. "Did you want to stop for a drink or rest?"

"I do, but no. Let's just get to fresh water and tonight's camp." Beth looked forward to being around other people, even if it meant more noise and crowding. She looked at Nicholas, reluctant to share his attentions with anyone else. Once united with his men and Amelia... She sighed, not wanting to think any more.

"We'll beat the sunset, I promise."

True to his word, she noticed Independence Rock eventually loomed large. She saw people going about their business. "Where will we sleep tonight? Every spot seems taken."

"We'll go out of the way. Most people won't backtrack for anything."

"Thank you," she said, squeezing his arm for emphasis.

Nicholas glanced back at her, grinning. "You're very welcome. Also, I'm very selfish like that. You'll be all mine tonight."

"I don't know..." she stammered, leaning away from him. Beth knew she might have been too forward in touching his arm.

"We're friends, correct?"

Had she heard a little clip to his tone? "Yes we are, and can spend the night together, but not quite together." She waited for a reply, but he didn't respond for a long while.

Nudging the horse into a fast walk, he said, "I'm eager to find Sam's message. So, when we get there, could you please lead Buck to the water and maybe some grass."

"Of course." Beth examined the ground passing underneath them. She hoped better grazing lay past the Rock and closer to the river. A few minutes passed until the smell of cooking, cattle, and people overpowered the light scent of sage. "How do you know where to find the message in all this?"

"Sam and I have a place we like. It's out of the way, where people usually have to pay young men to climb."

"Isn't getting up there dangerous?"

He helped steady her as Beth slid off the horse. "A little for me, a lot if a person is reckless. But I'm not."

"I'm glad and will see to Buck while you find your secret

message." She waited until he dismounted. "Please be careful."

He grinned, chiding her, "Why, Miss Roberts, I'm beginning to suspect you like me. Let's meet here later." With a tip of his hat to her, he walked towards Independence Rock, now a huge wall of stone in front of him.

Beth wanted to watch him climb but Buck stamped at the ground, distracting her. "Let's go, boy." She led him past various campsites. He picked up the pace, pulling her to the river. She smiled at the beast's impatience. The animal stopped hard at the water's edge and nosed down to drink. While Buck kept busy, she searched for Nick and spotted him near the top. Fear froze her in place. If he fell from that height, Beth knew he'd not survive. She turned away from the monolith and back to the serene horse. He'd reassured her, but still, accidents followed no schedule. Beth couldn't imagine her grief if he lost his grip on the rock and died. For a brief instant, she shared a taste of the pain both Nicholas and Daggart held every day.

She swallowed back the lump forming in her throat. Imagining a world without him tempted her into accepting any condition he'd place on their relationship. Beth shook her head, knowing being Nicholas's consolation prize in life wouldn't be enough for her. She turned to scan the stone for him but didn't see him. Had he already fallen and she'd not noticed? Terror gripped her. She took a deep breath, forcing herself to be calm and look for him again.

Panic set in when she didn't see him, and she focused on the rock surface to keep the fear at bay. Time stretched like hot taffy during her search. Each flicker of movement caught Beth's attention until she saw it wasn't Nicholas and dismissed the motion to resume scanning for him.

"Interesting, huh?" said Nicholas in her ear.

He startled her with his proximity. She'd been searching so hard for him at a distance she'd not seen him approach. Relief filled her and she hugged him tight. "You made it! I'm so glad you didn't fall!"

"Me, too." He snuggled into her, adding, "They're one, maybe two days ahead of us."

"Is that good?" She slipped from his arms when Buck nuzzled her back.

"Yes. We'll catch up, get your belongings, and settle this mess of who you're married to once and for all." He took the reins from her hands. "We can eat, maybe visit with others around here, and sleep, then start fresh in the morning." He stopped at a spot close to the water but not so near anyone else. "We don't have a lot of daylight left. Would you like to freshen up first? Maybe I can trade for some meat to go with the rice."

"Very well, I'll take the opportunity. Is there anything else I can help you with in the meantime?"

"No, not until you're done at the river. "I'd like for you to wash up before dark."

"I will, and thank you." Beth pulled down saddlebags from Buck's back while Nicholas unsaddled him. He walked away with a wave, and she tied off their horse for the night. Finding the soap, Nicholas's hand cloth, the cook pot, and the canteen, she went to the water.

Certain the spot she'd picked was well enough away from anyone else and she could see the riverbed, Beth took off her shoes and socks. She left everything but the canteen on the bank and strolled out to the middle of the river. She dumped out the stale water before filling the flask and drinking. Sweetwater lived up to its name. A few more gulps later, she refilled the container, capped it, and went to the bank. The sky grew ever darker, Beth noticed, so she hurried to wash herself. When she was as clean as a person could be while still dressed, she filled the cook pot half way for dinner. One hand held the water steady and with the other she held her boots stuffed full with socks, soap, and hand towel.

Nicholas still hadn't returned to their scant camp. Buck and the belongings remained just where he'd left them. Beth searched the gloaming to see if he approached. So many people loomed around the river that he must have found others he knew.

Hungry, she started a fire, letting it build while mixing up beans and rice. She took the time while the food cooked to set out their bedding for the night. Dinner smelled good, especially after the respite she'd had in eating it. Beth looked at the saddlebags. She wanted to read his Bible and reached for the book until remembering the picture of Sally lay between the pages. Was it the only one, she wondered? There had to be more. Beth shook her head. She had no need to see any more proof of how wrong Nicholas was for her. Impatient to get the day done, she dished up and ate her meal. He hadn't returned by her last bite. Beth sighed, placing his plate over the pan in case he wanted it later. She felt full and weary and laid down. A few blinks and she fell asleep.

Beth woke shivering in the predawn light. She sat up with a start and looked for Nicholas. He slept in his own bed, and she smiled when hearing his soft snore. She saw the clean dishes and knew he'd eaten. She settled back under the blanket and hoped to sleep. The cold seeped into her bones, chilling her too much to rest. The sky lightened enough to keep her awake, and she decided to get started on the day. She kindled the fire, enjoying the heat. Coffee sounded even better, so she took a quick trip to get water. Once the cook pot sat on the embers and she'd thrown in a few coffee beans, Beth began mixing biscuit dough in a cup.

In a short while, the rich smell of breakfast competed with the wet aroma of the sagebrush covered in morning dew. Nicholas sat up, rubbing his eyes like a little boy. "Good morning. Is it ready?"

She smiled at how drowsy he sounded. "Almost."

He got to his feet. "I'll see to the horse."

"This will be ready soon."

He nodded an assent and walked away. They shared a cup when he returned and then ate without much talk. Both used to the routine, they made quick work of cleaning and packing up the few belongings. Buck began a brisk walk at his owner's urging. After a while, Nicholas said, "I'm looking forward to tomorrow night. My bet is on us finding everyone else by then."

"I've been keeping a watch along the way for my trunk, in case Daggart discarded it like he discarded me." At Beth's admission, Nicholas reached back and patted her leg. She leaned against him in a silent thank you. His warmth in the morning chill made her sleepy and she yawned. She sat up and focused on the open landscape, intent on staying awake and not falling off the horse while asleep. Air and distance gave the rolling hills a blue haze, while the bright green shrubs offset the white seed heads of the prairie grass. She smiled at how the hills closest to them looked like a loaf of bread baking in the sun. Only, this loaf had a section cut out as if God himself wielded the knife. She pointed out the landmark to Nicholas. "Will we be going through that particular pass?"

"We can, but I don't think you'd care to ride through Devil's Gate. It's a channel for the river."

"That's the name of it?" she asked and continued after his nod, "Oh, then no, we won't."

Still grinning, he looked back at her. "We can walk around and even up to it. There's a pool on the other side. Shallow, sandy, but nice. You'll get a good look without having to get in the river itself."

"Your plan is much more pleasant. Let's do that."

Nicholas laughed at her answering the question before he'd had a chance to ask. "Yes, ma'am."

They walked on, skirting the Gate. Others, some pushing carts, already took advantage of the water at the south side. He continued on a little ways, passing the crowds. Beth gave his arm a squeeze. They resumed after a quick stop for drinks and to stretch their legs.

The trio hugged the Sweetwater River as the route eased from southwest to straight west in direction. The sun shone so bright, it whitened the sky to blinding. The snow in the higher parts of the low mountains to the west of them surprised her. She speculated that must be why the stiff breeze blew so cold from that direction. The low, granite hills shimmered in the late morning sun. Every so often a warmed crosswind seemed to thaw her. She wanted to stop for noon but preferred waiting until Nicholas found something to hunt.

The abundant pronghorn compelled them to wait. Nicholas pulled Buck up short, seeing a herd to the right. He pointed to the west. "Did you enjoy the antelope from yesterday?"

Following his direction, she smiled as she saw the herd grazing in the distance. "Yes, so when you have the chance, please do."

He withdrew his rifle from the holster and took aim. She felt him tap the horse in a warning, leveling the weapon. Both seemed to hold their breath. She heard him whisper, "One, two," and the loud blast of the gun. In a couple of seconds, the animal he sighted dropped dead.

The herd scattered as Beth exclaimed, "Good shot!"

"Thank you, ma'am. I hope you wanted antelope for dinner."

"I did, very much." She waited until he secured the rifle and then leaned forward, wrapping her arms around him. "How soon can we eat?"

"As soon as we get there." He nudged the horse into a gallop. She hopped off first, him following when they reached the animal. "I'll cut what I can. We'll ride back closer to Sweetwater for camp."

She nodded, not squeamish, but still not wanting to watch him gut their hunt. "We're rather low on everything. Dinner might be all meat and some coffee."

"Do we have enough for tomorrow morning?"

"Yes, but only just."

"We can skip coffee this evening and make up what's left of the flour for tomorrow." He cut more of the flank. "That way, we can leave out early and catch up sooner."

She nodded. "I might take Buck back to the river, if you can carry everything."

"Yes, leave me the cook pot." She placed the pan next to him and he put the cut meat into it. "Thank you, I can use this while you get us some water."

"Very well." She left, leading Buck a couple of hundred yards back to the river. She eased to the water's edge to let the horse drink. While the horse drank, she checked if Nicholas could see her. His back was to them as he continued to butcher the antelope. Counting on his distraction, she removed her dress while still wearing her underclothes and began washing her bodice. She took the chance to rinse her lower skirt as much as she could without getting in herself. After wringing out the water, she spread her dress out to dry. Her underclothes, though thin, still kept her decent, so she took Buck back to their new camp a little ways up the bank. She cared for the horse, and just as she finished staking out Buck, Nicholas returned with a pot full of meat. She felt guilty for not fetching water or starting a fire. "The task didn't take you very long."

His easy grin reassured her. "I've had practice." He knelt, digging around in his saddlebags for his flint kit. Once a small flame burned, Nicholas stood. "If you don't mind, I can get the water while I'm taking my turn to clean up. I feel like my mouth is coated with dust."

She walked with him to the river's edge. "Don't worry about supper. I'll bring back the water and get it started while you're washing."

He pulled off his boots, leaving on his socks. While shrugging off his shirt, he stretched, saying, "You could help me bathe." He grinned at her while undoing his pants.

Beth's cheeks burned. His offer tempted, but she shook her head. "Maybe I will wait until you return."

He laughed. "If you must. Otherwise, feel free to join me."

She took the chance to fill both of their cups. Beth eased her way back to camp, minding every drop. Her face still hot, she very much wanted to join him, but her stomach growled. First food, and later maybe something else. She cut up the meat so it would cook tender, adding rice, the water, and a little bit of salt. Satisfied with dinner simmering, she began setting up their beds.

Beth heard him approach after a while and turned to make sure. His dark hair turned black with dampness brought out the steel blue of his eyes.

He spread his shirt out over a nearby sagebrush. "Smells good."

She dished him up a plate of meat. "Try this and see if you think it's finished. The rice is still cooking. It's too chewy."

"I'm hungry enough to not care." He settled in beside her and took a bite, nodding. "Very good. We should keep a herd of antelope with us always for just this reason."

"Thank you." She ate a bite, her breath catching when she glanced at him. Nicholas stared at her, desire in his eyes. Beth's face heated and she stirred their food as if doing so would make the rice cook any faster. She shared his need but focused on their dinner as she heard him move closer to her. Seeing him without his shirt distracted her from everything.

He moved behind her and leaned in against her back, putting a hand on Beth's shoulder. Nicholas caressed down to where her hand led the spoon. "I think this will do fine on its own." Moving the pan a little away from the fire, he added, "Now, where was I? Ah, yes." His lips pressed against her neck, under Beth's earlobe.

She leaned into his kiss. "I don't know if we should."

"I do, and I'm tired of waiting." He wrapped his arms around her, holding her tight.

Her skin tingled through the thin undergarment, feeling his bare chest warming her back like the flames warmed her front. "We're so close to everyone."

"I'm trying to care about them, I am." He moved to her side, pulling her onto him and away from the fire. "But right now, I want to kiss you so much, I can't think of anything else."

She braced herself against him, hands resting on the ground above his shoulders. How odd to think passersby might suppose she had him trapped. Beth felt how ready he was for her and shivered. "I've tried to remember what I must do as well. This might not be wise." He felt so inviting, her slip and his pants the only fabric between them. "Just a kiss or two couldn't hurt," she whispered.

Nicholas held her head with both hands, kissing her so her toes curled. Oh Lord, she thought, what had she just allowed? Just their lips meeting felt so good, it had to be wrong. She struggled to stay coherent by remembering Nicholas's prediction. Tomorrow, they'd reach Daggart and the others. She'd retrieve her belongings, maybe have enough to reach Oregon by herself. Maybe once there she'd find a widower willing to marry her. A sharp sound of fabric ripping caught her attention.

"Beth! I'm so sorry!" Nicholas's hand rested on her upper arm, her undergarment torn at her cleavage where he'd tried to ease down the material. "I just wanted...I'm sorry, sweetheart."

She sat upright, smiling at his remorseful expression. Beth loved him so very much and this might be the last night for them to be truly alone. "I can fix this." A quick glance around reassured her no one else lurked close by. Satisfied of their privacy, she lifted the back of the shift, bringing it over her head and forward. She slipped her arms out and held the garment in front of her. "This might be better for you and my clothing."

He also sat up, letting her legs continue to straddle his hips. "I agree, but...." Nicholas caressed her bared upper arms and shoulders. "It's still pretty light out here, I don't know...."

His lips forming words tempted her so much, she kissed him with a feather light touch. "We can cover with a blanket. I don't care. I need you."

He nuzzled her neck while blindly reaching for the other blankets to create one bed. Nicholas used his foot to get the far end beside them as well before leaning back, pulling her with him. He held her secure, rolling over to where she lay on the bottom. Beth laughed at his actions. He asked, "Is this all right with you?"

"Very, thank you."

Nicholas covered them both with her blanket, letting it settle around his shoulders and slide down to his middle back. He sheltered her chest with his, hiding her from even his own gaze. He nestled closer and kissed her neck, behind her ear, and moved to her mouth.

Her body ached for him. She spread her knees a little to allow him nearer, sharing his sentiment when hearing his pained groan. She opened her eyes, ending their kiss. When he looked at her, Beth asked, "How about I help you out of those constricting trousers?"

"Please do." He lifted his hips from hers. "Does this help?"

She smiled at him in answer, undoing the belt and buttons, sliding down his pants until his hardness caught the waistband. Beth felt shy touching him there and knew how silly she was. She'd touched him much more intimately than this. She reached in and held him. He felt like an iron bar wrapped in the silkiest material. Surprised at how something so hard could be so soft, she looked up into his eyes. He frowned as if in pain. "Does that hurt?"

He rested his forehead against her shoulder, gasping, "No. Feels too good to be true."

She smiled, enjoying the power her touch held over him. "I might have to help you inside me."

"Please."

"Kiss me?" she asked and he answered with a harsh meeting of their lips, as if he intended to mark her as his forever. He pulled back, pressing the tip of his tongue against her lips, parting them as he pressed his hardness into her. Both projections overwhelmed Beth with the sensation. She groaned, the pleasure unexpected and too much. Remembering their last time together, she wrapped one leg, then the other, around his waist. The action allowed him deeper access into her.

Nicholas pulled his mouth from hers to say, "Damn it woman, you don't make this easy." He lifted from elbows to hands. He resumed his easy thrusts into her. Cupping a breast, he said, "How did I resist you all this time? I can't imagine leaving you alone ever again." He lowered to rest on his left elbow, his right hand still holding her so intimately, and his thumb caressing her nipple.

Beth held onto his shoulders, sliding her hands down to his upper arms. One bicep hard, holding his weight, the other soft as he caressed her, sending ripples of gratification throughout her body. Each movement of his pushed her closer to the release. As he eased to rest on both elbows, his lips reaching hers, she stifled a gasp. Beth wanted him to move lower, kissing where his thumb had touched her nipple. The thought of him doing so thrilled her more. She wrapped her arms around him, lost in the lovemaking.

His breathing became faster, each exhale almost a moan in her ear. "I can't keep going like this." His lips pressed against her skin, Nicholas said, "Slide your hands and feet lower on my body."

The request intrigued her. Was this his attempt to make their union better, and if so, how could such a thing be possible? Yet, Beth complied, her level of tension kept constant by his relentless thrusting. She didn't notice her feet reaching his calves so much as when her hands touched his lower back. Beth stopped, feeling his hips under her fingers.

"Yes!" Nicholas gasped before adding, "No, no. Just...lower."

She complied by lifting her shoulders a little to reach further down his body. Upon feeling his muscles providing the momentum, the string holding her passion at bay snapped. Her fingernails dug into his flesh before she could help herself. "Nicholas! More! Harder! Love me, please love me!"

He gave a strangled cry and she felt his own pleasure adding to hers. The summit they reached seemed unbearable with the rapture between them. Beth clung to him as much as he did her, their bodies rigid with the mutual release.

Several minutes passed before their heartbeats slowed. He relaxed a little, letting his body rest against hers. "Do you want more?"

Beth felt the desire in him filling her and replied, "I don't know. There can't be more."

"There is." He scooped up her leg so the back of her knee rested in the crook of his arm. "I can't last for long this time," he said as he began moving inside her.

"We could do this again?" she asked, seeing him frown as if in pain. His expression and her leg being pulled so wide for his entry felt amazing. Unable to reach his lower back again, Beth settled for burying her fingers in his hair. She pulled his face closer, kissing him. Beth moaned as his tongue raked her teeth. In a move she considered bold, she touched his tongue with her own. He shivered and she suppressed a smile at his pleasure. Beth wondered how much control Nicholas had over his own release. She wanted to tease him and lifted her hips repeatedly to meet his every thrust.

His words always brought on her satisfaction. Maybe hers could hasten his as well. She broke the kiss to whisper in his ear. "I didn't know a man could be so, so much, before you." A hard pant escaped her at his sudden thrust. "I'd only ever seen stallions so large."

He cried out, "No!" and pressed his lips against her forehead. Muffled, he stopped moving while his body tensed. "Damn, Elizabeth! I can't."

His agony delighted her more than she'd thought. "I don't want to hurt you. Just please you."

"That's the problem. I'm too pleased."

She ran her palms up and down his body. "You feel just right to me."

He let go of her leg and rose to his elbows to look down at her. "So beautiful, loving me like this." He closed his eyes, letting his head drop. "I can't see you like this without losing control. You're my fever and only this will cure me." He lifted his chin, staring into her eyes. "I can think of a future remedy I'd like to try."

The idea of another episode like this thrilled Beth. "A future remedy?"

"One where I kiss every inch of your body." He withdrew and pressed into her a little harder than before. "Even here."

The very idea of a touch so unimagined shocked her. His kiss, there? Nicholas resumed his movements as a rush of pleasure cascaded through Beth. Each pulse through her body was more intense than the one before it. This time, she was unable to say anything, so she just held him tight and panted wordlessly with his every stroke.

"That's my girl. That's what I want." He wrapped his arms under her. "You want me to kiss you everywhere, don't you?"

"Yes!" Recovered a little, she added, "I want to do the same. Kiss you everywhere."

"Do you...?"

"Everywhere, every inch," she said and smiled when he responded with a shudder. Beth felt an impending release building in his every muscle. She wanted to shove him over the edge like he had her. "Please let me kiss you there."

He gave a strangled cry, body tensed. "So good." His every movement made as if under duress, at last he melted against her.

After catching his breath a little, he said, "Every time we're done, I think nothing can ever be as good. And the next time we're together, you prove me wrong."

She kissed his neck. "Likewise, sir."

Raising so his weight rested on his hands, he asked, "Are you hungry?"

"Starving and not for you this time." She grinned at his chuckle. "I can warm up our food while you settle in Buck for the night."

"I might get dressed first."

Beth laughed at the thought of him running around with pants around his ankles. As he fastened his trousers, she said, "At least you weren't too naked."

He reached over to retrieve and hand Beth her slip. "Between my clothes and your shoes, we're almost fully clothed."

She looked at her feet, still wearing her boots. Had they really been together and she'd been fully shod? Her face heated to an unbearable degree. "I wasn't aware..."

Kneeling in front of her, he said, "I'm glad. It shows me our passion is mutual." Nicholas stood. "Caring for our animal is first, dinner second."

Beth nodded at his retreating form. She shook herself from a sleepy daze and pulled on her slip before poking at the fire. A few flames flared, and she pushed the cooling food back in to warm. She shivered, her body still tingling from their act.

Being together this way hadn't been ideal. She loved him more each time they were intimate. Living without him had been difficult to imagine in the beginning, unbearable now, and would be impossible if they continued. She busied herself with the food, not wanting to think about tomorrow. She dished out their remaining dinner as he strolled up, sitting beside her.

He held up the canteen. "I've brought fresh water. It's the finest wine this country has to offer."

She took a drink and replied, "This is very good, but could be any sort of wine and I couldn't guess at the quality."

He took a bite and swallowed. "You've never had wine?"

"No." Beth gave him back the canteen. "Not unless you include overripe fruit sometimes."

"I'll have to introduce you to the taste when we get home."

"Oh?" His assumptions and cheerful expression hurt. She

looked away, unhappy he continued to ignore her decision.

"It's a treat when we indulge, especially at Christmas and New Years."

Her food lost its taste. "The holidays seem very far from now," she managed to say before forcing herself to eat one last bite.

"Now they do, but before you know it, we'll be knee deep in snow." He looked from the fire to her and caressed her face. "I'm already looking forward to winter nights with you." She choked at his words, and he asked, "Are you alright?"

After gulping down water, she answered him, "Yes, I'm fine. I just don't know what will happen in the future."

Patting her back, he reassured her, "No one does, but I'm certain we'll be married soon after reaching the others."

Beth shook her head, regaining her voice with a final cough. "We won't be married at all."

Nicholas laughed. "You sound as if you're certain and you can't be. We'll most likely be married by this time tomorrow."

"No, we won't." The effort to say the words aloud hurt her as if she had a physical pain. She pressed on, hoping to make him understand. "I will not marry you, not now, not ever."

"Good Lord." He stood. "I think you're serious."

She gathered the plates and also stood. "I am very serious." Beth glanced away when seeing the hurt in his face. She refused to let her feelings and sympathy sway her decision. "I won't marry you, so please don't ask again."

"Is it just me in particular, or marriage in general?"

The upset in his voice pierced her heart. She wanted to hold him and agree to anything he suggested no matter how much it harmed her later. "I don't think I should answer."

"So it is me, then." He looked west at the horizon. "Have I done something wrong?"

"No." Beth put the dishes near the fire, unhappy at having to wash them tomorrow. "You've done nothing wrong."

"No? This is illogical." He took her by the shoulders, far more gently than Daggart ever did. "Every time we make love convinces me that we belong together. I can't imagine anyone else I'd rather have in my life than you."

"Yes, you can." She paused before staring into his eyes. "You can imagine Sally."

He released Beth, running a hand through his hair in frustration. "She's not here."

Any weakness she might have had vanished with his answer. His words confirmed in her mind what she already thought. "And you love me only because I am?"

He laughed without humor. "You being here is a large part of it, yes. Otherwise, I'd find it very difficult to love you."

She shook her head. Nicholas loved Sally despite the circumstances, while his feelings for Beth were circumstantial. She seemed doomed to always fill the shoes of a deceased wife. "I absolutely will not marry you, Nicholas. Not now, not ever. I plan on marrying someone else when we arrive, saying you were the perfect gentleman. I'll tell them you believed I was married to someone else and respected me."

"You are not married to Bartlett and you will not marry anyone else but me." He ground out between gritted teeth, "Not now, not ever."

His order angered her and Beth put her hands on her hips, close to raising her voice. "Again, I will marry someone else, anyone else suitable for me." She searched her memory for someone they knew to be a widower. "Mr. Calhoon, maybe. He's still grieving but might need help with the children."

"Calhoon?" Nicholas squinted, each word enunciated from fury. "Have you even spoken to him? Touched him like you have me?"

His suggestion shocked and repulsed Beth. "Goodness no! I've chatted with him in passing, but never…not like with you, no."

He crossed his arms, a smug expression on his face. "And yet you prefer him to me?"

No, she preferred no one in this world to him. Unlike how he preferred her because Sally was dead. "Yes, I do want him, and will marry him if he'll have me."

Letting his arms fall to his side as if in defeat, he stated, "Tell me why and I'll abide by your decision."

The sadness displayed in Nicholas's expression upset her too. Beth tried to think of how best to tell him her plan. "Mr. Calhoon is a fine man who needs a woman to help his family. With being a replacement wife to first Daggart and then you, I'd prefer to go on and be a replacement wife to him."

"A replacement wife is what you'd call yourself?"

"Yes." She waited for him to say more. When he remained silent, Beth continued. "Mr. Calhoon is my second choice for a husband, which, from what I've learned, is what I need. That way, we're both a consolation prize in our marriage."

"This is assuming Calhoon is interested in a second wife. And assuming I'll let you marry him at all, which won't happen."

She smiled a little, knowing he wasn't as much the boss of her as he thought. "You don't have a choice."

"I'm beginning to believe you." He straightened out their rumpled bedrolls. "What I don't understand is how you love me, yet are willing to marry anyone else."

Beth shook her head and had to argue with him, "Not just anyone else."

His eyes narrowed. "But not me."

"No, Nicholas, not you. I refuse to marry you because you're my first love and I'm not yours. I've been down this path and refuse to live a life in love with a man who's using me as a bookmark in his life."

"My loving you doesn't matter?"

"It does, yes." She saw the triumphant expression in his face and had to continue, "But not enough for a lifetime together."

He had their beds fixed by now and lay in his. "I don't think you're being very rational. I can't undo the past. I can't stop loving Sally just because you're jealous."

"Excuse me? I'm not jealous." Beth sat to remove her shoes and socks. Knowing she lied, she had to confess. "All right, yes, I'm jealous, but not of her specifically."

"Oh?" He held open her bed so Beth could slide between the covers.

She lay face up, looking at the night sky. "I'm jealous that I'll never be your first love, the one you love more than anyone else."

After a moment, he said, "I can't change my history."

"I know." She heard him lie down and get comfortable in his own bed. Beth wondered if he'd want a good night from her now.

"I still love and want to marry you."

She paused; wanting to trust him, believe he'd love her for herself. "I know you think that."

"I think I love you?" He shook his head. "I'm glad you admit that much." Nicholas thought for a moment before saying, "We have an interesting day tomorrow. I suggest we get some sleep."

Beth didn't reply but stared into the dying fire for a long while, unable to relax. The too quiet breathing of her companion told her Nicholas was awake as well. At long last she whispered, "I do adore you."

"Good night, Elizabeth."

She opened her eyes to the smell of coffee. Seeing Nicholas sitting across the fire, Beth sat. "Good morning."

"Good morning. We'll need to skip breakfast and get an early start. I'm impatient to reach the others."

"I understand."

"You don't seem to, but will soon." He held out her full cup. "We'll leave when you're finished drinking this."

"Should I hurry?"

He sighed, "Don't scald yourself but don't stall, either. Mr. Calhoon might not like to be kept waiting, even if he doesn't know it."

"He doesn't know, not yet." Beth watched as he rolled up his bedding, saddled Buck, and brought over her dry dress. "Thank you." He nodded an acknowledgement and she blew on her coffee to cool it faster. Their time together grew ever shorter. She hesitated to do anything to hasten their departure, but her need to settle things with Daggart propelled her forward.

Beth drained her cup and shrugged into her dress. She carried the two items to the river. Catching sight of him leading Buck to the water, she felt a lump rose in her throat. She loved him, loved the smallest glimpse of him. Tears threatened to spill. Doubt crept into her mind. Was living a life without him better than living a life as a replacement, she wondered. How long would they have before he realized she could never be his Sally? Beth wiped the tears from her face in a hurry before he caught her crying. She'd made her decision and it was the right one for them. Nicholas needed a woman who pined for her first love as well, not her.

He turned to her as she approached. "Ready? So am I, so let's get going. The sooner we find the others, the sooner we can have Sam fix us something to eat." They did the near dance of getting on Buck and started west.

Neither talked and Beth enjoyed the silence. She wanted to hold him this last time. If the group traveled as close as Nicholas speculated, she thought better of arriving in an intimate embrace.

The sun-warmed smell of his shirt and skin enticed her to press her lips against his shoulder just to smell his skin. With temptation this close to her, the miles crept past as if they raced snails and turtles.

"I see them!" Nicholas leaned over so Beth could see as well. "Right there! We'll be caught up by dinner, maybe even mid afternoon."

"Good."

"It will be. I want this settled once and for all."

"So do I."

Giving her a glare, he turned to the west. "In fact, hold on and I'll see how fast Buck wants to go."

"I don't know if that's—" she managed to say before he nudged the horse into a slow gallop. She hollered "Whoa!" and grabbed Nicholas around the waist when Buck lunged forward.

He laughed and nudged his horse into a faster pace. "I warned you."

The speed blinded her. Had she ever gone so fast in her life, she wondered. Beth held tight, the ride somewhat smooth but unsettling. "How far?" she managed to holler out at him.

"A couple of miles! Are you doing well? Shall I slow us?"

"No, keep going." She grit her teeth and held tighter as he laughed.

"That's my girl!"

Beth almost started arguing about being his anything but decided to show versus telling him yet again. War whoops from the Granville men Lucky and Chuck caused her to open her eyes. Nicholas slowed Buck to a slow gallop then fast walk as the duo reached them. She let go of him as everyone began talking at once. The noise and attention as the men gathered their horses around overwhelmed her.

Mr. Lucky spoke the loudest and fastest. "We're almost to Split Rock and didn't know if you'd catch up by then."

"Who's going to lose the most money with us arriving now?" Nicholas asked.

"We didn't bet nothing," Chuck said.

Nicholas laughed, asking, "How much?"

Lucky glanced at the other man as they both flanked the couple. "Maybe Claude might lose a little bit. He'd bet on you reaching us at Independence Rock. Everyone else bet later if you found her alive." He tipped his hat at Beth. "Everyone will be rightly pleased to see you so sound, ma'am."

"Thank you, I'm glad." She caught the look passing between him and Chuck, wondering at its meaning. "How is Mr. Bartlett?"

Lucky stared at his boots and muttered, "I don't know if that's something you'll want to know, ma'am. We're not quite sure how he is at the moment."

She didn't like how uncomfortable both of the men seemed to be. An odd feeling of foreboding crept over her. "Why not?"

Chuck replied, "Because he's gone."

Beth's blood seemed to drain from her body. Had Daggart died in her absence? She swallowed and croaked out, "Gone?"

Lawrence punched the other man on the arm in disapproval. "Oh, not very gone, ma'am, not at all! Or at least not gone like we thought you were."

As he gave a massaging rub to his bicep, Chuck added, "He traded everything for a horse."

Lucky added, "The day Mr. Granville left, Bartlett said he needed a faster way to California. So Mr. Sam made him a deal, a horse and provisions for everything else Bartlett owned."

"So he's not dead, ma'am," Chuck finished.

"Mr. Granville owns my belongings?" Beth bit her lip, unable to think of a solution to her problems. She didn't know if Calhoon would not only marry her but also give her the money to buy back her family heirlooms.

The two looked at Nicholas before Lawrence replied, "I'm sure he'd share with you, or something, ma'am. I mean, we're all still wearing the socks you made us. Maybe you could have a bargain or something."

"Maybe so." She sighed, scared and frustrated at the mess Daggart left her. "I'll have to think about this for a while."

"Sure, ma'am," Chuck said, taking off his hat and twisting it in his hands.

Lawrence tugged at the bandana around his neck. "We're real glad you're alive. The way Mr. Nick took off and Mr. Daggart's trading, well, we're just glad."

"Thank you." She didn't know what else to say, upset by her brother-in-law's abrupt leaving and the fact she only owned what she wore. Beth glanced at Nicholas. She had a sudden urge to marry him for the security he provided, even if she never measured up to Sally's memory.

Nicholas leaned in as if knowing her thoughts and said, "I have a solution for you, Miss Roberts."

She could say yes, Beth knew, and trade one set of problems for another. "No." The answer left her like a curse word. She shook her head. "My answer will always be no."

"All right." He waved a few seconds later as Samuel approached.

"You found her!" Granville hollered as soon as within earshot. He galloped to them, swinging off his horse and running to them. "Get down here and let me see you."

Nicholas held out his hand for her and she swung off the horse. Before she could turn to him, Samuel had her in a bear hug and Beth croaked out, "Oh goodness, Mr. Granville!"

Giving her an extra squeeze, he held her at arm's length and said, "Don't Mr. me young lady, I'm Sam to you, now. You heard about Bartlett?" At her nod in assent, he went on, "And about his deal with me?"

"A little. You own everything of mine?"

"Until now, yes. Consider me keeping it safe until your return."

"You didn't know I'd return."

He hugged her again, squishing the breath from Beth. "I didn't but am glad Nick found you." To the three others watching them, he said, "We'll walk, you all can go ahead. The poor girl needs me to catch her up on everything."

Nicholas stated, "She can ride with me."

Appealing to Samuel, she said, "I'd rather walk, if you don't mind."

"Suit yourself," the eldest Granville scowled at them. "I'm riding ahead."

Beth started to reply in agreement, stopping short when he galloped away. "He's either hungry or angry."

"I could guess," Samuel laughed. "The hungry I can understand. You must be as well."

"We had to miss breakfast."

"You're not walking another step. Here," he got on his horse and held out his hand like his brother had. "We can ride in so you'll have something to eat."

She followed him up, already missing the usual buffer against the cantle. "We can also discuss how much I owe you for everything."

"Sounds good. Although," he looked back at her with a grin, "if you're my sister-in-law, you could consider it a wedding present."

She hoped Samuel lacked Nicholas's stubbornness. "I won't be so I can't."

"He didn't propose?" Samuel faced the front and nudged his horse into a fast walk. "He must be waiting for a more romantic time and place."

Bracing for an argument, Beth replied in an even tone, "He proposed. I said no."

"I see." They rode for a few minutes before he asked, "I suppose you had a good reason?"

"A very good one."

"That's too bad."

She wanted to agree but kept quiet. At first, she longed to cry on Samuel's shoulder. He'd been trustworthy and she wanted someone to reassure her. But from an objective point of view, Beth saw no need in telling him her thoughts. The time would be better spent in setting her sights on Mr. Calhoon.

They reached and rode into the wagon circle. Everyone on foot and a few on horses came over to see her, having heard the news. The greetings and well wishes ran together in their frequency. She enjoyed the excitement, happy to receive it.

Once the fuss died a little, Samuel said in a quiet voice, "No matter what you'd like to do concerning Nick, I do need someone to care for your wagon. I've had to juggle three myself and need the help."

"Of course! I'd be glad to do so." She'd struggled to help Daggart with their wagon. Samuel must have had a horrible time of it these several days. "Maybe I could be the group's cook, do laundry, and care for the animals too."

"I like that idea. You're hired."

Nicholas rode up to them. "Everyone thinks we're getting married, we're stopping for noon, and I found your wagon."

"It's Samuel's wagon, not mine." She took the younger man's hand and slid from horseback.

"Samuel?" He exhaled and also dismounted at the same time as his brother. "How nice you're so unattached and so familiar with him already."

Samuel dismounted and nudged her, grinning. "Don't mind him. He's very often jealous of me. I'm much more handsome."

"Shut it," Nicholas all but yelled at the other man. He pointed at Beth, "You're not marrying anyone else but me."

Crossing her arms, she said, "You know my plan."

He stepped up and stood almost nose to nose with her. Teeth gritted, he asked, "Shall I tell you what to do with that plan?"

She enunciated each word so he would better understand. "You wouldn't dare!"

"Yes. I. Would. Because this no longer amuses me. Everyone in camp assumes I'll do right and make an honest woman of you. I don't intend on proving them wrong."

A part of her liked how close his face was to hers, within kissing distance. She took a deep breath, determined to not accept being second choice. "You'll have to because I'm marrying anyone else in camp besides you."

Nicholas leaned away as if she'd slapped him. "Anyone else?" He pointed at his brother, "How about Sam? You'll marry him? He's anyone else." His voice rose as he pointed out the nearby men. "How about Chuck, Lawrence, Mr. Chatillon? They're all eligible and certainly anyone else but me."

She bit her lip, not wanting to hurt any of the bystanders' feelings, but not wanting to propose marriage to them in such a backhanded way. "None of them, no. Sam's too much like a brother, and the others are nice, but not likely to find me interesting."

"So it's Calhoon, then? He is the *anyone else* you mean? He's the only one you've mentioned by name. Do you even remember his appearance? His age?"

"Of course I do." What she remembered of Calhoon seemed pale and dreary when an impassioned Nicholas faced her. "But he's a widower and that's what counts."

Samuel interjected, "How is him being a widower important?"

Nicholas snorted, replying, "It's not. Beth thinks there's something wrong with me and needs an excuse."

His assessment angered her. She'd never thought of him as less than an ideal man. "I do not! There is nothing wrong with you. You're perfect and I love you dearly, but I'm not spending the rest of my life in Sally's shadow with you wishing I was her or hating me because I'm not. Two years of being a second rate Lizzy was enough for a lifetime. I refuse to be in love with a man who is in love with a ghost. So no, Mr. Granville, I will not marry you, ever."

Samuel began laughing, more so when Beth heard and gave him a fierce look. He stopped upon seeing Nicholas glaring at him as well. "Miss Roberts doesn't know, does she?"

Wound up too much from irritation, she said, "I know enough, thank you."

"I'm not sure." Samuel shook his head, grinning despite the tense atmosphere between them. "You've argued more with Nick just now than I've ever seen you do anyone else. It's amazing, really. I'm very impressed."

Nicholas retorted, "Good, because your good opinion is the objective."

"If you could see past that haze of infatuation, you'd realize how much she loves you as well."

"Not enough to marry me," Nicholas said in a quiet tone.

Samuel put his arm around her, asking, "Is that true, Beth?"

She nodded, not looking at Nicholas. "I meant what I said about taking another woman's place."

"Very well," Samuel said. "Come with me. I'll fix our meal and have a task for you both in the meantime."

Beth glanced at Nicholas to see what he thought.

He caught her silent query and retorted, "I don't know, but if it means he feeds us, let's go along."

"If it means food..." She felt like an errant child as they followed Samuel to the Granvilles' wagon.

"Nick, you sit here. Miss Roberts, here." They both sat facing him while he stood. "Ah, now here's the trick. Don't look at me but at each other. Turn around to make it easier. Do this the entire time and once you're done, you're done."

This seemed like a game the two men had played before and Beth wondered about the rules. "Can we talk or just look?"

"Of course you can talk, in fact, please do." Samuel tapped his brother on the head for emphasis. "Just no fisticuffs."

Nicholas laughed. "Don't tell me, tell her. She's the one being ornery."

Beth smiled at his choice of words before retorting, "You're the one not listening, so Sam might have to tell you all this again."

"Sam, huh?"

The jealousy in his voice amused her. "You're correct. I

should call him Mr. Sam since I'm in his employ now."

"Since when?"

"Since I decided I need something more than your horse's back to ride to Oregon and what few belongings I have." Her voice caught despite her best efforts to maintain an even tone. She knew he'd heard her sadness when his stubborn expression softened.

"You're not returning to Independence?"

"I suppose I could. It depends…" She didn't want to continue, saying her future hinged on what Mr. Calhoon decided. She smoothed her skirt, wondering when would be a good time to tell the other man her plan. Beth looked up at Nicholas through her eyelashes to find him staring at her. Embarrassed, she gave him a slight smile.

Nicholas sighed and reached out to take her hands in his. "Elizabeth, please marry me. I promise to be the best husband possible." He stared at her. "After losing Sally, I didn't think I would ever love again until meeting you for the first time that day. My heart almost hurts with happiness whenever I hear your voice or see your face. Every word, every touch, has branded me as yours for the rest of my life."

His mention of their first sight caught her by surprise. As if a portrait painted in her mind, she recalled the sorrow in his eyes and the unhappiness during their time together. Now, when she stared at him, she saw hope and love, the same as she felt. "I remember that day." She caressed his cheek.

He kissed her hand, saying against her skin, "I want us to have so many days together, they blend into one long lifetime. You're wrong about being my second choice wife. I'm a man twice blessed and don't intend on letting the last love of my life go."

"I'm a love of your lifetime, almost as much as Sally was?"

"Yes, almost." Before she could reply, he added, "You and I aren't even engaged and we'd need to be married just to make sure."

"Need to be, hm?" She smiled at his flimsy argument. "I'm not so sure about marrying a man just to prove him right."

Samuel startled them by asking, "Beth, Do I need to get Calhoon over here to marry you?"

"She is not ever marrying that man, Sam," he replied with a smile. "I forbid it."

He squatted down to his brother's eye level and retorted,

"He's the only minister in a twenty mile range, and his feelings might be hurt if you refuse to let him."

"Oh."

Beth pulled away from Nicholas and stood, straightening out her skirt. Saying yes would be the easy thing for her to do. They'd not discussed a future together. Daggart's very existence had forbidden them. She bit her lip, and saw him still sitting there, looking up at her like a lost puppy. She didn't want to say no but didn't feel comfortable accepting a proposal. "I'm not sure."

He hopped to his feet. "What can I do to help you decide in my favor? Shall I draw up a list of my assets, my educational history, my family tree, or even have Sam speak for me?"

Samuel wore an evil grin. "You know I won't be kind to him."

Both men stared at her as if willing Beth to give them the answer Nicholas wanted. All this would be much more amusing if she weren't so tired and hungry all of a sudden. "Gentlemen, let's discuss this after dinner."

"I don't want to wait." Nicholas crossed his arms. "I love you, can provide whatever you need, and have a solid family in Oregon. We could even move back to Missouri. I have a house there."

Samuel laughed. "Make him take you to Oregon. He has more land there and can build you a bigger shack than the house he has in Missouri."

"You're not helping," Nicholas growled.

"Neither are you. Let's feed Miss...?"

"Roberts," offered Beth.

"Roberts, and then pester her into accepting you. Tell her how much land our family has, how much our mother wanted a daughter, and don't forget to mention that you won't be home much. That'll convince her."

"Sam."

She frowned. If she did marry him, she wanted him with her most days. "Why won't you be home?"

The younger brother stepped between them, telling Beth, "He's not been back since Sally died and won't be used to taking orders from a woman."

Behind him, Nicholas tapped his brother on the shoulder. "Don't you have something else to do that's anywhere but here?"

"I'm going, I'm going." Samuel headed out toward the wagon party, hollering, "Be sure to tell her you're kinder to everyone else than you are to me," as he left.

Once certain his brother was gone, Nicholas's cheek brushed hers as he leaned forward then back to take her hands. "Elizabeth, we're only a third of the way home, and yes, our home is in Oregon. Before you can argue, you need to know that anything can happen between here and there. Most of it will be bad while some of it might be good. The only certainty I have about the trail ahead is that I want to travel it as your husband." Keeping hold of her hands, he knelt on one knee. "I need you in my life and can promise you'll always be first in my heart."

Beth's heart pleaded with her to believe him. Seeing how his eyes echoed her own feelings added to the argument. "I don't know if you can say that. Daggart wanted—"

"He isn't me, Elizabeth. I want you for yourself, not as some sad replacement for Sally. I can never be her husband again, but I can be yours and that's all I want for the rest of my life. If we're married, I'll prove it to you every day."

She wanted to take him in her arms and never let go. "Well, then. It looks like Mr. Calhoon is marrying me after all." She helped up her groom. "Or rather, marrying us. Let's go find him and make arrangements for the ceremony."

On his feet, he asked, "To be clear, you're saying yes to marrying me?"

She wrapped her arms around Nicholas, kissing his face. "I'm saying yes very much, so shall we go?"

"Of course, my future Mrs. Granville." He laughed when she tickled him by nuzzling his neck. "Sam was right about everything except my being away from you. After suffering through one night of not knowing where you were, I'm never letting that happen again."

She pulled away to squint at him. "Are you sure your mother won't mind your marrying me and you have enough land for Erleen, maybe some chickens, and a garden?"

"Horses, more than one cow, crops, a pond, a good well, all of it." He kissed her forehead before moving to the tip of her nose and lips. "And my mother is going to love you."

A little premonition of a wonderful future with Nicholas went through her thoughts when she stared into his eyes. No other doubts clouded her mind and she smiled before taking a step back, pulling him with her. "Then let's get married. I'll need to make an honest man out of you, so we can start enjoying our nights together.

OTHER BOOKS BY LAURA STAPLETON

The Oregon Trail Series

The Oregon Trail Short Stories
Undeniable
Undesirable
Uncivilized

The Very Manly Series

The Very Best Man
The Very Worst Man
The Very Rich Man
The Very Poor Man

Nova Scotia Murder Mysteries

Betrayal
Impatience
Pleasures
Surplus
Appearances
Rage
Honeymoon